SUMMER OF THE HAWTHORN

Anne Doughty

HEADLINE

First published in 1999
by HEADLINE BOOK PUBLISHING

10 9 8 7 6 5 4 3 2 1

British Library Cataloguing in Publication Data

Doughty, Anne
Summer of the hawthorn
I. Title
823.9'14 [F]

ISBN 0 7472 7360 X

Typeset by
CBS, Martlesham Heath, Ipswich, Suffolk

Printed and bound in Great Britain by
Clays Ltd, St Ives PLC

HEADLINE BOOK PUBLISHING
A division of Hodder Headline PLC
338 Euston Road
London NW1 3BH

www.headline.co.uk
www.hodderheadline.com

For all those who have cherished
hope for peace in Ireland

'Do what you can, do it in love and be sure that it will be more
than you ever imagined.'

Deara, fifth century
healer from Emain

Acknowledgement

It is not appropriate to provide a bibliography with a work of fiction, but I would like to say how grateful I am to the scholars whose work illuminated and inspired this story. Where it is possible to establish facts I have tried to be accurate: the story, however, makes use of the spaces between what is known and what scholars were still debating in 1986.

I am particularly grateful to the Patrician scholars who argued so fiercely in the volumes of *Studia Hibernica* of 1961, as to how many Patricks there were, the archaeologists who have worked so extensively on the material culture of both the Celts and the Romans, and the Irish scholars who translated stories and poems, as well as the fascinating law tracts from the fifth century.

An old friend told me of the discovery of the skull of a Barbary ape at Emain long before the result of that excavation was available and a much-loved teacher gave me the volumes of Joyce referred to in the text.

My mistakes are my own and I hope will not detract from the truth of the fiction which is for each individual reader to decide.

Anne Doughty
Belfast 1999

1

ARMAGH, 1986

This morning, after the most ghastly ten minutes in Mother's bedroom, I went to Emain. I just took off, as Sandy would say. And the moment I crossed the main road and set foot in the lane that weaves its way between the scatter of farms and strikes west to run along the foot of the great mound, I felt better, so much better I could hardly imagine the waves of nausea that almost overcame me the minute I'd pushed open her door.

I walked quickly, my eyes eagerly seeking out the familiar features, once the focus of my childhood imaginings: the oak where Robin Hood crouched ready to pounce on the Sheriff of Nottingham, the hazel bush whose fruit bestowed wisdom on those who partook of it, the twisted hawthorn beneath whose branches the little people danced on moonlit nights. Smiling to myself as the memories flooded back to me, I turned aside into McCreesh's field and tramped through the rough grass by the hedgebank.

'Oh wonderful,' I said aloud, as I found the primroses, the patch I'd known for thirty of my thirty-five years. Last autumn the hedges had been brutally cut back by a machine that left the branches bruised and torn. I feared the primroses might have gone. But here they were in full flower, the pale leaves offering the faintest perfume to the morning sun as I bent to touch their soft petals.

The flutter and scuffle of birds followed me all the way down the lane. A blackbird was singing its heart out on the pointed gatepost of Toner's farm. I glimpsed a wren, minute and secretive, hopping through the ground ivy at the foot of the hedgerow.

Had I not caught sight of a man perched on the low roof of a cottage painting the inside of the chimney stack, I would have danced for joy. I had been let out. I had escaped. From what I had escaped, or from where, I could not say, but the feeling of freedom buoyed me up like a following wind, my feet barely touched the ground as I sailed along the lane heading for the familiar green gate.

'It's because these are *my* hedgerows,' I confided to a thrush, so absorbed in smashing a snailshell that he didn't hear me coming. Other places were all very well. I could enjoy Hampstead Heath or St James's Park, and Matthew's home village in Norfolk was wonderful with those great skies arcing over the marshes and the heathlands. But this was my own place, this was part of me, and I had been lonely for it for so long.

As I closed the small, green gate carefully behind me, I wondered how I could possibly be lonely for a place I had had to visit regularly in the last eight years, even more often this last year, the year of my mother's dying. But no answer came to me as I began the climb along the outer ramparts, across the ditch and up to the top of the great mound.

Every time I begin the climb, I feel just as excited as I did the very first time my father took me there. I'm so convinced that this time will be even more exciting than before that I forget how very steep the mound is. In my enthusiasm I move far too fast. By the time I reach the top, I'm always out of breath.

This morning, I pushed it so hard I had to flop down on the grass to recover myself. For ages, I just sat there, not quite believing it. Suddenly, summer had come and here was I, at Emain. The sun was warm on my skin, its brilliant light spilled over all the little fields and the patches of woodland spread out below me, bringing them alive, picking out every soft, new leaf, every fresh-painted farm and cottage.

The top of the mound is completely healed again after the excavations. For years, I longed for them to be over. I could not bear the nakedness of those scraped surfaces, the rubble walls dated and labelled, the post-holes numbered and colour-coded. Now I had my Emain back, soft and green, keeping its own secrets and sharing mine.

When finally I did get my breath back, I stood up and scanned the horizon. Whatever the weather, however clear or misty the day, I'm always aware how for millennia, men and women have stood on this high point. Here they have stood in pride and hope, in fear and expectation, century after century, their eyes turned north to the glitter of Lough Neagh, or west to the hills of Tyrone and Donegal, or south and east towards the lowlands of the Bann and the Lagan, where the old road goes through the mountains to Tara.

On my very first visit, my father had told me how the warrior princess Macha had traced in the dust with the pin of her brooch the outline of the citadel. For Emain was the heart of the country of the Ullaid, the old Kingdom of Ulster, the setting for the great stories about Cuchullain and the Knights of the Red Branch.

Intensely aware of the long past, I stood in sheer delight, watching the high white clouds stream out of the west against a pure blue sky, their fleeting shadows racing across the grass like companies of phantom horsemen summoned into battle.

'You've a great imagination.'

I could hear my mother's voice, as clearly as if she had been standing beside me. If you wrote the words on a page, they would look harmless enough. They might even be read as a compliment. But the written word can't conjure up that characteristic intonation, that inflection of the voice, that habitual edge of criticism; nor can it show the tightening of the lips, the ironic smile, the upward movement of the chin and the dismissive shake of the head.

The last thing you ever did where Mother was concerned was take what she said at its face value.

And now she is gone. After all the months of waiting, of knowing the diagnosis she refused to acknowledge, the months of phoning and visiting hospital and then hospice, of trying to behave better than one felt. Yet when the end came, it was still a shock. I didn't even suspect anything from Sandy's tone when I picked up the phone last Friday evening.

'I've been trying to get you since five-thirty. I tried Robert Fairclough's, but you'd gone.'

'Yes, I went for a drink with Pat at the Festival Hall. She's over for the Tyroneweave Exhibition.'

The pause at the other end was only momentary.

'Mother passed away at twenty-five past five.'

Passed away. To write that the men and women who once stood upon this mound had passed away was appropriate enough, but for my plain-speaking sister to use the words was more of a sudden shock than the news itself. But we choose our words to match our feelings and when it came to the point, Sandy's feelings were clearly not what she had expected. Waiting in the queue for security at Heathrow next morning she still sounded totally distraught.

'I'm sorry, Dee, I haven't the remotest idea what to do at a time like this. There's a *Which* paperback I meant to buy.'

She looked so uneasy and so unhappy I'd have liked to put my arms round her, but that's not something you can do with Sandy. I couldn't do it when she was nine, or nineteen, and I certainly couldn't do it now she was twenty-nine.

Our mother's fierce hostility to physical contact of any kind between women had gone deep with Sandy and this was no time to upset her any further. All I could do was reassure her that I knew the rules, the unwritten ones that guide the community at times like this. I knew every line that would have to be spoken and every gesture that would have to be made from years of observation and hours of listening to Mother as she assessed the relative success or otherwise of the many funerals she had attended.

'I'm prepared to do it their way, if I can manage it,' I said, as we crossed the wet and windy tarmac. 'How do you feel about it?'

3

'I don't,' she shouted back over the whine of the engines. 'Just let's get it over with. Tell me what to do and I'll do it. I won't be happy till I'm walking back up that corridor.'

Sandy was as good as her word and Matthew, my husband, as reliable as ever. We performed the prescribed rituals in the prescribed fashion. Even Mother might have admitted that her funeral 'went off very well.' After it was all over I was left with no more than a handful of fragments and images flickering inside my head like the fleeing shadows on the grass.

I didn't get much sleep in the two nights before the funeral, so on the day itself I seemed to see everything in the brightest Technicolor, with the sound turned up. The incredible noise of elderly relatives drinking tea or whiskey, according to sex, in the sitting room. The fallen petals from the wreaths tramped into the hall carpet. The bright green wing of Sandy's eyeshadow. The frayed ends hanging down from the giant umbrella produced by the funeral director.

I felt slightly drunk most of the time, though I left the actual alcohol to Sandy and Matthew. Nevertheless, I felt very much in command of the situation. Like an anthropologist who has studied her tribe long and hard, I knew exactly what I should do at each point as the elaborate ritual unwound. I think I even managed to play my part with conviction. Matthew said I did it very well. Sandy was quite unambiguous in her praise: 'You were just fantastic, Dee. Given how you really feel, you were incredible. I don't know how you did it.'

In one way, it was all very easy. You simply didn't allow your true feelings to get in the way. You let people have what they wanted, say what they wanted to say, believe what they wanted to believe, because that was what was important for them. Truth of any kind was the enemy, not to be allowed within the charmed circle of mourners and mourned.

In particular, Mother's dying, lengthy, painful and diminishing, had to be rewritten to their liking. She had fought every step of the way, refused all the help and support the hospice had so richly offered, been critical and unpleasant to everyone she had come in contact with and repeated endlessly that her only wish was 'to be out of this damn place and back to work'. But such facts, however true, are not relevant to those who gather to mourn.

The church was very full and very hushed. In contrast, the minister's voice was very loud. It seemed to oscillate in harmony with the sudden drumming of rain on the roof and against the windows of the north aisle. I found its resonant boom strangely soothing. But the more it went on, the sleepier I got. I was listening to poetry in a foreign language. I was sure it was very good and no doubt apt to the occasion, but what was I supposed to say at the end of it all?

I sang the hymn vigorously, took deep breaths as I had been taught at choir practice and hoped that would help me to get through the address. We were asked to be seated. I composed myself.

'Pearl Henderson, our dearly beloved sister in Christ, devout member of the church, unfailing servant of the Lord, whose triumph over death, whose courage in adversity was surely an inspiration to us all, goes before us into glory . . .'

As the words cascaded down upon me, I couldn't quite grasp what was happening. I just kept looking at the toes of my new black patent shoes. Even though I had polished them the previous evening, they seemed to be very dusty. I wondered if it was the shininess that attracted the dust and whether they would have been less dusty if I hadn't polished them.

'Ashes to ashes, dust to dust, if the Lord doesn't have her the devil must.' I was in the school playground, on a March day, bright with sun, the dust blowing in a sudden breeze, the long arc of a skipping rope curving before me, the chant of children's voices.

But it was not children's voices I was hearing, it was still the minister. Quieter now, more conversational, he was reading from his notes: 'Pearl Henderson was the youngest member of a churchgoing family. Hers was a home where Jesus Christ was known and loved and Pearl brought that knowledge to her family life here in Armagh after her marriage. It was the faith and care of Christ that sustained her when, with her two children still very young, she lost her husband and bravely took up the role of breadwinner.'

One of the undertaker's men had a dreadful cough. I looked across at him as he tried to muffle it in a huge striped handkerchief, but the more he tried the worse it got. By the time he'd recovered himself, the well-articulated voice had reached the 1980s. Mother's active phase of building up the business gives way to 'the opportunity for further public service through the Business and Professional Women's Club of which she was secretary for many years'.

'Cheerfulness, industry and efficiency. These were the keynotes of Pearl's personality. Whenever she did something she did it well, and the Church had good cause to be grateful for her gifts, for who but Pearl could have organised so efficiently the Christmas bazaar. She would long be remembered for her magnificent needlework and tapestry, for her Swiss rolls and her Christmas puddings.'

I had forgotten the Christmas puddings. We dreaded them. I could see so vividly before me the huge bowl of sticky ingredients, the row of ready-greased containers, and hear the sharp edge in her voice should either of us dare come into the kitchen while she was preparing them. There were boiled eggs for supper when she cooked the puddings for the bazaar. She'd had enough of cooking and washing up for one day, she always said.

I was quite upset when the voice telling me the story about this wonderful woman stopped and instructed me to lift up my heart and sing another hymn. Halfway through, the undertaker's men smartly turned the coffin through 180 degrees like a military manoeuvre, summoned Matthew to take his place at its leading edge, and left Sandy and me to our own devices.

'Come on, Deirdre,' I said to myself, as the funeral director caught my eye. 'You're back on parade. Get Sandy moving down that aisle beside you. No one else can move till you do. Another two hours and it'll all be over.'

It was raining more gently as we stood on the muddy, tramped grass by the open grave. A sheet of plastic grass covered the mound of excavated earth. Like a model of Emain itself, it dominated the wet ditch into which minute rivulets dripped and splashed.

The coffin bore a shiny, brass plaque: 'Pearl Henderson, Born 21 January 1926, Died 16 May 1986'. The saturated earth fell upon it and obliterated her lifespan.

The funeral director moved us on. Behind us, the undertaker's men in black coats and well-polished shoes, were filling in the grave as if they were hard at work in their own back gardens. As we reached the paved path at the edge of the churchyard, I saw the departing mourners pause, turn and adjust their face muscles ready to address a member of the immediate family with the customary, 'I'm sorry for your trouble.'

Rather like going to church each Sunday, even if you never sang, never listened and left it to the minister to do all the praying, to speak these words now would ensure your presence had been noted, a tick entered in the register that mattered most to you – God's or your neighbour's.

After the words had been spoken, it was equally important to draw a response from the family member in question, preferably a comment the deceased had made in happier times. This comment would be repeated when the funeral was discussed in those circles where Mother was known, exchanged for similar comments, leaving the speakers confident that they had done justice to the event.

'Miss Henderson, I'm sorry for your trouble.'

Those who knew me called me Deirdre, but those who didn't followed the old custom of not allowing marriage to intervene between a daughter and the death of a parent. They lined up and said their piece as they shook my hand.

'Parker. Fred and Mary. We knew your Mother *very* well. So sad. *Such* a loss to the Church. And what a wonderful new shop she made after the bombing. *Such* energy. I wish there were more like her.'

I nodded and smiled, thinking of Malvolio. 'Mother often spoke of you. You used to help on the cake stall, didn't you?'

There were dozens of them, all ready to present the speech they'd prepared. I've always had a good memory for detail and as my mother was voluble about her activities and concerns, I found I could place nearly all of them. Unfortunately, so much of my life passed before me as I did so that I felt like the proverbial drowning man.

At some point, the minister excused himself for another engagement and I became aware of the fact that Sandy and Matthew were nowhere to be seen.

The last hands were shaken, and then, only then, did I realise that the funeral director had been standing behind me all this time, his huge umbrella angled into the drifting mizzle so that it didn't get in the way, but still protected me from the worst of the rain.

'It's a hard day for you'n yer sister. She's very upset, the young lady is. Yer good man thought he'd best take her back to the house. I daresay they'll have a nice, hot cup of tea waitin' for you. You'll feel more yerself after that.'

That was the only time I lost hold of the proceedings. I mumbled my thanks and as he put me into the back seat of the funeral car I burst into tears and cried the whole way back to Anacarrig. Not for Mother. For a little man with a red nose and a country accent who had held an umbrella over me when he needn't have bothered.

2

Beyond my bedroom window the swifts wheel and cry in a clear sky. Blackbirds are hunting on the lawn below. It has been a warm, sunny day and now, when my lamp would be lit if I were in London, it is still bright enough to read. I had forgotten how long the light lingers in Ulster. I am further north and further west. It feels like a different world.

A week now since I arrived with Matthew and Sandy, the house cold and dank, closed up since Sandy's last visit, the rain pouring down as if it would go on for ever. I'll never forget that Saturday evening with the phone ringing and visitors arriving and all the awfulness of the funeral still to be faced. Now it seems so far away. Even the person I was that evening, the one who said the right things to neighbours and relatives, who handed round cups of tea and glasses of whiskey, seems someone I hardly recognise.

I am beginning to feel different, but I'm not sure in what way. I do know I don't feel so panic-stricken when I go into Mother's room any more, certainly not like that first morning when I was determined to stick it out and then turned tail and ran. I don't push my luck, I don't stay in there very long at any one time, but I have been managing better.

I've made this long list of things I must do, most of which I dread having to do, but I bribe myself, just as I did during all those years of revision for exams, the mugging up of boring stuff for the sake of the results I needed.

My secret weapon is the garden. Two days after the funeral, I took a mug of tea outside and had a look around while it was cooling. I got a nasty shock. The lawns had been cut and the edges trimmed, but nothing else had been done. Mr Neill, who does the grass, was sure to have offered to keep things tidy, but Mother would have insisted she'd be home in no time, so there was no need at all to bother.

There were huge stems of groundsel poking up through the splashes of purple aubrietia and pink saxifrage. The rockery was full of buttercups and sprouting thistles. Before I quite realised it, I had a pile of weeds on the terrace and my tea was stone cold.

It was that first head of groundsel that did it. 'Out you come,' I

9

said, as I tweaked it from the rain-softened earth. That's what my father always said.

The garden had been Mother's big thing. Even more than her baking, her tapestry, her pickles and preserves, the immaculateness of her garden was one more demonstration of her superiority over the locals. But it was my father who designed and laid it out.

I always assumed it was because she came from Belfast that she felt she had to show the locals she could do just as well as any country person, but maybe that's not the reason at all. Certainly, however much anyone might argue for Armagh's historic status as a city, Mother always insisted it was just a country town and its inhabitants were only country people. When my father commented that Armagh was the ancient capital of Ulster and the ecclesiastical capital of all Ireland, she only laughed. Big words and grand phrases were always 'a lot o' nonsense'.

My father, of course, was only a countryman, in her terms. She had been quick to forget that this particular countryman had designed and created both the house and its garden. Indeed, after all the years in which it was 'her house' and 'her garden', I had almost forgotten myself how much I loved the garden I had helped him to make. Since I stood looking over the familiar flowerbeds, the mug of tea still in my hand, I have wanted to be nowhere else. Through all the hours I've spent there, I've been so happy, working and listening, remembering things I haven't thought of for years.

It was Great-aunt Minnie who used to tell me stories about my father. Back in the 1920s, he used to pass the site on which the house is built on his way from the small cottage where he lived to the primary school in Armagh. In the days before school buses, he had plenty of time to think as he walked. She said he started to plan a house on this hillside even then.

The year I was born, 1951, he bought the land. Steeply sloping and without planning permission, it was going cheap. Minnie said my mother thought he was mad. Even if he could ever afford to build on the land, the position was quite unsuitable. It was too far out of town, inconvenient for the shops and school. Worse still, it wasn't among her own sort. All the neighbours would be Catholic. Later, when building did begin, she said her kitchen would be overlooked by cottages at the top of the hill and that the sitting room had a view of a dreadful old farmyard with a rusting, corrugated-iron hayshed. The other sort, of course. As one would expect.

He met her objections one by one. He bought her a small car and went on using his ancient bicycle to pedal to the shop in English Street where he sold seeds and fertilisers to men in big boots. He worked all the hours there were. If he wasn't in the shop, he was in the garden. He terraced the slope to the road, built the stonewalls and the rockery, began planting trees and shrubs, laid out the rose garden and the vegetable plot, screened the cottages at the top with willows and the farm at the bottom with chestnuts and sycamores.

I learnt their names before I'd even started school. Sitting on the wheelbarrow drinking tea from his Thermos, I listened while he told me where all the different shrubs and trees were to go, what they liked, how they would grow and what a big girl I would be when they were all just right. That was before the building work started, of course. Once that began, we had our tea with the workmen in their stuffy wooden hut with its paraffin stove. One of them became a great friend of mine, an elderly Catholic called Mick from some unknown place called Mill Row. Until Mother found out, that was.

He was such a silent man, my father. Silent in himself, I mean. Beyond his work and Anacarrig, his greatest pleasure was his books. History and natural history were his great love, but he also enjoyed some poetry. I remember him reciting 'Under the Spreading Chestnut Tree', one day when William Coulter from Tamlaght came to call and found us planting saplings down by the road.

The other thing my father enjoyed was talking to country people like William Coulter. He was slow to get started, and so indeed was William, but with a little encouragement they would tell the most marvellous stories. I had no greater delight in those days than to sit in William's forge, or the garden, or some unfinished room in the new house and listen to them talk of 'the olden days'. Never 'the good old days', always 'the olden days'.

My mother hated it when my father told his stories. Whether it was about the olden days or the events of everyday, immediately she got irritated, behaved as if he was somehow wasting time, idling when there was work to be done, and not looking to the future, to a bigger shop with a greater turnover and a higher income. Yet all the time he was creating a house well ahead of its time, stocking seeds and tubers of the newest varieties and planting a garden that only the future would reveal in its full character.

I supposed then it was because she was such a townie and so proud of being brought up in the city with all its life and bustle, that she objected to what she thought were 'country ways', but I'm not sure any more. Her hostility seems too deep for that. Sometimes I think she was standing over against the man himself, rejecting the deep sense of self from which all his actions flowed. It's one of the puzzles in my life that I may never resolve.

It is almost dark now and the cars on the road below me are using dipped headlights. I can see them only momentarily as they pass the bottom of the drive. The seclusion of the garden is complete, as he said it would be.

The house was finished in 1958, when I was seven and Sandy just two. A year later, at the beginning of June, with the garden full of blossom, apple, pear, damson, flowering cherry and hawthorn, he collapsed behind the wooden counter of his shop in English Street, packets of seeds still in his large, square hands. He was dead before the ambulance got down the hill from the hospital.

Mother never forgave him.

And now the garden blossoms again. Another week and it will have reached the same point of growth he left behind that June morning. Some sprays of flowering cherry are out already, and the apple trees in the shelter of the house, and the hawthorn, the May blossom, blooming late in the very last week of the month.

That was one of the worst rows they ever had. If you can call it a row with someone as silently imperturbable as my father. Over the three ancient hawthorns on the right-hand side of the front garden and the broad damp area in front of them. Mother insisted the hawthorns were making the whole corner wet. Nothing would ever grow there, she said, and the gnarled roots were unsightly. Why didn't he cut them down and clear the place up? He wasn't surely going to let some ridiculous old superstition stop him. She'd never heard worse, a man with a bit of education talking about fairy-thorns.

But he didn't cut them down. For a long time he searched around, hoping to discover the source of the spring he was sure was there. But all he found were two large pieces of worked stone that might once have fitted together. So he sank the two pieces in the bare ground among the hawthorn roots to make a sitting place for me. Then he created a small water garden, planting fern and marsh marigold, irises and kingcups.

I have one of those kingcups on my table in the window where I write my letters to Matthew and scribble notes for my work, a brilliant golden eye, looking at me, unblinking, bringing back memories long hidden away. All through my childhood, that small marsh garden with its two smooth, worn pieces of stone was where I played. I had almost completely forgotten the long hours I would spend there absorbed in conversation with one of my 'friends'.

These friends were seldom actual children from my class at school, or from the cottages and farms nearby. My mother didn't encourage Sandy or me to bring playmates home. But not having a real person never seemed to trouble me. I'd settle myself on one stone and talk to whichever friend had come to sit on the one opposite to me.

Once there was a little Red Indian girl. That must have been after I'd read the story of Pochahontas and her journey to England. Later, there was a girl who'd been with the children of the New Forest, but who didn't get into the story. Then there was a Scottish lass who served in the kitchens of Dunluce Castle where my father had taken us on a summer outing.

The more I thought about my stones, the more I recalled the peaceful hours I'd spent sitting lost in reverie. How precious those solitary hours had been. As precious in their special way as the comfort and joy brought by those imaginary friends. Out of sight of the house and my mother's critical eye I felt safe, yes, but there was more to it than that. There was a calmness about that small corner that made it seem quieter than the rest of the garden. It had, too, a feeling of security that enfolded me without any sense of enclosure. Certainly, I was never happier than when I was there, talking to my friend or just sitting dreaming, wandering through an inner world all of my own making, a world that grew and extended with everything I read or saw and with every story I ever chanced to hear.

And indeed, the slope where my stones rested in the shade of the old thorns was as special to my father as it was to me. He had little cause to go there, there being no grass to mow and no shrubs to prune, but he had done one thing that left me in no doubt at all about his feelings. He had named the dwelling he had long dreamed of building 'Anacarrig', and in the tongue of the olden days, 'Anacarrig' is 'the small marsh of the stones'.

3

On the night Mother died, I phoned my dear friend Joan to tell her the news. Joan lives in the ground floor flat below us – a sturdy, silver-haired lady who has lived through eight decades, but only owns up to the fact on rare occasions because she says people treat you as if you have lost your wits if they find out you are over eighty. And Joan is most certainly in full possession of hers. She is more shrewd and wise in her judgement of people and what happens to them than anyone I have ever known.

Matthew and I carried down all our houseplants for her to look after while we were away. We found her waiting for us by her door, a freshly opened bottle of whiskey in her hand.

'Drink up, my dears, it'll help you sleep,' she insisted, pouring generous measures for us both. 'The most important thing to do in the face of death is to celebrate life,' she pronounced, as she eased her stiff limbs into her special upright armchair. 'You must be willing to accept how you feel. There's no use pretending you're coping if you're not. If misery is inevitable, relax and get on with it. It will pass. All things pass, however ghastly.'

With her strong voice and Cheltenham Ladies' College accent, Joan could strike you as quite overbearing when she holds forth, but I had long ago grasped the true character of what lay behind the briskness of manner. Joan's life had been full of difficulties and her struggles had left their mark, but she was a musician of great talent and when she played for you she revealed herself, a woman of deep sensitivity and compassion.

'You'll ring me, won't you, Deirdre, if I can be any use whatever. Going through your mother's things won't be easy. You never know what's going to come upon you, my dear, especially if it's someone close. Things you've forgotten, or things you never knew, just pop up. You may find it very trying, especially as you'll be on your own,' she said firmly, as we stepped out into the hallway and said our goodbyes.

A week later, four hundred miles away, kneeling on a pink bedroom carpet, tears trickling down my face, I heard her words echo in my ears and longed for the comfort of her overcrowded sitting room and the hiss and bubble of its antiquated gas fire.

Armagh Gazette, it said, in Gothic script on the paper bag I held in

15

my hands. 'Newspaper and General Printing Offices, Office Requisites and Stationery Stockists, Largest stock of books in the City.'

At the bottom of the deepest drawer in Mother's dressing table, hidden underneath a leather handbag full of receipts and the spare parts for her heated rollers, I'd found this paper bag: it contained two unused hardbacked notebooks. I had bought them with my prize money from the 'Living in Armagh' essay competition. The same paper bag the assistant slid them into, fresh and shiny as the day I bought them.

I wiped my eyes crossly and counted on my fingers. Yes, 1969. That would have been it. The Easter holiday before my A level. I could almost feel the chill of the early April day when I cycled into Armagh to see what I could find to spend my prize money on. I went into the *Gazette* office and at first I just couldn't make up my mind. I was so confused by the array of exercise books, notebooks, files and folders laid out on the broad counters, I turned away and went and looked at the books instead.

I walked up and down the tall display cases where I had spent my tokens and chosen my prizes since I was old enough to read. And then, on a counter right at the furthest end of the shop, I saw the pile of blue notebooks. 'Challenge', they said, in gold lettering on the spine.

'That's what I want,' I said out loud, and a woman buying paper doilies stared at me, as I pounced on one of them to find out how much they were. To my delight the prize money would pay for two.

My joy was unbounded. Those two shiny notebooks, full of smooth, unwritten pages, were a hope and a dream. I had such plans for filling all the space they offered me. As I cycled back to Anacarrig with the blustering east wind behind me, my jacket billowing, thinking of what I might write in them, my spirits soared so high that I felt I might take off into the dazzling sky and make a circuit of the city.

'What kept you?'

I could see the anger in her face, because she thought I'd been gone too long. Then came the inquisition as to where I'd been, who I'd met. She hadn't believed me when I said I'd just been looking at books and buying some notebooks.

'Not surprising they disappeared, is it?' I said to the empty room, as I wiped my eyes again. 'That was in another country and besides the wench is dead.' She was hardly a wench, but she was certainly dead.

Joan was right. You really couldn't guess what was going to jump up and hit you and there was no use pretending it didn't hurt. Here in my hands I held a dream that had been taken away, not just by the loss of my precious notebooks which I couldn't afford to replace, but by all the pressures and obliqueness a mother can bring to bear on a daughter.

16

If I were being charitable I might try to justify her action by saying she was simply ensuring I had no possible distraction from my work for A level. But the facts wouldn't support me even if I tried, for no matter what I wrote, she always found a way of suggesting that my writing, like my reading, was a self-indulgent activity even when school and exams were long behind me. It could have no value whatever, because she could never see any connection between it and earning my living.

'Have a bit of sense, Deirdre. When did reading a book ever pay an electric bill? Tell me that? An' where would you'n Sandy be today if I'd sat on my backside and scribbled at stories or read books?'

I put the notebooks down where my dripping tears could not spatter the bright covers and hunted in the pockets of my jeans for a hanky. There wasn't one, only a screwed up pink tissue with a lipstick print on it. I unfolded it meticulously, wiped my eyes and blew my nose.

Then, suddenly, I heard my own voice echo in the empty room, a voice I barely recognised. Strong and firm, with no trace of tears or the choke I could still feel in my throat, it said: 'So what are you going to do now, Deirdre Weston? You've got your notebooks back. You've got a life of your own. There's no one to stop you now. What about it?'

I hadn't got an answer, but I got to my feet, picked them up and carried them along the landing to the table in my own room. As I set them down, I nodded reassuringly to the golden eye of the kingcup I'd brought up from the small marsh of the stones. Something would come to help me.

4

I still don't know what possessed me, whether I was over-confident, or curious, or prompted by some inner need I couldn't explain, but on the Sunday morning after the funeral, I decided to do what I hadn't done since I'd packed my bags and left home for good. I rang Mr Neill, our one and only Protestant neighbour and asked for a lift to church.

The short journey into the city was no problem. It was a beautiful sunny morning, the light spilling through the newly-leafed trees. William Neill is a retired farmer who knew my father well. He talked about the weather and the sudden surge of growth in the fields and gardens in just the way my father would have done. It was as we drove down the Mall, I realised I should never have come. It was seeing Mother's parking space that did it.

The moment we drove past the spot, waves of nausea hit me, my light spring suit felt like tweed and the strong white shape of the Courthouse began to waver uncertainly. It was here, under the trees, by the side of the broad, green oblong that lies like an oasis in the heart of the city, close by the grey-faced church where she worshipped that we arrived well before the service was due to begin for the express purpose of 'seeing all the style'. No one who passed within range escaped her comment. She knew everyone and everything about their affairs.

'See you later, Deirdre. I'll leave her parked opposite the Orange Hall in case you're out first. I never lock her. The boyos would be afraid to steal her, she only goes for me.'

I just about managed to say a thank-you as William drove off to the parish church in a cloud of fumes, leaving me standing at the foot of the worn stone steps that led steeply up to the dark vestibule of the plain, square Presbyterian edifice I had been forced to visit week after week, month after month, for all the years I had lived at Anacarrig.

By the wrought-iron railings children were eyeing each other. Newly released from Sunday school, they shoved and pushed surreptitiously, while keeping a watchful eye out for their parents who would soon be arriving for the service.

'If anyone speaks to you and asks you how you are or how you're doing at school, just say, "Very well, thank you." That's quite enough.

Don't tell them any of your business. People only speak to you on account of me and they don't want to listen to any of your nonsense, especially on a Sunday.'

No, it was absolutely no use telling myself Mother was dead. Her presence was as tangible as if she were alive and well. And she'd be there inside as well, waiting for me.

I still wonder why I didn't turn and walk away then. Perhaps someone spoke to me, but it's more likely I simply lost all power to act. I just went on into the building, walked down the aisle as I'd done so many hundred times before, and sat down in our family pew. I even bowed my head in prayer. 'Only for a minute, of course. You don't keep your head down and pray for this one and that one, you can do that at home. People will think you're showing off if you do that. Just do what I do and you'll be right.'

I jerked my head upright and stared at the wooden pulpit, the focus of all that went on in this particular rite. No cross, no candles, no stained glass. Just a large wooden box of a pulpit and behind it, blocking the east end, the pipes of the organ. As a child, my eye had gone round and round the church looking for some interesting feature to rest upon. There had been nothing then and there was nothing now, except the broad pastel spaces of the unadorned walls and ceiling. Through endless hours of boredom I had covered those spaces in drawings and paintings. Bigger than the biggest drawing book, or the generous sheets of grey paper for free expression in school, those spaces were my comfort, my defence against the torrent of angry words which poured down upon us, Sunday after Sunday.

At the age of twelve, when I learned that Michelangelo had painted the ceiling of the Sistine Chapel, it came as no surprise to me. I simply assumed he had suffered as I had and had come up with the same solution to save his sanity.

A door clicked open at the foot of the pulpit and the choir filed in self-consciously. I had once been a member of that choir and a Sunday school teacher as well. I had read the lessons on Children's Sunday and sung solos at Harvest. I had been complimented afterwards by various old ladies and the good-natured verger and then I had been stripped down by Mother.

'You weren't nearly loud enough, couldn't hear you behind a wet newspaper. You must remember half those men at the back of the church are deaf.'

'Then why don't they sit at the front?'

'Don't you be cheeky with me. You know perfectly well that no one sits at the front.'

There were never any answers to Mother, only the answers she expected from you. And woe betide you when you couldn't come up with them.

She would sit throughout the service, her large family Bible unopened on her knee, a look of concentration on her face. Once home again, over lunch, she would declare her verdict on the congregation. It always seemed to me she was more acutely aware of the sins of her fellow men and women than the Almighty. Had He been a member of her staff and fulfilled His promises of retribution so ineffectually, He would most certainly have been given the push.

'I don't know how that man can sit there on a Sunday with his shoes shining, the way he's carrying on with your woman in Lonsdale Street. Bold as brass he is, goes in and out, doesn't care who sees him. Brings her bunches of flowers. At her age. And him with two good-looking sons and one of them the manager of Lipton's.'

A voluminous, black figure appeared at the foot of the pulpit stair, mounted purposefully, ran his eye over the congregation and threw his arms in the air.

'Brethren, let us ask forgiveness for our manifold sins.'

I bowed my head gratefully. I prayed for the energy to stand up and slip noiselessly down the aisle, now, when no one could stare at me too obviously, because they were supposed to be bowed in prayer.

But my prayer went unanswered. My legs received no strengthening power and my hands began to sweat profusely. I could shield my eyes from this ranting figure, but about my ears I could do nothing.

How I got through that service I shall never know. I remember I kept hallucinating on the sight of William Neill's battered car. I could see myself crossing the road, hurrying across the White Walk and along the side of the cricket pitch to where it would be parked, but instead I sat with my head throbbing for over an hour, unable to shut out anything going on around me or coming back to me from a past so painful I had been doing my best to forget it for years.

When the organ finally gave the signal to depart, I had to hold on to the pew in front of me as I got to my feet. Of walking back down the aisle, I remember nothing. A crush of bodies in the vestibule, words I couldn't distinguish. And then, the miracle. I have never stopped believing in miracles. Parked at the foot of the steps where no one except the minister ever parks was William Neill's car.

He'd spotted me before I was able to distinguish his bent figure among the departing worshippers.

'In you get, Deirdre,' he said as he opened the door for me. 'You got good value this mornin'. Our man must have been wantin' his lunch.'

Dear William Neill. The sight of his whiskery brown face did more to restore my faith in humanity than a visitation from a whole delegation of angels. I sat back in my seat and watched the dispersing crowds who wandered in front of the car as if we were parked in a pedestrian area rather than waiting at a stop line to cross the main Armagh to Portadown road.

21

'They're always like this on Sunday mornin',' he said cheerfully. 'So full o' the Holy Spirit they think nuthin can git them.'

I laughed then, but inside my head I added, 'Yes, that's the trouble with the belief business. That's why I want no part of it.' As far as I could see belief was all about insulating yourself from the reality of life and particularly from anything you'd rather not face up to. I was sure at that moment that nothing would ever get me back inside a church ever again.

'Look, Deirdre, look.'

We lurched to a halt with a disregard for the cars behind us equal to that of the pedestrians who had strolled across in front of us. I followed the pointing finger into the brilliant triangle of sky between the roof of the Courthouse and the distant twin spires of the Roman Catholic cathedral.

He said they were pigeons, but I could see only doves. Pure white against the blue, they were circling in close formation, rising and falling in an aerial ballet that was a pure delight.

Suddenly, I saw another dove and remembered immediately the small church where I had found it. Back last March, working on an article for *Travelling East*, I had driven around Norfolk and Suffolk visiting churches from a list the editor had made for me. The church with the dove was not a grand one, rather small as East Anglian parish churches go, with no beautiful glass or carving, but full of a marvellously clear light and a deep stillness. In the south aisle, on a tomb chest, I found a stone statue of St Francis and the dove was in his hands. At his feet someone had arranged a handful of violets in a piece of bark filled with moss.

I looked around me. The church was full of flowers, as it would be, the week after Easter. There were sprays of blossom, jugs of daffodils, some irises and forsythia and beech leaves just beginning to unfurl. Nothing from shops or garden centres. Some of the arrangements were in clean jam pots, some in metal troughs full of chickenwire, where fronds of ivy had been used to cover up disintegrating, much-used oasis and spots of rust. Offerings made in love that meant something to the people who made them. I so envied them.

As I knelt down to take my pictures of the gentle saint, whose story I have always loved, I thought of the generations of knees that had worn the chancel step, the bottoms that had polished smooth the ancient wooden benches. I knew I envied them too.

When I stood up, a great shaft of sunlight pierced the piled white cloud and filled the south aisle with sudden brightness, picking out every detail of the bareheaded saint. I lingered as long as I could, reluctant to go, but I got very cold and began to feel anxious about all I still had to do. I returned the key, as I had been instructed, to the peg basket in the garden shed of the cottage directly across the road, and drove off rather faster than I should have done.

'Home James and don't spare the horses,' said William as we drew up at the foot of the drive. 'Are you sure you won't come on down for a bit of lunch? There'll be a roast an shure only the two of us to eat it.'

I thanked him as I got out, explained I was expecting a call from Sandy and walked as quickly as my high heels would let me up the steep drive.

It may have been the fumes from the car, or the thought of a Sunday roast, but as I turned the key in the front door I had to make a dash for it. I just made it to the downstairs loo.

After I was sick, I did feel better though I looked absolutely dreadful. I took some tablets for my head, got out of my suit and wandered round the house drinking tumblers of cold water. I couldn't think what had brought on so bad a head.

The afternoon had clouded over and the empty rooms felt stuffy and chill at the same time. The dim light showed up the grubby windows and made the carpets look dull and cheerless. I felt my spirits droop. I knew I must find something to do.

That was when I got it wrong again. I went upstairs to my table, took up the first of the blue notebooks and filled my pen. I would write about what had happened in church. I would set it all down, describe all the people, all the unease in their manner and their being, the boom of the men who never looked at each other when they talked, the women who wore such elegant clothes and yet scurried into their pews as if they were doing their best not to be seen.

I sat and stared at the smooth page, the page which offered such promise only a day ago. Nausea overwhelmed me. How could I ever write about what I'd experienced, ever sort out the tangled feelings, the confusions that came upon me? How could I ever write about anything?

Pain oscillated in my head. The white page broke up into jagged fragments. I staggered to my feet, heard the crash as my chair fell over. 'No, no,' I cried. 'I can't write about it. I can't think about it. I can't bear what I see . . . Leave me alone . . . leave me alone.'

I ran from the room, tripped on the landing carpet and just managed not to fall downstairs. Ran through the hall and out of the house and on down the drive. Cars whizzed past continually on the main road but I scarcely noticed them as I ran on, not knowing what I was doing or where I was. The pain in my head was so bad nothing seemed to matter any more. I just kept on running.

5

The roar of the cars grew in my ears, louder and louder as I drew closer to the foot of the drive where the gates stood open to the road. I ran on. My chest felt tight, my breathing was hard and laboured, my head throbbed as if it were ready to explode. Suddenly, I turned aside and dived through the shrubbery, as if I'd hit an invisible wall, breaking twigs and scratching my hands as I fought my way through the overlapping branches. I pitched headlong out of their shadow and threw myself down on the sunken stones beneath the three ancient hawthorns my father refused to cut down.

I lay there sobbing violently, indifferent to the rub of the gnarled roots and the dampness of the grass. My tears dripped down on to one of the well-worn stones and blurred its familiar outline.

'You fool, you fool,' I whispered, despairingly. 'You should never have come. It's your own fault completely.'

Sandy and Matthew had urged me not to stay on at Anacarrig. The clearing-out could all be done in a week, they said, once Matthew was back from India, if the three of us did it together. But I'd had to cancel my flight to India because Mother was still with us and now she was gone I couldn't get another. I had the time; they hadn't. Besides, I argued, I'd masses of things I wanted to do as well as sort out the house. There were people I wanted to see, places I'd once known that I wanted to revisit and I was longing to spend time with Helen, my oldest friend. Besides, I said, I could work just as easily at Anacarrig as in London.

I meant every word I said, but neither Sandy nor Matthew were happy with my plan. Sandy simply announced I was mad to try it and left it at that; Matthew reasoned with me, as he would always do, questioned me closely and tried to understand why this staying on had suddenly become so important to me.

The night before he left, we lay awake in the moonlight after we'd made love. 'Promise me you'll be very careful, darling,' he said, anxiously. 'Promise me you won't stick it out, if it really should go bad on you. Promise me you'll just pack, go home and wait till I'm back.'

I turned in his arms and hugged him. Through all our time together I had suffered periods of depression, sometimes so bad I wasn't able to work, because the simplest phone call was more than I could manage.

We did what we could ourselves, exploring old memories and all manner of painful, half-forgotten things. We'd taken advice and had real help from a close friend of Matthew's – his contemporary at medical school. And with each year of our marriage, the depressions lessened in length and intensity. But they had never gone away completely. Matthew knew how vulnerable I still was. A word, a memory, a dream: it took so little to set the darkness going again.

'I won't do anything silly, love, you know I won't,' I reassured him. 'You know I'll never break my promise.'

I felt him shiver. I wished I hadn't mentioned that particular promise. Some years earlier, in the midst of a really black depression, I admitted that often, when it gripped me, I just wanted to run out into the darkness and never come back, because the sheer pain of existing was more than I could bear. If it were not for him, I'd said, nothing in the world would stop me.

He had been quite beside himself and I'd ended up having to comfort him. It was then I had solemnly promised him that I would never, never harm myself however bad the pain.

'Oh Matthew, my love,' I whispered, my tears pouring down ever faster onto the bare stone beneath my cheek, 'I promised you I'd be all right and I've got it all wrong. There's no one else can help me but you and you're far away.'

I clutched my aching head, racked by the violence of my sobs, absolutely at the end of my tether. 'What shall I do? What ever shall I do?'

How long I lay there I don't know, but after a time, I grew quieter and lay still, too exhausted to move, my cheek pressed to the surface of one piece of stone, my arm thrown out across the other. Quite suddenly, I had a sense that someone was watching me.

The idea was quite ridiculous. Besides, what did it matter if anyone did see me? No one could help me now. No one. But, despite my despair, my curiosity got the better of me. I rolled over and sat up, my eyes still wet with tears.

A girl stood looking down at me, her large, grey eyes full of concern. She was about sixteen or seventeen. She wore a light tunic of creamy-white fabric tied with a brightly-coloured woven girdle and she had long hair, as dark as my own but much longer. Her bare legs and arms were tanned to a warm honey colour. In the crook of her arm she carried a small pitcher and in her other hand she held a bunch of kingcups just like the ones coming into bloom a few yards from where I sat.

As our eyes met, she spoke to me, but I could make no sense of the words she used and nothing of what she said.

She went on talking to me, her voice light and pleasing, her tone reassuring. She must have thought I was troubled by her presence. But I wasn't. Just puzzled and confused.

After a little while, she set down her pitcher, placed the flowers gently on the grass beside it and held out her hands to me, the palms spread wide to show me they were empty. I stared at her fascinated, watching every graceful movement and gesture. Everything about her – the tunic, the thonged sandals, the pitcher she had carried, the words she spoke – came out of another age, yet she herself seemed so familiar, like someone I knew well but could not for the moment place.

I wiped my eyes and told her who I was. I could see she didn't understand me any more than I understood her, but as I watched, I saw her make up her mind about something and step towards me. To my astonishment, she put her hand on my forehead. It was so cool and comforting. Holding one hand steady on my forehead, she began to move the other gently across my neck and shoulders. She pressed lightly on the rigid muscles and worked her way down my spine to my waist.

The coolness of her hand eased the throbbing in my head so quickly I could scarcely believe it. Wherever she touched me there was a warm, tingling feeling which spread out as she went on talking to me. Although I still couldn't understand her actual words, it was obvious she was telling me who she was and how she came to be here, today, when I had such need of her.

Sitting there, her hands on my head and back, I realised I felt perfectly calm and at ease while the pain in my head had simply melted away. I closed my eyes. Instantly, as if I were viewing a film, I began to see the girl whose hands rested upon me moving through scene after scene of her own life. As I followed the images, I grasped what she'd been trying to tell me. Not the details, of course, but enough. I looked up at her and smiled. Her life had been no easier than mine.

When she smiled back at me, it was such a gentle, warm smile, the smile of someone I felt I had always known. Looking up at her, it was just like meeting someone you know so well in a context where you don't expect them. Once, in the Ladies at Euston Station I came face to face with a girl I'd been at school with. Instant recognition, but total puzzlement as to how and where we'd known each other.

Here and now, I just couldn't place this girl. I could give her no name. At the same time, I was absolutely sure her presence was bringing back to me some shared experience I had somehow managed to forget.

She folded her hands together, laid her head against them and closed her eyes. When she opened them again and nodded to me, her

meaning was quite clear. I ought to go and sleep. She was quite right.
I was absolutely exhausted. But I couldn't just get up and walk away
when she had been so kind to me.

I stretched out my hand to touch her. To my surprise she drew
back, a look of concern on her face. After a moment, she bent down,
chose a bloom from the bunch of kingcups she had laid so carefully
on the ground, and handed the flowering stem to me. Our fingers
brushed and she was gone.

I sat quite still, alone in the quiet of the afternoon, the whizz of
cars a distant mutter beyond the density of the shrubbery. I stared at
the bright golden eye of the kingcup with the single unfolding bud at
its side. I gazed around hopefully as if perhaps she might have moved
into the shrubbery, though I knew perfectly well she had gone.

I made an enormous effort, got up and walked unsteadily back to
the house, clutched the banisters as I climbed the stairs and went
into my room. I must have fallen asleep the moment my head touched
the pillow.

The heat of noonday burned in a cloudless sky. On the great mound
nothing moved but the shimmer of haze above the baked earth which
had been worn bare in the preceding weeks by the movements of
men and horses. Since the Festival of Beltane it had been fine. Day
followed day of warmth and sunshine with only the slightest of showers
in the night to settle the dust and bring freshness to the early dawn.

Deara had loved every moment of the unexpected fine spell. After
the raw chill of the previous months, the confinement to hut and
storeroom, the smoke of fires, the scratch of her heavy wool cloak
and the lingering odours of horses and penned cattle, she revelled in
the sudden freedom like the wild creatures themselves.

In the first weeks she covered miles everyday, doing the old woman's
bidding with pleasure. Coming back each evening footsore and wolf-
hungry for the evening stew, her arms and satchel full of bark and
flowers and leaves, she had trudged up the dusty path to the main
gate and known herself happy. It was the first time such happiness
had come to her. And it frightened her. Surely such joy was not given
to mortal kind. Perhaps it was some jest of the gods to make her thus
so happy that they might cast her down and humble her.

Now, as she reached the edge of the wood and began the short,
steep climb again, she knew joy had gone. Today, the sun was no
longer her friend. He, who had warmed her and brought flowers
blossoming from the damp earth, was now an enemy, a cruel white
eye, who mocked her sadness, who rejoiced at the end to her freedom,
who would shine on through the months of her sixteenth summer,
whether she were to survive the coming time or not.

She tossed back her long dark hair impatiently and ran a brown arm across her brow where beads of perspiration gleamed on her high, pale forehead. The flowers were wilting already though she had picked them only in the water-meadows beyond the wood. She cradled them in her right arm, pulled her tunic higher within her woven belt and stepped out of the cool shade of the wood.

Perhaps it was too late already, though she had been as quick as she could. Conor had said Merdaine would not see another sunset, and indeed, in the night, when she sat by the bedplace with her, she thought the old woman would not greet another dawn. But she had.

In the first dim light she had stirred and spoken to her, but Deara had not understood. The old woman seemed to be speaking another language, one she had never heard before. The words were perfectly clear, she was not wandering in her mind, like other old people she had seen die, nor was it like the wound fever of warriors when they called to comrades or lovers in their pain. No, Merdaine's words had meaning and they were meant for her, she felt sure, but she could make nothing of them.

And neither could Conor. She could tell that from his face. Not that Conor would ever admit to such a thing. How could he, a Druid, a King's Druid at that, skilled in all the knowledges of this world, the other world and the world beyond? How could he possibly admit that he did not understand?

Conor had simply pretended not to hear. He had busied himself with trimming the candles before the God, moving them so that the deep-set stone features took on their most benign aspect. Conor was a great believer in getting the patterns right. Merdaine was not and their wills had often clashed. 'No,' Merdaine would say, 'that is not the way, not for this man, in this place, in this time.' Yes, one must acknowledge the God and make due sacrifice, she would agree, but not all power lay in the hands of the God, even the mighty Nodons, the deity served by all who sought to heal men by words or deeds.

Deara toiled up the steep slope with all the speed she could manage. The guards on the gate were half asleep, but it was no matter. The air was so still and heavy you could feel the movement of a rider as far away as the river. Beyond the gate she threaded her way between crowded huts and empty cattle pens. Dogs stirred and went back to sleep again as she passed, her leather sandals making almost no noise in the deep dust. She looked neither to right nor left, her eyes firmly fixed on the low doorway of a larger wooden hut beyond and behind the King's Hall. With a sigh of relief she saw that the door-hanging was still in place. It had not been tied back to let the spirit go. Merdaine yet lived.

Without a sound, Deara entered the hut and knelt by the low couch now pulled out into the centre of the dim room. The candles had burned low, but Conor was asleep, his head hung down on his chest.

29

He snuffled rather than snored, like a sleeping dog hunting rabbits in a dream.

Deara took the old woman's hand and laid the flowers below it. They were kingcups, broad and gold, the flowers she had asked for when she roused at mid-morning. They gleamed even in the dim light.

Merdaine stirred, her eyes flickered open.

'Child, you are early back today, you cannot have finished your tasks, why is that?'

Deara looked at the dark eyes and saw in them a look she already knew. A look of slight preoccupation, as if already the eyes were fixed on something else, a person beyond this person, a place beyond this place.

To her great consternation Deara found her own eyes were full of tears. Tears. How could she? When Merdaine had taught her always to celebrate the going, to go herself as far as she might with the departing spirit, both for the sake of the departing one and for her own sake, that she should be wiser when the time of her own going should come to her.

Deara blinked in the vain hope that Merdaine would not have seen. But she knew that Merdaine had always been able to see whatever she chose to see. Even with her eyes closed, Merdaine could see with her heart.

Today the old woman did not rebuke her. Instead, she smiled a strange half smile and closed her fingers round the soft blooms, caressing them gently like something very precious to her.

'He sleeps still?' she asked softly.

Deara nodded.

'Then come close to me and listen. Come, let me whisper to you like I did when you were a child, when you crept to your bedplace and wept by yourself because others had mocked you. Come, for you see true. My work is finished in this place. It will soon be time for Conor to stir himself and do his part. Come now, lie close.'

Deara stretched out on the rushes, her arms above her head, her slim body as close to the old woman as the wooden frame of the couch permitted. Thus she had lain for all her sixteen years, to sleep and to weep, for often the two had come together in that only time in the long, busy day when she might turn her back upon the world, a world where she had no place except as Merdaine's handmaiden.

She felt the press of the rushes through her thin tunic. They were only a few days old and still had a smell of greenness about them. Like the water-meadows that morning. Tears once again welled in her eyes and she did not know whether it was the memory of all these golden days, now ended, or fear of the future, or the loss of the one person in all the world who had protected her.

'Do not weep, child.'

Deara had made no sound, no body movement, but Merdaine had put out a thin hand and touched her hair.

'Listen now, and hold to my words that they may guide you. Your heart is soft and quick to sorrow, but your head is strong and firm. Use your head as a warrior uses his shield. Harden it by use and by discipline as a warrior does, but never think it is the greatest part of you. For that which is weak and soft is your real strength. It will guide you in the darkest ways and in the strangest of unknown places. Remember when Emain is no more, when sword and fire seem masters of all the earth, that light grows out of darkness, that without evil we cannot know good. You are a child of light for you know darkness at noon. You will heal many, and many will speak the name of Emain with love for your sake. But a time will come when Emain will speak no longer . . . its kings and heroes gone . . .'

The voice faded to nothing and Deara felt the hand slip from her hair. She got up quickly and saw Merdaine struggle for breath.

'Up, child, up.'-

Merdaine's hand jerked imperiously, a familiar gesture of a woman accustomed to being obeyed, now in contrast to the whispered tones of her command.

Deara lifted her to a sitting position and supported the frail body in her arms.

'Two things more,' she gasped.

With an effort of will Merdaine drew breath into her lungs. Deara heard the ominous bubble of fluid and knew clearly, as Merdaine herself did, how little time remained. She felt the pain as if it were her own pain, the choking tightness as if it were her own lungs struggling for air, and the urgency as if it were her own need to speak.

'Gently, Merdaine, gently,' she whispered, as she stroked the damp grey hair from the old woman's brow.

'The Gods protect your gentleness, child. If I have been too hard on you, you will come to understand why it was so. I have taught you all I know of healing and the world. To heal others you must heal yourself first. That will ever take you into danger. But if you have done as your heart speaks then help will come in your sorest need. But you must trust that it will come. Remember that above all things.'

Merdaine paused, her head hanging forward on her chest. Her eyes flickered round the room, taking in the squat, sleeping figure of the Druid, the candles burning straight and sharp, the dark stone eyes of the God. They came to rest on a wooden chest in the shadows. The metal clasp reflected one of the candle flames.

'Take my brooch to Morrough. Tell him Merdaine asks that he keep his promise. He will make you an offer, or his brehon will. But

31

do not let him frighten you. Whatever he says, make up your own mind.'

Deara felt the tension relax in the narrow shoulders. Something had moved. Something was different. A darkness had passed, though she knew not what it was. She bent to kiss the old woman. She had never kissed her before.

At her touch the half-closed eyes opened. They seemed to focus on her face and yet Deara could not feel sure that it was she whom Merdaine actually saw. But suddenly Merdaine's eyes were smiling.

'Have a good journey, my little one, both you and your friend in another time. Here, I give you a parting gift of what you already have. For you both, and for all of your kind, who have love in your hearts, I give you the sign of healing.'

Deara felt the soft touch of the kingcups against her wrist and watched the pale tide gently erase from the familiar face both the brown of wind and weather and the lines of wisdom and experience.

The weight in her arms grew heavy. The spirit had flown like a lark into a summer sky, but the frail body breathed a little and swallowed before it was finally still.

Only then did Deara lay the old woman gently back on the couch and gather up the blooms which had slid from her open hand and scattered across the woven rug. For a moment she cradled the flowers in her hands as she would a newborn child. Then, looking down at the sharpening lines of Merdaine's face, she said over again to herself, 'If you do as your heart speaks, then in your sorest need, help will come. But you must trust that it will come.'

She put the kingcups into a pitcher of spring water in the farthest corner of the hut. Then, taking a deep breath, she crossed to the doorway, took up the corner of the door-hanging and standing on tiptoe, tied it up by its leather thongs.

The sunlight, lower now, but still fierce, dazzled her as it poured round her, filling the hut with light. For a moment, she shut her eyes and heard her heart cry out its own farewell. Then, only half aware of what she did, she knelt in the dust to the left of the door, turned towards the west and began to recite in a voice she barely recognised, the welcome to Nodons, the giver of life within life, the bringer of life beyond life.

When I woke it was quite dark and yet my eyes felt dazzled as if by strong sunlight. For a moment, I had no idea what had happened or where I was.

Gradually the dim outlines of my room took shape around me. It was much too dark to see the face of my watch, but beyond the undrawn curtains the sky was pricked with stars. Faint moonlight made pale patches on the wallpaper and caught the bright petals of a

32

kingcup in a glass vase on my table by the window.

Memory flowed back as I burrowed deeper into the soft hollow of the duvet where I had lain down, just as I was, when I staggered back from the garden exhausted after the throbbing pain of that fearsome headache. Startled, I realised that I'd had a full-blown migraine and not a trace of it was left. Not only had the pain completely vanished but there was no hint at all of the nausea that usually lingers long after the pain itself has gone. Apart from my cold arms, chilled by the flow of night air through the open window, I was so blissfully warm and comfortable that I felt I never wanted to move again.

For a little while I lay quite still just enjoying the wonderful sense of being free from pain. Then I began to recall the dream from which I'd woken, an intensely vivid dream full of detail still fresh in my mind. Unlike those dreams that evaporate the moment you wake up and try to catch them, this one was crystal clear and so absorbing I found I could rerun it like a video I had made.

'Now I know what her name is,' I said out loud, amazed that it had only just struck me.

Her name was Deara. She had just been bereaved, as I had. But how different her situation. She had loved the old woman who had died in her arms. With her gone, Deara would be lonely and vulnerable. I didn't see myself as having those problems as a result of losing my mother.

The old woman's name was Merdaine. I whispered it over and over again. I was sure I'd heard it before, somewhere. But nothing came to me. I always forget that the harder you try to remember something the less likely you are to succeed. So I tried to put it out of mind and hoped it would come of its own accord.

I still felt very reluctant to move and break the spell of comfort and well-being that enveloped me, but I had needs that would wait no longer. I was desperate for a pee and I was absolutely ravenous.

The fluorescent lights in the kitchen are hard on the eyes at the best of times. Tonight they were unbearable. Hastily, I poured myself a bowl of cornflakes, stuck it on a tray with a jug of milk and a spoon and carried it down the hall to the sitting room.

A small sliver of moon was rising above the trees down by the road. It cast long shadows across the lawn, as I stood by the window, munching devotedly. Outside, everything was still. Not a single car whizzed past on the road. Not even a bird rustled on its roost in the shrubbery. I thought of all that had happened since William Neill dropped me at the foot of the drive after church. I found it hard to believe I could have experienced so much, in such a short time, and feel so incredibly different at the end of it.

The sitting room clock struck twelve. I laughed aloud. No, my ball gown was not going to turn to rags. I felt quite clear in my mind that what I'd been given was not going to disappear. But I was equally sure that it was up to me to decide exactly what I did with it and whether I was willing to accept what might grow from my experience in the weeks to come, while I dealt with the business that had brought me back to this house and led me to re-encounter the life I had once lived within its limits.

Surprised at how very calm I felt, despite my rising sense of excitement at the prospect, I went back to the kitchen, made some coffee and spread a thick slice of bread with honey. I couldn't remember when bread and honey had tasted so good. I drank my coffee, left cup and crumby plate on the draining board with the empty cornflake bowl, rinsed my fingers and ran back upstairs to my room.

As I went in, it was bright enough to see the blue notebooks sitting on my table. I paused only for a moment before I drew the curtains together, switched on my Anglepoise, unscrewed the top of my pen and began to write.

This time, there was no problem. I had something to set down that I couldn't wait to begin. It must be written now, before even another minute should pass. The sharpness and vividness of what I had experienced today mustn't be lost or allowed to dull with the passage of time. And the words came without deliberate thought and almost without any effort at all.

6

It was two o'clock in the morning when I put down my pen, pulled off my clothes and crawled back under the crumpled duvet, but when I woke next morning and saw what I had written I was so excited by it I ran downstairs full of a bubbling sense of joy. It was so strong that even the dreary list of jobs I jotted down while I drank my second cup of coffee could not extinguish it.

'A touch of the Monday shit,' my friend Sheila would say. She has three children under ten and a husband passionate about all kinds of do-it-yourself. She dreads Monday morning. Left to face the wreckage of the weekend, she steels herself for that moment, back from school, when she pushes open the front door, walks through the empty house and sizes up the full enormity of the task that faces her.

Today I would be keeping her company. The estate agent was coming on Wednesday, so the debris generated by the funeral and our attempts at a preliminary sort would have to be dealt with and the whole house made clean and tidy. And then, there was the woodwork.

I sighed. Beautifully painted only two years ago, the white woodwork throughout the house had suffered a year of Mother's cigarette smoke and a year of neglect. Sandy and I had tried wiping a damp cloth over one of the worst bits. We'd produced a dirty streak and confirmed the source of the nasty smell we noticed the moment we stepped into the closed up rooms. There was masses of it; doors, skirtings, picture rails, banisters, windows, built-in shelves and assorted ledges.

I put on the immersion, heated up enough water for a home confinement and got stuck in. I really did surprise myself. Whether I was so far away inside my head that I didn't notice what I was doing, or whether I had a sudden burst of energy, I don't know, but by lunch time I'd done so well I reckoned I could allow myself to go out into the garden.

I'd already made a beginning, but the flowerbeds were still a sorry sight. Encouraged by the sudden warmth, weeds were growing even more vigorously than the carefully chosen perennials, tall plants leant at drunken angles or squashed less lofty specimens, while winter's damage had left behind empty spaces and dead foliage. My fingers itched to put things right, to restore the shape and form my father had created, a shape and form my mother had never troubled herself to modify. Somehow I felt I owed it to my father to restore what he had so lovingly created.

Morning and evening I did whatever needed doing indoors, but through most of the long hours of daylight I worked in the garden, following the shadows on the flowerbeds so I could move plants that were overcrowded and fill up the empty spaces that spoilt the overall effect. And from the moment I picked up a trowel everything I had learnt from my father came back to me.

'Yes, that's all very well' he would say, when I read out the instructions on the back of a packet of seeds. 'Not all plants have read the book, you know.'

That's what he used always to say when some job needed doing at the wrong time of day, or in the wrong season, or to the wrong plant.

'If you move a plant when it's in flower, it will die,' he would say cheerfully, as he dug it up and carried it carefully across the garden. 'Seedlings should be potted up when they are two inches high,' he would intone as he gently separated the roots from a flourishing boxful three times that height. 'A plant is more interested in growth than in obeying the rules,' he would say dryly. 'Plants can't read books, they just get on with what they need to do.'

He would have been proud of me those first few days when I pruned and moved and planted out with a gay abandon quite at odds with my normal caution. And not a single seedling wilted. Things grew as if they were grateful for being given the space they needed, the light and air they craved.

Everything I touched flourished as if by magic. And then the day the spirea bloomed, its branches weighed down with clusters of delicate white flowers, I suddenly remembered my old childhood fantasy.

'One day,' I said to myself, 'I shall have a magic ring, a huge ring set with masses of small white stones.'

I had picked a single blossom from the small spirea bush and held it between my fingers. Pretending the cluster of tiny flowers was the boss of my magic ring, I walked solemnly round the garden.

'Everything I point this ring at will grow especially well.' I picked up a broken twig and continued on my way. 'Everything I touch with this wand of willow will turn into whatever I want it to turn into and any one who's ill whom I touch with my hands will immediately get better.'

I looked up at the magnificent spirea towering above me and laughed to myself. Would a child in the 1980s entertain such imaginings? Or was it only that their fantasy moved in different directions, into space or time travelling?

I had no answer, but all through the day as I tucked self-sown seedlings into spaces I made for them and stroked their leaves as I

36

firmed in the soil around them – the way my father always did – I was acutely aware of what an imaginative child I must have been and how rudely my fantasy world was shattered when I lost my father's sheltering presence.

For my mother had no time at all for imagination. Indeed, she was actively hostile to even the mildest flights of fancy. I could even remember her objecting to an essay I'd been given for homework: 'A Day in the Life of a Penny.' I hadn't been much enamoured of it myself, but she had been quite virulent. Wasting time on such nonsense. That wasn't what she'd sent us to the High School for.

So what on earth would she make of the experience I'd had yesterday, when this girl called Deara came and healed my migraine, and then by some means I still couldn't even guess at, had begun to share her life with me through the images that came to me unbidden, asleep and awake?

As I worked my way round the garden, once more my mind filled with the images I'd had both sitting under the hawthorns and later while I slept. I found I could call them back so easily and as I went over them again and again I found I was asking questions of them, trying to fit together the fragments that had come to me. Who was this woman, Merdaine, for instance, of whom Deara seemed to be so fond? Clearly not her mother. So what had happened to her mother? And what about brothers and sisters? She seemed a solitary person and yet someone who could be very loving.

It was on my third afternoon in the garden that I started dropping things. I knocked the bloom off a plant I was tying carefully to a stake and was furious with myself. The more I tried to calm down, the more anxious and restless I became. Increasingly, I felt as if there was something terribly important I hadn't done. Something awful would happen if I didn't pay attention and do it right away.

I told myself to stop being silly. Things had been going well; the estate agent had come, spent two hours measuring and taking photographs and made a special note about the well-stocked garden. He'd even complimented me on how well the rockeries were looking. The house was immaculately tidy, the woodwork pristine and the only smell was a hint of lavender polish and the varied perfumes of jugs and vases of blossom and flowers.

In the end I put down my tools and walked straight across the lawn to the hawthorns. The moment I sat down on my stone under their shade, the agitation ceased. 'It's Deara,' I said to myself. 'She needs me. She's in some kind of trouble and I must try to help her.'

Without giving any thought to what I was doing, I propped myself against the trunk of the largest hawthorn, shut my eyes and tried to bring her to mind.

Immediately, there she was, leaving the hut where I had first seen her with the old woman, Merdaine. She walked slowly uphill towards a much larger building near the top of the great mound. I could tell by the way she walked that she was uneasy, reluctant and fearful. At the same time it was clear to me she was determined to do whatever it was she had to do.

I leaned back and concentrated all my attention on the slim figure walking slowly away from me.

It was three days after Merdaine's burial before the King held Council again. Although it was the custom to observe such a period of mourning on the death of a close relative, it was also Morrough's custom to disregard any observance which was not to his liking. So although Merdaine had been mother's sister to him, many were surprised that he made no attempt to go to the Hall of Council.

It was not only Morrough who acknowledged Merdaine's passing. An unfamiliar hush lay over the whole encampment. Deara noticed it as she took up her usual tasks again, waiting as best she might to see what her future would be. There was turbulence, foreboding almost, which made her think of those days when the thunderclouds mass and the Gods vent their wrath upon human kind.

Yet on the surface there was no visible change in the pattern of daily life. The weather continued warm and fine, the cattle grew fat on the lush pastures and the cooking pots were full every day. Women span in the sunshine and ground barley out of doors, their shifts or tunics drawn high in their kirtles to benefit from the sun. But their chatter seemed less noisy, their glances less direct. Many of them feared Merdaine, for she had a sharp tongue and tolerated little foolishness; nevertheless, she was part of their life, stable and secure. Her going left a space which few of them had the slightest idea how to fill.

For Deara, the days passed with incredible slowness. From first light till sundown seemed an eternity of time. She found it hard to sleep in the empty hut and lay wide-eyed in the darkness, seeing again the days of her childhood, her meeting with Merdaine, and all the hours she had spent by her side learning the herblore, making infusions, grinding willow bark, blending spices, repeating and repeating all the recipes, mixtures, prescriptions and laws which Merdaine herself knew. Often her head had ached and the words tangled till she thought she would never understand anything. But it had come. Like the welcome to Nodons, the words had finally stood still. They were hers for ever. As were the parting words Merdaine had spoken to her. She had repeated them to herself as often as any poem or prayer.

The words would stay with her. She would have need of them and of all Merdaine's wisdom, for on the third day after the burial fires she must go to the Hall of Council bearing Merdaine's brooch to Morrough, the King.

Deara had never before entered the Hall of Council for it was not a place where women might go, unless, of course, they had a petition to make, or were party to a dispute. Today, as she joined the groups of people making their way between the King's Hall and the storehouses, she felt full of dread. However much she had tried to master her feelings, she knew she was afraid. Lying awake in the short summer night, part of her wanted to run away, to slip out of the well-gate which was never guarded these days, and disappear into the Long Wood. Another part of her argued that it would be no use. There was nowhere to run to, no neighbouring encampment to shelter her. And besides, although she bore no slave mark, for Merdaine had refused to permit it, her situation would be obvious. A slave was a slave and the law tracts were quite specific as to how they were to be treated. No, there was no escape that way.

'Cumail, where do you think you are going?'

Deara stopped short by the doorway of the hall and turned to face the man who had spoken. It was Conor. Only he would call her 'slave' instead of using the name the woman who had nursed her had given her, or even the commonly used word, 'handmaiden'.

She looked him full in the face. 'I go to petition the King.'

'Oh ho, and by what right does a female cumail enter the Hall of Council?'

'By the right of pledge and token given. I act as the Lady Merdaine instructed me.'

'Pledge? Token?'

Conor's face grew red and he spluttered in fury. These days everyone was challenging his authority. The King rarely consulted him and then ignored his advice, the brehon looked through him, the bard had taken to making jokes at his expense, and now this slip of a girl was quoting the law tracts at him, looking at him quite directly, not even shading her eyes as a woman should when addressing a King's Druid.

'Show me the pledge. Here, let me see it,' he demanded angrily.

Deara regarded him steadily, her grey eyes taking in the deep flush which suffused his face, the pulsating veins at the side of his neck. This man was ill, wounded in spirit by his own weakness. But the illness could not be cured by medicine or healing. Only those disorders of spirit recognised by the sufferer could be treated. Conor would admit no weakness. So, like a wounded animal, he would defend himself by attacking anyone who crossed him.

'I am bidden to show the pledge only to the King. It is not for a cumail to disobey even for Conor, son of Art, chief of the Druids of the Ullaid.'

She cast her eyes to the ground and hoped the gesture might appease him. But the heavy body did not move aside. Not till a quiet, world-weary voice intervened.

'Let the girl go, Conor. The Council will deal with her.'

She looked up and saw a thin hand wave her past. Sennach, the brehon, a tall, emaciated man, pale like a plant grown in deep shade, an unsmiling man, meticulous, moderate in all things. She wondered how a man could live with so little joy.

The Hall was full as she took her place on the lowest bench, nearest the door. The heat was intense already and the smell of men and hounds made her long for the woods and fields. Almost immediately her thin linen tunic began to stick to her back where it touched the wall behind her. She fingered the brooch in the woven purse tied to her kirtle and settled to wait.

Because of the heat, the door of the Hall stood open and a broad shaft of sunlight fell amongst the gathering. It picked out the gold ornaments of the warriors, the worn clothes of the freedmen and the brindled fur of the hunting hounds who lay at the King's feet. As the morning moved on, so the beam of light moved from left to right. Deara thought of Merdaine's finger pointing at the patterns she had drawn in the ash with a piece of stick.

'Come now, child, the brehon sits on the King's right hand, the Druid on his left. Now who is this? And this? And this?'

Deara had learned their names, their ranks and titles, the position which each must occupy. She knew who might address the King, what decisions he would be asked to make, how agreements were made, sureties given, how the law was to be enforced. When other children played at seven stones or touch-and-run, Deara had moved stones in battles and raids fought long ago, had drawn in the dust the heroes and kings of every part of Ireland. She had sailed in willow bark ships to Albi and Gaul, Dalriada and the land of the Bretons, and always Merdaine was there asking her questions, punishing her if she forgot the genealogy of Niall, or Cui Roy, or Maeve of Connaught, the names of the tribes of Albi, or the rank order at a King's Council.

At noon, a woman left a pitcher of water by the door and a warrior took a drinking horn to the King. The heat grew steadily stronger as the Hall became less crowded. Throughout the morning clients had stated their cases. As time passed, the King had grown steadily more irritable. A big, heavy man, he sat with his head half-turned from his petitioners, as if his mind was somewhere else. From time to time he would interrupt, ask a question, pretend he had not understood what was said. Then he would shout and abuse both plaintiff and defendant, threatening what he would have done to such troublesome clients. The punishments he described were brutal, but they did not in themselves alarm Deara. Not only was it part of Morrough's usual

40

way of behaving, it was a tradition, a reminder of bloodier times past and a restatement of the King's enormous power. But it did remind Deara, if reminder she needed, that there was little in either law tract or tradition to protect a female slave.

It was late afternoon by the time her turn came. The water from the pitcher had long gone and her left arm was burning from where the sun had caught it as it moved across the open door. But she was grateful as she rose to her feet and crossed the now empty Hall to kneel before the King.

'The handmaiden of the Lady Merdaine begs by pledge and token to petition her Lord and King, Morrough, son of Ferdagh, ruler . . .'

'Enough girl, enough. The day has been long. What do you want of me?'

Deara bent to take the brooch from its place at her waist, and saw that Conor, who had dozed most of the afternoon, had stirred himself. He was now looking at her intently.

'Sire, the Lady Merdaine bade me give you this as token of the pledge made between you and her last Samain.'

'Pledge, what pledge?'

Morrough turned to look at her, as she held the inlaid brooch towards him.

'What's your name, girl?'

'Deara, my Lord.'

'No, my Lord it is not, the girl lies, as cumail always lie, her name is Deirdre.'

It was Conor who had spoken. Deara saw the familiar flush suffuse his face.

'Deirdre? What of it, Druid?'

'If my Lord would but give me leave to speak, then it would be clear to him. Was it not Art, my father, that warned Carrig Dhu, my Lord's brother, of the doom that awaited him in the wood of Carore? And was it not I that prophesied my Lord's taking of Emain and all the lands of the Ullaid?'

Deara watched the King's face, the brooch in her hand still proffered towards him.

'Speak then, Druid. Tell me what enchantment this Deirdre is to bring upon us.'

Morrough snatched the brooch from her and turned it over in his fingers, his body turned towards the Druid, his eyes still upon her.

'Lord, at your command I tended the Lady in her sickness that I might perform those rites which would restore her to health. But, Lord, I was defeated in my purposes. I, Conor, who have served at all the shrines and brought peace and prosperity to Emain these many years, I was defeated by this Deirdre who has lied in the Hall of Council. This girl bewitched the Lady Merdaine with hand passes

41

and with potions so that she was spirit lost. Then she tied back the hanging and called the God. I could not stop her for I was powerless to resist, held immobile as was the Lady by her wicked powers. And since the Lady's untimely death my Lord has had news, dark news I think, for my powers are not fully restored to me. Lord, this girl bears the name of sorrow. Sorrow she has brought and yet more will she bring. Evil she has done to the Lady Merdaine, evil she will bring to this place and to my Lord if she be not cast out. The Lady, sister to your good mother, nourished in her bosom a snake. Out of goodness, she took this outcast, a child spawned on a hillside, by a woman whose wickedness brought sorrow to Tara, death to our warriors and the breaking of a treaty, joined again only with the greatest of toil by the King and his loyal servants.

'Sire, I beg of you, for the vengeance of the Lady Merdaine and the safety of your people, do now what should have been done at birth.' Conor paused, his face livid with colour, a light in his eye that Deara had seen only in animals crazed with pain, in labour or mortally wounded. She felt sweat trickle between her shoulder blades. Yet somehow, now it had come, she breathed easier, as if there were some comfort in seeing the danger and facing it rather than anxiously wondering from whence and in what manner the threat would come.

'You would kill her, Druid? And what manner would you favour?'

The King turned his eyes from Deara and began to outline both torture and modes of death. As he spoke, so his large frame seemed to grow more ominous, his dark voice becoming yet more threatening.

'Come, Druid, what manner would you favour?'

''Tis of no matter, Lord, but that it were done quickly.'

'This evening, perhaps? Or shall you despatch her now? Fergus, your weapon, my friend.'

The King reached behind him and a warrior drew his sword and put it in his outstretched hand.

'Here, Druid, here is a sword.'

'This evening would do very well.'

Conor spoke hastily, his words muffled like a man who is parched. The light in his eye dimmed and he seemed to draw back from both the powerful questioning presence of the King and the proffered sword.

'This evening will do as well as any. Is that so, Druid?'

The King balanced the sword in his hand, narrowing his eyes as if he were testing its trueness. For a moment he looked at the inlay of the handgrip, examining the delicate workmanship in the beasts entwined there. When he spoke again, he spoke softly.

'And where would you suggest you kill this woman?'

Deara did not hear Conor's reply. She was watching the King's face, her body taut with tension. In the silence, she became aware of men moving like shadows along the walls. She waited for Conor to speak, to name the place of her execution. But Conor paused again.

Suddenly, it was the King's voice that thundered out. Warm and welcoming, free of the dark menace which had chilled her heart as he consulted the Druid about her death, it roared down the Hall.

'Welcome back, my brave warriors. Come, draw closer. I forgive you for leaving me thus to the business of Council. You would not have left me had I a sword in my hand and an enemy at my back. I know that well. Come, come closer and let you judge this case.'

The King rose to his feet and pointed the sword at Deara, as the men drew closer.

'Here is this girl, a slave, the handmaiden of the Lady Merdaine. She is accused by Conor, chief of the Druids in the Ullaid, of witchcraft, of causing the death of that Lady. He wishes her death, for all your sakes, to keep you safe from evil.'

The King paused. Deara felt at that moment, that if she took her eyes away from his face, he would toss her aside like a bone to his hound.

'Do not let him frighten you.'

As if the words had been spoken by someone present, Deara felt the memory touch her. She held her gaze and it was the King's eyes that moved away.

'What think you, my warriors?'

There was not a murmur from the warriors. They knew their King too well to answer a question that was purely rhetorical.

He raised the sword and looked at her again. Then he spoke once more, addressing himself to her in a strangely quiet manner.

'A rare thing is it not, handmaiden, for a Druid, a Druid of such mighty power and knowledge of magic, to require your death so unceremoniously? Think you not it more seemly for him to make sacrifice to the Gods, to ascertain the most auspicious time for your despatch, the most auspicious place, and the most pleasing method? Surely there are proper observances for the purification of the evil caused by one such as you – a witch?'

The warriors murmured. Even the slower-witted amongst them had seen the drift of the King's words. They had no love for Conor and his self-important ways, but, even if they had, it would be enough that the King's favour had turned against him.

'What say you, witch? Shall your King become your Druid? Shall I consult the magic lore and tell you what I see?'

The warriors roared their approval, and Morrough, smiling broadly, held out his hands to them.

'I see a fat man, and a long road,' he whispered loudly. 'And I see hounds baying and footsteps fleeing – and – I do believe – ah, the mists, the mists dim my vision, I cannot see as I should. My powers

43

are dimmed by a slavegirl – oh, what mischief is this . . . I am asleep again by her spells.'

There was laughter now, and the slapping of hands on thighs. Conor's face, Deara could not see, but within her grew a seed of hope. If only she kept her eyes on the King she might yet live.

The laughter died away as the King made a dramatic gesture with his raised arms. He closed his eyes.

'Ah, but hold, all is revealed to me. Why, it is Conor. Conor, the fat man, who boasts of the past and listens at doorcurtains, who feasts on the sacrifices the poor bring him out of fear. What say you, men, to my prediction? Shall I not be your Druid?'

'Surely, surely. Morrough, our Druid and our King.'

The Hall filled with noise, the bang of weapons on wooden benches and walls, the hammer of fist on collar and belt, the stamp of feet, the chanting shout: 'Morrough, Morrough.'

From the corner of her eye Deara glimpsed Conor's hasty movement as he ran from the chamber. The men, still laughing, drifted away.

Morrough filled his drinking horn and lowered it, his head thrown back, his eyes closed. He wiped his mouth with his hairy arm and threw himself back in his chair.

'So, brehon, what pledge did I give the Lady Merdaine? I have forgot.'

'Sire, I have the deed here and your mark upon it.'

'Get on then, man, would you have us here till Connaught wished us well?'

'Item, that the Lady Merdaine doth give all her property to the King for his sole use upon one condition.'

'Condition? I agreed to no condition. You are mistaken, man. You cannot make out your own marks.'

'Sire, it is not writ in my marks; the script is in the lady's hand.'

'Then how can you read it? Her hand she conned from a trader in my father's time. A rogue he kept about the place to play fidchell with.'

The brehon, who had throughout the day tolerated the King's irritability, seemed at last to lose patience.

'My Lord, the times are changing and we must change with them. It would not do if all of the King's servants dozed by the fire and lined their pockets. In these three winters, Lord, I too have conned this language that can be written down more easily than our own. By your leave, I read you the words you spoke to the Lady Merdaine:

'By the brooch of my mother brought in token, I swear that I will free the girl, Deara, give her dowry of twenty milk cows that she may be betrothed, or, if it be her wish, dowry in gold that she may pursue her studies with Alcelcius of Ard Macha into whose household she may enter.'

'Twenty milk cows!'

The King bellowed as if he had been stung by a wasp, his face dark with anger.

'Where in the name of all the Gods, man, would I find the price of twenty milk cows to dower a slave-girl? Had I a daughter of my own I might be hard-pressed to do as well.'

'Sire, may I remind you of the kist the Lady Merdaine left to you. It was her wish that you would benefit by her gift.'

The beam of sunlight that had filled the chamber all day finally moved westwards. Shadows sprang up in all the corners. Deara, still standing before the King, felt again the sense of desolation that had come to her as she tied back the hanging after Merdaine's death. Then, she had faced the blinding light of day with no protection from its strength, now, what strength she had seemed to be draining away with the light, as the King and brehon argued.

'Well, then, open it. If you have no key, let Fergus fetch Ulrann and his hammer from the forge.'

The brehon, however, had already produced the key. Like everything he had done, all day, he proceeded meticulously. Watching him, Deara realised that his manner was both a defence against the King's turbulence and a compliment to it. These two men, opposite as they seemed, were in some way bound to each other. It was not a bond of love, such as she saw amongst the young warriors. It was a bond of need, a defence against a loneliness which neither colleagues, nor warriors, wifes or concubine, could take away. In the midst of her own need, intensely aware of her own unprotected isolation, suddenly she saw a need just as great in two men who, it seemed, had everything that she lacked. They, who had position and power, who could dispose of her life by a word to a warrior, or a mark on a tablet, were in a way she could only dimly grasp, as weak, as vulnerable, as unsure of their place in the world, as she herself was.

'By all the Gods.'

The King turned to Deara from the open kist behind which the brehon still knelt.

'What do you know of this, girl?'

'Of what, my Lord?'

By way of answer, the King leaned down and showered at her feet a handful of coins and a cluster of armbands, beaten in gold and inlaid with bronze. In the dim light they gleamed like pale flowers at dusk.

The thin hands of the brehon set down on his table a silver drinking cup, a set of gold torcs, a terracotta figurine and a jewelled belt.

Deara looked from one to the other.

45

'Well, then, what do you say?'

'My Lord, it is the custom to bring an offering to the God when one comes to ask for his healing.'

'And do my people bring such gifts as these that I, their King, have not the least of them?'

'No, my Lord, the people of Emain bring food and drink, and neighbouring peoples bring cloth or skins. Only the traders bring such gifts as these.'

'Traders? The Lady Merdaine traded? With what?'

'Wound salves, sire.'

'To salve the wounds of our enemies?'

'No, my Lord. All that I could make went to Albi.'

'You? You made them?'

'Yes, my Lord, at the Lady's bidding. They are very good wound salves, the same as we use ourselves.'

The King sat down suddenly, filled the silver drinking horn from a pitcher of beer and downed it in one long swallow. He wiped his face and began to laugh.

It was a real laugh, not the hard, uneasy laugh Deara had heard so often that day. She glanced at the brehon, but his face had not relaxed its habitual close scrutiny. He was examining the final items from the bottom of the box and marking their value on a tally.

'Well, then?'

'Between 200 and 300 milk cows, Sire. I must consult to be sure.'

'So, Deara – that was your name, was it not?'

'Yes, my Lord.'

'So, you shall have your dowry. How say you to Marban, son of Dairmid, a brave young warrior? He lacks nothing but a wife to furnish him with new weapons, a good horse and a handful of sons.'

Deara's heart sank. She knew little of the young warriors, for the Lady never spared her to serve with the other young women in the King's Hall, so much was there to do in preparation for the coming of the traders. But Marban she knew of by repute, as did all in Emain. A small, swarthy man, boastful even beyond the custom of warriors, a man who took pleasure in cruelty to any weak creature, be it child or hound puppy. The thought of Marban made her tremble more than the threat of Conor.

The King was staring at her again, fiddling impatiently with the brooch she had brought as a token.

'Come then, girl, your word, and let Sennach draw up the agreement.'

'If it please my Lord, I would ask my dowry in gold, that I may enter the house of Alcelcius.'

'Alcelcius? What manner of man is this, Sennach, with such a name. Is he a trader?'

46

'No, my Lord, he is not of our people. He came here from Dalriada and was once a surgeon with the legions from Gaul.'

'And you would go to be his concubine?'

'No, my Lord, Alcelcius is an old man, who takes pleasure in books and writings. I would go to learn what the Lady Merdaine would not teach me.'

'And what was that?'

'To read and write, that I might set things down as she did.'

'And make wound salves?'

'If they are needed.'

The King swung away from her and thrust the sword by his chair into the earthen floor at its owner's feet. The man started and the King laughed, short and hard.

'Make your wound salves, Deara, aye and learn well to bind and splint – but pray to Lug that they will not be needed. D'ye hear, girl?'

Deara dropped her eyes from the King's face in acknowledgement of his command. She saw the glint of jewels at her feet. When she looked up again her fear disappeared, for in the King's eyes she saw a fear far greater than her own. Not for himself, but for his people, for all that was entrusted to him.

Morrough, the strong and mighty Morrough, King of Emain, ruler of all the Ullaid, sat in his carved chair, fondling the muzzle of his hound bitch and looking at her. What she had seen in his eyes was something she knew with her heart. This man stood alone. Alone in spirit and every bit as unprotected as she had known herself to be. She felt herself shiver and knew the flesh had roughened on her bare arms, though the Hall was thick with heat.

'D'ye hear me, girl?' he repeated more insistently. 'Pray to Lug. Wear this for the Lady Merdaine.'

Morrough pushed the brooch into her hand, roused a sleeping hound with his toe and left the chamber without a backward glance, followed by the dogs, the chief of the guard and a small group of warriors on duty by the door.

Deara stood staring at the precious object in her hands, unable to grasp what had happened to her.

She had entered the Hall of Council, a slave, a fearful slave, knowing that her life might be forfeited without the protection of Merdaine. And now in her hands, she held the Royal brooch of Emain. Worn by the Princesses of the Ullaid for as long as bard or Druid could remember, worn by the King's mother, and mother's mother and by his mother's youngest sister, Merdaine. Now hers. This thing of power and beauty and protection. No man of the Ullaid would dare raise a hand against her. Even the enemies of the tribe would heed such a token, if only in hope of the ransom money such a captive might bring.

47

'Deara.'

The sound of her name seemed to come from a long way away. She looked up, her eyes still held in the swirling tracery of the brooch. The Hall of Council was empty, except for one pale face, Sennach, the brehon. He sat at his table looking at her.

'You serve Nodons?'

She bowed her head in acknowledgement, for words seemed to have deserted her.

'Your God has been kind.'

His statement was matter-of-fact. The voice he used was no different from the voice he had used all day, to question, to clarify, to record. But something in his eyes spoke louder, less dispassionately. It told her what she was already coming to recognise, that something had come to help her in her deepest need. She had no idea what it was, but it had come, just as Merdaine had promised. Some would call it a miracle.

She looked at the brehon steadily and saw the weariness which dragged at his body. It looked as if his life was draining away. She who had been given back life, could not bear what she saw.

'Sir, I thank you for your kindness to me . . .'

She paused and grasped more firmly the brooch in her right hand.

'Sir, I would take an offering to the God and bring you back a draught from the well.'

The brehon laughed. The sound was short and brittle.

'Would you heal me then of the cares of office? Will you give me back sleep and pleasure in food? Have you a wound salve for the heart, then?'

'The God has all these things.'

'And he will give them to you, if the offering is large enough?'

'No, sir. The God gives, the God takes away. It is His wisdom, not the offering, but we who serve are permitted to ask, for those who will give us leave.'

The brehon glanced round the empty hall as if he were making an inventory of the blackened rafters, the wooden benches and the empty drinking horns.

'And if I say yes, what offering will you take?'

'I do not know, Sir. When I have held your need in my heart, the God may tell me what he wishes, and then I will go to the well.'

'And bring back healing in a pitcher?'

'If the God wishes.'

The brehon repeated the words thoughtfully and considered them, as he considered everything. On the face of it, it was quite obvious. The girl believed a traditional set of superstitions known to the tribe for centuries. Most women did. Quite unfounded in the face of any real danger, but no doubt useful for day-to-day ailments. One had to

48

admit some of these things worked. Some didn't. One could see that quite clearly. The girl herself was a different matter. Not clear at all. There was something unusual about her. She was almost enough to make one imagine the unimaginable.

'If I say yes, when will you go?'

'Tomorrow, Sir, as soon after the noon hour as I can finish my tasks.'

'Very well, then. Come to me at this hour and we shall see if your pitcher brings back my appetite. Go now and eat. May your food bring you strength.'

'Thank you, Sir. May your sleep bring you peace.'

Deara smiled at the brehon and bowed her head as she returned the evening greeting. Then she walked from the Hall of Council into the swirling woodsmoke of the cooking fires and the red flame of the sunset, carrying in her left hand the Royal brooch of Emain.

7

When I saw Deara walk from the Hall of Council, a free woman
under the protection of the King himself, after all the anxiety she had
suffered throughout that long day, I was so relieved and so excited I
wanted to stand up and cheer. I wanted to run after her and throw
my arms round her and challenge anyone who might have slighted
her, and tell them to their face, 'There, I told you so'.

What actually happened was very different. I opened my eyes only
to find myself under the hawthorns, exactly where I'd sat myself down
when the awful agitation came upon me and I'd started making a
mess of everything I tried to do.

Plainly, I couldn't chase after Deara, so I made no move at all, just
went on sitting in the dappled shade, looking out over the lawn and
enjoying the splashes and patches of colour in the flourishing borders.
But I was so grateful something had come to help Deara in her need.
At the same time, I couldn't help being totally absorbed and enthralled
by the remote world in which she lived. I found I was running through
the whole of her time in the Hall of Council once again, minute by
minute, detail by detail.

I was intrigued by the unwritten law Morrough administered in
such an extraordinary fashion and the customs and practices of the
people over whom he ruled. I was appalled by Conor the Druid,
curious about this person, Alcelcius, whose home was soon to be
Deara's, and absolutely intrigued by Sennach the brehon with his
tally system for reckoning wealth and his new language he had taught
himself over the last three winters.

There was so much more I wanted to know, so many questions I
was dying to ask. How I wished I'd been able to see those documents
on his table, particularly the one in Merdaine's hand. I love old
documents of any kind. Regardless of their content, I feel they bring
you so close to the person who wrote them. I've often imagined how
exciting it would be to touch something really old and precious, the
kind of thing now kept behind security glass with alarm systems like
the *Lindifarne Gospels*, or the *Book of Kells*, or the one I should like to
handle most of all, the *Book of Armagh* itself.

Sennach was such a precise character, meticulous and methodical.
His long, pale face reminded me of a man who used to work with

Daddy in the shop. Poor man, he never looked well, but he was still alive, able to dig his garden despite his eight decades while Daddy was long gone.

I sat on and on, with so much going through my head I couldn't begin to sort it all out. Suddenly, everything cleared and words took shape just as if someone had spoken them out loud. It was the advice Merdaine had given to Deara just before she died. 'If you do as your heart speaks, then in your sorest need, help will come. But you must trust that it will come.'

I repeated the words aloud to myself. They made perfect sense, however many centuries might have passed since Merdaine herself had spoken them. Help *would* come for Deara, but only if she believed that it would. And if it would come for Deara, then it would come for me were I to believe that it would. The more I thought about it, the more it seemed to me Merdaine's advice applied as much to me as to Deara. I had to confess to myself that I'd lost my hopefulness over the years, my confidence that things really would or could come out right for me. Oh yes, I'd achieved many things. I was successful after the fashion of my own world. I had a decent job and earned a reasonable income. But so much potential happiness was marred by my doubts and anxiety.

Suddenly and very sharply, I saw that Merdaine's words were telling me it would be better for me to cherish hope, to develop new confidence and take a chance on failure, than to go on in my normal, cautious and considered way.

As the shadows lengthened across the lawn, reluctantly I went back into the house. As I came through the kitchen into the hall I stopped in my tracks and stared at a striking, arched arrangement of pear blossom and dark petalled tulips, set against the well-polished mirror above the hall table, as if I'd never laid eyes on it before. I laughed at myself.

For days now, all I could think of was getting through the cleaning jobs in the house so I'd be free to go out into the garden. And without being quite aware of what I was up to, I'd brought the garden back in with me. All the rooms were fresh and full of light. With the windows open, the smell of blossom and flowers outdoors mingled with the perfume from the branches and posies I'd arranged and placed in every possible corner.

'No wonder the estate agent was so complimentary,' I said aloud, as I passed down the hall. I pushed wide the sitting room door. Gone was the electric fire Mother had parked in the hearth, the clutter of small tables that fell over at the slightest provocation, the assorted ashtrays and piles of product catalogues that were her constant companions. Out in the garage I'd found the wrought iron companion set from the hearth and the old willow basket that once served the

52

open fire. Filled with turf and logs from a dusty corner of the garden shed, it now stood ready for a wet afternoon or a chilly evening. To my amazement, I realised I was actually looking forward to sitting here, by a fire, in the lamplight.

Then I walked through the whole house and I wondered how I could ever have seen it as dark and dreary. I was amazed the effect a few well-placed objects retrieved from cupboards and drawers had had. I'd found them, stacked away like the fire irons and the log basket, things I'd once known and loved. Old-fashioned. Dustcatchers. Those were the words to describe any object that didn't meet with Mother's approval. Well, I'd certainly shifted plenty of dust, but as I stood looking over the banisters down into the heart of the house, it seemed to me that the light, warm summer breeze had swept something much more pervasive than dust out of Anacarrig, once and for all.

In the few dark hours of the short May night, Deara lay awake yet again. Despite the help the day had brought and the reassuring shape of Merdaine's brooch in a pouch beneath her pillow, she felt uneasy. The hut seemed strange and empty, bereft of Merdaine's spirit, untenanted, as if cold ash lay unswept in the hearth, food bowls stood unscoured and the strewn rushes browned with age as she had seen them often enough in homes abandoned after plague.

She looked up into the darkness. Through the smoke hole a single star shone in the deep midnight sky. Outside there were myriads of stars, so still and perfect the night, but from her bed she could see but one, solitary, in all that great gathering.

That was exactly how she felt. She was surrounded by people, she was close enough to touch them, speak to them, to share food with them, but all the time she remained separate. Isolated. She wondered if anyone in all Emain felt as she did, lying wide-eyed on her narrow wooden couch.

She turned onto her side, curling the woollen rug around her, seeking comfort more than warmth. She closed her eyes.

Immediately she stood again in the Hall of Council. She heard Conor's voice.

'You lie. Your name is not Deara. It is Deirdre.'

She shivered, the memory as fearful as the moment itself had been. Yes, she was Deirdre. She bore a name given to no girl-child in all the tribes of the land. Deirdre. Deirdre of the Sorrows. Any child old enough to sit by a campfire could tell you the tale by heart. It was not the name itself but the manner of her name-giving that called up anxiety and despair within her, an aching pain, which Merdaine herself had not been able to heal, the hurt of memories which Conor would never allow to rest.

53

Her mind began to fill with images. Now they had begun she had no power to stop them. She felt her body stiffen, her fingernails bite the softness of her palms, her chest tighten as if to restrain her racing heart.

The horses' hooves were drumming in her ears. Faster and faster they came, clods of earth thrown back as they galloped towards Emain and the safety of the stockades. But it was too far. With weapons flashing in the moonlight the warriors turned aside to the grove on the far hillside to make what defence they could against the assailants who had lain in wait for them almost at the entrance to their own encampment. They gathered close around a woman in their midst. Half-crazed by fear and noise the white mare crashed between the trees and stopped abruptly in the small clearing which surrounded the stone altar to the God. The woman, white as the mare she rode, half slid, half fell to the ground. She lay there writhing in pain as the warriors made what brief defence they could against the encircling host.

Tears streamed down Deara's face, her body began to shake uncontrollably. Let it come, said Merdaine. To heal the pain you must let yourself feel it. You must accept it. Do not fight it, do not deny it. Deny it and you give it power. Accept it and it becomes part of you, subject to your own power.

She had not understood. Nor did she understand now. And now there was no Merdaine to comfort her, to wipe away her tears and assure her that one day the images would go, that remembrance would no longer be like a knife in her heart.

She could see the woman now. She lay exhausted against the God's altar beyond the fallen lords of Emain. Across the valley horns rang out, the alarm was raised, but above the noise of warriors riding out in pursuit of the raiders came a far more menacing sound.

'There she is, there is the evil of which I warned you. The one for whom our best warriors have given their lives so worthlessly, their honour ensnared by her evil spells. Kill her, my friends. Avenge your dead comrades.'

Conor, his staff raised in his hands, his eyes glittering, burst into the clearing, a group of young warriors at his elbow. Swords drawn, ready to do battle with the whole host of Tara, they faltered as they saw in the moonlight the dark, still shapes which lay before them and the deadly-white face of a woman in a blood-soaked gown. In that moment of stillness they heard, as Deara now did, the tiny mewing cry of a newborn child.

'Why do you pause? Think you this is a woman? Nay, no woman this, but evil itself in woman's garb. See she spawns evil as she has spawned death on this hillside. Come despatch her and her cub. Let us make them a sacrifice to Lug that he will give us vengeance for Tagganath and all our brave kin. What use this Nodons, this mealy-

54

mouthed God who cures warts for hags and protects not our bravest and best? Away with them.'

The warriors surged forward. The woman raised her head. Her voice was but a whisper, but there was no fear in it. All there heard her speak.

'Kill me if you will – gladly I go – but not this child. Here do I name her Deirdre. Sorrow is her birthright and sorrow she shall know, but the greatest sorrow of all comes to him that shall wish her harm.'

With enormous effort the woman gathered herself, so that she sat upright, her back against the stone altar in front of the well, the child cradled in her lap.

'Send me a woman of your tribe.'

'Woman? To be your slave? A slave's slave?'

Conor roared in fury. He stepped from the darkness of the encircling trees into the moonlight, his dark shadow enlarged by the flicker of torches which had now been brought.

'Stand aside, Conor.'

It was Merdaine who spoke. It was she who wrapped the child in her cloak and waved the warriors away.

'This woman's blood is spilt already. Go home and comfort your wives and mothers. There are dead enough to carry to the fires.'

Deara wept.

She wept for her mother who died in Merdaine's arms. And she wept for Merdaine. She wept for the women who knelt by the bodies of husband, or son. She wept for the sorrow in the face of the brehon, the fear in the eyes of the King. She wept till her arms were damp with tears and the star had faded from the smoke hole. Then she fell asleep.

Long after dawn had broken she woke, her dream still alive in her memory. She had been walking in sunshine, across fields of kingcups. Green and gold. The colours beloved of the God. It was a sign. She knew now what she must do. Merdaine's parting gift, the kingcups, refreshed now in the cool shadows of the hut, must be offered for Sennach, for the healing of his spirit. She must make haste with her morning duties.

The God's well was not far from Emain. Beyond the outer rampart it lay just across the valley in a small hawthorn grove, the surviving trees of a wood which once covered the whole hillside.

At one time, individuals as well as those who served the God would visit the well. They would leave an offering, tie a scrap of fabric to the branches and ask for healing for the person from whose tunic the fragment had been cut. Merdaine could remember a time when the thorns had blossomed with tokens all the year round. Now, few people went there except herself.

Deara went often, either to fetch water for infusions, for the water from the God's well was pure and clear and had never failed, or to pray for the sick. It was many years now since Merdaine had come with her. As soon as Deara was strong enough to bear the water pitcher by herself she had sent her alone, saying that she would worship in her own place. So Deara had come to know hours of quiet, the only times in the crowded life of the encampment when she was alone. Alone, and yet never troubled by the loneliness which was her companion in the midst of the crowded encampment. Her visits to the God's well were always welcome. Today was no exception.

As she set off down the dusty path, Deara was aware of a sense of excitement. Some flicker of happiness had rekindled within her. Drawing warmth from the brilliant sunshine and power from the upturned faces of buttercups and daisies strewn amid the grass of the wayside, it grew stronger as she crossed the valley and made her way up the slope beyond.

It was five days since she had brought back the full pitcher to wash Merdaine's body. Now the hawthorns carried the first touch of blossom. The familiar heavy scent drifted towards her on heat-shimmered air as she followed the thread of a path through the encircling trees. The place was deserted and full of deep stillness. Before her lay the stone altar on which she would offer Merdaine's parting gift.

She bowed her head, closed her eyes and repeated the prayer of greeting. Its words were so very familiar. She had learnt them when she was seven years old, when Brega, wife of Dairmid, her foster-mother, had brought her to Merdaine to begin her service. On that very first day, she had stood at this spot and repeated them line by line after Merdaine. Today, it seemed as if she heard them for the first time. She asked the God for help, knowing without doubt that in some way her request would be granted.

She opened her eyes, then blinked them again in amazement. The altar had gone. The encircling thorn trees had gone. Everything known and familiar had disappeared. Where the wall had been there stood three old thorns. Beneath them, stretched out across a piece of stone lay a woman in strange clothes, her dark hair tangled about her. She was crying in sore distress, the fierceness of her sobs shaking her narrow shoulders.

Deara's first thought was of her mother.

But how could her mother wear such strange clothing? Besides, this woman was not with child. Her body was slim, her long, dark hair had not been braided as it would be were she betrothed or married. She wore the frayed and sun-bleached breeches that slaves usually wear, but her feet, which were bare like a slave's, were neither brown from the sun, nor broken from toil. Above the waist she wore a tunic, so short she had to put it inside the breeches, and of so fine a stuff that she could see the fine tracery of some undergarment that enfolded the woman's breasts.

Deara took a step forward. As she watched, the woman rolled over, sat up and wiped her eyes. Her face was red and blotched with crying. On her left wrist the woman wore a gold band set with a colourless gem. There were two rings on a finger of the same hand: one plain, one set with small blue gems. She couldn't possibly be a slave, for it was forbidden by law for a slave to wear gold. Indeed, it was even forbidden for them to carry gold for their master or mistress.

The woman's tears caught at Deara's heart. What could she do to heal such distress?

'Ask your heart what to do.'

Merdaine's words came to Deara just as they had come in the Hall of Council. She stepped forward. 'Have you come to be healed?' she asked softly.

The woman looked up, startled, her grey eyes full of amazement. She was much older than Deara had imagined from the shape of her body. The body was that of a maiden, but the lines in her face suggested that she was in her fourth decade.

Deara looked around the unfamiliar place as if it might somehow explain the presence of the woman. But there was not a single thing she recognised. Apart from the warmth of the sun and the blossom on the trees, everything seemed strange. Near the crest of the hill beyond the thorns was a building unlike any she had ever seen. The walls were of square red stones, all the same size, and they were pierced by dark shapes in which she could see not only reflections of trees which were behind her, but also objects which lay beyond the walls. Between her and this place was a shorn meadow. It had stripes upon it as when the wind blows, but they ran in contrary directions. Not a single wildflower grew on this space, which was the size of two cattle pens.

Beyond, there were flowers. Great, brilliant splashes of purple and white and gold. But all the flowers grew among boulders. How could there be nourishment for such profusion?

She looked down again at the woman. She had taken her hands from her face and had stopped crying. It was clear now what was wrong. The half-closed eyes were always a sign. She knew now what she must do.

She laid down the pitcher and the offering she was carrying and showed the woman her empty hands. Then she moved gently towards her, careful not to startle her. The woman did not move. The grey eyes regarded her steadily but without fear. Deara smiled and put her hand on the woman's forehead. No wonder she had cried. Beneath her hand, she felt the pain oscillate, pulsing and contracting. She put her other hand at the back of the woman's neck, closed her eyes, and began to pray to the God.

As she prayed she followed the lines of pain from temple, to neck and to shoulders. The lines were red and deep. Her fingers traced them, pressing gently, always keeping the body steady, the balance even, like a cup of wine that one carries over unraked rushes. The lines went all the way to the woman's waist. It was some time before they responded to her touch and she felt the patterns change. The hard, sore places began to dissolve, she felt them disperse as the darkness that had invaded the body dissolved and its own light grew again.

An image flickered into Deara's mind as it always did when she healed. However often it happened, it could still take her by surprise. The skill of release Merdaine had taught her and made her practice till she was able to read a back like a plan of a country, tracing out which paths led to which centres, which paths were near the surface, which buried deep, which revealed the pain and which concealed it. Reading the images that came as the pain went, however, was a very different matter. Reading these could not be taught, Merdaine had said, because they were the gift of the God. They could only be used with the guidance that came from her own heart.

She had tried to be open to what was given. Already she knew that what she saw was always related to the source of pain. If she spoke of her seeing to the one in pain, at first the pain would grow stronger, but then, if they could bear the distress and speak of what was revealed to them when the pain increased, the pain would fade away. Often it did not return.

Deara opened her eyes and looked down at the woman whose body she touched. She sat quite still, head slightly bowed, eyes closed. There were traces of blue eyepaint on her lids and dark smudges below her eyes. But the red swelling had gone, the skin was soft and smooth – not young, but not hardened as many women's faces were by hardship or bitterness.

She closed her eyes once again and let the images come.

A child. Running across the shorn meadow, in its hands a piece of blue parchment. The child kneels by the boulders, tears the parchment. From it drops seeds. One by one, with great care, the child makes holes with its finger, drops one seed into each hole, for there is after all soil between the boulders. Now a woman comes. Speaks words in anger. Sends the child away, scratches in the earth, finds the seeds and takes away the blue parchment.

The image fades. Another shapes. It is the same child grown taller. She is sitting by herself beneath trees talking to someone. But there is no playmate to be seen. The woman appears again. She moves silently behind the trees and listens to what the child is saying. Then she steps out. The child jumps in fright and the woman laughs, becomes angry, speaks quickly, and sends her away.

Deara lifted her right hand from the woman's shoulder and opened her eyes. The images she could not understand. Clearly the child was she who was in pain. The woman had harmed her in some way. But in what way she could not tell, for she could not share the image. She had no words this woman would understand, for she was of another tribe.

The pain, however, would go now. She could do no more. She addressed the God, spoke the prayer of thanksgiving, made the sign of the coiled snake for the woman's protection and took her left hand away.

The woman looked up, smiled and spoke.

They were words of thanks. Deara was quite clear about that. But the words themselves were quite unfamiliar. She thought of traders and travellers she had met, but not even they had spoken in this manner. She felt sad. Sad that this woman was not her mother, that she could not speak to her, or give her a draught from the God's well to speed her recovery.

She made a sign of lying down to sleep.

The woman nodded, but did not go on her way to her sleeping place. She had stretched out a hand towards her. It came to Deara that perhaps the woman needed a token from the God. She picked up the flowers of her offering, chose a bloom that had both a flower and a bud, and handed it to her.

For a moment she was intensely aware of this woman on whom she had laid her hands. She saw her as if from a very long way away, sensing a great space between them. But at the same time, she was also intensely aware that she knew this woman. She felt a familiarity, an intimacy, that she had never before known with any other person. It was as if her hands had touched some secret part of the woman's being, known to few, perhaps not even to the woman herself.

Deara watched the woman's hand reach out for the token she offered. She was aware of the grey eyes smiling, the touch of the woman's fingertips. In the same moment she experienced a strange, shimmering weariness and then knew herself to be alone.

She sighed and looked around her. Gone. Yes, she had gone. And everything else as well. The old trees, the stone on which she had sat, the shorn meadow and the strange dwelling place. In front of her stood the familiar worn stone coping of the God's well. The fading flowers of her last offering dropped their petals around the base of the small earthenware jug which held them. Driven by the warm breeze they fluttered into the lush grass which grew where the water always splashed down from newly drawn pitchers.

For a few moments Deara stood, poised between joy and sorrow, elated by hope and possibility, yet saddened by the brevity of this strange meeting.

Then, into the stillness of the deserted grove, where only birdsong broke the heavy somnolence of the afternoon, came words of comfort. Merdaine's words, spoken in this place, when she had talked to Deara about joy.

'Joy, true joy, comes but rarely, but when it does, cherish it. Cherish the moments you have without longing for others.'

Deara took the flowers of her offering and looked at them. It was the moments she had just been given that she must cherish. For them she would give thanks.

8

Two days after the estate agent's visit to Anacarrig, a lengthy communication dropped through the letterbox. He thanked me for my kind instructions, repeated all he'd said about the state of the market, the possibility of finding the right kind of buyer and the likelihood of achieving a satisfactory sale. He named a selling price which amazed me. But it was his final paragraph that left me feeling agitated and upset for the rest of the morning.

He regretted he'd been unable to advertise in this week's local papers because the photographs of the property were not available until Thursday afternoon. However, he'd gone ahead with putting the house in the *Belfast Telegraph*, as we'd agreed. Their weekend property guide had a wide circulation, he assured me, and as his firm's offices remained open all day on Saturdays he would no doubt be in touch with me to arrange viewing for this coming weekend.

Working so hard all week to get the house ready for viewing, it just hadn't struck me I could end up having to show people round so soon. The thought appalled me. I realised with a shock that I wanted to see no one here at Anacarrig.

For a whole week I'd hardly spoken to a soul. Apart from the estate agent, the only other person was the mechanic who was working on Mother's car. He'd called in on his way home from work to let me know why it was taking so long. A matter of a part that hadn't been sent when it was ordered. Mr Neill had rung to ask if I needed anything from the shops in Armagh, but I'd reassured him that Sandy had filled the freezer so full I'd have a job eating it all up before it was time to leave.

I would have phoned my dear friend, Helen, but she was still in Oxford on her course. Joan had gone to visit a cousin in Rye, Sandy was somewhere in France buying old farmhouses and my beloved Matthew was visiting hill villages north of Maharajpur a dozen miles at least from the nearest telephone.

I hadn't been aware of my solitariness at all. In fact, I had actually enjoyed being on my own. Tears of disappointment and frustration sprang to my eyes as I read the letter a second time and imagined what would happen when the phone started to ring.

And, of course, I had a rotten morning as a consequence, the kind where nothing you begin to do can be carried through. Some tool, or code number, or critical piece of information just isn't available and you can't get on without it. It got so bad at one point and I felt so irritable that I just couldn't keep going. I took myself off across the lawn and down to the hawthorns. I hoped if I sat down and composed myself something might come to comfort or inspire me. But nothing happened. All I was aware of was the scratch of the worn stone against the seat of my jeans, the buzz of an insect swooping around behind me, the clacking racket of some new piece of machinery in the farmyard across the road and a dull throb in my lower back. Of my friend, Deara, there was no trace. I simply couldn't reach her.

I gave up eventually, tramped back to the kitchen feeling thoroughly upset, climbed awkwardly up onto the work surface, took down the curtains and put them in the washing machine. After the morning's record of disasters, I could hardly believe my luck when I pulled the switch and it actually worked. I watched the curtains swoop and fall, swoop and fall, and was strangely comforted by the rhythmic swish of the rotating drum.

'All things pass, however ghastly.' The words took shape of their own accord. Yes, it was true. There was no doubt I'd feel better in an hour, or a day, or a couple of days. What I did while they did their passing was the problem.

Not surprisingly, I ended up in the garden and although I worked much more slowly than usual I made some progress. I trimmed my way along the sandstone path at the foot of the rockery, taking out the dead leaves from the flourishing succulents that spread over the warm flagstones. I touched their bright rosettes, each fat point tipped with red. I began to feel it was far better to get on like this and do what I could manage than to strain after something way beyond my present capacity.

After a time, I leaned back on my kneelers, stretched my aching neck and turned it towards the sun, so its warmth would be like a gentle hand on the tight muscles. The thought of Deara and the brooch she had carried from the Hall of Council came into my mind. I'd caught only a glimpse of it: dark, gleaming metal inset with bright points of colour.

I spread some loosened soil on the path in front of me and traced its circular outline with my finger, hoping I might recall the pattern of its subtle, intertwining spirals. But what happened was very different. My finger bit deeper into the soil, but it was not the soil of the Anacarrig garden.

Startled, I looked around me. The path had gone. There was no garden around me, no house perched on the terrace above me. I was kneeling on the soft, dusty edge of a small, sloping vineyard through which a stony path led upwards to the hilltop. A low colonnaded villa

62

with a tiled roof stood silent in the warm sun. There was no sign of anyone about.

I stood up and ran my eyes around the countryside spread out below me, hoping to find some familiar landmark. But there were none. Apart from the pink and gold touch of autumn on a cluster of chestnut trees nearby, there was nothing remotely familiar in the whole landscape to tell me where I might be.

The valley below was densely wooded. Only in the distance where I saw the gleam of water did the woodland give way to lush green meadows. Cattle were grazing there – angular, bony creatures, shaggy and hollow-chested, a far cry from the plump Frisians and the well-fed Shorthorns on the farms close to Anacarrig.

Apart from the villa, there were no other signs of human habitation, though there were trackways, criss-crossing the water-meadows and disappearing into the woodland. From where I stood, the path ran downhill and joined a more substantial causeway at the bottom. This stony track skirted the hill, cut through the woodland to the water-meadows and then disappeared again into more woodland away to my left.

Suddenly, a flash of light caught my eye. To my right, as far as the causeway reached before being enveloped in the woodland, a party of horsemen had just come into view and the sun glinted on their metal collars and the weapons they carried. They were moving fast. Moments later, over the thud of hooves, I heard the jingle of harness as they drew nearer.

Wanting to get a better look, I moved towards the rosemary hedge which bounded the vineyard. It was then I heard a rustle behind me. I turned and saw a young woman walking towards me, a wicker basket hung over one brown arm.

To be honest, I didn't recognise her, but the moment she saw me, she held out her hands and smiled. With those grey eyes, it could be no one else. She seemed taller, less waif-like, more confident than I had remembered her. Pinned to the left shoulder of her pale olive green tunic was the brooch.

'So you have come again as I prayed you would. You are so welcome. I hope the migraine troubles you no more.'

I was completely taken aback for the words she spoke were perfectly comprehensible.

'Thank you, it went away when I slept. It hasn't come back,' I heard myself reply, to my amazement, as easily as she had spoken. And then I realised why: it was neither Italian, nor Greek, of which I have only a smattering – it was Latin. Not exactly the Latin of Tacitus or Pliny I know well, closer to the late Latin poetry I'd loved so much, and a form I could certainly follow. And it was clear from her cry of delight that she had understood what I had said.

63

'But now you speak the tongue of Rome as I do. How is this? Come, let us sit in the shade. I have been waiting so long for you to come. But I had not thought we might speak words to each other that we might understand.'

She took my hand and led me to a stone bench below the colonnade. On either side of its fine-grained marble surface, two great wine amphora held single-petalled roses, one pink and one red. As I sat down I brushed against one of them and some petals fell, bright red splashes on the flagged terrace. I could see the veins in the rose, the grain in the quarried stone and feel the warmth of a brown hand holding mine.

Sitting there in the sunshine, her familiar-looking wicker basket at my feet, I felt both easy and excited. Easy, as with an old friend like Helen, whom I've known since our very first day at grammar school, and yet excited, like the first meetings with Matthew when it was so obvious to us both that all we wanted to do was be together.

There seemed so much we had to say to each other and yet a strange sense that we had shared so much already, as if we had been friends for a long time, but had been separated and now lived in different countries.

'Please, how is it that you speak the Roman tongue?'

'I learnt it at school in Ireland a long time ago.'

I thought my words sounded very stiff, rather like one of those guide books for eighteenth century travellers with phrases like: 'My postilion has been struck by lightning.' But if I was, it seemed not to bother her.

'But we are in Ireland now, not far from the God's well where I first met you. Do you not recognise this place? Over there to the west is Emain, and behind us is the town, Ard Macha, where the traders live. This is the villa of Alcelcius, my teacher.'

'Is Alcelcius a Roman?'

I could not conceal my curiosity or my excitement. I so hoped she would say he was.

'Yes, Alcelcius was a surgeon with the legions in Albi, but he came to Ireland disguised as an eye-doctor to spy for his general, who thought to conquer us. But Ireland conquered Alcelcius instead. He made his home here when he was discharged with honours.'

I laughed with delight. I knew it. I always knew it. I had been right after all. I was back at school, the soft voice of Miss Barbour in my ear. I had liked Miss Barbour very much, she was kind, hard-working and very fair. Without her, I would probably never have won my scholarship to university. But she would never accept a statement unless I could produce concrete evidence. I could still hear her steady, unperturbable tone.

'Well, yes, Deirdre, I can see the reasoning behind your suggestion.

The Romans were indeed adventurous, they do show a decided tendency to explore and document, but we have no evidence at all that they came to Ireland. It is true, Agricola did calculate that he could subdue the country with two legions, but the attempt was never made. As we all know, he shortly had to give his mind to more pressing problems.'

And with those quiet, bleak phrases, quite unknowingly she had snuffed out some possibility that was beginning to grow in my mind. I had felt such loss, such disappointment, and now suddenly that old hope returned.

'And are you also Roman?' I asked quickly, the words coming to me more easily now, in spite of my haste.

Her face, so full of pleasure and enthusiasm, changed instantly and I glimpsed a different Deara, vulnerable and ill at ease.

'I know nothing of my family,' she said uneasily. 'I was brought up by the Lady Merdaine of Emain, but she died some four years ago, a few days before you first came to me. After her death I came to study with Alcelcius. He is such a good, kind man. He has taught me Latin and Greek, as well as medicine and the ways and customs of the Romans. Have you come from Rome?'

I shook my head and smiled.

'No, I'm not a Roman. I've been to Rome once, many years ago, but there haven't been Romans in Britain for a very long time. I think you and I live in different ages rather than in different places. Can you tell me what year it is, here, at this moment?'

The grey eyes widened and she nodded slowly.

'This is the fourteenth year of the reign of Niall, son of Laoghaire, King of Tara and the tenth year of the reign of Morrough, son of Ferdagh, King of Emain.'

I shook my head and laughed, none the wiser.

'That sounds like a long time ago. Presumably the Romans are still in Britain?'

'Britain? Where is that, please?'

I tried to think what Britain was called in Roman times, but I just couldn't remember.

'Where Londinium is,' I offered helpfully.

'Ah yes, Londinium. Alcelcius served there before he went north to Eboracum. You know Londinium?'

'Yes, I live and work there, but it's rather larger now than it was in Alcelcius's day . . . or rather, I mean . . .'

'You mean that you have come from the future?'

'It looks like it. I know quite a lot about the Roman Empire and I've read Agricola, but his world was about nineteen centuries before the time in which I live.'

'So, how have you come? Why have you come?' she asked earnestly, pressing my hand, as if my answer was of the greatest importance to her.

'I don't know. Why did you come to me six days ago when I was sitting crying with my migraine?'

She shook her head gently and smiled, that lovely warm smile which banished all anxiety.

'My friend, for you the time was but six days, for me, four years and four months. It seems there is much we do not know. But some things are clear to us.'

'Such as?'

'Who we are. That we are friends.'

She leaned forward and kissed my cheek. I was terribly taken aback. Until I met my sister-in-law, Diana, I'd never been kissed by a woman. She's one of those Anglican clergy wives who kisses everyone, so it shouldn't have been a problem, particularly as I happen to like her. But it was. Every time Matthew and I went to visit I'd get worried I might react in spite of myself. Eventually we managed to work out what lay behind it. Mother, of course. As if we couldn't have guessed. She'd never held or kissed either Sandy or me, even when we were very little, and her comments were always quite vicious if she ever saw two women kiss each other.

'Please, tell me your name,' she said earnestly.

'Deirdre.'

'Oh . . . so . . .'

Her eyes grew round with amazement.

'What's so strange about that?' I asked, as I saw her begin to smile.

'I too am Deirdre, but only a few people know that, a Druid who bears me ill will and my foster-mother, who gave me the name Deara.'

'But why did she do that?'

'Because Deirdre was a name too hard to bear.'

She said it so softly that I wasn't sure I had heard her properly, and yet I felt it was the most important thing she could have said. Yes, it was too hard to bear, being Deirdre. Often enough, just existing could be too hard to bear.

I thought of the strange scenes and images I'd experienced when Deara had laid her hands upon me and all that had come to me in the days that had followed. Her life had been as full of anxious thoughts as mine seemed to be. I wanted to understand how and why this had happened to her. I asked her about the woman who had died by the God's well, about the Druid who had tried to have her executed. And she answered all my questions, quite easily and steadily, explaining both what had happened on the night of her birth and how Conor had behaved towards her as she was growing up.

'But, Deirdre, how is it you know these things about my life when we have not spoken of them until now?'

I was about to explain, when suddenly the warm stillness of the afternoon was broken by the most appalling noise, a kind of high-pitched scream, followed by shouts and a fierce metallic banging like the dustbin lid protests up the Falls Road in the early days of The Troubles.

I jumped and went rigid. Her hand tightened around mine and she said softly: 'It's all right, Deirdre. The King has arrived back at Emain with the ambassadors from Tara. That was the guard shout and the warrior greeting. I hate it too. When I'm up there and it happens, I hide in my workplace till the speeches begin. They go on a long time, but they're quiet. Did you see the King's party pass by?'

I nodded, not yet trusting my voice, for my heart had leapt into my mouth at the sudden jarring noise.

'Just a glimpse, before I saw you,' I managed to reply, my mouth suddenly dry. 'Was that the King at the front?'

'Yes, it would have been. He is always so happy to ride home. He's not overfond of Tara and he hates negotiations, but that is the only way to keep the peace. Without going to Tara, it would be easy for enemies to make trouble between Emain and Tara. Then many suffer, not just warriors. Do you live in a time of peace, Deirdre?'

I shook my head wearily. I could not bear to tell her of the killings, the car bombs, the ambushes and the thousands of innocent people the last years of bitterness and hatred had claimed.

Again, a violent clamour erupted from the west. I felt it like a physical blow, but before I could react she took my other hand. I saw the look of concern on her face as she explained gently and patiently, as one does to a frightened child, that the guest cup is offered to the ambassadors, and it is the children who make the noise with blunt swords and broken shields, a tradition which would not go on for more than a few minutes.

I seem always to have hated loud noises. Long before The Troubles began, with their real threat from bombs and bullets, I had jumped out of my skin at fireworks, or cars backfiring, or even some child bursting its paper bag at lunchtime. The racket had now died away. I took a deep breath and tried to forget it.

'Is it impolite if I ask what age you are, Deara?' I asked, knowing that I sounded formal again because I couldn't find a word for 'rude', only one for 'vulgar' and another for 'obscene'.

'Surely not. I was twenty-one in the fifth month of this year. And you, my friend?'

'I shall be thirty-five in a few months' time.'

'By then we shall have known each other a long time.'

'What do you mean?'

'I don't exactly know what I mean, but that is how it seems to me. We shall be good friends, shall we not?'

She looked at me with the warm smile which I found so utterly appealing. I was about to speak of the hope that was beginning to grow in me, born out of the strange situation in which we found ourselves. But I didn't manage it. Without any warning, a huge noise away to my right broke in on me, a noise that filled up all the space inside my head.

'That noise, Deara, that awful noise. Whatever is it? Make it stop. Oh, please make it stop. I can't bear it. It feels as if it will make my head burst.'

I covered my ears with my hands and felt tears spring to my eyes. She couldn't hear it. I knew she couldn't hear it. And she wouldn't believe me if she couldn't hear it. Nothing I could say would make her believe me. I wanted to scream and scream, but no sound would come. Everything was blotted out by pulsing waves of pressure. I couldn't even see her any more. Then I felt her hands on my wrists.

'Deirdre, my dear friend, I am here. Give me your hands. Do not shut out the noise. Listen to it. Let it speak to you. I will not let it harm you.'

There was a strength in her voice I had not heard before. It was firmer than reassurance, much firmer, it was the strength of one who speaks to command. She drew my hands away from my ears and held them firmly in her own.

'Listen, listen to it,' she insisted quietly. 'It cannot harm you now.'

As suddenly as it had begun, it stopped. I could see her face again. She was watching me with enormous concentration. She released my hand as I moved to get my hanky out of my pocket. I blew my nose and mopped up my tears.

'Are you all right now? Has the noise gone?'

'Yes, it's gone. I'm so sorry, I can't think what happened to me. It's so silly. Please forgive me.'

'Forgive you? What is there to forgive between us? It is you who must forgive the woman who harmed you in this way.'

'Woman? What woman?'

'A woman with glass in front of her eyes who crept up behind you when you were sitting on the stones by the God's well and talking to yourself. The same woman in a long bedgown who found you walking in your sleep and scolded you, and when you spoke of hearing a noise she said you were telling lies. A woman who did not comfort you when you wept.'

'That's my mother. She died the week before last.'

'Such women leave great burdens on the spirit. You must rest and pray to your God.'

'I have no God.'

'Then I shall pray to mine. It makes no difference,' she said, as she touched my cheek with her hand. 'You are very pale. Will you

68

drink a cup of wine? It would help you.'

Suddenly I became so aware of the blue threads in my jeans, the fallen petals of the rose and the soft, brown hand still holding mine.

'Thank you,' I said, nodding and looking up at her.

But she was gone. I was sitting on my stone under the hawthorns. Indoors, the phone was ringing. I didn't move. I let it ring until it stopped.

I sat on for quite a while, letting myself absorb what had happened. Then I realised how thirsty I was. I got up and walked across the garden to the path along the bottom edge of the rockery. There was the circle I had begun and not completed. I bent down and drew my finger through the soil to close it.

The phone rang again, that fierce, strident ring I could identify as the Anacarrig phone from wherever in the world I might hear it. I went in and picked it up.

'Deirdre Weston speaking.'

I heard my name as if it were the first time I'd ever used it. It was the estate agent with a query about the rateable value. I told him what he wanted to know and wished all queries could be dealt with so easily. And yet, as I filled the kettle, I felt sure that finding answers to the questions that were really important to me was going to be a whole lot easier. If there was something I had to do while I was here, then I was being helped to do it. There was no point asking for it all to be clear to me now: I just had to get on and do the best I could.

9

Despite the optimism of the estate agent, no prospective purchasers arrived to view Anacarrig the weekend after my meeting with Deara in Alcelcius's vineyard. I had a blissful two days. It was warm and sunny and working in the garden was a delight. I read a lot, wrote a massive letter to Matthew and short notes to some of my local friends suggesting that we meet.

More than once, I caught myself just sitting, lost in my own thoughts, beside a flowerbed I had set out to weed or a bookcase I had decided to sort and pack. Once, I even found myself sitting on the low wall near the back door unable to remember what I was supposed to be doing there until I saw the neatly tied bag of rubbish at my feet.

To my amazement, the peaceful quality of the weekend persisted into the following week. We all have good hours and good days, times when things go right beyond all reasonable expectation, but that whole week it appeared I could do no wrong. Whatever I put my hand to, some tedious job in the house or some piece of executor business, the problems just melted. Like the child who had once walked round the garden with a magic ring, making things happen, I appeared to be mistress of all I surveyed.

Entirely new to me was the sense of steadiness and purpose I felt. Sometimes I just marvelled at my good fortune; at other times, I found I was looking around for new worlds to conquer and had to laugh at myself.

I was able to finish a routine piece of work for Robert Fairclough in record time and I had lively phone calls from the friends to whom I'd written. I wrote page after page in my blue notebooks, sketched out thoughts for short stories, and developed an idea for a longer work. As if this were not joy enough, early one morning I even had a call from Matthew in Maharajpur.

We tripped over each other and said the most banal things in the few minutes that could be spared on the up-country hospital's one and only phone. There would be another opportunity for us to go to India together and work on the project we'd had to set aside this summer, he said. He sounded so excited at the prospect and both pleased and relieved that I was in such good spirits with things going so well at Anacarrig.

But beyond and behind all the objective things that had lifted my spirits, there was Deara. Unlike any friend I had ever had, however dear, her presence seemed to reassure me in a way I could not put words to as yet.

When I tried to puzzle it out, I told myself it was because she had survived a situation far, far more dangerous than anything I had ever experienced. With no one to care what happened to her, she had been totally vulnerable after Merdaine died. The actual threat from the Druid I would have found terrifying. And yet, despite everything being against her, she had won through, she had kept her nerve and ended up with Alcelcius, a man who was not only kind but one she could be sure would never let her down.

Day after day as I went on with the work in the garden, I thought about her, going over in my mind all I knew of her, putting together everything that first meeting had offered with what she herself had told me when we discovered we could talk to each other. I longed to see her again, and yet, as I moved through those memorable days, I felt she was with me, an active presence in my life, steadying me, showing me ways of being that were new to me, bringing me hope and confidence.

Whether it was thinking of Deara or the happy chance of Mother's car having arrived back from the garage, I really don't know, but on the Friday afternoon, I suddenly put down my trowel, abandoned my bucket of weeds, scrubbed my fingernails at the kitchen sink and set off for the library in Armagh.

The magic of the week was still at work when I got there. I almost burst out laughing when the librarian looked up from her filing in the empty reading room. It was Maureen Purdy. Years ago, at primary school, when we came top of the class in reading, Maureen and I had had the job of going to the library and choosing the weekly box of books for our class.

'Deirdre Henderson, how are you? When did I last see you?'

The reading room was unusually quiet that afternoon, so Maureen was free to talk to me. We spoke about our schooldays and she filled me in on the lives of school friends I hadn't heard of for years. Then I told her I'd got interested in the fifth century. By the time I left, she'd made me a list of titles for the early Christian era and suggested I go round and meet the curator of the museum who had made a special study of that period.

When I did track him down in his minute, congested office, I discovered his wife had been at Queen's with Sandy. I'd been working in London so long I'd almost forgotten what a close and intimate community I'd once been part of. As I watched him raiding his shelves and extracting material from his own files to photocopy for me, I felt quite overwhelmed by his generosity and his willingness to help. This responsiveness, this kindness, was once a familiar part of my experience. It was a part with which I had completely lost touch.

Back at Anacarrig I staggered into the house with my arms full and caught sight of myself in the hall mirror. I was wearing such a broad grin I reckoned I must look like the lucky winner of one of the 'Biggest Ever Prize Draws' that kept dropping through Mother's letterbox despite all my efforts to turn them off.

I laid out all my stuff in the sitting room, books and photocopies and lists of forthcoming publications. I was tempted to sit down and begin reading there and then, but I remembered I'd just dropped my tools and gone off into town, so I went back out into the garden.

The mixed perfumes of the newly opened perennials and the very first rosebuds lay on the warm air. All was quiet. I went on where I'd left off and when I tired I fetched some of my new books and sat under the hawthorns in the last of the sunshine. Soon I was so absorbed, had the phone not rung I'd probably have been there till it was too dark to see the print.

It was Helen, safely back from Oxford and looking forward to our meeting the next evening. As I put the phone down I thought of the calls I'd been putting off. I'm happy enough to talk on the phone once I get started, but I'm often reluctant about actually making them. I brought a chair into the hall and settled down to make up for my delays.

I rang the rectory in Norfolk, spoke to John and passed on Matthew's news from Maharajpur. Then a marvellous talk with my sister-in-law, Diana, which included her account of the latest episode in the long-running row among the flower ladies over the colour scheme for the patronal festival.

Still smiling, I rang Tanza Road and heard Joan's familiar voice. She had some really exciting news. Her great-niece Sarah had just been accepted for the Purcell School; the scholarship would give her the best possible opportunity to become the clarinet player she wanted to be. Joan questioned me most carefully and sympathetically about the trials of clearing the house. I felt so grateful I had a friend of her wisdom and experience, one who would actually speak about mortality and its effects upon you instead of merely uttering the conventional platitudes and cliches which made her feel comfortable.

I sat by the phone thinking about what she had said until I realised I was starving. I put together a tray, took it to the sitting room, and went back to my books. Soon, I was a very long way away.

Suddenly, the phone rang. I'd been so absorbed, I jumped inches out of my chair, my heart leapt and my stomach turned over. That damn bell, I cursed. Mother had chosen it deliberately so that she could hear it over the sound of her radio.

I hurried from the room, tripped over the flex of my reading lamp and just managed to stop it crashing to the floor. I picked up the receiver confused and breathless.

It was Sandy.

'I rang several times this afternoon, but you were out. I tried half the evening and you were engaged. I thought by now you'd have let me know how things were going.'

'But you were in France,' I protested weakly.

'I left you my number.'

I hadn't been paying enough attention to the business of getting the house sold. The agents should have been chased up when there was no immediate response. Had I checked they'd done a personalised mailing as well as the newspaper advertisements? Had I had confirmation from the solicitor's that the will we had found was valid or was there another one? Didn't I appreciate that an empty house costs money, is less saleable and is more likely to be vandalised, especially in a situation like Anacarrig?

There was a perfunctory enquiry about Matthew, an assurance that she'd deal with the agents herself in the morning and a promise to talk to me again as soon as she had sorted them out. She rang off. I felt torn between being furious with her for being so unpleasant and furious with myself for not having had the wit to do those things that would have kept her happy. I went to bed and had a predictably rotten night.

That was only the start of it.

Next morning, Saturday, as I was waiting for my coffee to drip, the postman rang with a recorded delivery parcel and a handful of letters. My heart sank when I took the bulky parcel, saw the postmark and the familiar heavy-duty packaging. I knew it was from Robert Fairclough and a brief glance at the contents told me it was one of those pieces of report writing whose only virtue is that it helps to pay the mortgage.

I had agreed to go on doing routine stuff while I was in Ulster, but when I started to unwrap it I found a 'Collect' label for the day Mother died, the day of my last visit to the Regent Street office. Someone had forgotten to give it to me then. Or perhaps, someone had been tactful in not sending it sooner. It really didn't matter which. What was relevant was the copy date, that ever-fixed mark by which Robert conducted his relationships with his writers. My heart sank further when I looked at it – the wretched thing would have to be finished by Wednesday morning and go back first class.

Drinking my lukewarm coffee, the parcel parked on the draining board, I suddenly felt such a revulsion that I nearly chucked it into the open black sack standing beside me. I'd been throwing out half-used packets years beyond their sell-by date, saved up pieces of wrapping paper, old carrier bags, ancient shopping lists and household receipts going back over the last twenty years. It would sink like a stone amongst the lighter material.

The old discipline of responsibility asserted itself. I just stood staring at it. Was my restraint a lamentable failure of nerve or a commendable acceptance of my commitments? I couldn't answer my own question.

I turned to the rest of the post hoping to find something to lift my spirits. What I found were two very good quality envelopes full of more bad news. The bank wished to inform me that they did not appear to have in their possession the relevant documents connected with Mother's selling out to the consortium. Without them, they said, there was a question of a tax liability. That would put Sandy into orbit, if not both of us into bankruptcy.

Meantime, at the solicitor's, an older will of Mother's had been found. It was certainly valid in terms of signatories, but a note attached to it in the hand of the senior partner indicated the existence of a further document lodged in the safe deposit at head office in Belfast. The senior partner, one Hector Anderson, an old friend of my father's I know very well, had just retired and was cruising with his wife in the Mediterranean. The said head office was being relocated. I would appreciate that in the circumstances some delays might be unavoidable.

I would appreciate and did understand, but I was pretty sure Sandy would not. I dreaded having to tell her when she rang.

I sat bleakly at the kitchen table trying to decide whether to make a decent cup of coffee to make up for the tepid one I'd just pushed aside, or get on with the morning's job. I wasn't looking forward to that either. One glance at the kitchen clock settled the question: it was after nine, the church ladies were due at ten thirty and not all the stuff was ready for them.

Earlier in the week, I'd had a phone call from one of the said ladies. Unlike her predecessors who had enquired about my health and how I was getting on sorting out the contents of the house, this one actually got to the point. Mother had made clear that all her personal possessions were to go to the church for fund-raising. What no one had told me until this phone call, was that the quarterly 'nearly new' sale, for which her clothes were now available, was on this coming Saturday afternoon. They would, of course, come and collect them as soon as it was convenient.

I knew Mother had a lot of clothes. Clothes seem quite innocuous when they're hanging in cupboards and wardrobes. It's when you take them out the trouble starts. I'd made a start the previous morning while still in good spirits. I'd arranged them neatly on all the beds except my own, ready to be picked up by their hangers. All I had left to do was the hats.

I humped the stepladder upstairs, opened the double doors of the first overcupboard and was greeted by an avalanche. Dozens of hats tumbled past me, piling up in a drift around the foot of my ladder. Straw hats, felt hats, hats for weddings, hats to match suits, plain hats, hats with floral trims, winter hats, summer hats. I kicked them off the aluminium treads, climbed down and found they'd spread themselves over the entire space on one side of the bed. There were two more overcupboards as well as this one. I cursed myself for not checking them earlier and hurried down to the garage to collect cardboard boxes. There wasn't a box in sight.

To begin with I couldn't believe my eyes. Mr Neill had brought me dozens of boxes from his brother's supermarket. I hurried back upstairs, scanned the other bedrooms in case I'd left them ready somewhere else and ran back again to Mother's room. For a moment, I stood helpless in the middle of the floor, then something inside me gave way. I chose the largest, shiniest black straw hat and smashed my fist through its crown. It crumpled effortlessly, denying me all satisfaction.

Furiously, I swept aside all the hats that had fallen on the bed, kicked and punched them where they fell, flung them into corners, tramped on them. It didn't help. Mostly, they bounced back like ping-pong balls or gave way with no resistance. Desperately, I looked around for something to smash. There wasn't anything. The bottles from the dressing table and the tortoiseshell brushes were already packed in one of the boxes stacked in the hall.

Then I had a thought. I snatched out the drawers of the dressing table one after another till I found the one I'd put it in. Mother's photograph, face down. I grabbed it, bent it across my thigh and heard the glass crack in the silver frame.

Splinters fell to the carpet with a minute tinkle, except for one, which remained embedded vertically in the ball of my thumb. I dropped the photograph and pulled it out. Blood oozed up, trickled across my wrist and fell on to the splinters below. Beside them, on the thick pile of the pink carpet, Mother looked up from her glassless, bent silver frame, unruffled, undamaged, indifferent to the drips of falling blood.

Hastily, I tied my hanky round my hand to stop the blood splashing on to the carpet. How typical, I thought, how like you, to stop yourself bleeding for the sake of the carpet. I threw myself down on the dressing stool and wept until I was exhausted. Then I just sat.

After a while I was aware my tears had dried because my cheeks felt tight. The blood had dried on my hanky as well. But still I did not move. I was right out of myself, sitting there like a petrified object. My mind was working, but it seemed to have no power to initiate action. The church ladies would come and go without getting any response from me.

I was aware of a stream of negative thoughts: I had been a fool to stay. It was hubris to think I could ever escape from my past, from the damage I had suffered. Virginia Woolf had got it right. The burden was to great to inflict on another human being. She had filled her pockets with stones and gone to the river. She was quite right. That's what I should do, too. No one could save me. Not even Matthew.

Only Deara.

As the words jumped into my mind something changed. I'm sure it was a positive change, but I'll never know for sure, because the phone rang only seconds later. Before I knew it, I'd answered it. The petrified object had moved, had freed itself – or had been freed.

It wasn't Matthew phoning from India, miraculously on cue, nor even Helen, nor anyone who could conveniently fit the miracle scenario. It was the estate agent. But I had to admit there was still something quite miraculous about that. Given the state of inertia I'd been locked into for nearly an hour, to be able to move, to understand words spoken, to pick up a Biro and make notes, to suggest times and refuse to see anyone else after four-thirty was something quite exceptional.

I was truly delighted by my release, but as the call went on I found both my patience and my ability to concentrate was running out. I desperately wanted to be left alone and I was gasping for a drink of water. But the voice showed not the slightest sign of going away and leaving me to collect myself. I hung on grimly. Eventually it got to the point.

'I'm afraid my secretary should have telephoned you yesterday, Mrs Weston. I have Major and Mrs Andscombe here in reception. Mrs Andscombe flew over last night especially so they could visit Anacarrig this morning before their afternoon engagement in Derry. They are most interested. Of course, as cash buyers, it would be very much . . .'

'Robert Andscombe?'

'Major Robert Andscombe, yes. He visited on Tuesday, you may remember.'

I remembered very well. One more of the pleasures in the week. An Englishman in his early forties, who read Irish poetry, was delighted by the garden and spoke openly and with real affection about his family.

'What time?'

'Ten-thirty.'

I glanced at my watch. Ten o'clock. I looked at the battered hats, the smashed glass, the angry cut on my hand. Downstairs the breakfast dishes were still in the sink, the elderly washing machine was making a noise like a Mississippi paddle steamer and the hall was full of packed boxes. It wouldn't bother Robert Andscombe. I'd take a chance on his wife.

'Ten-thirty will be fine.'

I cut short the expressions of gratitude, dropped the phone and went into action. I gathered up the hats which were little the worse for my treatment and lined them up on the bed – small ones in front, big ones behind, just like a school photograph. Then I picked up the discreetly tinted full plate print and the broken glass and dropped them back into an empty drawer. I dragged some of the waiting boxes to one side so you could get into the bedroom without having to climb over them. The place still looked like a second-hand clothes shop, but it couldn't be helped.

Across the landing, the bath was full of net curtains I had put to soak in Ariel the previous evening. The grey water looked revolting. I pulled out the plug, prodded them, then left the taps running as I dashed into my own room. I picked up the knickers and shirt I had dropped on the floor after Sandy's call, ran back with them to the basket in the bathroom and straightened out the guest towels. The curtains now lay decently obscured under deep water. I pushed in the plug, turned off the taps, hurried back to my room, shook the duvet, put away my blue notebook and tidied up the books on my table.

As I paused for breath I heard a car change gear at the foot of the drive. Only a quarter past, but it was them. I pushed my bare feet into my sandals and walked downstairs as steadily as I could. Perhaps I had been moving a bit too fast.

'Mrs Weston, sorry to land on you like this. This is Carol, my wife. There seems to have a breakdown of communication somewhere. And we're early as well. Can you bear it?'

I held out my hand to a pleasant, dark-haired girl of about my own age and found my eyes full of tears. Looking at the two of them standing together on my doorstep, I understood exactly why Robert Andscombe had asked the questions he did. He knew what they wanted, the sort of house that could be a real home for their two children, the Cairn terrier and the stray kitten. I knew then that Anacarrig would be theirs.

I wasn't sure whether the tears were tears of joy that Anacarrig would soon be just the sort of home I had always wanted myself, or distress that I was about to lose something I had only just found. But I was sure that Carol Andscombe was a woman I could like.

'I'm sorry about the chaos. It's even worse upstairs,' I said apologetically, taking them to the kitchen to make coffee.

As I leaned forward to fill the kettle I felt very peculiar and had to lean against the sink.

'Are you all right, Mrs Weston?'

There was a hint of the West Country in Carol Andscombe's voice and a gentleness that almost had me in tears again. Robert

78

Andscombe's face seemed rather blurred.

'I think you ought to sit down and let Carol have a look at that cut,' he said quietly.

I remember saying something feeble about making coffee and telling Robert where the medical kit was, but it was only after Carol had done a neat job on my cut hand and Robert had put a mug of coffee into my other one that I began to feel steadier.

'It's a rotten job,' said Carol sympathetically. 'I had to do it last year when Robert's mother died and he only had three days' compassionate leave from Germany. I had Alison and Peter with me, but even with them around it felt grim. I still can't understand why it was so bad. It's not as if I was very fond of Olive – I hardly knew her because we've been abroad so much.'

Robert Andscombe was leaning easily against the sink unit, his coffee in his hand. I remember thinking how strange it was that he looked younger in full regimentals than he had done in the comfortable tweed jacket he'd worn on Tuesday.

'Mortality usually gets you when you least expect it,' he said thoughtfully. 'You're ready for it at a funeral or when you see bodies being loaded into ambulances. But that's not when it comes. That's when you have responsibilities, commitments, and you have to act, and you're so caught up there's no space left for the feelings.'

'I think you're right,' I said slowly.

Carol nodded. 'Yes, he usually is about things like that. He said what he's just said to you when we talked about Olive last year, but I didn't grasp it then. It was when I saw the boxes piled up in your hall it all came back to me. I think I couldn't see the difference between Olive dying and the fact of mortality itself.'

The conversation moved on, Carol mentioned Alison and Peter and I asked how they would feel about coming to Ulster. I was amused and delighted by her openness and the honest way she talked about them. Peter was at that stage where he was incapable of going through a door without damaging himself or the door, while Alison spent all her time reading Welsh myths and was trying to decide whether to change her name to Angharrad or Bronwen.

'Poor child,' said Carol. 'Her parents are a sad disappointment to her. They have no imagination.'

I looked across at her and smiled. Her easy manner and lively style had cheered me up enormously. I suddenly found myself wondering how she would have responded to Alison if she'd found her in the garden planting seeds of Morning Glory.

At least three times in the last week I'd dreamed about planting those seeds. Mrs Curry had given them to me when I went to fetch the eggs. They'd come free with her husband's gardening magazine, she said, but he only grew vegetables and dahlias. Would I like them?

79

I was ten at the time, exactly Alison's age.

I was so thrilled with the picture of the extravagant blue trumpets and their wonderful name. Ipomea. When I pressed the seeds gently into the ground I could already see them, full-grown, turning to the morning sun. Like Alison, I had a vivid imagination. But Mother had caught me. I'd got such a telling off for bringing 'old weeds' into her garden that I'd never planted anything again.

No, I couldn't see Carol Andscombe doing a thing like that. I stood up and smiled at them both, aware of the long drive to Derry. I felt sure we were going to meet again. When we did I might even tell them about the Morning Glory.

'You've both been quite marvellous. Thank you for patching me up. In all respects. Now please go and look round. I'm feeling very guilty about that drive to Derry. You must be way behind schedule.'

'Don't worry. It's such a big do they won't miss us. Provided I'm in time to get my name on the guest list with my lady wife, all will be well.'

Still smiling, they went out into the hall. As Robert stood aside to let Carol negotiate the pile of boxes at the foot of the stairs, the musical chimes echoed forth.

'That's all I need,' I said under my breath, as I put the coffee mugs in the sink. 'It has to be the church ladies.'

To be honest, the church ladies were no trouble at all. If I had expected them to chat, to speak of Mother or to extract recyclable news from me or the house, I had certainly got it wrong. All they were concerned about was getting everything into the large Peugeot estate parked behind the Andscombes' Volvo.

Carol and Robert left before they did. It didn't surprise me they were so quick, nor that they had made up their minds. I walked into the garden with them to avoid the scurrying figures and Robert said all the proper things about informing the agent and instructing his solicitor. I nodded silently and Carol put a sympathetic hand on my arm and asked if this was really awful for me.

I told her that it made it easier that Anacarrig was going to people I liked, but even as I spoke I wasn't sure it was strictly true. Selling the house was one thing, but after only three weeks I had come to see the garden as mine. I felt I would have a long way to go before I could come to terms with that particular parting.

I waved them goodbye and turned my attention to the figures who were poking and prodding the last items into the back of the Peugeot. It was touch and go, but they managed it. Box after box, armful after armful of stuff on hangers, carrier bags full to overflowing. And the hats. As they drove cautiously down the drive, the back window totally obscured, my last image of Mother's clothes was a collage composed of assorted hats, decorated with random flowers and feathers.

10

The red Peugeot with its cargo of clothes and church ladies lurched perilously across the main road, swung right towards Armagh and disappeared. I turned away and walked slowly back into a house that would very shortly belong to Carol and Robert Andscombe.

I paused by the telephone in the hall. I should ring the estate agent and confirm what I had said to Robert, I thought. Then I remembered Pat Dunbar was coming to lunch and I hadn't even thought yet what to give her. I hadn't seen Pat since the day mother died and I wished I could put her off till another time. But I couldn't. I'd done that once already. Whatever we were going to eat probably needed to start defrosting an hour ago.

Instead of picking up the phone or heading for the freezer as I should have done, were I being my responsible, sensible self, I turned my back on the empty hall, hurried across the terrace and down the steps. I almost ran across the lawn to my sitting place under the hawthorns.

I wasn't distraught or in tears, but, suddenly, being in the house was just unbearable. I breathed a sigh of relief as I settled myself on the bigger of the two pieces of stone, the one that lets you rest your back against the twisted trunk of the largest of the three trees. I took a deep breath of the cool morning air and drew in the heady perfume from the blossom that now weighed down the richly clothed branches above my head.

I did have a headache, but mercifully, it was nothing like the one Deara had come and healed for me.

'Deara,' I whispered to myself. 'I wish you were here. I could do with a friend.'

I laughed at myself, knowing perfectly well that the more I wanted something, the less likely it was to happen. I flexed my aching shoulders, leaned back and promised myself five minutes peace and quiet. In five minutes I would go back and face what had to be done.

The moment I closed my eyes, I felt the sudden buffet of wind. Not a cold, wintry wind, but a blustery, rain-spattered turbulence, the kind you get in springtime. I opened my eyes and found myself outside the villa where only a few days ago I had sat in warm autumn sunshine with Deara. Now, under leaden grey skies, fragments of

81

tender new leaves were blowing around the terrace. In the inner courtyard, a climbing rose had broken loose from its support. Long branches bright with the red shoots of new growth were trailing across the wet flags of the pathway.

From a storeroom at the far end of the rain-sodden courtyard, a young man emerged. He was dressed in a short tunic and carried two heavy metal stands. After him hurried an elderly woman with iron-grey hair, with two well-polished lamps in her hands.

Although I had no sense of having followed them, a few seconds later I found myself in the room where they were fitting the lamps onto the stands and adding wood to the recently kindled fire. As the glow of the lamps increased and they moved on to trim the candles on the table, the dim room sprang to life.

The broad table, spread for a meal and decorated with both fruit and flowers, dominated the other pieces of carved wooden furniture. The walls were hung with strange scimitar-like weapons incised with exotic lettering and with woven rugs which reminded me of those I had seen from Bokhara and Samarkand. At my feet, birds and fishes made a jewel-bright pattern in a circular mosaic.

Shadows flickered as the fire burnt up and I glanced back at the table. There, to my surprise, three figures, two men and a woman, sat eating, drinking and talking animatedly. The woman was Deara. Dressed in a most lovely white gown with a gold belt, embroidered around the neck and cuffs with gold thread, she looked so happy, her eyes bright in the candlelight, her mouth softened with laughter. I had to stop myself calling out to her for something told me she would not hear me. I could watch, I could listen, but this time, while I had come to Deara, she had not come to me.

'Come, Sennach, my good friend,' Alcelcius began vigorously, 'another glass of wine. We will have none of your wretched moderation this evening. You'll taste nothing like this for many a day. Come now, pour your own and Deara's as well; my hand is too shaky for old wine.'

Sennach refilled the goblets, sipped his wine and nodded his agreement. I could see that he had tasted nothing as good even at the King's table. But he wasn't unduly surprised. He would certainly know, as I did, how passionate Alcelcius was about growing his vines and making wine. Deara had told me how much he loved to welcome any wine-merchant from his native Gaul, for he enjoyed not only making his own wine but sampling what others made as well.

'Now, Sennach, we must drink to this young lady,' he declared. 'It is a special occasion. Do you know why?'

I could understand now why Deara was so devoted to her teacher. He was so full of life. His deeply wrinkled, bearded face was alive with delight as he turned from one to the other, his tone light and teasing.

'Is it not always a special occasion when we old men are roused from sober thoughts by our young friend here?' Sennach responded dryly.

'Old men, Sennach?' Alcelcius exploded. 'Old men? Why lad, you're only a stripling. What, forty or fifty? No age, man. Though I wager this evening you wished yourself twenty years younger. Eh?'

He winked at his friend and glanced towards Deara who laughed and blushed slightly.

Sennach really was a strange looking figure, very pale and thin, with long bony fingers that seemed barely covered with skin. He looked rather formidable, but I saw the firm lines of his face relax as he gazed across the table at Deara and nodded.

She returned his smile and I wondered if perhaps she was remembering the day she had gone to the Hall of Council to petition Morrough, the day she had offered him a draught of water from the God's well.

'Come, Alcelcius, I shall drink Deara's health without more ado, unless you tell me at once what we celebrate,' he insisted with mock severity, as he raised his glass.

'Well then, I must. But it is the first time I have known you forget any date since the day we met.'

Alcelcius raised his glass. 'That is what we celebrate, my friend. It is seven years today, this last day of May, since you brought this dear child to my house, to become my pupil and my teacher. And this very day she has completed my manuscript for me. My "History of the Celtic Peoples" is finished at last. Half my lifetime it's taken to put together and it would not be half the book without her. Besides, no scribe in the world could read my spider marks.'

'Splendid, Alcelcius, splendid. My congratulations on your work. How say you then, shall we drink to "the fairest of amanuenses?"'

'Oh yes, I like that. Very good. That's very good.'

Alcelcius drank his toast with Sennach, then turned to Deara and took her hand.

'There is more,' he said, nodding to himself. 'Tonight I wish to tell you both. Deara has been my pupil and my teacher; she has also long been my heir. All I possess is hers, both here and in Albi and in Gaul. My will is drawn up in the Roman manner, Sennach. Now I ask you to do what is fitting under your brehon law. I want no difficulties for my dear girl when I go to meet my God.'

He paused, breathless, released her hand and raised his goblet again. 'My dearest girl, your health, wealth and happiness.'

I was watching Deara closely. Suddenly I knew she was overcome with sadness. Here, in the midst of celebration, I saw her eyes mist with tears and knew she was thinking that one day soon she must lose

Alcelcius and perhaps Sennach too – two men who had offered her their love and protection.

As I looked across at her, seeing her struggle to respond, to sustain the lightness of celebration, I was sharply aware of the young girl I had met only three weeks ago on the calendar I reckoned by. I could see her sitting at this same table poring over the letters and words on her wax tablet, struggling to master the new language he was teaching her, the language which meant that we had been able to talk to each other.

How strange for her after the huts of the encampment and the continuous presence of Merdaine, to enter a world where everything was unfamiliar: the language the servants spoke, the God they worshipped, even the tasks they performed each day to provide food and clothes for the household. She must have been amazed at how often people bathed. She might even have been uneasy about stepping naked into hot water. Did she miss the rushes on her bedroom floor and the animal skins on her bed in winter? Was she homesick for familiar things, even for the things she had disliked, the daily tasks like smooring the fire at night and blowing it into life in the morning?

As I watched the grown woman across the table, I wondered if the strangeness had been offset by the excitement, the delight, of writing her first words on the wax tablet. I could still feel my own excitement when as a 'senior infant' I first managed joined up writing and then, years afterwards when we were asked to write 'compositions'. Later, at secondary school, I had loved translating from French or Latin, imagining myself a detective cracking a code, or an archaeologist unravelling a long forgotten language, turning what was unknown into something everyone could understand.

I saw Deara collect herself. She began to speak quietly: 'I shall drink a toast too,' she said firmly, 'but I wish tonight I could stand in the midst of Emain to drink it. I, who hate the crowds and the council and the market place, would tonight climb even the Hill of Tara, when all the chieftains of Ireland come to greet Niall. There would I drink my toast, that all might hear me.'

She raised her goblet and looked from one to the other: 'To my teachers, Alcelcius and Sennach, from whom I have learnt far more than they taught. May I always be a credit to their wisdom, as well as to their knowledge.'

Alcelcius was silent for a moment while Sennach studied minutely the oak grain of the table.

'You rogue, Sennach, you rogue! Why did you not tell me you were teaching her oratory as well as law?'

I heard their laughter and for a moment was envious. Such love and trust, such companionship. How I wished there had been such figures in my own life to advise and guide me. I would have valued the friendship of a man like Alcelcius more than all his wealth in Ireland, or England, or France.

'Sennach, my lad, clap your hands for that fine fellow of mine. Bid him bring my box,' Alcelcius requested. 'Then he may conduct me to my chamber before I fall asleep.'

He raised a hand in protest as Sennach got to his feet. 'No, do not you go. It is early yet, far too early for the litters to be called, except for old men and dull women, as the saying is. Stay and finish the flask. Tell Deara that tale you told me earlier about the Christian slave who came to the King today.'

He stretched out his hands for the battered metal box his servant had brought him.

'Been all over the east, this box,' he said, striking it affectionately. 'Used to keep my instruments in it, until I put down roots here and had a shelf. Didn't often see a shelf in those days, bit of a luxury in a transit camp, or the desert, or up country in Galatia.'

He scuffled ineffectively amongst the parchment scrolls. I watched Deara remove his wine goblet to a safe distance before he caught it with his elbow.

'It's in here somewhere,' he muttered. 'I put it here myself.'

He picked up one scroll after another, examined the seals, the inscriptions and the bindings.

'Here you are, this is the will.'

He handed the document triumphantly to Sennach, then peered again at a discoloured parchment in his other hand. He struck his forehead and closed his eyes.

'Deara, I must beg your pardon and I do so most humbly. This bears your name and I was charged to give it to you when you could read it for yourself. You could have done it three or four years ago. But I put it away for safety and forgot.'

Deara shook her head gently. 'It is of no matter. I shall read it by and by,' she said soothingly.

'I remember, she was most insistent you should read it for yourself, when you had mastered the Roman tongue,' he went on. 'She made me promise I would not assist you, and if you did not come to me, or if you did not complete your studies, I was to destroy it. That's why I put it in my box.'

Deara fingered the seal and the linen bindings beside where her name was written. 'Thank you for your care, Alcelcius, it could not have had a safer home.'

'And now goodnight, my dear, and God bless you,' he said as he stood up. 'And you, Sennach, may He bless you, too, even if your heart is not His. May your sleep bring you peace.'

'Do you really want to hear about the Christian slave, or shall we have a game of fidchell?' Sennach asked, as the door closed behind him.

'I should like to hear,' she replied, 'if you have a mind to tell me. More wine?'

'Do you think that wise?'

'That you must ask your stomach, Sennach, not me. But whatever it says, a glass of spring water might indeed be wise.'

Sennach poured a draught from the covered pitcher and looked at it thoughtfully before drinking it down.

'It is also seven years since I was healed by just such a draught of water from your hand,' he said. 'Not instantly, that would misrepresent the facts; nevertheless, that same week, I did eat at the King's table for the first time in months.'

'The God was kind.'

'Perhaps, and perhaps not,' he retorted dryly. 'What is indisputable, however, is that his handmaiden was remarkably perceptive and very persistent in her ministrations. You were quite unwilling to accept what seemed to me the overwhelmingly negative import of the evidence.'

He took up the wine flask and raised it towards her. When she nodded, he refilled both their goblets.

'On reflection, I am most surprised I forgot that today was the day of your coming to Alcelcius,' he continued. 'You were very much in my thoughts while I was questioning that Christian slave Alcelcius spoke of. I recalled more than once another occasion, when a slave stood thus before the King.'

As they rose from the table and crossed to the hearth, I slipped deeper into the shadows of the room. I watched Sennach settle back in a handsome carved chair and begin to speak.

I was quite amazed by Sennach's story. To begin with he was not at all the sort of man I would have imagined to be a storyteller. He hardly moved a muscle as he spoke and there was little variation in his voice quality, but there was something about his steady tone, his attention to detail and his passion for accuracy that was compelling in its own way. As I listened, Sennach's words turned themselves into the very scene itself and I followed it step by step as if I had been standing among the crowd of clients waiting their turn at the back of the large chamber.

'Name?'

'Patricius Claudius, son of Calpurnius of Bannem Tabernae, sir.'

'State your business with this Council.'

'I come to petition the King, to give me leave to right a wrong which I have done.'

'You're a Briton, aren't you?' interrupted Morrough.

'Yes, Sire, I am.'

86

'Where did you say you came from?'

'Bannem Tabernae, Sire.'

'Where in the name of all the Gods is that?'

'It is nowhere, Sire,' the man replied quite coolly. 'It is a heap of stones by a river flowing to the sea. But it was once a village of two hundred souls, the place of my father and grandfather. It was destroyed by fire and sword when I was taken captive seventeen years ago.'

Morrough's brows darkened. 'So you are a slave, are you? Where is your master, then? Let him step forward.'

'I left my master eleven years ago,' Patricius replied. 'I know not if he yet lives, but I would pay my debt to him, if he does live, or to his kin, if he does not.'

'You mean you want to go back and spare yourself a whipping, is that it?'

Morrough's tone was harsh and the look on his face perilous.

'No, Sire, I wish to be free as all men are born and should remain.'

I saw Deara catch her breath and indeed it did sound as if the slave was living dangerously by speaking to Morrough so directly. Seeing her startled look, Sennach paused and told her that Patricius had shown not the slightest sign of anxiety or fear. He had just gone on quietly with what he wanted to say.

'I would repay my master the price he paid for me that he would not be wronged because by my flight I had sought to right a wrong.'

At that point Morrough had asked Sennach what the man was worth and Sennach had said that he couldn't say until he had questioned him further.

'Then pray question him further,' he said testily.

'What did your master employ you to do?'

'I tended his sheep, sir.'

'For how long?'

'Six years, sir.'

'And did you care for the sheep, or merely keep them from straying?'

'I learnt to care for them, to help at birth, to shear and dip, to puncture if they gorged new grass. It was a large flock, two hundred ewes, in a land of many streams and rough woodland where they would often break their legs.'

'Did you perform any other services for your master?'

'I kept his accounts and I delivered his son in the bad winter, when there was no woman to help.'

Sennach raised an eyebrow at Deara, clearly surprised by both these skills.

'You kept accounts with tallies?' he asked quickly.

'No, sir, I cannot understand the way of tallies, but I can read and write in my own tongue.'

'*Quod annum Caesar in Britannicum arriverat est?*' he threw out at him.

'*Annum quattor tres post natum domine Jesu Christus*' came the immediate reply.

'What are you saying, brehon?' broke in Morrough furiously, staring at them both. 'Why is he calling on his God?'

'I asked him, Sire, a question in his own tongue,' Sennach explained, 'to see if he lied.'

'And did he?'

'No, Sire, I think not. I asked him in what year Caesar came to Albi. Any schoolboy would know the answer.'

'And what does that prove?'

'That he has been to school and can probably read and write, as he says he can.'

'Then why was he calling on his God?'

Morrough turned in his seat to look directly at Patricius, his face like a thundercloud. 'You, man, why did you call on your God?'

Patricius was not troubled at all by this outburst. He continued to meet the King's gaze without flinching.

'Sire, I call on my God in every hour of every day, that he may guide me in His way. But when I spoke just now, it was but in answer to the question I was asked.'

'Sennach, this man speaks in riddles,' the King protested. 'I heard him call on his God, I swear. I have heard . . . others . . . use those words.'

'You mean the words "*domine Jesu Christus*", Sire?'

'Some such words, yes,' he replied shortly.

'Sire, Christians use the date of birth of their Lord in their calendars. My question required a date. So this man replied, "Forty-three years after the birth of our Lord, Jesus Christ". Just as I would have said, "In the eighteenth year of the reign of Niall of Tara and the fourteenth year of the reign of Morrough".'

Sennach paused and I looked across at Deara. She was sitting so still she might as well have been a statue. The colour had drained from her face and I could see the effort she was making not to twist her hands together.

'You know the penalty for a slave who runs away?'

'I do, Sire,' came the firm reply.

'Where have you been hiding . . . how long did you say you'd been hiding?' The question was deliberately and brutally insulting.

'I have not been hiding, Sire,' came the reply, as steady and composed as before. 'I escaped by ship to Gaul eleven years ago. I came thence to my kinsfolk in Albi and now I am come to Emain.'

Sennach raised his eyebrows and when he went on it was clear that the King's tone had softened somewhat.

88

'What is your master's name?'

'My master was Milchu of Foclut.'

'Eleven years? You escaped and came back of your own free will to face death? Are you mad? Or do you think to make fools of us all?'

'Sire, for many years I did not wish to come, because I was afraid,' Patricius admitted. 'But always in my dreams I saw Ireland and her people. I knew I had committed a sin, for our Lord tells us we must not steal. And by my flight I had stolen myself from my master, who is a good man. Here, Sire, I have brought gold that I may wipe out this sin I have committed, for it preys upon my conscience. If you would take my life, then I ask only that this debt be paid first.'

'How much is he worth, brehon?'

'Between six and eight milk cows, Sire, if he can indeed read and write and is as strong as he looks.'

'How much in gold?'

'That depends on the quality and kind, Sire.'

'Show us your gold, man,' the King ordered.

Patricius placed his leather satchel on Sennach's table and opened it.

'And where did you steal this?' Morrough demanded roughly as he tipped out the gold coins from a small leather pouch.

'I stole but once, Sire,' came the level reply. 'And that was when I stole my body to join my spirit which will ever be free, though my body be in chains.'

Sennach stopped speaking, drank a few sips of wine and looked sharply at Deara. Her face had grown sombre and she sighed deeply as if she had been so absorbed in his tale that she had forgotten to breathe properly.

'Can you imagine what happened next?' he asked.

'No, Sennach, I can't. But I pray Morrough didn't take up the idea of chains and make him prove it.'

He smiled wryly. 'That was in my mind too,' he said, as he continued. 'Morrough was as restless as a young colt. He even pushed away the hound that always goes to him when he is fretful. But that slave was not to be disturbed by anyone's manner towards him, not even Morrough. He just continued to say what he felt he had to say. I do not have your gift, my dear, but I'll try to recall his words, as accurately as I can remember them.

Sire, a man has one body. It is given to him with whatever faults and failings it may have. And with it he must bear heat and cold and the wounds of battle or of toil. It is not his to choose his body or its lot. But the spirit is a different matter. By the grace of God we can make ourselves whole and unblemished in spirit, we can rise above the hardships of this life, and find a courage we did not know we had and a love for our fellowmen that we thought impossible. I came to understand these things while I was tending my master's sheep, but it has taken me these eleven years to see clearly what it is I have to do. I ask you to let me pay my debt to free my spirit of the taint of sin. My life you may take at your will, but my spirit belongs to my God.'

Sennach shook his head in disbelief, as he recalled the firmness and clarity of Patricius's words: 'And then the man kneels down quite calmly in front of Morrough, raises his arms in the air and calls upon his God to bless Morrough and all his people.'

'And what did Morrough do then?'

Deara's voice had dropped to a whisper as she watched Sennach's face.

He bade me send for Milchu with all possible haste and see that our guest was made comfortable during his stay.'

'Your guest?'

Deara's voice was full of amazement and relief.

Sennech held her gaze and smiled his wryest smile. 'Yes, indeed, my dear. Patricius Claudius of Bannem Tabernae dines with Morrough this evening in the King's Hall. Had I been guest to anyone else but Alcelcius and yourself, I would have made my excuses and claimed my place, where I might have heard more of this man.'

Deara was silent for a moment.

'You think he was speaking the truth, Sennach, don't you?'

'Yes, I do.'

'What do you think will happen now?' she asked.

Sennach deliberated for a moment, and then he said: 'I think that depends on a number of factors I can see and just as many I cannot. The evidence of Milchu will be important, especially the character he gives the man. How the man conducts himself in the next week or more will be equally important, for a herald will take several days to ride to Foclut in this weather and more still for the farmer to return unless he has a better horse than most farmers can lay claim to. Then there is Morrough himself. You know well enough how hard it is to read his mind. When he first claimed his brother's throne, often enough I saw him act both harshly and unexpectedly, but he has not done so of late. Perhaps his heart is mellowing with the years.'

'Perhaps, indeed, though your tone makes me doubt it,' she said uneasily. 'But will it save this slave, Sennach?'

'That I do not know. The reprieve may be a trick, or a trial, or both. But with all my heart, I wish the man free.'

Deara looked surprised and indeed I could see why she should find Sennach's words uncharacteristic. He seemed to me to be such a controlled man, so balanced in his views and so cool in his judgement.

90

But he was being far from cool at this moment.

'Why, Sennach, why do you wish that?' she asked.

He shook his head as he reached for his goblet and drained it. 'It is a weakness I have, Deara, one of many you will almost certainly have detected. I admire in others that which I would most dearly like for myself. That man has courage and certainty. Never in my life have I felt I had sufficient of either.'

He stood up quickly as if he were reluctant to say more, half regretting that he had revealed so much of himself.

'And now, my dear, it grows late, my servant will be asleep, or will have gambled away his substance with that lad of Alcelcius, and I must be gone. Shall I see you tomorrow?'

'Yes, indeed, I have much to do. Morrough himself has need of new dressings for that wound he took at the boar hunt.'

'It heals well?'

'It heals,' she replied. 'But all too slowly for my liking. It would not go well with Morrough at this time were he to take a serious wound.'

Sennach nodded sharply. 'Like our slave, Morrough has no lack of courage, but unlike our slave, I think he is often uncertain of himself and he bears a great burden, without support.'

'It would be the heavier, Sennach, had he not your care. You must think to yourself as much as he should.'

Sennach waved his hand dismissively as he called his servant and pinned his cloak in place. 'I shall seek you out as soon as I have news of this man.'

'I would be glad indeed to know how he fares. Go carefully, Sennach. May your sleep bring you peace.'

'Goodnight, my dear. Greet Alcelcius for me.'

Deara followed him to the door and I felt the flurry of cold air as it swept past her and flared some red embers in the dying fire. I listened as she closed the outer door, spoke to a servant who came to see if she wanted him to put out the candles and lamps. She made her way back to the fire. I waited, not wanting to startle her by speaking as she leaned forward, her back to me, raking the embers to make a tiny blaze. She stretched out her hands to the flickering flames and shivered.

I shivered too. Something had touched my cheek and as I put up my hand to brush it away, I caught the rich perfume of hawthorn and felt the sudden stirring of the morning breeze that had tossed a tiny fragment of blossom into my lap.

91

11

For a moment I just didn't know where I was. Then the familiar sounds of an ordinary Saturday morning began to come in upon me: the whizz of cars, the bellowing of a cow, the scuffle of a blackbird turning over dead leaves and then the sudden staccato chatter of a helicopter on a surveillance run over the west side of the city.

Sound first and then recollection, the order just the same as when I woke up in the London flat. I'd hear the central heating come on, the moan of plumbing as a neighbour ran a bath, the whistle of an early passer-by. And only then would the detail of the day start to print out: 'Monday – Robert – town by ten – article and illustrations – skirt and high heels'; or perhaps, 'Friday, thank goodness. Work at home – draft new report – vacuum flat – cook casserole for freezer – type up article'.

The details of my present life at Anacarrig came with a rush. At first I was stunned, then I panicked. Questions assaulted me from every direction. How long had I been sitting here? What time was Pat due? What was I going to do about her lunch? Was there any tonic?

Confused and anxious, I glared at my watch. I thought it must have stopped. I put it to my ear and it ticked reassuringly. I studied the tiny second hand: it was going round exactly as it always did. How could it possibly be that no time at all had passed when I had spent a whole evening in another place?

'Some things we do know. We know we are friends.'

Deara's words came back to me, comforting me. My stomach lurched back into place and I collected myself.

I wished yet again that Pat weren't coming to lunch. I'd felt I had to ask her when she couldn't come to the funeral. Now I had to remind myself I'd put it off once already so there was no way out. I scuffled in the freezer and found a couple of individual fish pies. 'Best cooked from frozen' they said. I blessed Sandy for her foresight and forgave her for the awful night she'd given me.

'Tonic, Deirdre, tonic. Keep your mind on the job. Just for an hour or two, then you'll have all the time you need.'

I knelt in front of the drinks cabinet and began my search. There was the unopened bottle of gin I'd remembered, one of several Sandy had bought before the funeral. I lifted out whiskey, vodka and Pimm's.

Further back, I came on remnants of past lives, a bottle of sweet sherry Mother used to give her girlfriends when they came to play whist, a bottle of liqueur that only emerged at Christmas and a bottle half full of rum.

Rum was Uncle George's tipple. Of all Mother's admirers, George was the only one I really liked. Widowed and retired early from the police force because of a back injury, he'd been around since my sixth form year. A tall, angular man, kind-hearted and full of good stories, I was always grateful for his presence and the modifying effect it had on Mother. Sometimes, with Uncle George providing the treats and outings which she enjoyed, I could even pretend for a few hours that we were a happy family.

In my last year at university he'd had a heart attack and died suddenly. She didn't tell me till after the funeral. When I protested that I would have gone if I had known, she simply announced that she didn't go herself and she certainly wasn't having Sandy or me go. That was all that was needed to give people something to talk about.

I was right about the tonic. There wasn't any. And Robert Andscombe was right about mortality. He said it came at you in unexpected ways. It did. I sat there with the bottle of rum in my hands, tears pouring down my cheeks, overwhelmed by the loss of Uncle George.

It should have taken about fifteen minutes to drive into town and fetch the tonic, but there was an Army checkpoint a little way along the road and long queues of traffic in both directions. On the way in the young soldier waved me through without checking my identity, my licence, or the ownership of the car I was driving, but queueing up on the way back, I watched the minutes click past as another young soldier did it by the book.

'Licence, please, Madam.'

His accent was Midlands, he looked barely eighteen and he had very bad acne. I wondered who it was who said you know you're getting old when the policemen start looking young.

'Are you staying locally, Madam?'

'Yes, up there.'

I pointed along the road to where Anacarrig stood on the hillside. His eyes never left my face.

'Are you the owner of this car?'

'No, it belonged to my mother, but she has just died.'

'What was the purpose of your journey?'

'To buy a bottle of tonic.'

He was totally taken aback. For a moment, I really did think he was going to refer to his instruction manual; instead, he waved me on with a hasty gesture. I put the car into gear. It stalled. I stalled twice before I remembered that was third on Mother's car.

Ten minutes later, the pies in the oven, I went through to the sitting room for the best glasses and saw Arthur's Porsche drop Pat unceremoniously at the foot of the drive. All the tension and unease I'd been feeling about her visit came together. She had dyed her hair red. I knew then our friendship was over.

A week or two earlier I'd have been outraged at the unprompted thought. I'd have dismissed it as silly, ridiculous, unreasonable and illogical. But today I didn't. It occurred to me I had developed a habit of sweeping aside thoughts that came unbidden as this one had and it was a very bad habit. What would have happened to my friendship with Deara if I'd insisted on behaving as if she didn't exist. The effects of Pat's newly dyed hair upon me wouldn't fit any obvious scheme of logic, any more than my being certain that Carol Andscombe would soon be mistress of Anacarrig, but I'd have to give such thoughts more respect, I decided, as I went out to greet Pat.

I'd known Pat Dunbar for exactly ten years. We'd met on the landing below the attic rooms in Duke Street from which Robert Fairclough ran his agency when I first signed up with him. A tall building that got progressively more old-fashioned as you went up, it had a luxurious office furnishing concern on the ground floor, a travel agent's on the first floor, a textile company on the second and Robert under the roof.

Ninety-two stairs, carpeted at first, then linoleumed, curved around the shaft of the ancient lift that was always somewhere else, its gates open, its automatic cut-out permanently in place. I had reached the point where the linoleum gave way to bare wood and the chipped cream tiles and low light level made the place feel like the exit from a public convenience when a sharp, familiar-sounding voice interrupted my stream of thought.

'Can ye get past atall? Am sorry about all this stuff. It wasn't supposed to be here till tomarra an a can't move it till one of the boys comes in from the warehouse.'

The ring of an Ulster voice had been such a delight I'd laughed aloud, sat down on the nearest bale of cloth and asked its owner where she was from. In two moves we had established mutual friends in Dungannon and a mutual dislike for Robert Fairclough who earlier that morning had complained most unpleasantly about the cloth.

We arranged to meet that evening. The only option was a coffee bar because we were both so short of money. Within two months, we were sharing a tiny flat. We supported each other through one of the worst bits of both our lives and parted good friends eighteen months later when I met Matthew and Pat decided to move in with Arthur.

I took the drinks tray outside to the small white table at the end of the terrace and sat where I could look down the garden to the laden branches of the hawthorns and the deep pool of midday shadow at their feet.

'Well then, what's it like to be in the money?' she asked, as I unscrewed the metal cap of the gin bottle.

'You mean the gin?' I said, laughing, as she disappeared into her striped carry-all in search of her cigarettes.

I thought of all the times at the flat when we'd just managed to scrape together the price of a bottle of wine because we had friends coming for a meal.

'That was Sandy,' I went on, 'she's been very generous. She stocked up the freezer and checked the booze after the funeral. She left me so much stuff you'd have thought I was going to give a party.'

She re-emerged with her cigarettes and stared at me blankly.

'I meant the house. Haf o' six figures will come in handy. Have ye had an offer yet?'

'Yes.'

'Too low?'

'No, the full amount.'

'Ye don't seem very happy 'bout it. Is there somethin' wrong wi' the people?'

I did my best to explain that the Andscombes were very nice people, that I really liked them, but that it had all been a bit sudden. I suppose I must have sounded rather flat. Clearly Pat was not remotely interested in either the Andscombes or my problem with the speed at which things were moving.

'What are ye goin' to do with yer money? Ye'll hardly go on workin' for oul man Fairclough?'

'You mean the money from the house?'

'What else would I be talkin' about?' she asked, sharply. 'Is there more forby?'

'There isn't any money, Pat. Mother's left everything to the church, I thought I'd told you that years ago.'

'Get away wi' you.'

She tossed her head so fiercely that her earrings, pink and yellow parrots, swung madly on their plastic perches.

'It's true. She gave us both some money back in 1980 after she'd had the compensation for the bomb. That's how Matthew and I managed the deposit on the flat. She told us then not to expect anything more. We never have.'

'An what has Sandy to say 'bout all this? She's surely goin' to contest the will.'

'I didn't know you could.'

'Of course ye can, if ye know as much 'bout it as Sandy. Don't tell me she's not on to that wi' all her legal experience?'

Her words hit me like a blow. I had no idea what to say. With a presence of mind that afterwards left me amazed, I gasped, jumped to my feet, said I'd left the oven on full and dashed into the kitchen without answering her question.

Standing breathless with my back against the kitchen door I tried to calm myself. I thought of last night's phone call, the sharp questions, the inquisition about the search for another will. Sandy had been so preoccupied with prospective buyers and those six figures, a sum that still seemed enormous to me. However upset I'd been with her, I'd still imagined she was just trying to get the job finished. She'd told me weeks back that she wanted it done with so she could forget it and get on with her own life. Knowing Sandy, that made perfect sense. But this was quite another way of seeing things. What 'contesting the will' might do to our relationship and to my equilibrium was more than I could bear to think about.

I took some very deep breaths, crisped some rolls under the grill and took my time putting lunch on a tray. It would be two hours at least before Arthur reappeared to take Pat off to the golf club and another three before I was free to go and meet Helen for our evening together. The time would pass, as all things pass. It would have to be endured. That was not the problem. What troubled me was how I could keep my temper if Pat went on talking about money.

The things we fear are never as bad as we think they're going to be. Pat did go on talking about money, but she moved her attention to the large sum she had in mind for herself. Arthur, she explained, needed OPM for floating a new company and she had been able to put him on the right track for getting it. He really was going to make a killing.

I'd listened to Pat talking like this since first she met Arthur and as she warmed to her story I wondered why it was she always behaved as if I was an idiot about money. Years ago, the first time she mentioned OPM I'd asked her what it meant. For the first time in our relationship I had felt foolish and uncomfortable when she replied.

'OPM? Fancy you not knowin' that, Dee. Shure, I thought you were supposed to know what goes on in the world. OPM is Other People's Money.'

As I sat watching Pat down her gin, I decided to stop worrying about why I hate discussing money. Perhaps I do have a hang-up about it, but it doesn't mean I can't handle money sensibly. Halfway through my fish pie light dawned. What Pat was saying was nothing to do with my being able to handle money effectively, she was telling me I was a fool not to grab any possibility of getting rich as quickly as possible.

Yes, I'd confess to being a fool, but not about getting rich. For years I'd assumed Pat just didn't see the dubiousness of Arthur's activities. But I was wrong. Pat could see exactly what Arthur was doing: stockpiling fabric in anonymous warehouses, junking his creditors, relaunching new companies from the wreckage of his previous ones. She'd been actively encouraging him because what she wanted most was an easy life, and an easy life needs lots of money.

Now I'd faced it, I could see that the big money talk had begun the very moment she met Arthur. I'd made allowances then, because I knew how very poor she'd been and when she treated me as if I were an idiot about money, I'd ended up blaming myself for my unease. Money, business and profits were my mother's main preoccupation in life. I'd been forced to listen, hour upon hour, to the stories of her engagements and her triumphs. No wonder I was allergic to the whole topic of money. But that made no difference now. I couldn't give Pat the benefit of my weakness any longer and I could never feel easy again with someone for whom money was as important as it was to Pat.

I watched the parrots swing as the gin made her yet more animated. As the meal went on, I found listening to her actually got easier because I'd made up my mind this was indeed the very last time I would have to listen to her.

Hours later, as I drove out of Armagh on my way to meet Helen, I found the turbulence of the day simply melting away. The countryside was at its loveliest. Although it was warm and sunny the air had not yet lost the freshness of springtime; the new foliage was still soft, translucent where the sunlight shone through the tender leaves. The wisp of evening breeze was heavy with the scent of apple blossom and of hawthorn as it moved among the laden branches of the orchards and great hawthorn hedges which divide up this part of Ulster into a patchwork of irregular fields.

I'd never seen the hawthorns so weighed down with creamy blossom. I thought at once of the game Matthew and I always play when we travel. We look out for the plant, or animal, or insect that is having a special year. One April, after a bitter winter in London, we drove up to Norfolk for Easter and found pools of stunning colour, purple and mauve, in every rockery and garden from Suffolk to the north coast. We'd agreed that was the 'Spring of the Aubrietia'. If Matthew were with me now, he'd be sure to say this had to be the 'Summer of the Hawthorn'.

I am always glad to see Helen, but that evening outside the restaurant in Hillsborough I think I must have clutched her as if I would never let her go. Of all the people I know, she is the steadiest and the most reliable, as well as being the friend who has known me longest.

Helen and I met when we were eleven. Standing side by side in the line of third formers drawn up across the gym in the still-new High School, we were waiting self-consciously for the Headmistress to come and take assembly. Helen's family had just arrived in Armagh from Downpatrick, her father the new manager of the Bank of Ireland. We became friends there and then.

Without Helen's friendship in those years when my mother was building up the business, I would have been even more lonely and unhappy than I was. We were constant companions in school. We sat together, were partners for games and projects, but we saw little of each other outside school. Helen's mother was an asthmatic and often unwell. I seldom visited the tall house in Abbey Street where they lived and Helen's visits to Anacarrig were equally infrequent. Mother thought all this visiting was a lot of nonsense and only made work.

It's not simply because of all the shared experience, nor even the like-mindedness which is so often there, that I value Helen so much. What is even more important to me is that Helen alone among the friends I have, always seems to know when what I'm saying is right for me. She had that capacity, even when we were in the third form, and I hate to think what I would have done without it.

It was Helen who helped me when I panicked over choosing my subjects for A level and couldn't decide whether to try for a scholarship to Queen's or to just go to the teacher training college with most of our contemporaries. But that was not the most important of Helen's rescue jobs. There was one much more desperate than that.

It was Helen who rescued me from Robin, the well-known local sportsman and dynamic young businessman, when our marriage turned out to be disastrously wrong. Emotionally and physically bruised, with my mind like jelly and my decision-making ability nil, she worked out how I could get away and prevent him from finding me. It was she who bought my one-way ticket to London and she who borrowed her brother's car so she could wait unrecognised on the road close to our bungalow until Robin went out. Then she helped me pack and drove me to the airport.

'You don't think I'm going off my trolley, do you?' I asked as lightly as I could, when I finished my story.

She shook her head vigorously and pointed at the very good rum baba which I'd hardly begun.

'No, you're far lighter in yourself than you've been for a long time. And you look better.'

'That's all the fresh air and gardening,' I explained, as I tucked in to my favourite dessert.

She raised an eyebrow and I knew she wasn't convinced. But I also knew she was pleased.

'Are you going to go on writing?'

'You mean the blue notebooks and Deara's story?'

'Yes, the Fairclough stuff is different, it's job work. It's your own work that matters.'

'Yes, I think I'll be going on. I'm not sure I could actually stop if I wanted to. It's a bit like the cork coming out of the bottle . . . I think there's more to come.'

'Oh yes. Yes, there's more to come all right,' she said firmly as she made a space for the waiter to put down the tray with our coffee.

I smiled as I saw the familiar creasing of her forehead as she poured. What I really wanted to know was whether Deara was real or some sort of figment of my fevered imagination. I'd put the question to her in different ways in the course of telling her all that had happened, but there'd been no response as yet. I knew from long experience that nothing in this world would get Helen to answer a question till she was good and ready.

She'd listened patiently to all I had to say. I didn't suppress the nasty bits, but I told her all the good things as well, about the way the writing just flowed and the excitement of the books on early Christian Ireland and meeting Maureen Purdy in the library.

I'd been very anxious when I began to speak of Deara. There have been times when I've heard myself talk to Matthew with a kind of driving compulsiveness that has both saddened and frightened me. But that evening, after the first few moments, there was none of that. The story came out quietly and steadily. I even managed to laugh at myself over some of the confusions I'd had and the funny things I'd thought.

As we drank our coffee, Helen asked a lot of questions. Her brother Richard is a lecturer in archaeology and Helen, who read history, is very knowledgeable about both the Roman and the Early Irish period. At one point she tried to place Deara in time by the style of her dresses. She told me too that some recent discoveries of coins and artefacts had begun to cast doubts on the old idea that the Romans never came to Ireland.

It was not till the very end of the evening, when we were leaving the restaurant, that Helen finally said what she thought.

'Deara's real all right, Dee. What's more real than someone who can influence your decisions and open up new possibilities for you? She's probably the best thing that could have happened to you.'

She squeezed my arm as we stepped out of the brightly lit restaurant and paused to look at the last golden streaks of the sunset away to the west.

'She can do what I can't and thank God for that,' she went on. 'I was really worried about you. You've not been yourself this last year and I knew it wasn't just all the backwards and forwards visiting your mother. You'd gone flat, as if the life were draining out of you. I've racked my brains to think what I might do, but you have your answer now. Deara's already done what I couldn't have done. Don't go worrying about what's going to happen, just get on with it. It'll be all right. I'm sure it will.'

We talked for a few moments more by the side of her car and then we hugged each other and I walked away up the village street to where I'd found a parking place. I was feeling so light and easy I could have broken into a dance routine on the spot. It wasn't exactly appropriate for such a fine, warm evening, but after all that Helen had said, 'Singing In The Rain' summed up just how I was feeling.

The car was right at the far end of the main street and as I passed the pub I had to step aside sharply. A heavy figure lurched unsteadily towards me, his arm round a slim, blonde girl in very high heels. For one awful, sickening moment the bloodshot eyes looked straight at me. There was no sign of recognition as he staggered past, but I couldn't fail to recognise him. It was Robin, my first husband. I ran the rest of the way to the car, flung open the door and dropped shaking into the driver's seat.

The journey home was a nightmare. Traffic was heavy and the twilight between dusk and darkness made driving difficult. I had a couple of sharp reminders that many of the drivers whizzing past me would send a breathalyser needle right off the scale. Here in Ulster, Saturday night was boozing night. It was also pub-bombing night with the police and the security forces on full alert, a fact that the drinkers knew only too well.

I could not stop the stream of memory, the replay of all the awful detail of our brief, disastrous marriage. The shock of that one glimpse of Robin brought it all upon me so suddenly, so unexpectedly, that when I got back to Anacarrig I could hardly stand when I got out of the car. I didn't even think of putting it away and how I ever got myself upstairs and into bed I shall never know.

I lay shaking on the bed, pursued by the violent images I'd hoped I would never have to remember again. I was damp with perspiration and had a blinding headache, but nothing I did could stop the replay. Each time I shut my eyes, all I could see was Robin's face full of the jealous rage that terrified me and finally drove me away.

For years after we parted I had tried to understand what had happened between us. Robin had left me with an anxiety about sudden unprovoked violence, physical or verbal, that I had been quite unable to dissolve. I had escaped the man but I was still the victim of my own fear. I had read books and case studies and talked endlessly, compulsively to Matthew when first we were together. I had gone to see Tim, a psychiatrist who is one of Matthew's colleagues. Tim had explained most clearly what Robin's problems were and what the probable outcomes of his situation were, but no explanations, no understanding, had touched my fear.

Yet for three weeks at Anacarrig I had slept in the empty house without a second thought. Tonight, I was driven to get up and go round the whole place checking every window and door. I looked at the phone in the hall and thought of calling Helen. But I couldn't do it. The call would almost certainly wake her mother and that would make problems for Helen. I couldn't spoil her evening just because I wasn't coping.

I went back upstairs, collected my books and papers from my table and got back into bed with them. It was after midnight now. It would be dawn in a few hours' time. If I could just sit out the short night, somehow I felt I'd be able to get myself together in the morning, There was no point trying to sleep, but if I could keep myself occupied finding out about life in a different century it might help me shut out that angry face and that bullying, hectoring voice.

Probably I would have managed, but the question never arose. As I propped myself up on my pillows and found my place in one of the library volumes, I heard a tiny sound. I looked up and saw the dearest of faces. It was Deara, looking like an angel in the white dress with the gold embroidery. Except that she was crying. I jumped out of bed and held out my arms to her.

12

It was quite unbearable, seeing Deara in tears. I could think of nothing but how I could comfort her.

'Let me take that for you, Deara,' I said, as I sat her down on the bed beside me.

I held out my hand for the rolled up parchment she was clutching. She was gripping it so tightly that tiny fragments of dark wax from the broken seals were falling on her dress.

I waited patiently as she stared at the cylinder with its fabric bindings as if she could not bear to let it go. Then, suddenly, she put it down beside her and threw herself into my arms. I held her close and felt the softness of her body against me, her hair sliding down over my bare arms, her damp cheek against my neck.

Beyond the tide of her dark hair I could read the inscription on the scroll which lay close by in a hollow of my crumpled duvet. 'Deirdre, daughter of Angharrad' it said in dark, spiky letters.

Slowly her sobs subsided. She began to tell me what she had found when she unrolled the parchment Alcelcius had retrieved from his strong box. There were two parchments, she said, both written by Merdaine. One of them she'd written on the night that Angharrad died, the other she had added some sixteen years later when she herself knew she had not long to live.

Deara had never known her mother's name before. Now it was clear she knew much more, but the knowledge was painful. Still weeping and with many pauses to collect herself, she told me how it was that she had been born by the God's well at Emain and not in a coastal village on the British mainland. Once she began to speak, her voice was remarkably steady, though very, very soft.

'My mother was forty and had not thought to have another child, for my brothers were grown and my sisters betrothed. At first she did not tell my father she was with child, but when she did he begged her to go inland to her own people for there had been raids on our coast to both north and south and he feared for her safety. But she would not leave him. She loved him dearly and he was a good deal older than she was. She felt he needed her care.'

Tears poured down her face again and she did not protest when I wiped them away with a tissue.

'The raid came unexpectedly, Such raids seldom happen in winter, but the weather was mild and the sea calm. It was swift and murderous. My father tried to reach an old sword hung above the hearth, but he was cut down as my mother tried to shield him. They even killed the old woman who was my mother's nurse and has sat in a chair by the fire for many years. My brothers were bound, my sisters carried off screaming, my mother abused so that she fell senseless by the fireplace . . .'

Her voice failed her and I found tears streaming down my own face. I thought of all the women in Ulster who had tried to protect the men they loved from gunmen who had burst into their homes. I thought of men murdered in front of their children, at bedtime, or bathtime, or while they watched cartoons on television. I remembered people I knew dragged from burning restaurants by husbands or wives, lovers or friends, a girl I was at school with rushed to hospital from a Cricket Club dance, minus one leg, a boy I once went out with shot in the head by a murder squad, a young couple riddled with bullets while making love in their parked car, their only crime that one was a Catholic, the other a Protestant. I wept for all those who had died and were still dying in what others chose to call, euphemistically, Ulster's 'Troubles'.

I could feel Angharrad's helpless despair as the man she loved fell at her side. I sobbed aloud. Then I was seized by an even more fearful vision. What if I were to lose Matthew? How could I bear it if any harm should come to him?

The world was no safer for Matthew than for Angharrad's husband. My mind filled with images: the random bullets of hijackers at some foreign airport, the bomb blast that would turn his return flight into one more front page disaster. How could I exist were I to be left friendless, as Angharrad had been? I might not be plucked from my home and family, abused and bound, thrown in the bottom of a boat, another slave for the Irish market, but my world would be equally shattered, my well-being destroyed, were I to be left so desolate. I clung to Deara and wept, our tears mingled and made damp patches on each other's warm skin.

I was so ashamed that I was crying from fear and not from loss that I made an enormous effort to collect myself.

'Please go on, Deara, please tell me what happened to your mother after that.'

Distressed as I was, I can still remember being overwhelmed by the courage of this woman who even as she was dying told her story to Merdaine so that her child would one day know what had happened.

When she found herself at sea, Angharrad had wanted to die. She had felt sure that God would forgive her if she cast herself overboard, but she was so weak she had not even the strength to wipe the blood from her face.

I was moved by her honesty about wanting to kill herself and overwhelmed by the despair she felt at having lost, in one brief hour, everything she loved and valued, her husband Calpurnius, her children, her home, her country. And yet, this woman had somehow managed to get to Emain so that she could leave Deara in the care of Merdaine. I just couldn't imagine how she found the courage to go on living in such circumstances.

It was some time before I realised that Deara had dried her tears and was now trying to comfort me.

'Yes, my friend, it is cruel. The world is full of such cruelty and it is right that we should grieve. But we must take courage as well. Our being together has grown out of this disaster. Of this I am sure. Listen, my friend, there are things I must tell you so you may hold them in your heart.'

I shivered violently. The room was stone cold, for it was long after midnight, there was not a cloud in the sky and the central heating hadn't been working properly for days. Deara looked so pale, I picked up the Donegal rug that sits at the foot of my bed and draped it round her shoulders. She drew it closer, grateful for its warmth.

It's a lovely rug, woven in fine wool, blue and purple, the colours of the summer sea blended with the blaze of mountain heather. I stepped back from her, struck by the contrast with her white and gold dress.

'Stand up a moment, Deara, please.'

She smiled, puzzled, but stood up straight and tall, one hand on her breast to hold the rug in place, the fullness of the fabric falling like a cloak about her.

'You look lovely,' I burst out. 'Those colours suit you. You look like the Queen of Ulster. I could see you with great power.'

To my surprise she laughed. Often, I had seen her smile, seen her eyes shine when she was pleased or intrigued, but laughter was a rare thing with Deara. It was hardly surprising. I had heard only part of her story and that had been heartbreak enough for anyone.

I shivered again and glanced around the room. My white towelling gown was hanging on the back of the bedroom door and there was a cardigan draped over the back of the chair where I write. But I ignored them both, went to the wardrobe and took out the dressing gown Great-uncle Matthew had sent me from India as a wedding present. I love it so dearly that I want it to last for ever, so I wear it only on special occasions. I drew it on, yards and yards of pale green watered silk embroidered all over with exotic birds and flowers in deeper hues of green, the detail picked out in gold.

Deara watched me as I tied the broad belt. She nodded slowly.

'And that suits you too, Deirdre. You look like a sage, or a sybil, mysterious but powerful.'

It was my turn to laugh. It came to me then that even if my story was so much less dramatic than hers, in my life I'd had as little cause to laugh as she had.

'Please go on,' I said, as I came back to sit down close beside her, 'I want to know all that happened, everything that's in the manuscripts . . . if it's not too painful, that is,' I added hastily.

She was silent for a few moments and I saw her glance quickly at the rolled up documents lying beside her.

'Yes, I should like to tell you the whole story, my friend. It *is* painful. It will be painful for a long time, but Merdaine taught me that in the pain is the healing. She told me too, that pain of this kind will heal all the sooner if you choose wisely the person to whom you speak of it. So it is you I must tell,' she ended simply.

Her mother, with other captive women of her age, was brought to the kitchens in Tara. There, she was not ill-treated, but because of her pregnancy, the smell of food kept making her sick and the other women complained. When it was known that she was skilled in herblore, she was sent to Aillech, oldest and wisest of the healers at the court. And there Angharrad found comfort and a kindness she thought had gone for ever from her life.

It was clear from what Deara said that Aillech had been drawn to the younger woman. She had not only valued her skill, but had sought her company. Affection as well as trust had grown between them. Indeed, as Deara spoke, I could almost imagine them sitting side by side, as close as we were, one woman old in years, the other far gone in pregnancy.

'As my mother's time grew close,' Deara went on, 'Aillech laid her hands on her to ease her pain. She said then that she experienced great power flowing from my mother's body. Images had come to her in a way she had never experienced before, though she had heard of other healers who were so gifted. She told my mother she would not live to see her child grow and because of that she would tell her what I would look like and what my manner would be. And this she did.'

Deara paused and looked at me very directly.

'After Aillech had spoken to my mother about me, she went on to speak of you,' she said calmly.

'Of me?'

How could a wise woman at least fifteen centuries before my time possibly speak of me? Yet, at the very moment the question came to my mind, my incredulity was replaced by delight. I found myself holding my breath, waiting anxiously for what was to come, waves of excitement lapping over me. I felt sure that whatever Deara was going to say next would change my life in some way I could never have imagined.

'Aillech said I would be much alone and love few,' she went on, after what seemed like an eternity of time. 'One of those I loved was a woman from another time, a woman who never grew old, who wore strange clothes and spoke another tongue, but who shared with me a common gift.'

I opened my mouth in amazement.

'You are that woman, Deirdre. I am sure it cannot be otherwise. She said that we both had to struggle against some great danger. She could not describe exactly what the danger was, but she said it weighed upon her like a dark cloud. She also said that we carried a seed, that together we might defeat this threat, that indeed we might even light a fire in the heart of Tara.'

She spread out her hands and looked at me closely. 'Can you think what she might mean by that, Deirdre?'

'I've never even been to Tara,' I said blankly. 'Have you?'

Deara had gone to Tara once with Merdaine, shortly before she died, but clearly the visit gave her no clue as to what Aillech could possibly have meant. We sat silently for a little.

'Why are you so sure that Aillech meant me?' I asked at last.

'Because Merdaine mentions you as well.'

'What?'

Deara took my hands. They had gone stone cold. When she felt them, she took them one by one between her own warm hands and rubbed them gently.

'Deirdre, you must believe me. I don't know why it is so very important, I can give you no good reasons, but I am just as sure you are the woman Aillech speaks of as that I am my mother's child. Please, will you read Merdaine's letter for yourself?'

She caught up the manuscripts and unrolled them, letting the longer one fall unheeded on the bed.

'See, it is written in the Roman tongue,' she insisted. 'Her hand shakes in places, but I will read you the words you cannot make out for yourself.'

Twice, I began to read and the heavy parchment sprang out of my hand and rolled itself up again. Then Deara took it, smoothed it flat for me and held the corners firmly as we sat poring over it.

'My dearest child,' I read.

'At your hand you have the parchment I wrote at your mother's bidding on the night she died. When I came to her, she was near to death. I did not trouble her with questions, only gave her water from the well. After some time, she asked if I had my rock rose, which I always have. Its use you know as well as I do.

'I gave it to her and after a little she stirred and begged me to listen to her. She asked me to write down what she said and

107

give it to you should you learn the Roman tongue, the tongue she herself spoke. But she begged me to care for you and see that you were instructed in all the ways of the Celts, that you should learn herblore and healing and that you should carry all you learnt in your heart and in your head in the manner of the Druids.

'These things I promised her willingly, because of the tale she told, and because I knew she spoke the truth. Nevertheless, I should still have been bound by her words for she was a Christian, as I am. You did not know that, Deara, my child. I kept it secret, though it pained me greatly to do so.

'There are things that must wait upon their time. And the time was not yet. As I think you will come to understand, time is a mysterious thing. There is the time of the body which you have observed. But there is also the time of the heart which may make a man or woman old or young at any season. And there is time which only exists when events conspire together and create an opportunity for change that is like the lighting of a well-made campfire.

'If it is well-made, one spark and it will burst into life, and bring immediately light and warmth. But if it is ill-made, the wood too green or too closely laid, then the spark will fail, and all will remain dark and cold. This is the time that may never come to be, and the time that has the power to change all future time, should it come about. Like love, it comes of itself, or not at all. It is given and cannot be made.

'I have loved you dearly, my child. At times the love I bore you threatened to overwhelm my promises to she whose courage has supported me in my darkest hours. But I have done my part. It was for you to choose. And you have chosen well, as I prayed you would.

'May the blessing of our Lord be upon you. If the spirits of the dead have work to do among the living, as some men hold, then know that I will ever wish to be near you and she whom you will surely meet, the woman who is truly kin to you, though she live in another and future time.

'Your loving teacher,
Merdaine'

I was holding myself so still and so tense I positively gasped for air as I finished reading the letter. Then I read the last sentence over again.

'There is something else Merdaine said as well.'

Deara's voice was perfectly steady now. It made a complete contrast with my own agitated state.

'When I told you about Merdaine's death I think I did not tell you her parting words.'

'No, I don't think you did.'

Even if she had, at this moment my mind was in such a turmoil I couldn't be sure of remembering my own name. Sitting there, running my finger along under the words Merdaine had written centuries ago, stumbling over one or two that were unfamiliar or hard to decipher, I had felt so close to the woman herself I could easily imagine her scolding me for not remembering what she had taught me.

Her words, with their formality and precision, spoke so directly those centuries might as well have not existed. Here was a woman I could respect and learn from. She had been Deara's teacher; now, perhaps she might also be mine.

'That morning,' Deara went on, as I looked up at her, 'she asked me to fetch kingcups from the further pastures. I thought it was a whim, or even some confusion brought on by her fever, but when I brought the flowers back to her she seemed pleased and her mind was perfectly clear then. Just before she died, she said: "Have a good journey, my little one, both you and your friend in another time. Here, I give you a parting gift of what you already have. For you both, and for all of your kind, who have love in your hearts, I give you the sign of healing".'

'What do you think she could have meant by that?'

'That we both have the power to heal.'

'Well you certainly have, but I don't. I'd never make a nurse or a doctor. I can't even stand the sight of blood,' I protested.

She smiled and shook her head.

'There are more ways of healing than with herbs or medicine or surgery. Don't try to understand. Just hold the words in your heart and let understanding come to you. So many, many things Merdaine told me over the years I couldn't understand, but as time has passed they return to me and bring understanding with them. I have seldom found her mistaken. So it may be with you.'

She said it so gently and yet so firmly I had not the heart to argue or protest. Deara was convinced that I was the person Aillech and Merdaine had both mentioned and I had to admit that however strange that might seem it was no stranger than the fact that Deara and I were sitting here together, as intimate as if we were very old friends. Indeed, despite the strangeness of our situation, I had to admit I felt closer to Deara than to any person I had ever known, even Matthew.

I nodded slowly and watched Merdaine's letter roll itself up when we took our hands away. There were so many questions in my mind I didn't know where to start.

'But how did your mother come to Emain?' I said at last.

'On horseback.'

109

I shook my head. That wasn't what I meant, but it was one more amazing fact about this woman, nine months pregnant and prepared to ride all the way from Tara to Emain.

'I mean, why did she come? What prompted her to come?'

'It was Aillech's advice to her. After Aillech had laid hands on her, she sat alone for a long time. Then she sent for my mother and said she had had a seeing, that the God had counselled her and she thought she would die as soon as she had done what he asked. And she did die. Later that night, after she'd got the King's permission for my mother to go to Emain with a party of ambassadors returning the next day, she died peacefully in her chair by the fireside.'

I watched as Deara took up again the long scroll that had lain on my bed for all this time.

'I can find the place easily, it is very near the end,' she said, as she unrolled the stiff parchment.

'Look, read it for yourself. Her hand was steadier the night I was born and the ink she used has not faded at all. Begin here, where Aillech speaks to my mother.'

'Angharrad, I have never seen as I have seen today,' I began slowly, a kind of reluctance flowing over me, as if I did not want to know what came next.

'I feel my life draining away from me, but I do not regret it. The God has given me a great gift in this seeing and I think he will come to me, when I finish the task he has laid upon me. I hope my wisdom is great enough for what is at stake.'

I stopped, uneasy. If I were part of some prediction for the future and did not play my part, then the opportunity for change that Merdaine had spoken of would fail. How awful it would be to fail after all the effort, all the courage and love of Aillech, and Angharrad, and Merdaine.

Deara's voice picked up the text where I had left off. Quietly and steadily she read her way down the parchment.

'It seems to me this child of yours carries the line of your mother and grandmother, whose names we all know. But they were of the old faith, you are of the new, and your child must live in the future. She must go where the new faith will grow, but she must carry with her the wisdom that was born of the old. A man summoned by a dream will bring the faith to Emain and that is where this child must be reared. This is my advice: Take her to Merdaine, daughter of Ferghal. Let Merdaine teach her all she knows, let her follow the woman's side, till she is old enough to choose for herself the way she is called upon to follow.

If she chooses to learn the Roman tongue, to embrace the new faith and the new learning, then she brings together old and new, woman's side and man's side, past and future. But it is she who must choose. Ask Merdaine not to speak of Bannem Tabernae, till the girl has already chosen.'

Suddenly, as she read the last line of the long paragraph, Deara's voice gave way to a choking sob.

'What is it, Deara, what is it?' I cried, startled by the suddenness of her distress. 'What's wrong?'

She sat shaking her head and there were tears in her eyes again as she looked up at me.

'You have brought me such comfort and it has eased me so much to tell you of my mother's fate, but I have forgotten something very important, someone who is in great danger, whose life may be at risk if I cannot help him.'

'But who is this?'

'A slave came to the Hall of Council today to petition Morrough. He came from Bannem Tabernae, my mother's village. And his father's name was the same as one of my father's names. He must surely be my kinsman. It is even possible he is one of my brothers . . .'

She wept silently and I tried hard to recall the conversation I had listened to when I had suddenly found myself in Alcelcius's villa.

By the calendar that ruled my life, it was only this morning, but so much had happened I could remember nothing of Sennach's story that might help me to comfort her.

'What was the slave's name?'

'Patricius, son of Calpurnius Claudius.'

'Was he a Christian?'

Her eyes opened wide in amazement.

'But how could you know that?'

'I'm not sure . . .'

And then it all came back to me. I could see my school exercise book, open at a double page spread. 'The Life of St Patrick' by Deirdre Henderson, Lower 3. My saint was lopsided, and my shamrocks a rather livid green, but the neatly written account of his life was detailed and liberally underlined in red wherever my study of the encyclopedia had yielded a name or a date. That was why Bannem Tabernae sounded familiar.

'There are very few Christians in Ireland,' Deara began, 'and none at Emain. That is why Merdaine kept her secret and why he is an such great danger. There are many who fear the new religion, especially the Druids, who still have great power throughout the country, though not at Emain. I could help him to escape, but that is full of risk for everyone involved.'

111

She was so agitated that the rug fell from around her shoulders and I had to put it back.

'Oh Deirdre, I cannot bear that he should die when I might help him live. What am I to do? What am I to do?'

The obvious thing to do was to tell her it was going to be all right. I could take her over to the window, where the first hints of dawn were creeping into the room and show her the square tower of the Protestant cathedral and the twin spires of the Catholic cathedral, clearly visible on their opposing hills. I could point out that they were both sacred to the memory of her kinsman. But that didn't seem quite right.

'What would Merdaine say to you, Deara?'

'She would say that I should listen to my heart.'

'And what does your heart say?'

'I cannot hear my heart because I am anxious and fearful. That is ever the way. You must help me, Deirdre.'

I would have done anything to take away the look of utter desolation that had come over her. She looked like someone who had lost everything dear to them.

A few moments later, to my complete surprise, I grasped her hands and started to speak. Not only did my voice sound unfamiliar to me, but what I said had a ring of confidence about it that was quite extraordinary.

'Deara, it is not your part to help this man escape. He has listened to his heart. He has come because that is right for him. If good is to follow from his act, then the help you give must come from your heart also. Probably you will not even know when you are called on to act, you will simply do what seems right to you because you are Deara and no one else.'

She looked at me steadily and nodded slowly.

'When I saw I had come to you, I knew that you would help me. Each time we have met, I have felt your strength and your courage. They have sustained me when my own has failed. I have lost all my family, I have few friends and those elderly or at risk, but set against that, I have you.'

I shook my head in amazement.

'But Deara, the first time we met I had a migraine, the second time, I was frightened by a loud noise.'

I was about to add 'and tonight I was upset by a drunken man who once threatened and abused me', but it all seemed to have happened so long ago, it was no longer worth mentioning.

She smiled so gently.

'I tend the wounds of warriors and the bleeding of women in labour. I see beyond such momentary weakness. It is the injuries of spirit that cause the death of hope. These injuries can only be healed by courage and by strength and you have both.'

'And what of love and comfort, Deara, what is their part in healing?'

'They are precious, they sustain, they give time and opportunity, but in themselves they cannot heal.'

I felt a great weariness come over me as if I had been hard at work in the garden and had just sat down to rest. But it was not weariness. It was something which moved inside me. She had spoken words that had been waiting to be spoken. Perhaps I had always known love was not enough. But I had so wanted it to be otherwise.

'Do you always know when someone is going to die?'

She shook her head.

'What I know about is healing. Living and dying are different. A person can be cured of an injury or an illness, but if they are wounded in spirit they may never be healed. They will live or die as circumstances dictate, but if they remain unhealed, their life will be limited, crippled by what has happened to them.'

'That all sounds very wise, Deara, but I'm not sure I can quite follow.'

'Do not try. These are Merdaine's words. I know they are true, because I have discovered the truth of her words so many times, but they are not yet my words. Hold them in your heart and understanding will come to you, as it is beginning to come to me.'

At that moment, a tiny beam of light glinted through the join in the drawn curtains and caught the gold decoration on her dress. I told her then how Helen had tried to date her century from the dress she had worn in Alcelcius's vineyard. The story delighted her. She clasped her hands together, her eyes shining.

'Tell your friend that is a dangerous method. That gown was the fashion in Rome about a century ago. It belonged to Calpurnia's mother when she was a girl.'

She gestured towards the dress she wore and shook her head.

'This one is even more deceiving. Alcelcius had it copied from a painting which pleased him.'

'So how can I tell which century you live in, Deara? I've been reading books and I have sheets of genealogies. I've searched everywhere for Morrough. He's not mentioned at all.'

Deara laughed unexpectedly.

'Do not look so serious, my friend. It was ever thus. Alcelcius would have sympathy with you. He has had copies made of document after document, at great expense, and he still cannot resolve the movements of the Celtic peoples. Sometimes scribes disagree, and sometimes they think they know better than the people who were there at the time. Have you ever heard two people give their account of the same quarrel?'

We both laughed. Perhaps my search was not so important after all. What would it prove if I found Morrough in a genealogy. What mattered was what Deara and I had to share, here and now.

'You must put it down to my education, Deara. My teachers had a way of insisting that you begin at the beginning, proceed through the middle, step by step, till you reached the end. No digressions or diversions, only the relevant facts. And those facts were to be the facts you had been given by them, not any you discovered for yourself. It was very limiting. It still is very limiting. I still think in that old, logical, linear way and I don't want to any more.'

I could see I'd said something that had intrigued her. She was concentrating her gaze upon me. I was intensely aware of her physical presence, of her pale skin and her grey eyes.

'My friend,' she said, 'you are weary, you must sleep. This need of yours must be put before what Merdaine always called the Council of the Night. In sleep such healing can be given if you but ask.'

And then she was gone. The Donegal rug had slipped from her shoulders and lay on the bed curved round the small depression in the duvet where she had been sitting. I picked it up, still warm from her body, held it in my arms and laid it on the pillow beside me as I climbed into bed and fell into a deep sleep.

13

Despite the wind and driving rain that hurled itself at the west side of the villa and the even greater turbulence stirred up by Merdaine's letters, Deara slept in peace through the short May night. Only when she mounted her mare early next morning and the billowing of her cloak startled the poor beast did she realise how wild the storm still raged.

Soft, green leaves had been torn from Alcelcius's precious vines and tiny fragments blew across the pathway as she and Claudio, her servant, picked their way between the rivulets that coursed down to the track below. More like autumn than spring, she thought, as they passed the place where the braziers were kept, to dull the edge of the frost should it come.

For eight years now the winters had been kind, the vineyard had flourished and Alcelcius gave thanks. Each springtime, rejoicing, he told how the frosts were so heavy when he first came that only the plants in the courtyard survived. Three times he had had to begin all over again from those cherished rootstocks. Now the vines were well enough established they'd withstand quite a severe winter should one come.

'Survival itself is an achievement,' he would say. 'Each year gives strength to meet a harsher time. And if that harsher time comes not, the greater the strength for blossoming.'

She wondered if it could be true of people. Deirdre had suffered fear and loneliness just as she herself had, but they had survived everything and now they had each other. That in itself was something to give thanks for. Beyond survival, there might yet be blossoming.

Her thoughts were cut short. Turning west across the causeway that spanned the stream, her mare, Sabu, began to toss her head at every flying leaf. As a dark-cloaked figure approached them, moving towards the town, she shied violently.

'Let me ride first, lady, she will not be so afraid.'

Claudio drew level with her as Deara stroked the mare's neck, encouraging her. She moved her close behind Claudio's mount, an old stallion no longer fit for battle. The mare steadied immediately.

Fear and aloneness, she thought. We are all prey to it. Horses and women and Kings. But some feel their burden more than others:

some have little strength to stand against them. A sickness of spirit grows in them that burns up hope and joy and takes away all pleasure in living. Merdaine insisted only one treatment for this disharmony of body and spirit ever truly healed the hurt: love. Love, freely offered, through care and comfort, to the right person, in the right place, at the right time.

Deara listened to her words and thought she understood. But last night, in her deep distress, Deirdre had offered her love and care and comfort. And it was only in that moment, she now realised, that she was at last able to grasp what Merdaine's words really meant.

They moved into the shelter of the trees. She wiped the rain from her face and threw back her hood. Joy welled up within her as if the day had filled with sunlight and her path with fresh-bloomed flowers. Her spirits soared: she had a home, a place to do her work, people she loved dearly. And were she to lose all of them, she still had Deirdre.

Three times now in seven years, twice in time of great need, they had met. A kinswoman. A part of her, linked by a bond that could not be broken, by the seed that Aillech said they carried. How else could they be so close when time had parted them by so many centuries? She was sure, quite sure, that Deirdre would not change and grow distant as other women might. She would be a friend for all time, whatever was to become of them.

The roar of the wind subsided as the trackway moved deeper into the shelter of the wood. The trees rustled softly, the beech and the chestnut absorbed the force of the rain and allowed only a light mizzle to penetrate the heavy canopy of new leaves. Deara looked up, watched a fragment of leaf whirl towards her, brush her face damply and catch in the folds of her cloak. How good it was to be alive, to be riding from her home to a familiar place, where she would greet people she knew and embrace children who looked out for her. She, who had once been friendless and fearful, alone in the great encampment, not only had her place, but was valued and trusted.

'Your horse, lady. Your reins, lady. Let me. No, me. Please, lady, me.'

Deara laughed as she surveyed the gathering of eager faces that greeted every new arrival at the gates.

'Have a care,' she cautioned, as a small child grasped the mare's reins with more enthusiasm than skill. 'Let Claudio see to the mare. If you are patient he will let you ride on Brachu. Come, first tell me the news.'

Deara walked up the steep slope, her cloak held close as the children encircled her, shouting their stories. The warriors had come back late last night. The hunt was good. There was both meat and fowl awaiting her.

As she reached the hut behind the King's Hall, a hollow booming

116

cry echoed out across the sodden encampment. There was a muffled clatter of hooves and the whinny of horses. Like lapwings rising from a field, the children disappeared towards the gate, cloaks and shifts flapping in the wind, bare feet spattering in the mud, eager to see who the guards had thought it proper to challenge.

She turned to watch their headlong flight; children she had known from the moment of birth. It would please Merdaine to see them, strong and lively, for it had not always been so at Emain. In her own childhood, there were few playmates and no babies. Often, playmates died suddenly, women wept and murmured to each other. Sometimes she caught their hostile glances and hid herself away. Only later, when she was fourteen and went for the first time to serve in the Place of Birth did she begin to understand the absence of those years. Even Merdaine could not fully account for what had happened.

Hunger is always a cause, she said, as she drew Deara aside in the dimness, after they had prayed with the labouring woman who lay on the fresh strewn rushes. But not the most important one. After the great losses at the battle of Altcarrig, grief lay on Emain like a cloud. Women miscarried or aborted, or died in childbirth. Such a thing had happened before, but never as badly, because this time the women believed the God was angry with them. Then the cattle sickness began and the warriors returned, day after day, empty-handed from the hunt, though some said there was game to be had.

'When the summer fever came the year you were four years old, I sent you away to the sea with Brega. I had not touched a live newborn child for over a year. I knew that women feared to sleep with their husbands and the young girls did not want to be betrothed. I felt some evil presence striking at the heart of Emain. Against it my medicines and my hands were powerless. I could only pray.'

'And did the God answer your prayers, lady?'

'He did, child. But not in any way I had expected. He sent us Morrough, our King, in the place of his brother and that changed everything.'

Deara had listened, fascinated, as Merdaine spoke of the man she had seen only in the distance, on horseback, surrounded by warriors.

'Morrough came to Emain when things were at their worst. The huts and pens were empty and in disrepair, the herds small, the warriors quarrelsome and discontent. He stormed and raged. Everyone feared him, many people hated him and he did ridiculous and foolish things. Did Brega ever take you to see the dancing ape?'

'No, lady, but I have heard the stories.'

'But of course you have. And the more time passes, the larger the ape gets, the harder he dances and the more marvellous his tricks become,' she went on, laughing wryly. 'One day, child, you will understand the wisdom of foolishness, but it is not something I can teach you. Consider this: the tribe is hungry, the herds weak, the defences in disrepair, and the King spends his gold on a dancing ape from Africa. Can you think of greater foolishness?'

Deara had agreed that she could not.

'That poor beast. It only lived through one winter. But never has beast been more sought after. It was penned by the King's Hall and tethered with its keeper, a man with a black skin and a turban. There was always a crowd outside. If the beast only scratched itself, they would murmur and stare. And at night, the black man would bring it to the campfire, or into the King's Hall. It would dance and hold out its hands for sweetmeats. They marvelled over its hands, its hairy skin and its darting eyes. There was nothing to equal it, even at Tara, they said. Nothing in all Ireland, nothing in Albi, like the Beast of Emain.'

Merdaine shook her head.

'That ridiculous beast was a better salve than anything I could mix. It brought back a life and a hope that has never failed us since. When all your skills fail you, when there is no salve, no known treatment, remember this: first speak to the fear; then comfort the pain; and then pray for hope for yourself. Only if you have hope in your own heart can you do the God's work. I shall never know what is in Morrough's heart – I think he hardly knows himself – but I gave thanks for his foolishness. Through it, he did do the God's work.'

With the cries of the children still in her ears, Deara shook the raindrops from her cloak and turned uphill again towards the King's Hall.

'Greetings, lady, I have come to take my leave.'

Deara held out her hands to the woman who stood by the doorway of her workplace.

'So, all is well, your mare recovered.'

'The limp is gone, though I shall ride her gently. Darnon says I must spend the night at Lisbane and not try to reach Carnbanna before nightfall.'

Deara nodded. 'Are you sure you have all you need till you come again?'

'Yes, lady, except your blessing. Send me your prayers when I serve, lest I forget what you have taught me.'

'Grannia, you have learnt well. Your heart will teach you now. I shall think of you often, when I tend my garden. The God speed your way, for your people have need of you.'

Deara made the sign of the snake, kissed her on both cheeks and walked seven steps with her. She would miss Grannia most of her four pupils, though she had tried to show no sign of favouring any one of them.

'Farewell, Grannia.'

'Till Samain, lady. I shall greet you then.'

118

Deara went to her table, opened her box and began to replace its contents from the bottles and jars ranged on the shelves between and beneath the small-paned windows. She wondered what Merdaine would say if she could know of Morrough's part in Grannia's journey.

Three years ago, just at this hour, the King's herald had stood by her table.

'My Lord the King greets Deara, handmaiden of Nodons, and would speak with her as soon as possible, but only at the God's pleasure and as her ministry permits.'

She was not surprised that the man had tripped over his words. So uncharacteristic was the King's message, it surprised her almost as much as it disconcerted the herald. She was grateful there was no one in need waiting for her, for she could barely contain her curiosity.

There were four women in the King's Hall when she arrived. Two of them she knew by sight. All four were in their fifth decade. Morrough nodded to her as she knelt before him. He fidgeted and twisted in his chair, but he was quieter in manner than she had ever seen him before.

'Two warriors and a maiden you have brought to me this week and their mothers already sweeping their own hearths. But a week ago, a woman died. You were not there to help her. Why was that?'

'My Lord, two days in the week I ride out to the nearest of the new encampments to visit those who are not able to ride to Emain. The woman had a fall and was brought to the Place well before her time.'

'And there were only the old women to receive her?'

Deara bowed her head.

'Do you know what the treasure of Emain is, Deara, handmaiden of Nodons?'

'No, my Lord.'

'Do you? You, woman from Lisbane, or you of Carnbanna, you, sister of Ulrann, or you, wife of Dairmid?'

The women shook their heads. The King was famous for his riddles and anagrams, but this was clearly not a game of skill. They watched him silently.

'Not gold,' said Morrough, as he took four gold ornaments from a pouch at his waist. 'No, nor raiment,' he added, as he clapped his hands for his servant.

'No, nor sufficiency of all things useful. Cauldrons or weapons or made objects. Nor food, nor wine.'

The servant reappeared weighed down with an armful of woven cloaks. He hung them over the back of a carved chair, went out and returned carrying four wooden boxes.

Deara looked at them in surprise. The boxes were exact copies of the one she herself carried, the carved sandalwood container with rows of small compartments that Merdaine had given her when she was fourteen.

'Warriors,' he announced loudly. 'That is the treasure of Emain. Warriors and mothers of warriors.'

He studied the faces of the four women who stood motionless, their eyes glancing cautiously at the cloaks, boxes and ornaments he had produced.

'I will give each of you a horse such as your husbands will envy, a cloak and a box and an ornament, if you will learn to bring warriors and maidens safely into your own encampments. Strong maidens, mind you, cared for as well as the warriors by all the skills you shall learn. For if times go hard with us, the maidens shall go to the Long Field with the boys. We shall leave the spinning to the old women and let the maidens follow Macha. How say you?'

The women were shocked. It was one thing listening to the old stories of warrior princesses, but quite another to think of their own daughters' daughters riding alongside the young men. The King's gifts were another matter and not lightly to be refused. They watched him intently, the gold combs winking in his hands as he turned them back and forth.

'Go away and make up your minds. Walk out to the Long Field. Here, take these and try them on the way.'

He bundled a cloak into the hands of each woman and shooed them out as if they were straying chickens.

'Will you teach these women what they need to know?'

Deara bowed: 'If my Lord wishes.'

'How long will it take? A season, two seasons?'

'No, my Lord, longer, much longer. Two or three years.'

'Years? Years? But these women are mothers of mothers, twice your age, and you have delivered since you were fourteen. How can that be?'

'My Lord, I had the Lady Merdaine with all her skill beside me, behind me and within me. These women must walk alone, so they must be strong in knowledge. They must learn to read and write.'

'And what purpose does that serve in the Place of Birth?'

'The same purpose, my Lord, as the discipline and practise of the Long Field, when a warrior goes into battle.'

'Humph.'

The King considered her grimly: 'Well, so be it. They will have to live here and visit their kinsfolk every season till they are ready. Choose the best of the empty huts and ask Sennach to provide what you need for them. But you will ride out no more. I forbid it. I did not know that you rode out. Bid the new camps send their women here, well before their time.'

'And their dying too, my Lord? The injured child, the scalded woman, those with crab sickness, or pain in the chest? Shall they come too?'

Morrough looked up at the rafters, dropped a gold comb and picked it up again. 'If you must go, you will take six warriors. But let the women be brought here.'

'Thank you, my Lord.'

He looked down at the gold combs with which women loved to decorate their piled up hair.

'I have given you no ornament.'

'My Lord, you gave me this brooch, some four years past. I want no other ornament.'

Morrough shifted uneasily, his eyes resting momentarily on the brooch he had fingered as a child when he sat in his mother's arms. Essa should have worn it, but she and his mother died of fever in the same summer, before Essa had been delivered of their first child.

'Is there anything you have need of?' he asked abruptly.

'Yes, my Lord. I need a space of land as big as this hall.'

'For what?'

'To make a garden, Sire, such as women make for grain and roots. Then might I grow the herbs I need and have them by me when there is call upon them.'

'You have a place in mind?'

'Yes, my Lord. Between your Hall and my workplace the weeds grow tall, for seldom do horses, or cattle, or children, come to tramp them down. There would my plants thrive.'

'And you would not ride abroad so much to seek them?'

'No, my Lord.'

'So. The place is yours. My servants will clear it and till it. The wrath of Morrough will serve better than a ditch.'

Deara closed her box, peered through the rain-streaked windows and surveyed her garden. He had kept his word. Never had a straying animal trampled her plants or fouled the pathways. Someone was always there to drive them away.

The storm had done little damage, though she could see heavy heads of comfrey in need of tying up and marigolds blown sideways for want of a sharpened stick. Later, when her work was done, she would tend her plants. There was much to do making new, for in their saddlebags Grannia and her three companions had taken enough plants for four gardens. The loss must be made up with this summer's growth.

It was late afternoon when the King's servant came to fetch her. From the look on the man's face and the frequency with which he begged her to make haste, it was clear that Morrough was not in good spirits.

'Is the King taken ill then, Breddar?' she asked steadily, as she placed fresh dressings in her box.

'No, lady, he is well enough, but he would ride out and the brehon

121

says the dressing on his arm is soiled.'

'Ride out at this hour? Not to hunt, surely?'

'No, lady, not to hunt. There are ambassadors new arrived from Tara that he would speak with – pray, make haste, lady. Let me carry your box for you.'

'No, Breddar, I will carry it. Go before me. If you slipped and spilt my dressings, the King would have your life.'

'And what if you slip, lady?'

'Then he will have mine – come, pick the driest path.'

There was no dry path to pick, for the rain had turned all the paths to mud. It had stopped at last and now the lowering sun had broken through the heavy cloud. Pale and golden, flecked with bars of purple cloud, like islands in an ocean of light, the sky on the horizon was now clear.

It had gone quite still. The air was fresh, untouched yet by the first cooking fires. Nothing moved. Even the splash of the anxious servant could not break the sudden sense of peace that came to her, as she stepped from the dimness of the hut into the rain-washed world. If all life could be as this one moment, she thought, then all life would be joy itself.

Deara heard the King before she saw him. He was striding up and down his chamber, hurling abuse at the group of men who attended him. Sennach was there, his eyes steadily averted from the King's wrathful gaze; Alron, the chief of the guards; Deirchu, the King's half-brother and counsellor; and three young warriors. From the richness and style of their dress, they had come from Tara. One of them, a powerfully built young man with dark eyes, she had seen twice before with the King. He was Ferghal, son of Brendan, the King's youngest brother, one of the ambassadors who had died with Tagganath on the night she was born.

'Where in the name of all the Gods is that girl? Is the King to be kept from matters of state by a bramble scratch? Are his counsellors fit for nothing but to scold and worry like wet-nurses? Where's that boy gone? I'll have him whipped when he gets here.'

Deara took a deep breath, walked steadily across the chamber and knelt before the King.

'I pray you are in good health, my Lord, and the wound pains you not.'

'The wound pains me not at all. It is these fools who pain me. They would wrap me in cradle clothes and rock me in a crib did I but let them. Come, do what you have to do.'

'Would my Lord please to sit down?'

'Sit down, sit down? Am I a child that I should be treated thus? You do not ask a warrior on the battlefield to sit down.'

'My Lord, it is for my sake that I ask you to sit, that I may do what is to be done more quickly and not delay you from your ride, for the sky is gold and the air still and fresh.'

The King sat down with a thump on his carved wooden chair and scowled at the gathered courtiers. Sennach busied himself with some parchments. From the corner of her eye, Deara caught the merest flicker of a smile on the lips of Ferghal, who stood with his arms folded, in the manner of warriors who attend upon their Lord.

Deara removed the dressing. She did not like what she saw. The wound, healing slowly to begin with, had received another blow. The raised bruise had severed the lightly joined edges of the gash and the dressing was stained with fresh blood. But far more serious than the bleeding was the tightening of the skin and a change in its colour, a sure warning of suppuration.

She touched the bruised area and felt the pain coursing up the arm. The King was surely in great discomfort, but he was refusing to acknowledge it. If the arm were not cleaned and treated immediately, it would only be a matter of time before there was wound-fever. In his present state of distress and turbulence, there would be little to prevent it taking its lethal course.

'There is much pain flowing from the wound, my Lord.'

'Nonsense, girl, it's only a scratch. Bind it up and let us be away. Ferghal, bid that fool saddle my horse, and take your friends to the guest house. You and I shall ride out together.'

Deara spoke quietly and braced herself for the storm her words would provoke: 'My Lord, it would not be wise to ride tonight. Or tomorrow, or tomorrow's tomorrow.' From her box, she took out a small bowl of burnished copper. Keeping her voice as steady as she could, she continued: 'Pray, my Lord, ask your servant instead to bring me back this bowl, half full of boiling water.'

'Not ride for three days – for a scratch on the forearm? Is this what the Roman teaches you? No wonder indeed that their Empire fell. No wonder at all, if they ran to their tents every time they touched an edge of metal.'

He laughed harshly. 'I am no Roman, girl. I am Morrough, King of the Ullaid, subject to no man, and especially not to Niall of Tara, who has ever wished it so. Make haste and bind the scratch.'

Deara bent over her box as if she were about to begin her task without further question. She was quite sure now. If the King could not bend his will to the needs of his body, it would go ill with him, and there were enemies enough who would be ready to take advantage of the situation.

She took a deep breath and looked the King steadily in the face. In his eyes, she could see the weariness that comes with pain. There was anxiety, too, but she could not see whence that came. 'My Lord, let me speak but a moment before I bind the wound. I know the King is strong and of great courage, but even the mighty can be overwhelmed by a small thing, a nothing. Think, Sire, of the warrior who bears malice to his Lord. He is one man. One man among many good men. He is a nothing. But if this man speaks well and persuades others, and those others speak with their friends, – soon, my Lord, this one man, if the time be right, becomes a something. And this something, if left to grow, may overwhelm the strongest Lord. One may pick a bad apple from the storehouse, but if it is left untended, the whole gathering will be lost. The pain you feel and bear so bravely is the sign that this scratch is just such a nothing.'

The King shifted uncomfortably in his chair, glared at Deirchu and Sennach, picked up the copper bowl and threw it at Ferghal, who caught it deftly in one hand.

'Sennach,' he roared.

'My Lord.'

'Set it down in the record that in the fourteenth year of the reign of Morrough, Ferghal, brother's son, with his brothers-in-fosterage Laoghaire of Tara and Darmath of Thomond came from Tara bearing ill-tidings, and that for the space of three days, found Emain ruled by a woman who . . .'

Morrough paused to collect his thoughts while Sennach scribbled furiously.

'Who halted the King's horse,
Bound the King's swordarm,
And read the King's mind.

There now, let the chroniclers puzzle their heads over that one.'

Morrough laughed and repeated his riddle as Ferghal returned, the steaming copper bowl held in a cloth between his hands.

'Good, my Lord, very good. But you have not told us the name of the lady to whom we all must bow.'

He knelt before Deara, looked straight into her eyes and offered her the copper bowl, as if it were something of great value. His fingertips touched hers as he made sure the protecting cloth did not fall away from the hot vessel. She felt them speak to her as a man's touch speaks to a woman who has suddenly delighted him. She took the bowl and turned away, aware of the directness of his gaze and the fact that his eyes were following her every movement.

'Perhaps, my Lord, you might add a further clue to your riddle,' Ferghal continued quickly. 'A woman who came to heal the King only to wound Ferghal with her eyes.'

There was a murmur from the assembled company and a grunt

124

from Morrough. His voice was rough, but when he spoke it was clear he was not displeased.

'So that's the pretty speeches they teach you at Tara, is it? Beware of him, my girl, beware. The bees attended at his name-giving and dropped honey on his tongue. Now begone, all of you. I'll have no man see me bound.'

Morrough rose to his feet, waved his arms at the departing Lords, and sat down abruptly as soon as they had gone. He wiped the sweat from his forehead and wavered unsteadily in his chair.

'What now?'

'If my Lord would lighten his clothing and lie upon the couch. I must clean the wound and draw what pain I can from it.'

Morrough removed his cloak, his gold collar and the heavy inlaid belt which carried his sword. Obediently, he walked to the couch and lay down with a sigh like a child who admits at last it has played too long and too hard and wants only the comfort of its own bed.

Deara began her work. She cleaned the wound and put her hands upon it, seeking out the points where the pain pulsed deepest and strongest. She prayed. Slowly, very slowly, the pain began to weaken and to disperse.

'Why are your eyes shut?'

The voice was rough, but not abrasive.

'Because I pray for your healing.'

'And who do you pray to? Which one? Lug? Or Nodons? Or this other God whose servant was Christ? That slave who came worships him. I suppose that teacher of yours worships him too?'

The voice was hasty and the body movements restless. She felt the pain oscillate more strongly beneath her fingers.

'He does, my Lord.'

'And you?'

The words were spoken so quietly, with such uncharacteristic softness of tone, that she was quite taken aback. She could not be sure whether what he had said was a statement or a question.

From the wound beneath her fingers came a massive pulsing, a throbbing so intense that she could give no thought to anything else. Her whole attention was taken by this sign she could not interpret. Power was flowing from the arm in great waves like blood from an artery. She had never felt power flow out like this before. It must be stopped and stopped quickly.

She moved her fingers over the wound and prayed for guidance. It came to her instantly, in a single phrase: 'Tell him the truth'.

'My Lord, the Lady Merdaine taught me to pray to Nodons and out of love for her I have always prayed to him when I heal. But my heart told me there was a greater God. Now I have learnt that Merdaine was a follower of the Christ, I, too, shall follow that way with joy.'

125

'Merdaine? A follower?'

Morrough pulled his arm from her and sat bolt upright on the couch, his face red with fury.

'Why did you not tell me this?'

'I did not know till last evening, my Lord.'

Morrough wavered and beads of sweat broke on his face. He clasped his hands to his head.

'How is this? Tell me,' he insisted, his voice hoarse with distress, his anger quite gone.

Deara rose from her knees, moved his hands gently from his head and put her own on his hot, damp forehead. There was more throbbing pain. Violent, pulsing pain, as turbulent and intense as the power flowing from his right arm. It was not wound fever. It couldn't be for it was too soon. It was also too strong.

Grief. The word came to her, but there was no image to help her. No image would come till the pain eased and to ease this wracking pain was even more urgent now than to ease the arm. She put her hands on his temples and answered him quietly.

'The Lady Merdaine left a parchment for me written in the Latin tongue. It had been put away for safe keeping until Alcelcius found it last night.'

Morrough writhed in pain. There was enormous strength in his heavy body and as she tried to keep her hands in touch with his pain she could feel her own strength draining away from her.

'Why did she keep it secret? Why? I would not have persecuted her, my own mother's sister.'

The pain increased and she felt it as if it were her own: felt it, not as pain, but as a pressure that made her head feel as if it were about to burst. She knew the pressure would stop if she took her hands away from its source, but that she must not do; the pain had to be held.

'She said it was the wrong time; events must wait upon their season.'

Something moved. Beneath her hands, Deara felt the pain subside and die away to nothing. As she took away her hands to put them back on his arm, the pressure ceased and she was able to breathe freely again.

'Put your hand back on my brow.'

The colour had drained from Morrough's face. Beneath the brown of wind and sun, his skin had an ashen look.

Deara put one hand on his forehead, the other on his neck. She closed her eyes. Instantly, the image came. A young woman, far gone in pregnancy, lay on a couch. Beside her stood Merdaine, her hand on the woman's brow. The woman was dying. Her husband stood a little way off, his back half turned. It was Morrough.

A choking sob startled her. She opened her eyes as Morrough buried his face in his hands.

126

'I have wronged a good woman. I blamed Merdaine for letting Essa die. I thought she could heal anyone if she chose, except the very old. I avoided her, neglected her, dismissed her council, though she was almost my only kin. And when she died, she left me all her treasure. May God forgive me.'

Morrough broke down and wept. Deara put her arms around him and comforted him. After a few minutes, he clutched her hand and wiped the tears from his eyes with his sleeve. 'The pain in my head has gone. Why is that?'

'The hurt has been healed.'

'But why? Why, when I am not a good man, should I be healed by this God that you and Merdaine worship?'

'Because healing was what you needed and He heals by forgiving those who see what they have done.'

Morrough shook his head slowly, lay back on the couch and held out his arm to her. She touched the wound. The outflow of energy had ceased. She retraced the lines of pain with some difficulty, for they, too, were dissolving.

Slowly, she began to salve the wound. From Morrough's warm skin, the smell of herbs rose. Calendula and lemon balm. She thought of her garden, the heavy heads of comfrey and the wind-blown marigolds whose essence she would blend for others. Suddenly and unexpectedly, joy welled up within her. Once in the wood amongst the whirling leaves it had come, once in the rain-washed light of late afternoon and now, here at the heart of Emain, kneeling beside the King, the shadows from the lamps flickering around her, tall as a man.

She looked up from her work and saw that Morrough lay quite still. He was gazing around the room, his eyes resting on hangings and skins, carved furniture and ceremonial weapons, as if he had never noticed them before. She turned to her box and began binding the new dressing in place.

'Did you know there was a plot to kill me?'

'No, my Lord, I knew only that you were putting your own life at risk.'

'Was I?' He nodded to himself. 'There have been many plots to kill me and I have never felt their danger. Today, I did. I felt my strength desert me. I wanted an end to the pain in my heart. I would have welcomed death. And now my pain is gone. I have never felt more alive.'

'But weary, my Lord.'

'Yes, Deara, weary. But weary only for sleep. Not weary of life any more, or even of the burden of office.' He smiled, closed his eyes for a moment, then looked at her directly.

'Deara, if I bow to your command for three days and to your God

127

for what life is left to me, will you grant me a boon?'

'If it is in my power, my Lord,' she replied, as she released his bandaged arm and sat back to ease the ache in her own body.

'It is this, Deara. I wish you to be my counsellor in all matters. I shall listen to you with patience, for you have more courage than any warrior and more love than any woman I have known, save only Merdaine. You are her equal. You must take her place. You shall be the Lady of Emain. Come, tell me you will. I shall not rest till you do.'

For a moment, Deara could think of nothing to say. There was no greater honour Morrough could bestow on any woman, short of making her his Queen.

'My Lord . . .'

'Pray, Deara, do not call me "My Lord" when we are alone. It is not fitting for the Lady of Emain, unless she wishes me to address her as "My Lady".'

'Morrough.' She spoke the word quietly to test it. A noble name, strong and well-suited to the man who held Council and rode out with warriors to hunt. She shook her head and smiled at him: 'If I am to be the Lady of Emain, then in private, I shall call you "Bear", for truly you growl like a bear when you are wounded.'

Morrough grunted and laughed.

'Give me your hand on it, Deara. I have growled long enough; it is time for a different way.'

She looked down at her hands; they glistened with the oils from the wound salve she had used on his arm. She glanced towards him. For the second time that day, a pair of dark brown eyes were asking her to return their gaze and to give of her love and her friendship.

'They smell of marigolds, Bear.'

He took her hands and kissed the palms of each, curling them shut in his own large hands.

'In three days' time,' he began, speaking very quietly, 'I shall hold a great banquet. You will sit at my right hand with Ferghal on your right and on my left I shall place Laoghaire of Tara and Darmath of Thomond. In a special place of honour, of his own choosing, I shall seat Patricius with whatever followers he may wish for. Before the feasting begins, I shall kneel to your God and ask Patricius to bless not only the court of Emain, but the whole of this island of ours. We shall ask this God who forgives to forgive us the petty rivalries which have hurt and divided the people of this land. We shall ask for peace. Is it a good plan, Deara, or an old man's dream?'

'A dream, my friend, but a noble dream, the product of wisdom, not of age. And a good plan for setting out on a new path, to seek hope and strength beyond our own.'

'Will you take some gold ornaments I have by me and wear them for my sake?'

Deara nodded gently, knowing full well they were gifts he had once given to his bride. As she listened to him talk about his plans, in this new, thoughtful way, she suddenly remembered the woven rug Deirdre had wrapped round her like a cloak. She heard again her friend's words: 'I could see you with great power.'

Power had come to her, unlooked for, in the most unexpected of situations. Deirdre had been right. There was no one in all Emain who could be more certain of being heard by the King than she herself.

She put her finger to her lips: 'It is time you rested now. Even bears who do not growl have need of rest to bring them strength.'

'There is yet work for me to do, my little one, but it has waited so long, it can wait three days more. But give me leave to instruct Sennach before I sleep that the heralds may go forth at first light, and leave also to summon our guests from Tara to speak with me here tomorrow.'

She was about to protest at this second proposal, but he went on steadily. 'There are matters of great urgency, as you yourself will hear, for I wish you to be present. I promise I will listen to whatever you say.'

Deara nodded. Whatever eased his mind would help with the healing and she was sure now that he would keep his promise to rest. Suddenly aware of her aching weariness, she longed for the dark and quiet of the woods and the sheltering walls of her own room.

'Do you rest here tonight, or does Alcelcius await your coming?'

'He will be expecting me, but I will stay if you have need of me. Claudio will take him a message.'

Morrough nodded. 'I shall always have need of you, but tonight I shall sleep. Go to Alcelcius, but as you leave me, you must send in my guard so that I can arrange your escort. I will not have you ride even that short distance with only a servant. Rest a little before you go. I shall bid them bring your mare up here to save you walking down. Will you come early to me tomorrow?'

'Yes, I shall.'

He raised his head to be kissed, as children do before sleep. Beneath her lips his cheeks were brown and rough from sun and wind, the ashen colour quite gone. 'Goodnight, Bear. May your sleep bring you peace.'

She picked up her box and walked the length of the chamber, her steps silent on the woven rugs. The heavy door was pulled open for her the moment she set her hand upon the latch. Weary and absorbed in her own thoughts, she was quite unprepared for the sight that greeted her.

The antechamber was large, but never before had she seen it so crowded. The Lords and counsellors Morrough had sent from his chamber stood or sat in silence. With them were dozens of Morrough's guards and warriors and all the household servants. Sennach was writing at a small table and nearby Patricius knelt in prayer, a wooden cross in his hands.

Before she had time to collect herself Ferghal was standing in front of her. His brief bow was courteous, but his concern was clear: 'Your task was long, lady. How fares the King?'

Beyond the tall double doors at the far end of the antechamber, open except in the worst of weather, she could see that it was now quite dark. How long she had been with Morrough she could not tell.

'Better. Much better. The pain has gone. He bade me send him his guard. And he wishes to speak with Sennach before he sleeps.'

A sigh of relief rose from the assembled company. A hand touched her arm. It was Laoghaire, Prince of Tara. A heavy, carved chair had been brought to her side. As she sat down gratefully, he took her box from her hands and passed it to a servant.

'This is good news, indeed, lady,' Ferghal began, the relief on his face quite transparent. 'I am my Lord's guard while I am at Emain. I will go to him at once. My brothers Laoghaire and Darmath will stay with you till I come again.'

As she listened to his reply, she felt the colour drain from her cheeks and a heavy weariness envelop her whole body. It happened sometimes after a healing. She leaned back in her chair, watched Ferghal disappear into Morrough's chamber and the warriors and servants disappear into the darkness.

'You look very tired, my dear. You have had no supper. Come, what can we offer you?' asked Sennach, coming towards her.

Laoghaire indicated a tray and a glass which had been placed by her chair. 'Perhaps some blackberry cordial?'

Despite her exhaustion she was amused and intrigued. Of all the cordials made by the women of Emain, blackberry was her favourite. But who had brought it? She was sure that even Sennach, who knew so much of her taste, did not know about her love of blackberry cordial.

She sipped it slowly, grateful that no one expected her to say anything further. The antechamber was now empty and through the huge doors she glimpsed the moon rising into a clear sky. From the hall beyond came the shouts and laughter of warriors, gathered to drink and sing. The cordial, honey-sweetened with a rich, autumn tang began to restore her failing energy and she felt steadier.

She drained the glass and found Laoghaire, who stood easily at her side, his eyes upon the door of the King's chamber, waiting to take it from her. Suddenly, she shivered violently. It was not with cold, but from the release of tension, something else that often happened after a long or difficult healing. Before she could say a word, Laoghaire had unclasped the gold pin of his short blue cloak and wrapped it round her shoulders. It was warm from his body and smelt faintly of lavender.

Yet again, Deara thought of Deirdre and the rug she had placed round her shoulders only last night. What would Deirdre say if she could see her sitting here wrapped in the blue cloak of the Prince of Tara?

They waited in silence.

Moments later, Ferghal reappeared, his face composed to meet a crowded room. Surprised, he looked around, and finding that only Sennach and his foster-brothers remained with Deara, he smiled broadly.

'The King has relieved me of my duties; for the next three days, he says he will have no guard but the Lady of Emain. So as to spare my feelings at being dismissed from my post, however, he has given me instead the task, together with my brothers, of guarding the Lady herself.'

'But who, pray, is the Lady of Emain?' asked Darmath.

Ferghal exchanged a glance with Laoghaire and smiled. He stood before Deara and bowed deeply. 'Good brother, this is the Lady of Emain. Is she not well worth our guarding?'

Deara felt herself blush beneath her pallor and was grateful that Ferghal had turned immediately to Sennach.

'Sir, the King would speak with you before he takes his rest. I promise you will find him in good spirits. I vow I have never seen any man benefit so much merely from the dressing of a wounded arm.'

Sennach nodded thoughtfully. 'It is not uncommon, my Lord, here at Emain. I once knew a man given new life by the application of a glass of water.'

With a fleeting glance at Deara, he raised his hand in farewell and disappeared through the heavy oak door to the King's chamber.

Four warriors rode ahead and four behind, as Deara and the party from Tara set out for Alcelcius's villa. The moon was high as they passed through the gates of Emain, the night air fresh and crisp after the smoke of the lamps and the candles in the King's chamber and his anteroom. They rode in silence, four abreast, on the broad trackway leading towards the woods, but as they passed under the first branches and the path narrowed, Laoghaire and Darmath reined back, allowing Ferghal to move ahead to Deara's side.

Suddenly, as the two animals matched their stride, it came to her that she would ride often thus, this man at her side, his eyes upon her, eyes that were always able to meet her gaze, willing to let her see what was in his heart.

'Deara?'

His voice was soft but clear. She looked towards him, his face bright in the moonlight.

'Will you share your thoughts?'

'They were hardly thoughts, feelings, rather. The darkness so often conjures up dreams that vanish with the light of day.'

'But some dreams remain, do they not, images of what might be. How are we to judge between what is fantasy and what is inspiration?'

'Time tests for us, I think. If a dream persists and refuses to be forgotten, then it is inspiration that speaks.'

'And will be heard?'

They emerged from the wood and moved in single file across the narrow causeway to where the four advance riders awaited them at the foot of the trackway leading up through Alcelcius's vineyard.

'Wait here,' he instructed them. 'I shall return in a few minutes.'

Deara and Ferghal passed on up the steep track to the villa in silence. At the top, he dropped lightly to the ground and gave her his hand to dismount. The house lay behind them, its white pillars casting shadows in the brightness of the moonlight. Beyond the villa and the vineyard, deep patches of darkness lay. The tiny noises of bridles and harness came up to them from the horsemen waiting below.

'Deara, I have only three days left to me, before I must return to Tara. I will tell you my dream. It is to ride ever at your side, in body or in spirit. And truly, that dream will never leave me. It came to me, when you looked at me over the copper bowl in the King's chamber and it grows stronger by the hour. Whatever becomes of me, you will ever have my heart. I shall return here tomorrow, to ride with you to Emain. May your rest bring you peace.'

Without another word, he swung into the saddle and made his way downhill to where Laoghaire and Darmath waited with the warriors of her guard.

14

Alone at last, in the quiet of her room, Deara stood looking up at the moon now high in the clear sky. On the terrace below, the old amphora that held the roses Alcelcius had brought from Gaul stood in shadow. Beyond, moonlight glanced on the rain-scoured stones at the crest of the path where she had dismounted a little time ago. Ferghal had given her his hand, gazed at her as if his eyes would never leave her, but had not embraced her.

She had never felt a young man's arms around her. Since she was fourteen years old, she'd salved and bound their injuries from the hunting field. She'd shown their mothers and sisters how to tend them if they fell ill with fever, but unlike the rest of the unmarried girls at Emain, she had never served in the King's Hall where the young men and the boys joked and teased with them and arranged trysts in the unfrequented parts of the woodland or the quiet reaches of the riverbank.

Merdaine had always had other tasks for her and never allowed her to share in the entertainments or games the other young people enjoyed. She had seldom even spoken to a man of her own age except when he lay ill or wounded. In Alcelcius's house, she was free to do whatever she wished when she was not studying with him, but there she had given all her time to reading. She was scarcely aware that the only person she really knew of the same age as herself was Claudio, grandson of Alcelcius's housekeeper, Calpurnia, her own servant.

Clear on the night air, she heard the whinny of her mare, Sabu. She saw herself riding through the woodland, Ferghal at her side. How easy she'd felt then; as if they had always ridden together thus, old friends who had been childhood playmates, when truth to tell she had seen him only in the distance on his infrequent visits to Emain. Now she no longer felt easy.

His feelings for her he had made plain. He wanted her for his wife and if she were to say yes to him, her whole life would change. She would ride where he rode, live the life that fate and fortune brought to him, just as all the women she had ever known had had to do.

Yes, she had thought of loving a man and having a companion, as all women did. She had known, too, the aching longing of her body in the night hours, but she had never before thought what marriage might mean. Loving a man had seemed to her to be about one's feelings, about the mutuality of love and pleasure and of companionship. But much more was involved. Committing oneself to share a life was more complex than she had thought. Love would not only give, it would also take away.

She looked around the familiar room where she had studied and slept for seven years. Every object was precious to her, from the well-worn table where she read and made her notes, to the tiny terracotta figures that were Alcelcius's first gifts to her. How could she leave him, leave Emain and go with Ferghal to Tara? However much she might love him, or come to love him, how could she ever bring herself to live at Tara, place of such bitter memories; Tara, where her mother worked as a slave in the kitchens and from whence she had ridden north to her death.

Deara shuddered and felt tears spring to her eyes. This morning, life had seemed so good. Thinking of Deirdre as she rode the woodland path in the mizzling rain, greeting the children at the gates of Emain, wishing godspeed to Grannia, doing her work in her own place; all these parts of her life had come together, bringing her joy. Later, she had felt the loneliness that seemed lodged forever in her heart dissolve as Morrough reached out to her in love and friendship. How was it that the pleasure of a ride by moonlight could call up the very shadows it should have driven away?

Overcome by weariness, she sat on the edge of her bed, tears streaming unheeded down her face.

'Deirdre, Deirdre, my friend, I need you so. Please come to me. Please come to me.'

She went over the events of the day again and again, twisting her hands in her distress. She felt suddenly chill and reached for the woollen rug at the foot of her bed. As she pulled it round her, she remembered Deirdre's. She closed her eyes and tried to call up the touch of her hands, the sound of her voice, all they had said to each other. She sat quite still, as if by remaining motionless she would be able to feel again Deirdre sitting beside her. Then, very quietly, words shaped in her mind, Deirdre's words: 'What would Merdaine say?'

Deara knew perfectly well what Merdaine would say. First she would say that many fears are bred out of ordinary human weariness. Then she would say that Deara had overspent her healing power. Finally she would prescribe: 'Whatever the problem, it is always wise to seek the Council of the Night.'

Deara woke very early next morning and lay quite still, watching.the pale fingers of the rising sun cast long shadows on the marble-topped table, where her mirror and combs lay ready beside the tall copper jug and basin. The light strengthened and struck the well-polished rim of the jug. Like the burnished bowl in her box, returned to her hands with a tenderness she had never before known, it dazzled her with its radiance. She was filled with a longing she could not name. Ferghal came into her mind and she was still thinking of him as she was pinning up her hair and heard the jingle of harness and the clatter of horses on the path below the terrace.

'The King greets Alcelcius and sends Ferghal as his messenger. If it is too early we will await his pleasure.'

His voice surprised her. It was firm and courteous, but strangely flat. Surely she could not have misremembered the liveliness of his normal tone.

'Come in, young men, come in. You are early indeed. I hope the King fares well. I heard of his injury, but it seemed yesterday that he was mending.'

Deara smiled as she heard Alcelcius's reply, his voice warm with welcome as he hurried along the terrace from his vineyard.

'Well, indeed, Sir. Tomorrow's morrow, he hopes to give a great banquet. He would be honoured if you would come. He says . . .'

But what Morrough had said, Deara did not hear, for the voices were lost to her as Alcelcius led his visitors between the slender columns of the terrace and into the courtyard beyond. There, by the small rectangular pool at its centre, she found them when she had finished dressing; Alcelcius seated on a stone bench, while the three young men stood before him with folded arms, a gesture of great courtesy usually reserved only for Kings and Princes.

The old man's eyes were bright as he studied his visitors and returned their courtesy with talk of their journey to Emain. To enquire of its purpose would be quite improper, but a man like Alcelcius, alert to every nuance of language and gesture, could glean much from commonplace questions about the state of roads and tracks, the speed at which they had travelled and their expectations for their return journey.

Despite the depth of his curiosity, which by his own admission was his chief vice, Alcelcius was aware of Deara's presence the moment she entered the courtyard.

'My dear, come, we have guests. Your friends have arrived to escort you to the King. And they have brought us a bidding to a banquet.'

As she came towards the little group, Ferghal turned to greet her, such a look of sadness on his face that she stumbled over her own greeting to Darmath and Laoghaire. And when Claudio brought Sabu from the stable, it was Laoghaire who helped her mount, not Ferghal. He remained distant, courteous and composed, but weighed down by some distress which she could neither grasp nor ignore.

As they rode, she wondered what could have happened to affect him so deeply. She almost resolved to ask him if he were unwell, when she saw Laoghaire was watching them both, while Darmath pointed to the flight of a heron, as if nothing were amiss.

'The banquet is to be a splendid affair,' said Laoghaire softly. 'Already the heralds have departed to summon the guests and to ensure the provision of the kitchens. It must truly delight all Emain that Morrough has found a Queen.'

Deara stared at him in amazement. He regarded her steadily. She was aware of his blue eyes and his fair skin, his ease of manner, his hand so light on his reins. In contrast, Ferghal was pale and strained, dark hair thrown back, eyes fixed on the track ahead.

'Oh no.' Deara's voice was a mere whisper, but Ferghal heard it and turned towards her. For a moment, their eyes met. Deara felt the colour drain from her face as everything became clear to her.

'The King awaits you,' said Ferghal quietly, as they reached the outer defences of Emain and reined in their mounts for the climb to the King's Hall.

Deara's mare picked her way sure-footedly up the steep track, rutted and difficult after the scouring it had received in the previous day's storm. Later, she remembered nothing of that slow ascent. Her sense of rising panic must be stilled before she greeted Morrough. She struggled to steady herself, but as she dismounted and took her box from Claudio, she knew she had no plan in her head, nor wisdom to call upon. All she could do was keep up hope that all would be well.

Morrough was alone when she entered his chamber and a single glance told her he was in good spirits. An empty cup, a flask and a plate sat by his chair, his beard and hair had been dressed and he rose and came to meet her, smiling, his damaged arm outstretched towards her.

'Come in, my Lady of Emain,' he said, bowing to her. 'I have been waiting for you. Look, the arm moves again without pain.'

He waved it up and down, took her hand and kissed her cheek. 'See, I have brought you a gift. You said you would wear these trinkets for me. Let me see you put them on, Deara, before you dress the arm. It would please me so.'

Deara followed his gaze. Spread out on the table, gleaming in the sunlight which now filled the chamber, lay a gold necklace, a belt of gold links inset with enamel work, two heavy bracelets and the two jewelled discs which, when placed in her hair and secured with gold pins, would announce the honour the King had bestowed upon her.

He waited patiently as she stared at the beautiful objects that had not seen the sunlight for many a long year.

'Tell him the truth.'

These same words had come to her first less than a day ago, as she felt the flow of energy from his body like a haemorrhage that would prove fatal.

'My Lord,' she began hesitantly.

'Deara, we are alone.'

She looked up at him and saw his good spirits fade. Like a child whose gift is rejected, his face was puzzled and sad. Suddenly, she felt such a warmth towards him that it seemed only foolishness not to accept what he was offering her so freely. This was the man who had given her life itself, when Conor, the Druid, had urged him to take it from her. He had given her more than life – a place to work, her freedom to go to live and study with Alcelcius. She owed him so much. And she knew without doubt, were she to be his Queen, she would have the power and the opportunity to make life so much better for many.

But not for Ferghal.

Her resolve crumbled the moment she thought of Ferghal. She turned to Morrough, touching his hand: 'You are dear to me, Bear, and I would do anything in my power to bring you joy. But I cannot be your Queen.'

'My Queen?'

There was such surprise in his voice that her heart leapt with hope. He began to smile broadly. 'And why can you not be my Queen? Do you think Ferghal would object?'

His tone was light and easy. Deara blushed, in spite of herself. Morrough shook his head.

'Deara, Deara, my little one. I do not need a woman to warm my bed, rather, a woman to warm my heart. That you do and no other. I shall not tie you to me, nor to Emain, if your heart would take you elsewhere, as I think it might. Who brought you this news?'

'Laoghaire of Tara.'

Morrough nodded and beamed broadly. 'Then all is as clear as a summer pool. There is no news comes to Laoghaire of Tara that Ferghal of Emain does not hear of in an instant, and equally Laoghaire of Ferghal, for that pair are closer than brothers. This morning, early, I bade Ferghal fetch the gold from a hiding place known to few and I told him it would be worn tomorrow's morrow. And then I bade him bring you to me with all speed.'

He drew her gently towards the table.

'Ferghal is quick of mind. His feelings go deep and though he has learnt to master them, he has not learnt to hide them. I'm not sure he'll ever make a King. Kings cannot afford to feel, Deara. Or so I have always thought. Perhaps I'm wrong. In any case, such things are for the future and for others to decide. But for a little space, Deara, till I have tested out my thoughts, will you be my Queen as well as my friend?'

She nodded easily and stood still while he lifted the heavy necklace carefully over her bent head, clasped the gold belt round her narrow waist and handed her the bracelets to slip over her long fingers. To her great surprise, he then made her sit in his carved chair, so that he himself could place and pin the matching jewelled discs around the curved pleat of her hair.

When he had finished, he brought her his mirror. She was suddenly strangely reluctant to look in it. The weight of the gold and its cold feel through the light fabric of a summer gown made her stiff and ill at ease, but she could not disappoint him. And when she did, it was the Deara she knew she was who looked back. She smiled at him. Then she stood up and walked slowly round the room for his benefit, turning her face and arms to the light so that the precious metal flashed and gleamed.

His face beamed with pleasure. She raised her arms so that he could see the inlaid work of her belt and as she lowered them, for a moment, she remembered the touch of a woollen rug and saw again the smile of a woman friend in another time.

'Now, my Lady, as we have settled that little matter to our satisfaction, let us see if we can turn this misunderstanding to our gain. Do I take it Ferghal is cast down, torn between his loyalty to his kinsman and overlord and his new found love for the woman he expects to become his kinsman and overlord's Queen?'

Deara had seldom seen Morrough in such good spirits, his dark eyes flashing with pleasure and amusement, his shoulders high, as if some great burden had been removed from them. It was she herself who now felt weak, confused and made anxious by what was happening. All she could manage by way of reply was to agree that, yes indeed, Ferghal was certainly cast down.

'He was ever thus, Deara, from ever he could understand a harsh word. He will meet joy and disaster in a day, indeed even in an hour, but he changes thus only in mood, never in loyalty. If you take him, he will be yours forever.'

Deara bowed her head and hesitated.

'Bear . . .'

'Does that thought trouble you?' he asked quietly, seeing her distress.

'I know so little of men. I have no mother, no woman friend. And Merdaine . . .'

'Warned you, no doubt, of their passions, their getting of children under bushes and in other men's bedplaces.'

Deara smiled wryly. Merdaine had indeed been scathing about the men of Emain.

'A small fault in a good woman, Deara. I know not the story behind it. She never seems to have wanted a man for herself, or perhaps the man she wanted spurned her, Lady though she was. And her tongue grew sharper with years. Even I feared it.'

He paused and looked at her thoughtfully.

'But what is it you need to know of men? Not how to get children, surely.'

Deara laughed and considered his question.

'No, it's not really that I know little of men. They have their feelings and wishes and desires, just as I have. They feel the same pain of body, the same pain of mind, as I do. No, it is not knowledge I lack.'

'Then what?'

She hesitated, completely at a loss to explain herself. 'I could not give up the life I have here at Emain,' she began abruptly. 'I could not leave those I have come to love,' her voice faltered, 'and go and dwell in a different place.'

'Oh yes, you could, if you loved the man enough. But any man that loved you enough to deserve you would not want to ask it of you.'

She took a deep breath and looked at the heavy bracelets on her bare arms. Suddenly, she saw what he was saying. Like the bracelets on her arms, love was a gift, a beautiful gift, even though it would prove heavy to carry at times, or a burden, a thing limiting what you did with your life, how you could behave. And the difference was all in the manner of the giving. She came to him, put her arms round him and kissed his cheeks.

'Thank you, Bear, I think I understand. And now you said we had a task to perform. As well as the dressing of your arm,' she reminded him gently.

'Yes, we have. First, the easy one, This, I beg you, leave to me and say not a word. Now, please, sit in my chair.'

She sat down as she was bidden, watched him cross the chamber in a few strides, fling wide the door and bellow for his guard. She heard the name Ferghal, but the rest of what he said was lost to her. He had scarcely come back from the antechamber when Ferghal himself appeared.

He stopped dead when he saw her and looked for a moment as if he would turn and fly, pursued by all the hounds of hell. But it was a moment only. With his customary courtesy he approached her, bowed and said, 'Your servant, Lady.'

Morrough looked from one to the other and clapped his hands: 'Ferghal, we have a riddle for you. It goes like this:

> Fateful is the silence of the Lady
> Loud speaks the gold of Emain
> Honoured is the gift of the King
> Unanswered the suit of the Prince.'

He looked from one to the other, delighted with his impromptu effort: 'Work it out between you, for I have a task no man can undertake for me.'

Smiling to himself, Morrough left the chamber by the small door leading to the latrines at the back of the nearby guest house.

There was a short, tense silence before Ferghal burst out with: 'Why are you silent?'

Deara laughed and stood up.

'Because he asked me to be. I could not spoil his pleasure in teasing us.'

'But you are not to be his Queen, even though you wear the treasure of Emain?'

She shook her head and lifted the heavy necklace from around her neck. 'No, Ferghal, I am not.'

She unclasped the belt and slid the bracelets over her wrists. Carefully, she laid them on the table and raised her hands to unpin the jewelled discs that still encircled her hair.

But before she could begin, Ferghal had taken her in his arms and kissed her. Gently, but firmly, he held her against him. She did not move away. To be in Ferghal's arms was to feel safe, to feel loved and cherished as she had never felt loved and cherished before. It was also to know without doubt or hesitation that she could return his love with a passion and commitment that matched in every way what he offered.

She drew away reluctantly at the sound of a step in the antechamber. But no one appeared. Ferghal heard the step, too, and knew time was short.

'Deara, my love, listen to me. I would have asked you to be my wife at the banquet, but I cannot wait till tomorrow's morrow to know if there is hope for me. I must know today. I have encountered many women, Deara, some I thought I loved, but never before have I felt a love such as you call up in me. Will you ride with me later and give me your answer?'

'Yes, I will.'

They drew apart hastily as Morrough strode into the chamber. But he chose to behave as if he were quite oblivious of their presence. Except that the ghost of a smile played at the corner of his mouth.

15

Morrough's preparations for his meeting with the three young men from Tara surprised Deara greatly. When he sent for the Captain of the Guard and ordered a thorough search of the whole area surrounding the Great Hall and the adjoining building where his own chamber was located, it dawned on her why he had been so anxious to ride out the previous day. Only after repeated searches of storehouses, latrines and cellars was he satisfied that there could be no possible eavesdropper.

Guards were posted at some distance from the hall and orders given that neither man, woman or child was to pass within two bowshots of their meeting place until he himself heard the news which brought Laoghaire of Tara to Emain.

And when it was spoken, it was grim indeed. Quietly and without any apparent emotion, Laoghaire told of seaborne attacks upon the south-eastern areas of the country and of a growing hostile strength in the west, stirred up by Niall's half-brother, Fiachna. Much was unclear, but the unexpected force of Fiachna's raids suggested an alliance with powers beyond the sea, if not with the actual raiders of the south.

Morrough listened silently. Deara had never seen him so still, nor meet eye to eye with any speaker as frequently as with Laoghaire. While he spoke, Ferghal listened intently, but Darmath fidgeted restlessly, looking now to the partly shuttered window, now to the colourful wall hangings. It was only when he began to speak himself that Deara understood the source of his distress.

'It is in Thomond that the worst raids have taken place,' concluded Laoghaire. 'I leave it to Darmath to tell you what we know.'

'We have always suffered raiders on the shores of my home territory,' he began matter-of-factly. 'From Albi, from Dumna, even from Gaul. But nothing like this.'

Deara watched him closely; the man was quite changed, the earlier expression of lightness quite gone, his face drawn and pale as he continued.

'We had no warning of the first raids. They fell on a remote area where we seldom send scouts. A ship bringing goods to the settlements had seen them burning and brought word that something was amiss.

I rode south with a company and found ruin all along the coast, close to where my father's stronghold lies – the men slain on the shore, every hut burnt, and not so much as a chicken left behind. No sign of life, only the charred bones of the old.'

He paused and swallowed hard. Deara felt tears pricking her eyes. She sat straighter in her chair: the memories flooding into her mind must not be allowed to disable her. But what came next broke through her strongest resolve.

'We made camp and searched the shore, the woodland, the hills beyond, for anything that might help us. All we found was yet more destruction and not a fragment of any kind that might put some name on the source of this evil. We would still know nothing at all, had it not been for the child.'

'Child?'

Deara spoke before she could stop herself, but when Darmath turned towards her, she saw his eyes glittered with moisture.

'Yes, the child,' he continued. 'She was only four or five years old, a little scrap of a thing in a torn shift, with a face like an angel's, her small body covered with scratches and grazes. She walked into the light of our campfire, unseen by any of the guards we had posted. She had listened to our talk and when she knew we were of Thomond, she came to ask for food. She and her brother had eaten only berries for three days, she said, and they were so hungry. Yes, she had a younger brother hidden nearby, so well hidden we had searched the place and found nothing. They had been on the hillside picking berries when the raiders came. She saw all that happened and told us much of value. But the boy has not uttered a word since they saw the settlement burn. The little girl weeps, because he cannot speak. She says he used to talk all the time.'

It was too much. Tears ran down Deara's face and fell on her folded hands. As she strove to blink them away, she saw Ferghal looking straight at her. To her amazement, she felt no shame that he should see her weakness.

'And what manner of men were they?' Morrough asked roughly.

'It seems there were two kinds. She says the big ones had yellow hair. She called them giants. We know children exaggerate, but she said she saw them carrying animals on their shoulders and that when they first came to the shore, they carried their ship up out of the water as if it were but a coracle.'

'Weapons?'

'Axes and some weapon with spikes, "like the top of a teazel", she said.'

'Armour?'

'The tall ones wore skins, but the small ones had little clothing. Their skin was very dark, almost black, and they moved very fast.'

Morrough shook his head and looked grim.

'Yes, we too have had reports that bear out all you tell. Some time back, a party of these tall, yellow-haired men was surprised, up on the north coast. A single small ship it was, and discovered more by luck than judgement. But the fool of a Captain attacked them there and then though he was short-handed. The raiders were all slain, but only at the cost of six of our best men and others were left so sorely wounded they died before any aid could reach them. They were Donal of Edmond's men, but he and I agreed not to noise it abroad.'

Morrough turned to Deara.

'Deara, your good Alcelcius is a much-travelled man and keeps himself well-informed, so I am told. Can you cast any light upon our reports?'

'My Lord, I can,' she responded immediately. 'Alcelcius has spoken often of these northern men. He has met travellers who have visited their lands and speak of a poor country, where the soil is too thin for crops such as we grow, the mountains so high they are snow covered all the year, and the forests too dense and cold for the game our hunters can provide. These men have only the sea, its fish for food and its highway for trade or plunder. They are continually seeking out new land. Great numbers of them have already pressed south down the wide rivers of Rus, where as a young man Alcelcius met them himself. Others pass over the sea in their searchings.'

She paused, aware of Morrough's eyes upon her and of Ferghal's intent gaze.

'The small, dark people are more puzzling,' she continued. 'Just such a people were encountered by the Legions in the remoter parts of Albi when they first came. The Romans believed they had slain them to the last man, but this Alcelcius has never believed. By all the accounts he had heard, they were a resourceful people, well able to travel very long distances on foot and live off the land. He feels sure they retreated before the Legions and survived in the far north where they never ventured. If that were so, then they may well have made common cause with these other men of the north.'

Morrough nodded and shifted in his chair: 'Why would they start raiding now?'

'There is one reason I can think of,' said Deara, 'and I may be mistaken. Here, with us, numbers have been growing. Six new settlements made in the last ten years. Hunting parties go out each day and have to range further and further afield to find game. More land is tilled for grain; more wood cut for fires and for building. And they have none of these things at hand.'

'Aye. Hunger is a hard master,' declared Laoghaire. 'It makes men desperate, as these men are, and turns them into a powerful enemy. So how can we defend ourselves? We cannot take to the sea and search

143

them out for we are not a seafaring folk. And if we bring our settlements back from the coasts, they will go short of food. Nor can we safely increase our warrior force because we will not be able to provision them.'

Morrough looked from Laoghaire to Ferghal who had grown yet more silent as he listened.

'What say you, Ferghal? How solve you this riddle?'

'I say that there is but one answer and that is peace,' he replied abruptly.

There was a moment's stunned silence as Morrough, Darmath and Laoghaire turned to look at him.

He's right, of course, thought Deara. She did not know what arguments he would present, but she knew that whatever he said would be enormously important for the future.

She had experienced this sense of knowing even when she was still a child, though then it came but rarely. Most recently, it had come to her when she had been with Deirdre. More than once she'd found herself waiting with profound attention for words whose portent already lay like a shadow before they had even been spoken. She recognised the characteristic tightening of her body as Ferghal began to speak.

He began by outlining the long history of distrust between Tara and the west which had now sparked into open conflict. He spoke of the traditional unease between Tara and Emain and the internal tensions in both these kingdoms. Communications throughout the land were poor at every level, he continued, so that there were parts of the country where masterless men were able to form raiding parties at will and move on before they could be challenged.

All of these things pointed to one conclusion: it needed only the fall of Emain or Tara to leave the whole country open to an invader. If all parts of the island were vulnerable, then all parts of the island must cooperate to create a more active and mobile defence, unhampered by petty jealousies or lack of provision. Cooperation in the face of a common enemy was a necessity, he ended, but out of that necessity arose the real hope of a more lasting peace.

There was a silence. Morrough looked from one to another. Then he said quietly that he could find no fault with Ferghal's view; it was only the sheer size of the task that gave him pause. It would not be accomplished in his lifetime.

'So what say you, my Lords, to this plan of Ferghal's?' Morrough went on. 'Shall we be fool enough to hope and wise enough to see no other way?'

'Aye, Aye.' The response was heartfelt and unanimous.

Deara felt her eyes prick again. It seemed to her that here in this chamber at the heart of Emain, where yesterday she had knelt and

144

prayed for the healing of the King, some other and greater healing had been begun, a healing which would spread ripples far, far beyond this room, beyond even this kingdom and the boundaries of her own knowledge.

There was no explaining her sense of hope and joy, all she could be sure of was that she and Ferghal had some part to play in what was to come. What it would be, she could not guess, but that they must be together now in all things was clear to her beyond any shadow of doubt.

It was early in the afternoon before Morrough brought the Council to an end, dismissed the guard and summoned refreshment. By then, he had made it plain to Laoghaire he would cooperate with Niall and hold firm the whole northern coast of the Ullaid as well as the eastern coast as far south as the boundary between Lecale and Oriel. In return, he wished Ferghal released from all bonds of fosterage and free to return to Emain as Captain of Horse. He asked also for breeding stock to improve the speed and the carrying power of the horses of Emain and outlined a plan to improve the sending of messages between Emain, Tara and their allies. They should borrow from the Romans by setting up signalling stations, together with hostels along the main tracks where heralds could be sure of provisions and fresh horses.

Morrough also pledged to make the raiding of territory by the men of the Ullaid a treasonable offence and it was Laoghaire's hope that Niall would be willing to make a similar undertaking. For Deara, this further pledge brought great joy. It seemed to her that beyond the necessity of defence, this pledge was a real step towards a lasting peace for all Ireland.

'Do you think Niall will let you go?' asked Deara, as they rode side by side along the river bank in the late afternoon sunshine.

'Yes, I do,' he replied. 'Niall is no man's fool. He knows he cannot fight on two fronts. He may not want to, but he will do whatever is expedient. And it is.'

The day had been warm and the smell of hawthorn blossom lay on the heavy air. But here by the river, there was freshness. Above the swollen waters, deep and brown after the torrential rain, dragonflies flitted and shimmered, the light striking a glowing iridescence from their fragile bodies.

She looked across at him, her eyes dazzled by the strong light. 'You have been a hostage all your life,' she said slowly.

'Yes, I have,' he agreed. 'Were it not for Laoghaire and Darmath, I would have had little joy of most of it. Though these last years have been easier. Even Niall has chosen to forget exactly what my status is at Tara. What made you think of that?'

'It was the dragonflies,' she replied, smiling. 'I thought of the blue of Tara and how the red cloak of Emain must mark you out.' She hesitated a moment. 'How it must feel to be one among so many.'

'That is something I share with you, Deara. Have you not been alone as I for most of your life? You have no kin but those you choose to love; nor have I, excepting only Morrough, whom I seldom see.'

The path they had been following grew narrow where the lush vegetation pushed leaves and fronds outwards with all the vigour of summer.

'Shall we go on?' she asked, 'Or would you like to ride to Brolla? The view will be clear today.'

'Yes, it will. Let's go to Brolla. It's a long time since I've set foot there.'

They turned aside and struck out across the water-meadows to pass beyond the great mound of Emain on the north side. As they rode, the shadows lengthened and the quiet hush that falls upon the land in the early evening began to enfold them, so that even the sound of their horses' hooves seemed part of the silence.

Brolla was not far away and the climb through the trees to the top of the low hill was much gentler than the climb up to the Great Hall at Emain. On the broad grassy summit they dismounted and embraced.

For a little time, they held each other and then they walked to the highest point, arms still entwined. There among the buttercups, which swayed in the slight evening breeze, the ground had been marked out with staves and cords. They passed through a space between them and looked out over the spreading meadows and woodland to the north. Beyond, lay the calm waters of the great lake, and beyond again, the shimmering blue mountains of the Ullaid.

'I love this place,' said Deara quietly, 'and I love Emain and my home with Alcelcius, but I think they would be small comfort to me now, if I thought I would never see you again.'

And there on the Hill of Brolla, she pledged herself to him, a man whose dream she understood, a man in whose arms she had found passion and true homecoming, a man who had promised always to ride at her side.

146

16

There are points of change in every relationship. Sometimes they pass unseen, at others they stand out, a line drawn between what has gone before and what comes after. The long night when Deara and I shared our distress and puzzled over the strange predictions of Aillech was such a line. When I awoke next day I was just as fascinated by her life as I had been before, just as curious about all she had told me, but in the light of morning I no longer felt her life as separate from my own. A bond had been forged that was precious to both of us.

It seemed to me that if I could understand the problems and dilemmas in Deara's life it might help me to cope better with the difficulties in my own. I had no idea how I might bring this about, but I kept remembering Deara's gentle but firm insistence that I hold in my heart whatever was not yet clear to me and wait for understanding to come.

I did my best to use her advice in the days that followed and even when it brought me no immediate or obvious insight, it certainly comforted me. I felt her presence almost palpably as I struggled with the legal tangles that beset me. The more difficult things became the more I shaped questions and the answers I imagined she'd have offered me had we been together. But despite the reassurance of her palpable presence, I longed to see her again. I spent many hours quietly beneath the hawthorns, hoping to give her a chance to come to me, but for all my wishing and hoping the middle weeks of June passed without us meeting again.

Those weeks were blessed with a blissful warmth and sunshine that turned the garden into a haze of blending colours and textures. Each morning I walked out into the freshness of another day to find new blooms on shrubs or buds unfurling in the flourishing borders. As the sun grew stronger with the day, the perfume of hawthorn and Bride's Blossom would blend with the deeper scents of the dark red roses. The dew sparkled in the shadows for no more than an hour or two and then was gone. By midday the colours blazed, lilies opened and the birds retreated to the shadows to preen and doze in the coolness.

Painfully, I tore myself away from the garden. I was continually amazed at the amount there was to do. I asked myself how other people ever managed to clear out a house and wind up the trailing ends of the life that was lived there, when they had to go to work each day as usual? After all, living at Anacarrig ought to have been easy compared with London. No long journeys by tube, no traffic roar filling your head, day in and day out, no hassle with colleagues or printers, and above all, no deadlines, my time apparently my own to command. Given the particularly fine weather and the delights of the garden surely I ought to be feeling on top of the world. But I wasn't. I felt deeply weary, tired out as if I had been working very long hours at some endless, back-breaking task. All I wanted to do was just sit in the garden and read or shut my eyes and dream.

It's true, I did have a succession of boring commissions from Robert Fairclough and I certainly blamed them for the continuous sense of pressure I felt. Like everything that arrived through the letterbox, Robert's commissions had to be turned round quickly and there was always some complication with them that involved tedious phone calls and awkward redrafting. What I found even more dispiriting than the long hours at my table were the prospective buyers the estate agents insisted on sending 'just in case', although Carol and Robert had instructed their solicitors to proceed immediately after their first visit.

If it hadn't been for Helen and her regular phone calls, I'm sure I should have gone on berating myself for idleness. But she pointed out crisply that I wasn't just doing a house clearance: I was rearranging myself. I was beginning to ask questions about my past I'd never asked before. Inevitably, that was changing my relationship to the present and the future. And that kind of changing, she insisted, was a very demanding and exhausting task.

Thinking over what she'd said after the most recent call, I had to laugh at myself even though it's no laughing matter that we berate ourselves for being idle when we're working as hard as we can in ways we can't possibly see. Rearranging the furniture in a house, or clearing out a cupboard, or disposing of items you no longer want, lets you stand back and admire the result. But rearranging your inner life gives you no real clue as to what is going on: you can't see what you're doing and you certainly can't stand back and admire the result, because if you're successful the result is going to be somewhere in the future.

Helen can be very persistent and very persuasive. As the days passed, I found I was not being so hard on myself. Lighting a fire late in the evening, just to hear the crackle of wood and smell the turf, I'd watch the flames, or stare into the orange and blue caverns of the glowing embers for an hour or more. When I looked down at the pen in my hand and the unmarked pad on my knee, I'd just smile and remember her wise words.

My dereliction of duty was even worse once I let myself go out into the garden. Give me a patch of sunshine, a warm step or the stones under the hawthorns and I was away. 'Just sittin' dreamin' when ye could be doing somethin' useful', as my mother would say. More precisely, the exact words she always said whenever she caught me.

Helped by my new found insight, I saw how regularly guilt was one of my companions. It turned up after breakfast as reliably as the postman and it accompanied me upstairs at the end of the day if I should remember a task unfinished, or not even begun. And with guilt came its close cousin: anxiety. The cream inlaid envelopes that brought missives from the solicitor or the bank set it going each morning. Sometimes I ripped them open before I'd had time to think what they might contain. More often, I left them on the breakfast table until I'd cleared up the kitchen. Then I'd look at them and wonder whether I was being wise and protecting myself until I'd got the day going, or merely prevaricating. Perhaps I was 'only putting off the evil day'. That was another of my mother's favourite expressions.

One lovely early morning, sunshine streaming into the house, roses blooming in the garden, a blackbird bathing luxuriously in the stone bath in the middle of the lawn, I stood looking out of my bedroom window, a pile of laundry in my arms: 'Why should a day be evil?' I asked aloud.

Until that moment, I'd never appreciated how pessimistic the atmosphere that surrounded me all through my childhood and my growing up had been. It had to be its long shadow that led me to assume those envelopes I'd left on the kitchen table were full of problems. And even if they did turn out to be, surely it was the same long shadow which was persuading me there would be no one to help me deal with them.

I went downstairs and out into the garden, filled a watering can and sprinkled some newly transplanted seedlings. I was staring down at the small bushy fragments, absorbed in thought, when I heard a small whooshing sound behind me. Cautiously, I turned round. The pair of collared doves had just flown down from their regular morning perch on the roof ridge and were now walking slowly towards me. Since I'd arrived I'd been feeding them the remains of mother's crunchy bran muesli.

'Do I take it this is a hint?' I asked them quietly.

They paused, looked around and stood still, eyeing me.

'All right. You wait here and I'll see what I can find.'

I backed away gently and ran lightly up the steps, along the terrace and round to the kitchen. They'd finished off the muesli by now, but I'd bought seed for them in the pet shop in Armagh. I took the jar from the shelf and went out again.

To my amazement they were exactly where I'd left them. I walked towards them.

'Here you are, best mixed seed, bought at great expense,'I said, holding out the jar so they could see it.

I poured out a handful and knelt down, stretching out my arm as far as I could towards them.

'Come on then, here you are. You may have all the time in the world, but I've got to get to work. Come on,' I said, encouraging them.

First one and then the other came to my hand, pecked cheerfully at the mixed grain and scattered it liberally onto the lawn. I stayed on my knees till my back started to protest, then I let the rest of the grain slip through my fingers and left them to it. They didn't even fly off when I stood up, put the lid back on the jar and walked away.

Feeling quite ridiculously pleased with myself, I went back into the kitchen and put out my hand for the cream envelopes.

'Trust, that's it,' I said aloud. Those doves had never had any cause to fear me. From my first days at Anacarrig, I had fed them, called to them on the roof, talked to them on the ground. They had seen me in the garden and they had sunbathed on the warm stone by the bird bath while I moved backwards and forwards at my work. I had never startled them or made loud noises, or chased them away. What cause had they to be anxious?

As I picked up the envelopes, a penny dropped with a massive clonk. Was it any wonder I had problems with people and situations that were new to me? Was it any wonder I doubted my own judgement, my own experience and my own interpretation of events? What cause had I to trust and feel confident that nothing nasty would happen to me, when it so regularly had?

I blessed my little doves for the insight they had given me, opened the envelopes and found nothing to jump up and hit me. Then I sat down to see if I could work out just where we had got to without getting myself upset.

The problems of my mother's estate had been grumbling on since the week after the funeral when the first documents turned up for signing. Firstly, there was this business over an earlier will of mother's which hadn't been found. I really couldn't make sense of that. I thought a 'last will and testament' was your final effort, so that no previous wills were relevant, but the solicitor's office with whom Sandy had deposited mother's will appeared to think differently.

Then there was the bank. Mother 'sold out to a consortium' some years earlier. Now there seemed to be a question of tax unpaid. Apparently there should have been a document which made clear what had and what had not been done at the time of the sale. And the said document couldn't be found. In its absence, it looked as if somebody would have to stump up for underpaid tax and who was there but Sandy and me?

I had worried regularly about both these problems, but as surely as I settled on any one course of action, there would be a new development and I'd have to start all over again. Even worse than this frustration was a nagging sense of anxiety that I wasn't doing the right thing, or saying the right thing, or consulting the right people.

My deliberations that morning didn't get me much further with the practical problems, but I did at least manage to stay calm. Sadly, however, that didn't last for very long.

Although Mother 'left everything to the church,' she didn't trust the church to get the market price for either the house or its contents. She'd made arrangements with a firm of auctioneers to do the job properly as regards the contents. Next morning their letter arrived, offering me minimal condolences and a choice of making the inventory for the auction myself or letting their valuer come and do it.

After all those prospective buyers, I hated the thought of one more person poking round the house, so I said I'd make the inventory myself. Only when I got started did I grasp how much stuff there was to list and how much I hated listing it the way their instructions required. By the end of the day, I was depressed and irritable, too physically exhausted to do any more of it and too weary even to enjoy the quiet hour with my books I'd promised myself.

I may have dozed off by the fire, I may even have been dreaming, but suddenly I found myself wide awake and gripped by a panic that took me over completely.

Facing me, in the matching alcove bookcases on either side of the chimney breast where once my father kept his books, I saw row upon row of china figures I had not even begun to list on the schedule. They stared across at me, the firelight winking on their polished faces, their eyes glazed and malevolent, arms uplifted as if they were about to take off and fly into my face and tear out my eyes.

I shuddered and shrank back into the cushions of the sofa, staring back at them as if my only defence was to outstare them. Cavaliers and crinoline ladies, flower sellers and grenadiers, clothes colourful and perfect, uncreased, unmarked by any contact with the real world. Even the urchins, the match sellers and game keepers were modelled to enhance their quaintness of character – all raggedness of dress, all effects of too much hard work and too little food so carefully smoothed over.

Waves of anger surged over me. How dare they threaten me. How dare they. I jumped to my feet and grabbed the largest piece within reach. I hurled it into the fireplace, heard it explode and stood staring down at the hot embers of the fire. They sparked and protested under a shower of fragments as it shattered, the larger bits ricochetting onto the hearthrug and dispersing themselves round my feet.

Two ringleted ladies playing a musical instrument had been beheaded. Their music master, a pompous twit in a powdered wig, had been pulverised. A large chunk of the piano bounced across the carpet and came to rest among the cables at the back of the television.

I reached for another.

'No, that is not the way.'

For a moment, I was so sure Deara had spoken that tears of disappointment came to my eyes when I turned round and saw the room was empty. I put the piece of china down carefully on the sofa beside me, buried my head in my arms and began to sob.

But not for long. Even before the fire had finished its hissing and spitting, a calm and a stillness seemed to fill the whole room. Like a hand on my arm, I felt a kindly presence steady me, telling me not to be silly and pointing out that I was safe now.

'She can't harm you any longer.'

I spoke the words out loud just as they came to me, unsure whether I believed them or not. But the moment I'd said them, I felt better.

I mopped myself up and glanced at the piece of china by my side. I laughed aloud. A leafy branch bore a robin, a blue tit, a chaffinch and a wren. In heaven's name, when would any self-respecting wren share a branch with even one other bird? The robin's breast was a ridiculous vermilion red, its look coy, its outline rounded like the images on cheap Christmas cards. I thought of the pair of slim, rather tattered robins who'd been feeding from my hand for over a week now and the endless journeys they flew from morning till night, feeding the fledglings who waited open-mouthed in the beautifully constructed nest on the shrubbery side of the spirea. And then I promptly burst into tears again.

It was Mother. Mother making over the world in her own image. Neither bird, nor bush, object or animal or person, known or unknown, could ever be allowed a character different from the one it suited her to construct for them. Everything in her world had to conform to her specification, regardless of what violence that version did to the person, the object or the situation in question. Only when she could thus control the real world did she feel comfortable with it.

Of course, there was a sense in which I'd known that for years. Even as a little girl I grasped that only a cleaned up and rearranged version of the person I really was would do for her. Like the robin, I must be brightened up and rounded out to meet her view of what a daughter ought to be. And yet, if I had always known this, why was I so angry now?

I had no answer, so I mopped myself up, crawled under the television table and retrieved the fragment of piano. Limoges, it said, on the base of the bit that had survived. I went and had a look at the other pieces lined up along the deep set shelves. Most of them were Dresden. A few small pieces were Meissen. She'd been collecting them since Daddy died. It took me ages to sweep up all the bits of the piano players with a dustpan and brush, but by the time I'd finished., the anger had completely gone and I'd decided to summon the valuer. No doubt he would enjoy making the inventory himself.

I emptied the shelves, piece by piece, and carried the whole lot, trayful after trayful, upstairs to the spare room. There were so many I had to park them on the floor, leaving a pathway between the serried ranks so I could still get to the window to open it each morning. I stood looking down at them, feeling like Gulliver in Lilliput, then went out and closed the door firmly behind me.

I collected up some old glass sweetie jars I'd found in the course of sorting through the garage. Then I walked round the house, opening all the cupboards and adding to my collection any container that would hold flowers. In the morning, I'd fill the whole lot and put them on those empty shelves in the sitting room with my handful of books.

17

The phone was ringing its head off as I came back into the house next morning, my arms full of Philadelphus, or Bride's Blossom; 'when it's at home,' as my father used to say.

'Deirdre Weston.'

'Good morning, my dear. This is Uncle Hector.'

'Ticker!'

'The very man. How are you, my dear? Mary and I arrived back last night. We are so sorry we weren't here when you needed us. I'm afraid we didn't even know about your mother till we arrived in Armagh and it really was too late to phone you then or I most certainly would have done.'

I almost burst into tears as I listened to the dear kind voice. Hector Anderson was another old friend of my father. They had met on field excursions of the Archaeological Society and the Naturalist's Club and got on well with each other. But their friendship really flourished when they discovered their shared passion for roses. They had both known the McGredys of Portadown and followed the welfare of every new rose the brothers ever developed. I had known Uncle Hector since before I could manage to say the word 'Hector,' which was why he'd ended up with a nickname that very few people knew.

'There was a note waiting for me from Dot. You remember Dot, don't you? Dear girl. She's senior clerk with your mother's solicitors, McVitie, Wilson and Gardiner now. She thought you might be having some problems, so I've rung right away just in case you were.'

Hector is a small, rather prim looking man, with a toothbrush moustache. As long as I've known him, he's given the appearance of being rather old-fashioned. But the polite and amenable manner is deceptive. As another character once said of Miss Marple, he has 'a mind like a bacon slicer.'

Though now seventy-five, he has only just retired from his own firm of solicitors and he only did it for the sake of Aunt Mary who is younger than Hector, but who is still recovering from a major operation some years ago. Mary and Hector are one of the few happily married couples I have ever encountered and the very thought of seeing them really lifted my spirits.

'Oh, Ticker, I'm so pleased to hear you. I am in a bit of a mess, but

I don't want to bother you the minute you arrive back. Did you have a nice time?'

'Absolutely splendid, my dear. But Mary will want to tell you all about that, I'm sure,' he said firmly. 'I should like to know, if I may, what seems to be the problem.'

I explained as best I could the legal complexities that surrounded Mother's affairs. I thought I detected a sharp intake of breath at the other end of the phone. There was certainly a moment's silence after I stopped speaking.

'Well, my dear, I think we need to have a long talk, but I can certainly make some comments which will ease your mind. Are you quite sure McVitie, Wilson and Gardiner said there was another will of your mother's? Do you have that in writing?'

'No, I don't. It was Sandy who took them Mother's will when we found it. She said there was a problem about an earlier will. Then I had a letter from them saying they were searching for it and had contacted your firm, but, of course, you were away. No one else at Anderson and Long seemed to know anything about it.'

'Deirdre, my dear. This is most upsetting. I'm afraid you've been worried most unnecessarily. Firstly, there is no question of your being responsible for your mother's tax, if indeed there is a question of unpaid tax. But there are a number of things we must resolve before we consider that. May I ask you a question about your mother's will?'

'Of course you can.'

'I assume you looked at the document?'

'Oh yes, she got us both to read it before we signed it. Sandy and I are the executors.'

'You both signed it?'

'Yes. She said she wanted no arguments after she was gone. She had left everything to the church, except for five hundred pounds to each of us, to cover the funeral expenses. We were sole executors and she wasn't having any bank or solicitor making money out of her.'

'She said that, did she?'

Uncle Hector has a way of getting a wealth of meaning into an unexceptional phrase. Mother had never been able to stand him. Despite his impeccable manners, I rather wondered if the feeling were not mutual.

'Deirdre, who were the other signatories?'

'There weren't any.'

'Are you quite sure of that?'

'Absolutely. She said two would be quite enough, she wasn't having other people knowing her business.'

'Deirdre, did Sandra not make any objection to that arrangement?'

'No. Why, is there something wrong?' I tried to keep my voice steady, but it wobbled dangerously as I suddenly remembered Pat's throwaway

156

remark about Sandy contesting the will.

'I wouldn't quite put it that way, Deirdre. But I do have to tell you that if there is no earlier will of your mother's with the necessary *four* signatures and an appropriate deed of family arrangement, then we would have to deal with her estate under the intestacy laws.'

For a moment, I panicked. It sounded as if things were going from bad to worse. But what Uncle Hector said next changed everything.

'I think I should tell you, Deirdre, that when I drew up your dear father's will, he made provision for you and your sister in the event of your mother's death. Naturally, I cannot tell you the exact provision from memory, but I am entitled to make what enquiries I think fit, as his executor, and give you whatever advice is necessary. I am also now at liberty to tell you that he also gave into my keeping three volumes from his small library which he particularly wished you to have. I take it your mother disposed of the rest.'

'Yes, she did.'

'I think he rather expected she would. Do you remember P.W. Joyce's *Irish Names of Places*, in three volumes?'

'Yes, of course I do. Green. With a twist of gold shamrock on the spine and a round tower on the front cover and pale brown spots on the flyleaves.'

'My dear, what a memory! I am amazed. You can't have seen those volumes since you were nine.'

'I know, but I loved them so. They have all the old names with their origins and their meanings. That's where he got Anacarrig from, though he had to change it from Anna to Ana, because Anna means ford and all he had was a small marsh.'

'Yes, I do remember him telling me that, but when he explained it to me I was rather more than five years old. You become more and more your father's daughter, my dear.'

'Ticker, I'm so thrilled. I've always been so sad about Daddy's books. I can't think of anything I'd love more than the Joyce.'

Before he handed me over to Mary to make a date for supper, he said in his very firm way: 'Now Deirdre, there may be some problems over your mother's estate, but I see no reason for any anxiety. I don't know your sister very well, but if she'd like to talk to me I'd be very happy to assist in any way I can. In any case, as your father's executor, I shall certainly be involved. I shall have a copy of his will for you when you come.'

If I had inherited the whole land of Ireland from my father, I could not have been more pleased than finding those three precious volumes in Hector's safe keeping. When I put down the phone after talking to Aunt Mary and gathered up again the scented blossom still misted with dew, it came to me that that was exactly what he had left me. Joyce was the key to the land he loved, for it was full of the names men and women had put upon each small corner in the 'olden days', that time to which the Irish refer with such a fine disregard for the distinctions between decades, centuries or millennia.

Two days after my call from Uncle Hector, I arrived back from shopping in Armagh and found that a 'Sold' notice had been nailed across the 'For Sale' board at the foot of the drive. I was so taken aback I stalled the car and had to do a hill start in my own drive. I got out at the top of the slope and walked back down to stare at the bright red letters on a white background. It said the same as it said on the way in. Sold.

'Surely it should be 'Sold, subject to contract', I muttered to myself, as I stood gazing up at it. 'Sold' was so final. After all I'd heard from friends about interminable delays in conveyancing, it couldn't possibly have got this far so soon. Could it?

But it had. When I rang the agents they said the contract was expected at any moment. Neither party had raised any objections over the 'Questions before contract,' so it wasn't worth sending out the man with the hammer and nails twice.

I should have been pleased, but I wasn't. The only possible good thing I could see about this sudden move forward was that I could phone Sandy in Germany and win back some of the brownie points I'd lost before she went. I tried to reach her on and off for the rest of the week, but I didn't catch her till Thursday evening when I rang her London flat just before I went for supper with Mary and Hector.

The call was a disaster. Driving into Armagh afterwards, I didn't know whether to laugh or cry. Because of the awful stew I'd been in before Uncle Hector bailed me out, I'd spent ages rehearsing exactly what I was going to say to her. I fully intended to sound competent as I brought her up to date and then told her the good news of the sale. But what happens? She says 'Oh good,' in an offhand way and proceeds to tell me in some detail about her meeting with a young Euro-broker called Paul, who is an absolute dish. Married, of course. A minor detail as far as Sandy's concerned, if not actually a positive requirement.

I did my best to show some enthusiasm about this most recent encounter, but when she paused for breath and I dutifully mentioned Mother's will, she laughed at me.

'What on earth made you think it was a will of Mummy's we were talking about? I told you it was Daddy's. What were you thinking about? Don't tell me you didn't even know that a will has to have four signatures?'

Sandy has a habit of treating me like some teachers treat conscientious pupils who are not very bright and can only achieve decent results by great expenditure of effort on their own part. But not this evening. She made it clear she wasn't in the mood for explaining anything to anyone so limited in their grasp of the basic facts of existence.

I felt myself getting angry, but I do try not to get angry with Sandy. I'm the only person who knows how very unhappy she can be when she's not 'riding the maribou board,' as Matthew puts it. She is either madly in love and on top of the world or fed up with everything, including herself. Given her violent swings of mood, how she ever manages to hold down such a responsible, well-paid job I'll never know.

So I took a deep breath and told her about the three volumes of Joyce Daddy had left me. I ought to have known better. All she could manage was a dismissive: 'Oh, that's nice. Is it a first edition? I didn't know Daddy was a fan of James Joyce.'

Mary and Hector live in one of the tall, Georgian houses that look out over The Mall. Before our meal, we sat by the open windows of their first floor sitting room drinking white wine and listening to the crack of ball on wood as the local cricket team played another match in the midweek league.

Mary said she really was feeling much better since the cruise and Hector was full of stories about the places they had visited. But what was such a delight to me was that they were just so pleased to see me. When they asked me how Matthew was getting on with his Indian project, or about my own work, or our life together in London, they were not just making conversation, they really wanted to know.

I thought as they listened to all I had to tell them how lucky I was to have them thinking about me and caring about me even when they don't see me very often. I have often wished they had been a real aunt and uncle rather than friends of my father, but as we carried our wineglasses down to the dining room and settled at the small table overlooking the back garden, it struck me that it would have made very little difference where Mother was concerned.

Sandy and I don't have many relatives, but even those we do have seem quite indifferent to our existence and that has to be because Mother made it so clear she hadn't much time for them. She always said she was far too busy.

As Hector refilled our glasses, it came to me that Mother wasn't prepared to have anyone around, relative or otherwise, who didn't share her views on the bringing up of children. Two people like Mary and Hector who actually talked to them as if they had something to say would never find a welcome at Anacarrig.

After the meal, Aunt Mary excused herself for a little. When she had gone, Hector handed me my father's will.

As I held it unopened in my hand, I thought of Deara and the parchment Merdaine had left her. I think I hoped I would discover something I didn't know as she had done. And then I remembered how painful opening the parchment had turned out to be.

I knew Uncle Hector was watching me as I unfolded it and read its simple message. I recognised the handwriting. It was strange to see it again after all these years, but what brought sudden tears to my eyes was a tiny blot. I remembered Daddy's favourite pen had always had a tendency to blot, but because he was so fond of it, he would never buy another one.

I blinked furiously and managed to stop my tears. Hector tactfully ignored them, but when he spoke his voice was so gentle. 'I can assure you, my dear, this is now the only will relevant to your situation. As you see, your father left Anacarrig to you, jointly with your sister. It was your mother's for her lifetime only. Had she died before your twenty-first birthday, I should have had the pleasure of being your guardian. Perhaps I might still make application for that privilege. Without the legal implications, needless to say.'

I went over and hugged him and accepted the large, spotless hanky he offered me. I sat close beside him while he explained what I needed to know. There were only a few sentences in my father's flowing hand. One about the house, one about the Joyce for his elder daughter, Deirdre, and one about the guardianship he laid upon his friend and executor, Hector Anderson.

No revelations, no secrets, just a strange intimacy, as if my touching what he had once touched completed some unknown process I couldn't even guess at. Then Hector handed over the Joyce.

It was exactly as I remembered it. I looked up Anacarrig and found it after Anacloan and Annaboe, and before Annagelliff, which means 'marsh of the storm'. The names were like music, but there was more to them than beauty, each one had its meaning, a quite specific meaning that told you much about the history of the place, a history already disappearing under the debris of the present century.

'The old storytellers used to believe that a story had the power to heal,' I said suddenly, as I leafed through the pages of his introduction. 'Did you know that, Hector?'

'Now that you remind me, I do. Your father once told me of an old man, a storyteller, who no longer had an audience. Instead he used to tell his stories to his cows. When someone asked him why he did it, he said it was a waste of a good story not to tell it, for its healing could only work through its telling. If the story were not told, it would die, and with it, its power to heal. So long as it survived, someone might still hear it, one day, and be healed by its telling.'

'Oh, I like that, Hector. "Someone might hear and be healed by its telling". It has a kind of ring about it. I've been thinking I might try writing some stories.'

160

'You used to tell me wonderful stories when you were a child.'

'Did I?'

'Oh yes. Where you got it all from I cannot imagine. I know your father read to you a great deal and you used to bribe other people to read to you, until you could read yourself, but you seemed to me to have a complete world at your fingertips.'

'So, I bribed people, did I?' I asked, incredulous.

'Oh yes, you used to save your sweeties. I can remember quite well being propositioned when I came to collect your father for our excursions.'

'How extraordinary, Hector, I remember nothing at all about that, yet I remember so clearly all sorts of other things from quite early on in my life.'

'Memory is selective, you know, my dear. Sometimes whole areas of one's life lie dormant until someone or something wakes them up. It's amazing what turns up when they do. Ask your Aunt Mary about filling the kettle in the stream sometime. She did it on a camping holiday when the boys were young and it brought back a whole history. Very interesting story.'

It was, too, so much so that it was well after midnight when I finally got back to Anacarrig. But going to bed seemed out of the question. I was too elated, too delighted, altogether too excited. And yet what about, I could not tell. So I sat down at my table and wrote for an hour or more: I wrote about the past, about Hector and my father, about having people who really love and cherish you.

Feeling suddenly very tired, I put down my pen and reread what I had written. I came to the last lines:

What does it matter if I do only have a handful of people that care about me. I'm lucky to have even them. If it only needs one person to save a story from dying and losing its healing power then maybe there only needs to have been one person to have loved you long ago to keep you from losing your hope.

I stared at the words on the page, read them again and yawned. I wasn't sure whether they made sense or not, but they were the words that had been given to me, just like the words that were given to me when I smashed the piece of china.

I closed the notebook, peeled off my clothes and draped them over a chair. It came to me as I crawled under my duvet that my father had not only left me the materials out of which I might make a story, but that he had also given me the love that might enable me to do it.

18

I came downstairs to find a long, fat envelope on the hall carpet. I knew exactly what it was. I laid it carefully on the kitchen table till I'd had breakfast, then I slit it open, took out the contract, fetched my pen and wrote my name in all the places marked with a pencilled cross.

In the space of two minutes, I signed away the ownership of half a house that had been mine for a mere two days and a garden I'd loved from the minute I'd pulled out that first flourishing head of groundsel. What I planned to do next was really very simple. I would walk along the main road to the postbox, send the contract on its way and then follow the familiar route down the lane, along the side of the great mound and through that small green gate with the silvered metal signboard with the words I know by heart.

I was opening the front door when the phone rang. I hesitated and then picked it up. It was Sandy. The moment I heard her voice, I knew something was wrong, though all she did to begin with was enquire irritably if I'd been out last evening as well as the one before because she hadn't been able to get me.

I explained I'd been in the garden till dusk, but she was not remotely interested in anything I might have been doing. Something had upset her, but what it was, either she didn't know herself, or she wasn't going to tell me. My first thought was the dish called Paul, but I said nothing. I'd struggled with Sandy and men for years, but I never seemed to get any further towards understanding. Sunlight and birdsong flowed through the open front door, beckoning me. I felt my patience give way.

'Have you had the contract, then?' she demanded.

'Yes, I was just on my way to post it.'

'Aren't you taking it in to them?'

'Well, there's not much point. They won't act on it till Monday anyway.'

There was a only moment's pause before she shot the next question at me.

'You've remembered to cancel the auction, haven't you?'

'Cancel it?' I was quite taken aback. 'Why cancel it?'

'Oh, for God's sake, Deirdre, now they've found Daddy's will we don't have to go through with all that rigmarole. We'll get far more for the good stuff in Belfast and a straight house clearance'll deal with the rest. Couldn't be simpler.'

For a moment, I didn't grasp what she was saying. She'd never mentioned the auction when I phoned to tell her the contracts were almost ready. Given she wanted nothing from the house and the table from my room was the only thing I'd thought of keeping, the auction seemed as good a way as any of disposing of the contents, especially as it was already arranged, catalogued and advertised.

'Who had you in mind in Belfast?' I said slowly, to give myself time to collect my wits.

'Oh, any of the really good ones,' she replied hastily, naming several firms I'd never heard of.

'Will they collect the stuff?'

'Collect? For heaven's sake there's not that much is there? You could stick it all in the back of the car easy enough.'

I thought of the roomful of china, the amount of packing it would need, driving to Belfast, and having to find somewhere to park near any of the places she'd mentioned. The thought appalled me. Besides, I never wanted to see any of those stupid faces ever again.

'There's more than you think, Sandy,' I said uneasily. 'And there's still a lot to do here.'

'Well, perhaps you could cut down a bit on your gardening. No wonder you're always short of money when you can't even be bothered to run up to Belfast for the sake of five or six thou.'

'Five or six thousand?' I repeated blankly.

'Surely you know what that china's worth. Your half would be a tidy sum if you could see your way to taking a little trouble over it,' she ended nastily.

'But Mother wanted it to go to the church,' I protested.

There was a pause. Then she began to spell out the new situation very slowly in her instructing-a-backward-child mode. It just never occurred to her I had no wish to inherit anything from Mother that she didn't want me to have. The house was different. It was Daddy's. He planned it, he helped build it and working so hard on it probably shortened his life. He'd left it to us when Mother would no longer have any need of it. That was fine and I was grateful. But that china was hers. It had never been any part of my life. If she wanted it to go to the church, as far as I was concerned, that is where it should go.

I took a deep breath and told Sandy just what I felt. If she wanted the china sold in Belfast that was up to her. She could arrange for it to be collected. I was not prepared to lay hands on it again or to benefit in any way from its sale.

'You're out of your mind, Dee, just out of your mind. Principle is one thing, but you're just being ridiculous. If you want to throw away good money on the church that's up to you, but I've a bit more wit. I'll ring you back and tell you when the Belfast people can collect.'

She banged down the phone and left me shaking like a leaf.

'Oh you fool, you fool. Why did you answer the wretched thing? Now she's spoilt it all,' I cried, as I collapsed into the nearest chair, my head throbbing furiously. I felt so angry with myself. All my pleasure and excitement at going to Emain shattered. And for what? A stupid business about an auction. As if it mattered. But it did. Anything connected with money mattered to Sandy.

There was no way I was going to Emain in this state. I would have to do something to calm myself. I began sensibly enough by going upstairs and taking two Anadin for my head and sitting down quietly at my table by the open window of my room. But that was the beginning of one of the most awful hours I have ever had.

It was not being able to find my pad of A4 that finally did it. I had decided to pour out my fury on paper, say all the angry and bitter things I was feeling and then tear it up, so that no one would be any the wiser. But my A4 pad wasn't on my table where it should have ben. I pulled open the drawer and looked under my little pile of books, but it wasn't there either. And if it wasn't there, where was it? That was its place. I felt tears spring to my eyes. I wanted to lash out, to smash something, anything.

I dashed downstairs, rifled through a pile of newspapers in the sitting room, moved packed boxes in the dining room, pulled out the drawer in the kitchen table and emptied its contents on the draining board, scattering lists, documents and unanswered letters on the floor, and raced upstairs again. That pad of A4 was the only thing in the world that mattered. It had to be A4, big enough and strong enough to take the words I wanted to pour out.

'It can't have gone,' I screamed. 'It was here last night. There's no one to steal it now. It must be here. It must.'

I rushed to the door of Mother's room convinced she'd managed to spirit it away like the blue notebooks, wrenched at the handle and threw it open. There it was, sitting on her dressing table. I'd been using it for the inventory.

I ripped off the handwritten sheets, ran back into my room and took up my pen. Saturday 21 June. Twice I tried to write the 'S' of Saturday. Twice the dry nib scraped across the page. In a blind fury I stabbed the nib into the unwritten page, then broke the pen in two as easily as if it were a chocolate finger. Black ink poured over my hands. I wiped them on the page in front of me and burst into tears.

But I had to write. I had to. There was nothing else to help me. Tears running down my cheeks, I snatched up a Biro from my pen tray, wrote the date so fiercely that it rattled, so I flung it on the floor.

And then words abandoned me. I sat and stared at the empty lines.

What was I going to do? Nothing had stood between me and despair but the words that would fill this blank sheet of paper. And now even they had gone.

I looked at the scissors on my table, pointing towards me, dagger-like. Traced on their blades the words HOLLOW GROUND. Hollow indeed, it seemed, this life I lived. Ground had a cold, chill ring to it. Hollow ground, holy ground. Death. Death of spirit. That was it. At last they had come to me in my deepest need, the words to describe this despair, this grey chill of December at Midsummer.

I ached with loss as I sat there, blind to the sunlight, deaf to the birdsong. I ached for joy long gone, joy never experienced, never to be experienced. Hope had vanished and with it the promise of youth, all that seems possible, achievable when you are young.

Bleakly, I looked ahead at the residue of years to be lived through. No more than a toil and a burden, without light or texture, their weight seemed unendurable. And still words pressed up inside me, demanding to be put down. Pressing me till they seemed to choke me, as if they locked hands tighter and tighter into circles I could never break.

Could not? Or would not? The questions echoed round my head. I cursed the flat, empty page in front of me, deluding me with its promise that something might be said or done that would staunch my tears or assuage this ache. It was too bitter a cross to carry, this pressure of words. Oh, how I hated them. I felt the hate welling up in me. Or was it flowing into me?

Around me the stillness deepened. Not quiet, but stillness. The stillness of a flat, featureless calm: the stillness of absence. No simple human noise penetrated the grey blanket of my despair. I couldn't hear a dog bark, or a car pass, or even the moan of a distant lawnmower. All was silence. I felt totally abandoned. And I knew I couldn't go on, my body aching with the pain I myself had generated – feeling nothing, neither joy nor sorrow, only this blanket of nothingness enfolding me; so that the whole richness and variety of the world was null, gave nothing to me, asked nothing of me, could mean nothing to me ever again.

I looked at the sodden blank page spread open before me, my tears dripping onto it steadily. What use were words if they brought no relief? What use were they, words in my head, any words, if they brought no insight?

I flung down the Biro and tried to rip the pad of A4 across. It fell from my hands, so I grabbed my notebook, determined to rip it to pieces instead. It resisted. I took up the scissors, to prise the pages from the binding and shred them into fragments.

'No, that is not the way.'

I was so startled I dropped the book. I just couldn't believe that no one had actually spoken to me. I turned sharply and looked all round the room, but there was no one there. But as I bent to pick up the notebook, I saw it had fallen open at the record of one of my conversations with Deara:

'They are struggling against some great danger. I cannot see what that danger is, but I feel it like a dark despair. Each of these women, your daughter and her friend, carry a seed that may grow. They may kindle a fire in the heart of Tara.'

Written in my own hand, those words had a quite extraordinary effect upon me. I read them and reread them, even though I knew them by heart already. And as I read, I stopped crying. Then I saw the ink stains on my hands. I got up, went to the bathroom and scrubbed them with a nailbrush, but the black ink wouldn't shift. The lines on my hands, head line, heart line and life line, were now firmly etched.

Calm now, I went down to the kitchen to make a mug of tea. While I waited for the kettle to boil I cleared up the mess on the draining board and put all the stuff neatly back into the drawer I'd upturned.

Shortly after that, I set off for Emain.

I enjoyed every moment of the short walk across the road and down the lane. I felt intensely aware of the light, the fresh breeze, the bright patches of colour in the cottage gardens and the drift of falling hawthorn blossom on the lush, green verges. There was the familiar excitement as I pushed open the gate and said 'Good morning' to the old men who always sit on the wooden bench outside the custodian's machine shed. A smile still on my lips after their friendly greeting, I stepped onto the path to begin the climb, stumbled and gasped in horror.

'Oh no, please God, no.'

At my feet a man lay dead in a pool of blood, Half his head had been sliced away. As I stumbled against his legs, a cloud of bluebottles rose from the wound and then settled again. They crawled over his white face and into the open cavern of his mouth.

I put my hands over my face, but they couldn't shut out what I had seen. There were bodies everywhere, some clustered together, some lying separately. A few men were wearing body armour of leather or metal over bright woven clothes, but most of the dead were boys in tunics of white or brown, or old men wearing long robes. Amongst the tangled bodies of the boys, a man with a grey beard leant against a tree, his eyes staring unseeing into the far distance.

As the full meaning of what had happened dawned on me, I sank to my knees. Beyond the scattered bodies stood the charred remains of a gateway. From time to time, the crackle of flames was doused by

167

the crash of timbers and further plumes of smoke rose into the featureless grey sky, where the sun gleamed weakly through the pall of smoke.

Emain had been destroyed and with it my dream. What hope could there be now for any seed being planted in earth charred by fire and soaked with blood? I had lost my friend and with her the hope of healing, the hope of a future different from the past.

Somewhere in the smoking remnants of the buildings I would find Deara's body. I had seen burnt bodies before and the thought that I would not even be able to recognise her overwhelmed me. My cry of anguish pierced the stillness like the howl of an animal trapped and torn by hunters. Then a yet more fearful thought seized hold of me. Without Deara, how could I return to my own time? Always, it seemed it was the touch of her hands that parted us as well as drew us together. Now there were no hands to hold or to loose. I was alone, totally alone, in the midst of this desolation.

'Oh Matthew, Matthew, my darling.'

The tears poured down, splashing onto my jeans leaving deeper coloured spots on the faded fabric. There was no way back. I would perish and no one would ever know what had happened to me. It was all my own fault. I had not listened to good advice. I had thought I could face up to the past and all that it had cost me and come to understand it better. I had dared to hope. I had begun to write. Now I would die, before I had done anything with my life, as uselessly and pointlessly as these young boys in their bloodstained tunics.

'It is in your own hands.'

The words spoke themselves inside my head. I took my hands from my face and looked at them. I saw my own reflection in my wedding ring and the maze of dark lines on my hand where the black ink had refused to scrub off. As I stared at them, I remembered how I had tried to destroy my notebook and how when I bent to pick it up, the words on the page had given me hope. Now other words came to encourage me. 'When there is no salve, no treatment you know, first comfort the pain, then pray for hope for yourself.'

I couldn't remember whether they were Deara's words or whether she was quoting Merdaine. I couldn't remember when she'd said them either, but they seemed so right. Somewhere, there might be someone I could help. Until I had searched the ruins of Emain I would not say all hope had gone.

I had to step over some of the bodies to avoid making a long detour, but beyond the burnt out remains of the gates there were no more. The ground was dusty rather than charred and a fine rain of grey ash fell like flurries of snow in springtime. The acrid smell of burning thatch caught at the back of my throat and made me cough.

All that remained of the outer defences was a smoking earth bank.

Next to it, a broad open area had been churned up by the feet of animals. Wooden hurdles leaned drunkenly against each other or lay flat on the dusty ground. There was cow dung splattered everywhere. I picked my way through it, moving uphill all the time. Above me, at the top of the steep slope, I could see a high hall-like building, where massive roof timbers still stood, though fires burned inside its empty shell. Beyond and behind its smoking shape, I thought I could see a structure that had survived the fire, but my eyes were streaming so much I couldn't be sure.

As I stepped through the last of the cow dung and round a fallen hurdle, I saw something glint at my feet. I bent down and picked it up. Undamaged and unmarked by dust, or dung, or smoke, Deara's brooch gleamed in my hand. I didn't know whether to laugh or to cry. Touching what was hers brought me near to her, but finding her brooch only reminded me of what I might discover only a little further on.

I studied the brooch closely. The metal was grey, the engraving black, yet the whole thing gleamed and shone like silver. Small patches of bright enamel reflected the light like so many precious stones. The swirling patterns intrigued me. Each time I set out to trace any one of them, I found that it intertwined with all the others and led me back to my starting point.

With the brooch in my hand I continued my climb, but after a very short time I had to stop. Not only was my hand hot and sticky but I felt as awkward and unbalanced as if I were carrying something heavy and bulky. I thought of putting it in my jeans' pocket, but it was too large. Besides, one pocket had in it a large hanky of Matthew's and the other was still full of raisins I'd put there for the robins.

The only thing to do was to wear it, so I pinned it to the left shoulder of my shirt using the strap of my bra to give the heavy pin something to grip. With a sense of growing tension and excitement, I set out again, moving more quickly than before.

When I stopped to mop my eyes again, I thought I was imagining it, but I wasn't. Beside the burnt out ruin of the very large building, there were flowers in bloom. As I moved closer, a slight breeze sprang up. The swirls of smoke that had been drifting at ground level began to move higher and as I reached the ruin I saw the flowers were part of a flourishing herb garden, ablaze with summer colour. Marigolds and foxgloves, poppies and rock roses, thyme and rosemary and marjoram – flowers I knew and loved, mixed in with others I'd never seen before.

But I paused only for a moment. The garden ended with splashes of bright colour climbing up the sides of a large conical roofed hut which was still intact. At its entrance two red roses were growing in terracotta wine amphorae, each one supported in a metal frame. I recognised the roses from Alcelcius's villa. The hut had to be Deara's.

I hurried through the open door and nearly fell over a broken pitcher. The place had been ransacked. At my feet, manuscripts were scattered on the damp rushes. By the hearth, where the spilt water had made a grey paste of the fine ash, lay pages and pages of handwritten text. Objects had been thrown to the floor from the long bench which ran under the small windows. A chest had been overturned and its contents scattered. In the dark shadows at the back of the hut, cloaks and blankets were piled on a couch and some lay on the floor. But there was no sign of Deara.

My eyes stopped smarting and began to get used to the dimness. Although the hut was empty, I knew it was Deara's workplace. The documents, the papers, the rows of bottles under the small windows were hers, as surely as the herb garden and the roses were. Above my head, wisps of smoke were being drawn out of the enclosed space by the freshening breeze. As I looked up into the dark dome of the roof, through the smoke hole, I saw a gleam of sunlight.

I bent down and carefully gathered up the scattered sheets of paper. They were of thick parchment, written in Latin, with sketches and diagrams, in the same neat hand. I carried some of them to the open door. 'On the Circulation of the Blood,' said one title. 'Observations on the Symptoms and Treatments of Fevers,' said another. 'Infusions for the Treatment of Muscular Pain,' said a third.

I discovered that the pages were numbered with Roman numerals and that by picking them up so carefully I had kept much of the main work together. Delighted with this discovery, I set about making seven bundles, for I had found the final page and it was six hundred and eighty-six. I anchored the bundles with stone jars and empty flasks from the bench as I worked, for the breeze was freshening steadily.

By the time I was able to tie the seven bundles together with a piece of discoloured linen binding from one of the manuscripts, the air was once again clear and sweet in the hut, sunlight was pouring through the open door and falling on the damp rushes and scattered manuscripts.

I picked up the nearest one. It was large and yellowed and bore an inscription in a spiky script not at all like the neat hand of the notes I had just put together. I recognised it at once, for this was the manuscript Deara had brought to me two weeks earlier. 'Deirdre, daughter of Angharrad,' it said. I thought of us sitting side by side on my bed, our heads together as she helped me with the words I could not read. I wondered if I could manage it by myself.

To my surprise, I found it was quite easy. Neither the unfamiliarity of the Latin, nor the idiosyncrasies of Merdaine's hand seemed to trouble me at all. And the words, read only once before, were so familiar that I began to wonder if I had a gift for memorising what was truly important to me, just like Deara.

I realised I was scanning the text as if I were searching for something I had forgotten. When I came to Aillech's prophecy, I slowed down:

I see this child you carry as a young girl and as an old woman. She is holding out her hands to a woman of a different time, a woman who never grows old, who wears strange clothes, and who speaks another tongue. Your daughter is healing that woman, that she may heal in her own time. I see light grow round them as if together they are kindling a fire. They are struggling against some great danger. I cannot see what that danger is, but I feel it like a dark despair. Each of these women, your daughter and her friend, carry a seed that may grow. They may kindle a fire at the heart of Tara.

'I cannot see what that danger is, but I feel it like a dark despair,' I repeated, as if by speaking the words aloud I would be able to grasp their message better. And perhaps I was. Standing there in a pool of sunshine, holding the text that Merdaine had written for Angharrad's sake on the night she died, what came to me was that that danger is dark despair itself.

If you can avoid despair, then you can keep the danger at bay, even if it takes the shape of death, or the loss of what is precious to you, or the destruction of what you have struggled to create. Once you let yourself despair, you can't do anything. This was clear to me now. What was not clear was how you prevented yourself from despairing.

I had no answer, but as I went on reading the text, I realised there was something more written after Merdaine's signature.

I did have some difficulty with the text, this time, for there was a distinct shake in the hand that had written it and some of the words were completely unfamiliar to me. It said:

Since I have written this letter to you, my dear girl, I have had a dream. I have always taught you to pay attention to dreams for what they may reveal about the mental and spiritual state of the dreamer, but some dreams are also given for our guidance. So I offer this to you:

I found myself in a strange place, in a garden with flowers such as I have never seen. Under some trees, I found a woman writing with a pen that needed no ink, on parchment so thin the wind could blow it away.

She was old, older than I, her hair grey, her face lined, her limbs stiff. But her eyes were bright like a child's. She welcomed me by name, bade me sit down. I asked her how she knew my name and she answered thus: 'I know you because Deara is my

171

kinswoman and once for a little space of time I wore your brooch.'

And then I awoke.

I have held this dream in my heart and asked myself what it asked of me. What comes to me is this. You must tell your kinswoman, Deirdre, that she must not regret how little power she has to heal all the many hurts she sees. She must do what she can, do it in love and it will be more, much more than she thinks.

Greet your friend for me, you will meet her sooner than I have.

Merdaine

'Do what you can, do it in love and it will be more than you think.'

I repeated the words to myself and before I had even completed the sentence I knew that I had never done in love what I could do best. Yes, I was good at putting words together, but not since the long past, when I told stories to anyone who would listen, like my father and Uncle Hector, had I used words with love. Not until this summer. Striving with words was all I had done. I had bullied and browbeaten them, I had forced them to work for me in ways that were all wrong for them and for me.

'Deirdre.'

I spun round, startled by a hoarse whisper. On the couch at the back of the hut, now touched by a finger of light, an old woman had raised her head a few inches from the disorder of dark cloaks and blankets. Her hair was grey and her face a ghastly white. Below her listless eyes were deep, dark circles. There was blood on her left cheek. As I moved towards her she lay still.

'Deara, Deara my dear, you are wounded.'

I drew back the tangled hair from her face and saw that her eyes were closed. She lay so still I would have thought she was dead if I hadn't heard her speak. But I had heard her speak. I was not giving up so easily.

I looked around the hut for inspiration. There was none. Even if I had known how to use them, all those bottles of medicine were labelled in her own Celtic tongue. There wasn't even any water. I took out my hanky, spat on it and began to wipe the blood from her face. There seemed to be no wound, and as the blood began to disappear I realised that the dark circles were soot and smoke. The face which emerged was considerably older than when last we met, but still younger than I was myself.

Her eyes were still closed and when I drew away the cloak she had crawled under, I found her hands were covered in blood as well. They were stone cold.

I spat on my grubby hanky once more and remembered a favourite

172

phrase of my mother's: 'Sure you might as well spit on it.' It meant that whatever activity you were engaged upon, she considered your efforts futile. With the sound of that voice ringing in my ears, I knew nothing would stop me removing every last trace of blood from Deara's hands.

She was still unconscious and still just as cold so I covered her with all the cloaks and blankets I could find, while I worked on first one hand and then the other. I had found no wound, but the pallor of her clean face was ghastly. I told myself that I had set my heart against fear. However tenuous her hold on life might be, Deara was alive. Until I was sure she was dead, I would not give up hope.

I finished the second hand and realised that both hands were now warm, though Deara still had not moved. She looked as if she would never move again.

'Deara,' I said firmly. 'Deara, wake up.'

I saw a ghost of a smile pass across her face, but her eyes did not flicker.

'Come now. Time to wake up,' I said encouragingly.

Her eyes opened, but I don't think she actually saw me. She smiled a slow sweet smile and then stared at me, a look of horror on her face.

'My hands. My hands are covered in blood and my pitcher is broken. What shall I do, what shall I do?'

I put my arms round her and let her cry, then I showed her her hands. For the first time, she seemed to register who I was and where she was. She attempted to raise herself up. I helped her and she stared at the sunshine pouring into the hut in amazement.

'Deara, are you hurt? You were covered in blood.'

I saw her rub her tongue against her lips. They were black on the inside, where I had not cleaned them.

'Not hurt, Deirdre. So thirsty.'

She clung to me and I stroked her hair. The grey came off in my hands. It was ash.

'Tell me where the well is. I shall be very quick.'

She shook her head. With great difficulty, because her mouth was so dry, she said the well would be fouled.

'Let me go and see what I can do.'

Somewhere in my mind was the idea that I might find some rainwater in a gutter. But there were no gutters left. I had taken up a small copper bowl I had found sitting on the bench. In desperation, I went into the garden in search of cabbages. There weren't any cabbages either, but some plants that looked like giant rhubarb provided a few precious drops of unevaporated dew instead. Like beads of quicksilver at the base of the huge leaves, they barely damped the bottom of the bowl, but it was a start. I managed to collect about a tablespoonful and then, under some foxglove leaves,

173

I found a small pitcher. It was more than half full.

She was sitting up when I got back, looking ghastly, but alert.

'Do you think this would be all right?'

She nodded and I poured some into the copper bowl and gave it to her. She drank it all and held out the bowl for more.

'My garden has saved my life twice in one day,' she said in a whisper. 'Can you bring me my box?'

She was still too weak to open it, but when I opened it for her, she pointed out a small bottle: 'Four drops, please, in half a bowlful.'

The effect of the medicine was nothing short of miraculous. As she sat sipping it, she began to talk quite coherently, though when she made an attempt to stand up, she couldn't manage it. She said it would take a little longer and asked if I could sponge the bloodstains from her dress.

She sat drinking water very slowly from the little copper bowl as I sponged away at her dress. I seemed to be quite unaware that I can't stand the sight of blood.

'You came just in time, Deirdre. I lay down for a moment because the room began to move around me, but then I couldn't get up again. I dreamt of leaving my body, of looking down upon it from the smoke hole. But I saw you there, putting my book back together and picking up my manuscripts and I came back to greet you. I have heard such dreams are given to those close to death.'

'I thought you might be close to death at one point,' I confessed.

'I am well again now. My weakness is only from lack of food and sleep. That can be sustained. What I could not sustain was my despair.'

She looked down at the damp patch on her dress where I had managed to rinse away most of the blood.

'I came back for my box and found Claudio amongst the fallen. He was alive and he knew me. But after he had spoken to me, he died in my arms. The poor man had never held a sword in his life, but he went out to defend Emain with the boys from the school and a billet of wood in his hand.'

'He was dear to you?'

'Yes, he was. Alcelcius gave him to me as my servant. When Alcelcius died I freed him, but he asked to stay with me. He cared for my horse and carried my messages . . . oh, so many things he did for me. He had learnt to mix medicines and had begun to read and write. He was so pleased at his achievement.'

I saw the tears spring to her eyes, but she disregarded them.

'God rest his soul, and my dear Alcelcius too.'

'When did he die?'

'Almost seven years ago now, only a few months after he made me his heir, that night when you and I last met.'

A fortnight in my life and seven years in Deara's. I just nodded.

Some things I had learnt to accept and not to question.

She made another attempt to get to her feet, but after a few moments she had to sit down again. She asked for more water and a further four drops from the small bottle. It was then I remembered my pocketful of raisins.

Sometimes my pockets have soil and bits of leaf in them. The robins don't mind, but I couldn't give dirty raisins to Deara. To my great delight, they were still clean from the jar. I handed them to her and she looked at them in amazement.

'Dried grapes? I haven't had any since Alcelcius died. He used to grow some especially for drying. We will share them.'

'No,' I said firmly. 'I have eaten. They are all for you.'

She sat and ate them one by one, very slowly. Between each one, she took a sip from the small copper bowl. While she ate, she told me the story of her meeting with Ferghal and all that had flowed from those fateful three days at Emain when Morrough had accepted Patricius's mission and ambassadors had been sent again to Tara to seek a way towards peace and security.

I listened intently and was so absorbed in all she told me, I forgot where we were and what had happened. The questions I wanted to ask were never spoken.

'Did you hear that?'

I had heard nothing. But a few moments later, listening as intently as she herself was, I caught a sound on the breeze.

'A horn to the north-west. I cannot tell how far away,' she said, grasping my hands as she spoke.

Her tone was urgent and had a ring of authority. 'Deirdre, you must make me a promise. If the raiders return to scour the woods for the women and children, or to lie in wait for our warriors, you must leave me and go back to your own time. Take Merdaine's brooch with you. It will be the only way.'

'I cannot leave you now,' I protested, as I began to struggle with the stiff pin of the brooch. 'I found it on my way up from the gate. I'm sorry, I forgot I had it.'

'No, Deirdre, you must wear it. You must wear it, please,' she insisted.

I saw her hands cover the brooch to stop me unpinning it and I felt a strange drowsiness sweep over me. I had such a desire to close my eyes. Then I heard the horn again and I looked away quickly, through the door of the hut, to the smouldering ruins that lay beyond. The drowsiness disappeared.

'Yes. I shall wear it. But only till the danger is past.'

Deara had got to her feet again and now seemed quite steady. She poured water into glass bottles which fitted the compartment of her box and added other bottles from the rows beneath the windows. She looked around the disordered room, tossed aside the pile of dark cloaks and blankets which had been strewn around, and beneath them found a cloak woven of green and yellow wool, embroidered with sweeping designs in red.

'Here, you will need this. It was my husband's first warrior cloak. It is so old it has grown light, but it will serve for the passageway.'

I drew the cloak gratefully round me for even here in the sunlight, the thought of where we were going made cold sweat break out on my skin. There could be only one place reached by a passageway that was out of sight of the returning raiders. Deara was going to take me to the Place of Birth.

19

Deara asked me to help her move the couch where I had found her lying under the heap of cloaks. I was not surprised to find a trapdoor in the floor beneath, but the panic I felt when she moved aside the cover and I saw steps leading down into the darkness was a different story. Deara took up her box, showed me how to conceal and close the trapdoor behind me, reassured me that the steps were steep, but firm, and that there would be light in the chamber when we got there. Before I'd managed to think of anything to say, she'd already stepped down into the darkness and had her back to me as she descended.

I wanted to cry out, 'Deara, I can't. I'm terrified of the dark and of being shut in,' but my lips wouldn't move. Besides, I didn't need to ask what the sound of that horn might mean. This was the only way we could go.

I had the greatest difficulty following Deara's simple instructions, but I finally got the lid into place. That blocked out the last vestige of light and left me in total darkness.

Immediately, I was aware of a noise, deep and oppressive. Loud and rhythmic, it seemed to be growing louder and faster as each moment passed. I threw out my arm to ward it off and my hand struck the cold stone wall beside me. My legs shook so badly I crumpled to the ground on the broad step where I was standing, one leg scraping painfully against the wall as I went down. I sat quite still, certain that I was about to be overwhelmed by the noise or some malevolent presence accompanying it. But nothing happened. My lungs were almost bursting and I realised as I started to gasp that the air was both cool and fresh. I had been holding my breath. The noise was the beating of my own heart. Once I started breathing properly, it slowly faded and in the silence that followed I heard Deara's footsteps in the passageway below.

I mopped the sweat from my forehead with the end of Ferghal's cloak and groped around to find out where the walls and ceiling were and how deep the next step was. It was all perfectly sound, just as Deara said it was. Shakily, I got to my feet and continued the descent. By the time I reached the bottom and moved along the short passageway, I could see a gleam of light where Deara was holding open the door curtain to the chamber. I hurried towards her and we went into the chamber together.

As my eyes grew accustomed to the dim light, I saw how extraordinary the place was. To begin with, it was enormously large, a huge cavern with white stone walls, its roof held up by innumerable tree trunks. So many were there, so little trimmed or fashioned, and the floor so thick strewn with rushes, that it felt more like a woodland glade than anything made by human hands. Throughout the chamber, dozens of small lamps burned, sending strange flickering shadows dancing all over the walls and roof.

I followed Deara to the centre of the chamber, where a carved stone God stood with his back to a huge tree trunk, the central pillar of this forest. His deep stone eyes stared at me uncompromisingly, but he wore a garland of fresh flowers that did a little to soften their impact. The huge soaring trunk behind his squat and solid figure was deeply carved with entwined snakes. To it, crosses woven from rushes had been pinned as high as a tall woman could reach. Some of the crosses were beginning to fade with age, some were as green as the rushes on the floor below.

'Deara, what is this place? Surely not just a place for giving birth.'

'It is a strange place,' she began. 'I asked Merdaine the same question when I came here for the first time.'

'And what did she say?'

'She said it was a mystery. Some said the place had been a temple in the past and so had come to be a place of refuge. Many people do feel great security here. Others said it had been a dwelling of the Sidhe, the Little People, before they finally abandoned Ireland. There were also those who said it had been built in the past as a gift to the future, but the future would be left to discover how the gift should be used. As they saw it, it was made as an act of love.'

Against all my expectations, I had to confess I felt completely at ease in this strange place.

'Yes, I do feel great power here. I have never felt anything quite like it before,' I said quickly. 'There's something else too, but I can't describe it. Can we sit down for a little while?'

I wasn't feeling tired, but I couldn't quite bring myself to tell Deara the truth: that having got here, after frightening myself so badly in the passageway, I couldn't bear to leave. We sat down and I looked again at the deep set eyes of the God and thought of Patrick's mission to the court of Emain.

'Isn't worship of the old gods forbidden, now you've got Jesus?'

I stopped, surprised and upset by the bitter edge in my voice. I felt ashamed to have spoken so sharply, in a place so free from all bitter feelings. To my surprise, Deara did not appear to notice.

'Of course not. Each woman acknowledges the God of her heart. It is hard for anyone to face life without a power greater than their

178

own. And facing death is harder still.'

As she spoke, so simply and so gently, I felt tears run down my cheeks. It was something to do with that garland of flowers and the rush crosses and the pile of tumbled bodies at the gates of Emain. But quite what it was I couldn't express. All I could do was weep and cling to Deara, as if I couldn't bear to be parted from her ever again.

'My dear, my dear, what distresses you so? Tell me.'

'It's this gift of love you've spoken of, I think,' I sobbed. 'I just find love so painful. I cannot live without loving, but the pain of loving is too great for me to bear. Loving Matthew, loving anyone, even thinking about the hurts of people I love, the danger that faces Ferghal and Morrough, the death that awaited Claudio. These things are too much for me. Somehow I'm flawed, damaged. There is something wrong with me that cannot be healed. I fail myself and those who love me. It would be better if I died.'

She knelt beside me and held me in her arms and talked to me. I cannot recall a single word of what she said, but as she talked, slowly I grew calm. I wiped my face on the edge of my cloak and saw the concern in her eyes. But what she said then, that I do remember.

'Deirdre, you don't always have to know. You don't always have to understand with your head. The knowing of your head is like a lamp for your feet, but the knowing of the heart means you can walk in darkness. You can go where others are fearful, trusting in the power that is given to you. Deirdre, listen to me, in case we do not meet again. It is your mind that cannot bear the pain of loving. Your heart would be wiser and you would be stronger were you to listen to it. Merdaine told me that when I was only sixteen. It has taken me these fifteen years to come to understand what she meant. You are older than I and you have your own wisdom and courage. Take the gift of this place. Follow your heart.'

She hugged me and kissed my cheeks: 'Soon we must go, but you asked me to tell you what happened. Let me tell you now, for it may help me to clear my own thoughts. Then we must decide what to do. Come . . .'

We stood up and moved round to the other side of the great carved pillar so we could sit with our backs resting against it, the carpet of fresh rushes strewn around us.

'The years since last we met have been good years for Emain as well as for me. We have had less illness and fever and there has always been plenty to eat. Our numbers have grown and each year new settlements have been made. Some are nearby, beyond the trader's town. I can see them from Alcelcius's villa. Others are a morning's ride, some up to a day's ride. The largest are Lisbane and Carnbanna, to the north, on the shores of the great lake we call Iscamore. Do you know where I mean?'

I nodded. I wasn't surprised that the shores of Lough Neagh with fresh water, and fish, and wildfowl, had led to successful settlements.

'For some years now, our scouts have reported strange sea-going craft coming into the lake, craft with high prows and long bodies, unlike anything our own people fashion for fishing. And large, very large. Last year, their numbers increased and the encampments near the lake reported that cattle were taken at night. Some months ago, the settlements asked us for warriors to protect them and train their young men to fight. Morrough agreed. This spring Lisbane and Carnbanna strengthened their stockades and armed their able-bodied men.'

She paused, looked sad and continued.

'It was just in time. Three weeks ago, ships were seen in the river that flows north from Iscamore to the Northern Sea. More warriors were sent to Lisbane and Carnbanna. Three days ago, the ships crossed the lake and attacked Carnbanna. The battle was bloody and there were great losses on both sides. The surviving raiders managed to sail off, but by then scouts had brought news that a great mass of ships was coming south under sail with a favourable wind.

"Yesterday, at first light, Morrough sent heralds to all our allies and to every encampment in this part of the Ullaid, and gathered the entire strength of Emain, to ride to Iscamore. I know not what may have come to pass.'

She dropped her eyes and I knew she must be thinking of Ferghal, but I said nothing and waited for her to continue.

'I had to decide whether to ride out or not. All those now skilled in healing and herblore were following the warriors, knowing the need at Carnbanna and what was to come. I could have gone too. But I did not. There were three women already in labour and two close to their time. One of those in labour was Bregella. I knew the baby sat breechwise and might not turn. I could not be sure that anyone else I could leave with them would face what might have to be done.'

Deara's face looked so grim, I shuddered to think what Bregella's plight might be. It sounded to me as if Deara was talking about a Caesarean with no anaesthetic and no antiseptics, but I could not interrupt to satisfy my curiosity.

'By mid morning, all was ready. Ferghal sent his herald to me. I was watering the seedlings, while they were still in shade. I left my pitcher and ran down to him at the gate.'

She looked up at me, her eyes damp: 'I had never before seen the whole strength of Emain ride out at one time. A noble company, Deirdre. Pray God they will return.'

She paused. In the silence, I could see her walking back up the dusty track to her workplace, her mind full of what was to come.

'The day seemed long and the place so empty and quiet. I spent much of it here, for Bregella's labour was hard and it is her first child. Late in the afternoon, I went up to my workplace to wash and to change my gown, which was soiled. That is when I must have left my brooch on the bench, for my mind was still below and beyond. The fourth woman gave birth in the early evening and recovered very quickly. She was preparing to leave with the others when one of the scholars arrived. Poor boy, he had run so fast he could hardly speak and wished only to get his message out so that he could run back whence he had come.

'My Lady, Tassu, captain of the guard, greets you and sends this message: "We are outnumbered and cannot hold. Stay below and guard against smoke. Pray for our souls."'

She put her hands to her face. I thought for a moment she was crying, but she was only pushing her hair back from her forehead.

'God rest that good man's soul. He saved twelve of us.'

'Twelve?' I repeated gently.

She smiled. 'There were only ten to begin with, but we held hard to Sceto, who would have run to his death. I had to order him to stay, on the pretext that I might need him. Then we became twelve when Bregella finally gave birth. By then, the smoke was so thick in here that I had already sent the other women and Sceto into the passageway. When at last I was able to stand up with the child in my hands, I had to crouch down again so that we could breathe. Sceto and I dragged Bregella on a blanket into the passageway, because she was too exhausted to move and too heavy for us to lift.'

'And what then?'

'A long, dark night, with the smoke chasing us further and further along the passageway, until finally we were on the steps beneath my workplace. At one point, I heard footsteps overhead and my couch being dragged across the floor.'

In that same dark, confined space, I had been frightened when the air was sweet and my companion was a friend. I was holding my breath again as I asked: 'What did you do?'

She opened her hands. 'The only thing I could do. I prayed that no baby would cry and if we were to perish, it would be by smoke and not by the swords of our enemies.'

I waited anxiously for her to go on.

'Soon all was silent, except for the roar of flames. I ventured to lift the trapdoor a little. The flames from the King's Hall filled the whole sky. At times, when the wind blew, they swooped across towards my workplace. At other times, they rose straight up into the sky. Had it not been for my garden, the flames would have caught the thatch on the roof and we should have perished.

'We hid in the passageway until dawn and then found that the smoke was beginning to clear in the chamber. We crept out by the gallery that runs to the north-east and took the women to Brolla. Sceto and I carried two babies each so the four women could help Bregella and her little one. They had to carry her most of the way. I left Sceto to fetch them water from the well there. There is flour at Brolla to bake bread, but I told them not to make a cooking fire until I returned.

'I came back for my box and went amongst the fallen, until I found Claudio. His wound was not serious, any apprentice healer could have saved him. But I was too late, except to receive his greeting and to close his eyes when he died in my arms. I walked up through the encampment with his blood on my hands and found my pitcher broken. The rest you know.'

I reached out and took her hand. It was warm and firm.

'Deara, who was it attacked Emain?'

She shook her head and looked deeply troubled.

'Is it possible the lake raiders could get here? They would have to have horses, wouldn't they, to be so quick?'

'There would be horses in plenty if they had overwhelmed Lisbane, or Carnbanna, or our host.'

'Could that have happened so quickly?'

She nodded bleakly. 'By all accounts, these lake raiders are fierce fighters. We cannot tell how many these new ships are carrying. So far they have fought on foot, but that does not mean they have no skill in riding.'

From all that Deara had said, the raiders must be Vikings or at least some predecessor of northern origin, but I had just decided my knowledge of Vikings was so limited as to be useless, when a name came to me. Eric Bloodaxe. I knew nothing of the man, or when he lived, but it gave me an idea.

'Deara, those warriors at the gates; their wounds were great, were they not?'

She looked at me in surprise. 'You saw the fallen?'

'Yes, I saw them. The warriors, the old men and the boys. And the bearded man who sat amongst the boys.'

She gripped my hand more firmly. 'I did not know that you had seen them. I am sorry that it was so. The bearded man you saw was Finbarre. He was a poet and a storyteller, but unlike his famous predecessor who survived a great battle, he did not live to say: "I from my bleeding for my story's sake". The warriors you saw were the reserve guard, men with injuries or disabilities, unfit for battle. The old men were the teachers from the school. The boys were our scholars.'

'The wounds, Deara, were they . . . ?' I broke off, ashamed. I was forgetting that Deara knew every single soul who had lain strewn across my path.

182

'The wounds were as they always are, cruel and bloody,' she said, with a bitterness I had never heard before in her voice. 'Why do you ask?'

'It came to me that these lake raiders would fight with axes, and therefore the wounds would be different from the kind you know so well.'

To my amazement, she smiled.

'You are right, Deirdre. I have heard about the use of axes. What was done at Emain is a mystery, as well as a heartbreak, but it is unlikely to be the work of the raiders. If our settlements and our host have not been overwhelmed then we still have hope.'

We sat in silence for a little, then Deara asked me what I thought we should do. I shook my head and explained how difficult I found it to decide things, especially without knowing all the facts, particularly when there were so many variables.

'Then you must ask your heart, Deirdre, and not your head.'

'But how do I do that?'

'Just ask. But try not to strive as you ask.'

I wriggled uncomfortably on the rushes and felt myself resist what she was saying. It was all very well for people with a belief in God, a God, any God, to try asking their heart, they had something to bounce things off, but for an unbeliever, it just wouldn't work like that. I looked at Deara. She had shut her eyes and opened her hands. That was how Christians used to pray, wasn't it? Oh well, for her sake I would try. The minute I shut my eyes I was overwhelmed by booming voices, praying for my sins. They seemed to shut out all my own thoughts and feelings.

'Oh, go away. Go away. You are past and gone and have no right to be in this holy place.'

I spoke out loud, and in English, but the result was instantaneous. The booming voices stopped, the silence returned and then my heart spoke, or something did.

'Take courage. Go with Deara to Brolla. She may have need of you there.'

I opened my eyes and found Deara watching me, with a puzzled look on her face. I wondered what she'd made of my explosion in English.

'Well, what did your heart say?'

'Go to Brolla with Deara. She may have need of you there. What did yours say?'

'It said: "Do not ask to know where the journey ends, just take the next step. Go to Brolla and be of good cheer."'

We got up together and were about to cross to the leather curtain which closed off the exit passageway, when one of the small lamps nearby guttered and went out.

'Thank goodness for that. I almost forgot,' Deara said, as she gave me a pitcher of oil and showed me how to refill the lamps without putting them out. She herself relit the one that had run dry. Together, we worked our way round the chamber.

'Even if there is no oil for the King's Hall, these lamps stay lit, day and night,' she added, looking at me over her shoulder.

When the task was finished I was still reluctant to go, but this time it was not my fear of the passageway. This time Deara offered me a lamp, but I refused. The lamps belonged here. Besides, when she drew back the hanging, I could see a small pinprick of light at the end of the long slope upwards. She went ahead of me and paused for a long time at the entrance.

'Stay here while I venture out. The darkness which you feared has kept us safe. The light you crave is full of danger.'

I stood listening hard for any sound of movement or the distant note of a horn, but all was silent. In a little while, I heard her coming back.

'Come, my friend. For the moment all is well. Look, the sun and wind have come to cheer us on our way.'

20

On the north-western side of the great mound, there was no trace of the fate which had befallen Emain. The burnt out dwellings and scattered bodies were behind us, the pall of smoke had blown away. Ahead of us, the countryside was bathed in sunshine and green with fresh growth. Beyond the great lake, which shimmered in the dazzling light, the misty shapes of mountains receded, line upon line, to the furthest peaks of Donegal. The wild, warm breeze caught at our hair and cloaks and bent the tall, branching buttercups scattered through the lush grass that fringed our path.

We walked a little way and stopped again to listen, but danger it appeared had been blown away by the soughing wind. We moved down the lower slope of the great mound and continued along a well-trodden path into the light woodland where the ground flattened out.

We talked as we went. Deara asked me if I too had a husband. I told her about Matthew and his work, about his trip to India and how we planned one day to write a book about the 'barefoot doctor' scheme that Great-uncle Matthew had got going at Maharajpur thirty years earlier. She spoke of her children, Brendan and Alcelcia. By great good fortune, they had not been at Emain with her. Some years ago, she explained, on one of his many journeys, Patrick had come across Deara's eldest sister, Julia, alive and well, now the wife of an Ulster chieftain. He had last seen Julia only weeks before the raid which had carried them both to Ulster. After more than twenty years, they met at the foot of one of those mountains on the far horizon, by the shore of a deep inlet where Patrick had been given land to build a church. They had recognised each other immediately. Each summer now Deara's children went to visit Julia, while Julia herself came each autumn to Emain.

I asked Deara about the progress of Patrick's mission and about her good friend Sennach. I was relieved to hear that they, too, had been absent from Emain. Patrick, she said, had been given land to found and endow a church in Lecale and he and Sennach had gone there to draw up the documents.

'Where is Lecale, Deara? I don't know the name.'

'It is east of us, to the south of the large peninsula which faces Albi

185

and encloses the lake with the many small islands, where the seabirds come in winter.'

I nodded, so pleased that some things don't change. In my own time the Ards peninsula, with Strangford Lough on its landward side, was still a haven for migrating birds. I wondered if Sennach was drawing up the deed for the church at Downpatrick itself.

Absorbed in our talk and dazzled by the bright sun, neither of us saw a figure move to block our path. I was slightly ahead of Deara and I'm sure I cried out when a broad blade of dark blue metal almost touched my throat.

'Patrick . . .'

I could not understand what Deara was saying, for she was speaking her own language, but her tone had a ring of authority I was sure I had not heard until today. Immediately, the blade wavered and withdrew. What did not waver was the piercing look in the dark eyes of the sword's owner. Hardly more than a child, the sword was far too big for him, but I was sure that what he lacked in skill he would make up for in sheer determination. I was heartily relieved when he dropped to his knees in front of me and addressed me in very formal Latin.

'Lady, I beseech your pardon, I was in concealment and could perceive only dark and threatening figures.'

'Patrick, this is my kinswoman, Deirdre of Anacarrig. She has come to help us in our time of need. You must continue to speak Latin to her, as she does not speak our tongue.'

The dark eyes continued to gaze at me. For a moment, I wondered if my cloak had fallen open and he was puzzled by my unfamiliar clothes. But I quickly grasped that such things were immaterial to this boy. He was looking far beyond the mere surface of things.

'Finbarre would be pleased that you speak Latin to my friend,' said Deara gently.

'And Claudio, whose native tongue it was. Had he lived.'

Patrick's brave face crumpled a little, but did not give way. He hitched up the heavy sword belt, which was too loose for his slim body and in constant danger of slipping to the ground. Deara knelt down and put one arm around him.

'Now Patrick, what was it I said to you last night, when you saved us all? Have you forgotten?'

Patrick said nothing, but I saw his lips tighten and his body twitch. Deara looked up at me: 'Patrick's teachers and fellow scholars fell at the gates. He, too, would have fallen, but for the task he was given. It is hard for him to bear.'

'Why is that, Patrick?'

I was surprised to find I had spoken. There was something about this boy that was quite compelling. Courage, yes, but it was more than courage. There was loyalty and there was love. I found myself just as anxious to help him as Deara was. His burden was so clearly visible in his darting eyes, in his attempts to make a warrior out of his slight child's body and in his efforts to discipline his passionate and unruly feelings.

'My friends have all gone to God. They have gone with honour and will be received in glory.'

'And you were left behind?'

'I would have fought as bravely.'

'But of course you would,' I replied firmly.

I had no doubt in my mind Patrick would have done his best, and Deara would already have said as much, when she and the other women struggled to hold him from the fight. But something was needed to ease the burden of his grief. As I looked down at him I remembered from my own childhood how often the words of a stranger had more value than those of someone you knew.

'Patrick, in my time . . .' I began. 'In my encampment,' I corrected myself hastily, 'there is a wise man, the victor of many, many battles. He once said "It is easy to die for one's country, but far, far harder to live for it." Perhaps, Patrick, God has given you the harder task, to struggle for peace rather than fight for victory.'

Patrick's face lit up. He turned and looked at Deara, his eyes gleaming: 'But, my Lady, that is what you said last night.'

Deara nodded: 'It is, Patrick. And I promise you, my friend and I have not spoken of you, nor of what I said to you then. Come now, we must see how Bregella and her child fare.'

'My Lady, I will go and tell the women that you approach with your kinswoman, so they will not be afraid. God keep you safe, till your coming.'

He bowed to us both, hitched up his sword and ran down the path ahead of us. I looked at Deara in amazement. I'd never seen anyone move so fast in my life.

She laughed: 'You see why we call him Sceto, though he hates not to be called Patrick.'

'That must mean fast.'

'Yes it does, but more than simply fast moving. Rather, swift as with an arrow's flight. Direct, and always to the mark. And his mind carries him as fast as his feet, when he is himself.'

'What age is he?'

'Twelve, but small for his age. His mother was a very slight, gentle woman; she died some years ago. She was one of Father Patrick's first converts, hence Sceto's baptismal name which she chose for him when they were both baptised. Dairmid, his father, is a big, swarthy man. So are all his brothers. I pray they have answered our heralds and ridden out for the Ullaid, for they are all valiant warriors.'

'So Patrick is not of Emain?'

187

'No, he comes from Dalriada. North and east, about two days' ride. There's a strange, flat topped mountain near his home you can see from the King's Hall on a clear day, but Patrick never looks to it. He says Brolla is his home. His sweet hill, he calls it.'

I walked in silence for a little. I was trying to match what Deara had just told me with the fragments of history and legend her words had brought back to me. Much of what I remembered of the past was the stuff of Deara's future. But the facts underlined in red, in that old essay of mine, didn't seem to fit very well with what I was hearing. For once in my life, perhaps for the very first time, I didn't attempt to sort it out there and then. At that moment, what was important to me was the here and now, the part of both our lives we were sharing as we walked to Brolla.

'And your kinsman is Patrick, too, is he not?'

'Why, yes. That is the Father Patrick of whom I spoke just now. We call him Father, because he is now our Bishop, but also because his constant companion is Young Patrick.'

'Another Patrick?'

Deara laughed at the look of puzzlement on my face. 'When Father Patrick was sold as a slave he went to a farmer in the west. Milchu was his name. Father Patrick helped at the birth of Milchu's youngest son and his wife called him Patrick out of gratitude. But now this young Patrick is Father Patrick's devoted servant. "Young Patrick" is Patrick of Foclut or Patrick son of Milchu.'

'And so Sceto is therefore Patrick of Dalriada, or Patrick son of Dairmid?'

She laughed again, delighted by my attempt to understand the naming customs of her people.

'That's right, place, or parentage, or significant activity, like Ulrann the smith, or Tannach the herald, or Grannia the healer.'

'Or Patrick the scholar?' I suggested.

Deara looked at me quickly and gave a brief nod.

'Yes, very likely. He was the best scholar at Emain and now he is the only scholar. It's ironic isn't it, that the speed of his feet saved us the gift of his mind.'

'And eleven lives, too, including yours. And perhaps mine too,' I added, after a pause.

'How so, my friend?'

'When I saw what had happened at Emain, I thought you were dead. I despaired then. I thought I would be lost in time, because without you I could not go back to my own time. I thought I should die there, by the gate, along with the others. But then it came to me that I must do what I could, even if I should find you dead, so I set out to search for you. But when I got to your room, I couldn't even see you. It was you who saw me.'

188

'Yes, Deirdre, but you put yourself where I could see you. Had you stayed by the gates with the dead, I could not have called to you, and you could not have brought me back to life. Remember, I too had despaired.'

'It seems as if despair is our enemy.'

As I spoke the words, I remembered again what Aillech had said when she was talking to Deara's mother. The moment I mentioned it, Deara began to quote the whole passage. Her memory is so remarkable. I can't even recall things said last week unless I write them down, but she can quote whole documents without any effort and she appears to remember every word I have ever spoken to her.

'They are struggling against some great danger. I cannot see what that danger is, but I feel it like a dark despair,' she repeated. 'Each of these women, your daughter and her friend, carry a seed that may grow. They may kindle a fire at the heart of Tara.'

We stopped on the edge of the woodland and looked at each other.

'How does one heal despair, Deara?' I asked quietly.

Her face, so full of light and laughter when I'd struggled to separate out the three Patricks in her life, was now motionless. With the animation gone, I saw something I had not seen before. It was not so much that she looked older than her years, rather that she had already moved a long way along the road from knowledge towards wisdom, a journey which I had only just begun.

She thought for a little and answered slowly.

'Trust is part of it. So is love. And courage. But I do not know the proportions which make up the salve, and I do not know how one applies it. The important thing is to ask the question. Until you have a question, you cannot hope to find an answer. If we both hold it in our hearts, however, it will come to us in time. Perhaps Brolla will help us to find part of the answer.'

We stepped out from the edge of the woodland. A small stone building with a thatched roof stood at the highest point of a low, grassy knoll. Only when my eye fell upon a half-carved stone cross did I realise what the building was.

'Father Patrick's first church. The first of many, it seems,' said Deara. 'Small, but built in stone, which pleases him greatly. Many of his churches are built of wood or simply made out of turves. Come, let us go in.'

The door opened before either of us could touch it. The interior was very dim, except where shafts of sunlight fell from the narrow windows and made pools of light on the strewn rushes and reflected back from the clean white cloth that covered the altar.

I heard a movement behind me. Moments later, Sceto was kneeling before me once more. He had set aside his sword, washed his face, flattened his thick dark hair and tied a green sash round his smoke-

189

stained tunic. In the dim light, he looked almost clean. In his hands, a beautiful metal cup gleamed like dull silver. He held it out to me.

'In the name of the Lord, welcome, to all who come in peace and love.'

I took the cup and raised it to my lips. His eyes never left mine. Did I take a sip or empty the goblet? I was sure he read not only the simple question in my mind, but all the layers of doubt that lay beyond. One look at his face told me what I had to do. I drained the cup, returned it to him and thanked him. He disappeared as quickly as before.

'There are steps here, Deirdre.'

The sound of Deara's voice and the touch of her hand on my arm brought me back from somewhere a long way away. We moved along the south wall of the church towards a simple wooden altar. In a tiny side chapel, close by, were the five women. It was easy to see which was Bregella. Ashen-white, she lay full length, with her eyes closed, her baby close wrapped beside her. The other babies, naked, were slung between their mother's breasts. They slept or wriggled, supported but not confined by the fabric which held them close to their mother's warmth. Four pairs of eyes that turned towards us as we approached now turned to Bregella, as Deara knelt beside her, stroking her hands and speaking to her in her own tongue.

Bregella stirred, attempted to sit up and then caught sight of me. Without taking her eyes off me, she spoke to Deara, who turned to me and said quietly: 'Bregella wishes you to bless her child.'

I don't know how I managed to keep calm. Part of me was totally outraged. Me, bless a child. Me, an unbeliever, in this holy place. The poor woman must be delirious. But if she was, all the more reason to do what she wanted. I would bless the child. The question whether or not I was entitled to bless was unimportant. My only problem was how to do it.

I knelt down and picked up Bregella's child. As I began to unwrap the close wound linen bonds, the small parcel waved its arms and legs in the air. The last piece of fabric fell away and I held in my hands a tiny red creature with tight shut eyes. I had never held a newborn child before. I marvelled at the smallness of the curled fingers, at the vulnerability of this fragment of life, that might live and grow or falter and perish.

Suddenly, the baby opened its eyes and looked at me. Don't be silly, I said to myself, babies' eyes can't focus. But focused or unfocused, those eyes and those of the watching women were all asking something of me. I put the wrappings down on the rushes and placed the child, a girl, gently upon them. The arms and legs continued to move and the eyes to follow me, as I put my hands together. I had not put my hands together in prayer since the ritual of bath, prayers and bed insisted on by my mother. If I had prayed in my heart, then I had certainly never acknowledged it by this familiar gesture.

'God give me words.'

Before the request had even shaped itself in my mind, the answer had come. Out of the long past, from a time when singing in the church choir had also been insisted upon, came words which I had loved. Slowly, in my own language, I spoke them. They came as easily as if I used them every day of my life.

> 'The Lord bless you and keep you.
> The Lord make his face to shine upon you
> And be gracious unto you.
> The Lord lift up his countenance upon you
> And give you peace.'

Peace. The word echoed round the stone walls and vibrated back from the dark earth turves which lined the inside of the thatched roof.

'Peace?' asked Deara, repeating the word carefully in English.

'Pax,' I repeated, speaking in Latin.

'Slothan,' said Deara to the women, in their own tongue.

The four women held out their babies to me, one by one, and I repeated the words of blessing for each of them. It seemed not to matter whether you said 'peace' in English or in Latin, or in the Celtic language of the Ullaid, the word made its meaning clear by its effect on those who listened.

Deara spoke my name. I looked towards her and saw Bregella was sitting up, a hint of colour softening the pallor of her face. She was holding out her arms for the child. Moments later, in the sling which Deara had deftly tied, the child was asleep between its mother's breasts.

Without a word being exchanged between us, I knew Deara was well pleased. Bregella and her child could now heal the hurt of the shock and the pain they had endured in these last hard days. She touched my arm and drew me on towards the altar.

I had thought the altar bare except for a fresh white cloth, but when we drew near I saw what Deara had observed much sooner than I had. There on the altar was the sword I had encountered at much closer quarters on our way to Brolla. We looked at each other and were about to speak, when a woven hanging was drawn aside and the sword's owner appeared from a narrow doorway set in the stone wall. He was gasping for breath.

'Horses, my Lady.'

He mouthed the word without a sound. With her back turned away from the women, Deara made a gesture with her hands.

'Ten.'

I saw Sceto's eyes dart to the sword on the altar, but Deara was already signalling to us that we should move outside. The hanging dropped into place behind us as we stepped back into the dazzling sunlight.

'My Lady, one horseman has entered the wood, the others may follow behind. I did not wait, but came to warn you. My sword . . .'

'You did well to offer up your sword, Patrick. Let it rest in peace. Go, fill another pitcher of water for the women and come back to me here as soon as may be.'

As he disappeared, Deara turned to me and held out both her hands.

'My friend, we must cherish the hours we have had. It is time for you to go.'

For a moment, I just didn't understand what she meant. Then I heard the crackle of twigs in the wood and the sound of a horn. I had forgotten the raiders might return. The horn was very near and she was sending me away.

'No, Deara, I will not go. I can't leave you. I said I wouldn't go till all hope was gone.'

I turned my back on her, in case the sight of her outstretched hands might affect me as they appeared to have done once or twice before.

'Deirdre, please, you must go. If I am to perish, you must carry the seed for us. Please.'

I heard her voice above the growing sounds from the wood but I did not turn to look at her. If she had the courage to stand and await her fate, then I would stay, at least till I was sure there was no other way.

There was a high-pitched whinny from the wood, a final crash of branches and a horse burst into the clearing. It was riderless and breathing heavily. It faltered at the foot of the slope, caught sight of Deara and trotted gently towards her.

'Sabu, Sabu, how come you here?'

I saw Deara throw her arms round the grey mare and stroke its neck, but before I could speak, a larger black horse broke out of the wood. It was not riderless. Standing up in the stirrups, his hair flying, a frenzied look on his face, was the most fearsome warrior I had ever seen. The grey mare laid back her ears and rolled her eyes. My stomach lurched and my legs turned to jelly as I saw him lunge towards Deara. I was quite helpless as he threw himself to the ground in front of her and grasped the hem of her gown.

'Tassra, Tassra . . .'

I heard Deara speak a name and saw her kneel by the warrior. His body was shaking with great sobs and tears were streaming down his face. Gradually, my legs returned to normal. Whoever this warrior was, he was no threat to Deara. A few moments later Patrick appeared at my side. He had tethered the grey mare and the black stallion in the shadow of the church.

'Patrick, who is this man? What is happening?'

Tears unheeded, Tassra had risen to his knees, thrown wide his large brown hands and raised his voice to the sky.

'He is thanking God that the Lady Deara yet lives, for he had feared that she and all at Emain were dead and he is telling her that she is now Queen of Ulster.'

Deara was standing up now. She had gone deathly pale and stared at the warrior at her feet as if she was as bewildered by his actions as I was.

With a single gesture, Tassra drew his sword, whirled it in a great sweeping arc above his head, so that it flashed and sang, steadied it in his hands and then laid it at her feet. As Deara bent to pick it up, I saw that her cheeks too were wet with tears. Tassra's eyes were fixed upon her, his face transformed from grief to joy. She gave the naked sword back into his hands, made the sign of the cross above his bowed head and held out her hands in greeting when he had sheathed it.

'But how can that be?' I asked.

'That I do not know, but only to the Queen would a warrior wing his sword thus,' replied Patrick.

Then I saw how young the warrior was. If you took away the wild hair, the curled moustaches, the fierce grimace, and the pent up energy he had displayed as he exploded into the clearing, you could see he was not much more than twenty. He was standing now, quite easily, in front of Deara, answering her questions. With his arms folded, listening carefully to what she was saying, nodding often, I found it hard to imagine how terrifying his first appearance had been.

Apart from recognising the occasional name, I could make nothing of the conversation. Only once, when Ferghal was mentioned, could I see from the softening lines on Deara's face that the news was good. Patrick was nowhere to be seen.

To my surprise, it was when Deara spoke of Sabu that Tassra shook his head. He crossed his mouth with his hand in a gesture that said this was a matter of which he might not speak. Clearly, Deara accepted this. She nodded at some suggestion he made and then stood watching as he went to his horse and drew from beneath its gaily coloured trappings a delicately curved bronze horn.

As he raised it to his lips, a small figure sped across the open space in front of the west door and threw himself at Deara's feet. Tassra paused and lowered his horn. Although he was out of breath, Patrick's words were perfectly clear.

'My noble Lady, it is Tassra's joy and honour to be the first of all our warriors to set his sword at the feet of our Queen. I, Patrick, son of Dairmid, scholar of Emain, servant of God, I have no sword to offer. Nonetheless do I offer you my mind, my heart, my faith and my life, to serve you, as I serve God, until my life's end.'

He drew from his sash a rush cross, freshly woven, like those I had seen in the Place of Birth, and laid it at her feet.

Deara's tears had dried in the sunshine and some colour had returned to her pale face. Softly, but with a clarity I had not heard before, she began to speak.

'Patrick, son of Dairmid, scholar of Emain, servant of God, I, Deara, daughter of Angharrad, Queen of the Ullaid, servant of God, bid you rise.'

She knelt down, picked up the rush cross and turned it gently in her hands. Then she bent forward and kissed him on both cheeks.

'Take this cross, Patrick, the sign of love and peace. May it and you outlive all battles, all strivings, and all struggles for power. I accept your offer with gratitude.'

Patrick took the cross from her hands, tucked it in his sash, and bowed. Tassra raised his horn again. The sound that came from it made my heart leap. Strong and sweet, full of a tumultuous joy, it was not just a call to comrades, it was a call to celebrate life itself, to set aside all darkness and affirm what was good and true. From the direction of Emain, I heard the answering call. Short and swift, as their coming was to be.

I moved towards Deara as Tassra returned his horn to its place. She looked at me, but did not speak.

'Patrick, go softly. Tell the women that the news of their menfolk is good. Gallra is wounded, but not badly. Tell Bregella her husband is here, safe and well, and longs to see her and his daughter. He will come to her as soon as the herald and his escort arrive. I shall come myself presently.'

She turned to me and put out her hand for mine. I could see she was close to tears.

'Deirdre, you were right to stay. Please, don't leave me now. The only danger is that my strength will fail and there is more to hear. Stand near me when the herald comes.'

She squeezed my hand and managed a weak smile.

'Do you remember the night you put your rug round my shoulders and said you could see me Queen of Ulster? Could we ever have imagined, then, what has happened to me today?'

The noise of horns drowned my reply completely, but it was not important. Deara released my hand and stood up straight. Her gown was crumpled and grubby, her hair was tangled and still flecked with ash, she wore neither jewellery nor face paint, but she still looked every inch a Queen.

The drum of hooves and the snap and crack of twigs and branches reminded me rather too sharply of my earlier fear. But the warriors who rode up the grassy mound had none of the fierceness of Tassra. They circled the half-finished stone cross and dismounted, while one of their number, armed, but wearing no leather or metal plates over his brightly coloured tunic, made his way slowly towards the place where Deara and I stood.

Before he had reached us, Patrick reappeared. Deara spoke to him quickly and a moment later he was at my side.

'Lady, I must be your herald as you do not speak our tongue. The Queen wishes it so. But we must stand apart. It is the custom.'

I turned to move away, but Deara stopped us.

'Patrick, have you forgotten? Deirdre is my kinswoman and you are her herald. Do not draw apart.'

So I remained but a step behind this dearest of friends who had so suddenly become Queen of Ulster, as she waited to receive Tannach the herald.

Tannach was no older than Tassra, a slim, handsome young man, with neatly curled moustaches and a well-trimmed beard. As he knelt in front of Deara, I saw why he had moved so slowly across the grassy space between cross and church. On one leg, he wore a heavy metal brace. He began to speak and like a soft echo, Patrick followed, word by word, as if he were already familiar with the message.

'Deara, Queen of the Ullaid, I am charged by my master the King, Ferghal, son of Brendan, to bring you tidings and ask you this boon: "Deara, joy of my life, Queen of my heart, ruler of the realm that is Ferghal, come to me at Carnbanna. There let us give thanks to God for this great victory. Let us visit the wounded, comfort the bereaved, and further speak with those allies and friends whose speed in answering the call to arms has been our greatest weapon, excepting only our faith in God and the cause for which we strive. And if my pleading should fail because of the needs of others for whom you care, then I beseech you, if not for me, come for the sake of our dear friend, our father in spirit: Morrough, Lord of Emain, who has need of your greatest skills."'

Deara raised a hand to her lips and gasped: 'Morrough? Morrough? You mean the King yet lives?'

The herald bowed low. 'Ferghal is our King, my Lady. The Lord Morrough may live, or he may not.'

Deara sank to her knees and covered her face with her hands. The herald waited. I put my hand on her shoulder. I wished I could put my arms round her, but that would not have been right. It seemed that one shock followed another with hardly time to breathe. I sensed Deara making yet one more effort to compose herself.

She got to her feet, her hands folded in front of her, her face again damp with tears.

'I thought Morrough was dead, when Tassra winged his sword and called me Queen. I pray you herald, tell us all that has come to pass. I shall not again interrupt your telling, for which I ask your pardon, but I beg you, forget no detail, no smallest part that relates to Morrough, any more than you would to Ferghal, your King.'

The herald bowed low and began to speak. But not only to speak. For all my concern for Deara I could not take my eyes away from the herald's lithe figure. He moved, turned, gestured, grimaced with such feeling and sheer artistry that I was held captivated.

At moments, Patrick too was so absorbed that he forgot to translate the words, but so vivid was the herald's telling, I scarcely needed words at all. I was simply there, living the experience he had observed and turned into story on the long ride, begun at first light on a midsummer morning and ending long after noon on the grassy hill of Brolla.

No doubt, Tannach would recount 'The Battle of Carnbanna' many times in the future, in mead halls and by campfires, with new and more elaborate embellishments, but I doubt if he ever surpassed the verve and freshness of that first telling, made for a Queen to whom he was clearly devoted.

The battle itself had been no mere frontal assault on a known enemy. The raiders from the lake were unmounted but cunning, and they had had time to prepare themselves and to hide. Pits had been dug and covered with turves to trap both horses and riders. Valiant warriors were lost in the first assault, when they charged across the pitted ground against the massed enemy. But the courage of Morrough and the skill of Ferghal held the host to its purpose. Leaping over the writhing bodies of fallen horses and comrades, Morrough led the main body of warriors through the enemy, killing many and splitting their strength in two. He then slowed down and wheeled away from the battlefield as if he were retreating. The closer of the two groups of raiders reformed and began to pursue the horsemen. That was when Ferghal attacked from the flank, sending his fastest horses, carrying his most skilled warriors, to encircle first one portion of the divided company and then the other.

The raiders attacked the horses, swinging their axes to cripple them and bring their riders down. But they had never before fought against men who loved their horses as much as they loved their wives or their sweethearts. At the first cruel lunges from the axes, the horses reared. Then, held from above, moved by touch and pressure, they had attacked the enemy host themselves. Rearing and plunging, at one with their riders whose swords sang through the air, the well-loved beasts of Emain answered the battle cry as eagerly as any warrior. They pursued the dark figures who sprang up at them, thinking they could terrify them by their fierce cries and swinging axes. Many of the bodies dragged to the fires after the battle bore only the marks of hooves and teeth.

No raider escaped the whirling circles which Ferghal and his captains kept in motion, throwing fresh horsemen into the fight as allies came to join them, pulling back groups of comrades one by one to rest their horses, or remount, for every horse within a day's ride of Emain was at hand. Only Sabu and some of the youngest mares were held back for a final effort, which was never needed.

Having created the detail of the battle before our eyes, the herald paused, leaned on his sword, a warrior at the end of a great battle. I felt just as exhausted, as if I'd been fighting it myself.

'And then, herald, and then . . .' prompted Deara gently.

'Great was the singing, my Lady, and the greetings of comrade to comrade. Camp was made near Lisbane and some of the women who had been captured by the raiders and freed by our allies came to us bearing food and drink. Morrough commanded that cooking fires be made, that the horses be made much of and that all warriors report their wounds to the healers who rode with us or to the woman who had come bearing dressings with two maidens to whom she had taught her craft. It was she who bound Lord Ferghal's arm.'

'He is wounded, then?'

'A touch, my Lady; no more than a scratch, but he bent to the King's command that even the slightest wound be dressed.'

I thought I caught the hint of a smile on Deara's lips, but the set of her body did not alter. I felt her tension as if it were my own. She was waiting for some part of the story that was of great consequence to her and I could not guess what it might be.

'And then, herald?'

'Soon, it would have been time for the day meal, and indeed men drank from pitchers to keep off thoughts of hunger. But the King said: "Hold fast. There is yet work to be done before we take our well-earned rest." He called me to him and bade me ride to every campfire and call one man from each group of comrades to his side. And so I did, my Lady.'

He bowed low, then continued. 'That was when the blow came, Lady. As the King sat in friendship, with all our brave allies, to speak of things to come.'

He paused, clutched his chest, opened his mouth, gasped for air and sank to the ground. I was horrified, sure he'd had a heart attack, but he had bounced back to his feet before I had even cried out. Damn the man, he should be on the stage, I thought, for I had never seen anything so convincing in my life. I wiped perspiration from my forehead and tried to compose myself for what he would do next.

'Like an arrow in the heart, my Lady, and no enemy within miles.'

Deara nodded briefly. Her eyes closed for a second, but in a moment she was as wide-eyed as I. The herald had leapt to the ground and was tearing clothes from an imaginary body and beating his fists upon it.

'The woman I have seen walk in your garden, the woman who had presently dressed Lord Ferghal's arm, my Lady, fell upon the King, whose face was grey as ash. I would have sprung to the King's defence, but my Lord Ferghal was faster. "What are you doing, Grannia?" he cried. "My box, my Lord, in the name of God, quickly." She blew into the King's mouth, pressed his chest and then poured drops between his lips. The ashes fell from his face and he stirred again.'

Deara ignored the tears trickling down her face.

'The King made to rise, but the woman would not have it. She summoned cloaks from those nearby and raised him up a little that he might speak. His voice was but a whisper, yet clear to all. And these were his words: "That shaft was near its mark and may yet strike home. It clears my mind and underlines my judgement. Friends draw near."

'By now, my Lady, news had gone out to the whole company. The fires were smoored and every soul came to hear how the King fared. Beyond where he lay, circled by his own Lords, his captains and his allies, came all the warriors and the women who had been released and those who had come out from Lisbane and Carnbanna to greet us. They all waited in silence.

'"Ferghal, give me your hand," the King said. "Deirchu, unfasten my sword. Friends, hear me. By the grace of God, I may yet live to see peace in this land, to dandle children on my knee as old men do and fight them with wooden swords. But my part is done. It is time for change, for skill and wisdom to take their place with courage and loyalty and comradeship. I give you Ferghal for your King. Come, pledge him and I the first to bow to him."

'So, my Lady, the cry went up. And never have I heard a more joyous noise. "Ferghal," they shouted, "Ferghal," and again, "Ferghal." Then there was silence, my Lady, as Ferghal bound on the great sword of Emain and took the seal ring, and Morrough closed his eyes. The woman who sat by him was anxious for him, but when Ferghal spoke, Morrough stirred again.

'Thus spake Ferghal, King of the Ullaid. "Morrough, noble King, father of the Ullaid, I will bow to none except God, fight for nothing but the prospect of peace, and seek no gain, except wisdom, so that one day the bards may sing a new song, a song of peace, of healing and of love. May God and your counsel guide me."

'"Aye, Ferghal, and that of your Queen."

'And at that, my Lady, the warriors began to chant. "The Queen," they cried. "The Queen. Our dear Lady, Deara, Queen of the Ullaid." King Ferghal threw out his hands to his people and they raised him aloft, carried him through the camp, and back to where Morrough lay. There, at Morrough's side, the King took his rest, but in the camp singing and dancing went on all through the night and the fires burned till the dawn.'

The herald bowed, his arms crossed upon his chest, as if he had pronounced 'Amen' at the end of a long and complicated psalm.

'How does Morrough this morning?'

'I know not, my Lady, for I rode with the dawn. The King sent you also this.'

He drew from his pouch a fragment of parchment. He handed it to her as if it were a lizard he had drawn from his boot. She grasped it eagerly, ran her eyes over it again and again. Her face lightened as she read.

'Herald, I thank you for your journey, for your tidings and for your art. Greet the King. Tell him I shall come to him as fast as Sabu can carry me. And greet Morrough. Tell him I have received news of him and hasten to bring my dear Grannia relief from her task.'

The herald retreated three steps, bowed and unsheathed his sword. For a moment, he hesitated, and then with an awkwardness which I found amazing after the performance he had just given, he winged his sword as Tassra had done and laid it at Deara's feet.

He stood uneasily, his shoulders sloping, his weight held on one side of his body. Then he spoke. 'My Lady, Queen of Emain, I, Tannach, son of Ulrann, offer you my sword, my art and my life. Do what you will with them. It was you who gave me back life when all others had despaired. I will never forget.'

'Thank you, Tannach. I too shall never forget the offering you have made today. May you live to tell many a happier tale, though I doubt if you could tell any tale better. Go, rest in the shade while you may. Patrick will bring fresh water for you and your comrades.'

For all this time, Patrick had stood motionless at my side. Now he darted across the daisy-speckled turf and was gone in a moment. Deara turned towards me, her eyes misted with tears.

'Such joy, my friend, such joy, after all our sadness. Ferghal was made King in the manner of our people and not by Morrough's death, as I had feared. And Morrough seems like to live. He tries Grannia's patience already.'

There was laughter in her voice and relief and joy in her face. She grasped my hands and kissed my cheeks.

'Deirdre, my friend, you look so pale, let us go and sit together in the shade.'

Her voice was gentle, soft and comforting. I felt suddenly so tired. The heat, perhaps, or standing for so long with the wool cloak still about my shoulders.

'Deara,' I managed to say. 'Deara.'

'Yes, my dear, what is it?' She paused and looked at me closely. 'Are you feeling ill?'

'No, I feel very happy, very happy, just very tired. But there is something I have to do.'

I felt my strength ebbing away, told myself again it was the heat and put up my hand to release the clasp of the cloak. As I touched it, I felt Merdaine's brooch pinned to my left shoulder and that helped me to remember what it was I had to do. The cloak slid to the ground and I unpinned the brooch. I was surprised and grateful it came out so easily, I'd had such a job putting it on. I laughed.

'What amuses you so, my friend?'

Deara's voice sounded as if she had moved away from me, but she was still standing right beside me. I made a final effort to collect my weary body and straying thoughts to say what I had to say: 'Deara, daughter of Angharrad, Queen of Ulster, I, Deirdre of Anacarrig, have no sword to give you. I can give you only what is yours. Here, take this back, with my love, in hope and joy, and use it, as I did for a short time, as a weapon against despair.'

Our eyes met, our hands touched, the brooch was received and I found myself looking across the daisy-strewn grass of Emain at the summit of the great mound, still smiling. A short distance away, the custodian had just started his motor mower and was about to trim the grass.

21

Deara was constantly in my mind throughout the rest of the weekend, but this time I did recognise how preoccupied I was. When I sat down on Sunday morning to write my weekend letter to Matthew I couldn't even remember what had been happening at Anacarrig. I'd decided not to tell him about my meetings with Deara in case it might worry him, but although I shared my excitement over the garden, the prolific flowering of the Albertine on William Coulter's archway and the photographs I'd taken for him, I felt what I had written was flat and lifeless compared with what I'd written earlier about Deara's herb garden in the ruins of Emain.

When Monday morning came with the usual scatter of envelopes on the mat, however, I made a supreme effort to gather myself as best I could. As I waited for my breakfast coffee to filter, I ran my eye over the kitchen calendar and tried to put together a picture of the weeks ahead. I flipped back and forth between the months and looked at the colour photographs as if somehow they could help me work out what had to happen. They brought back memories, certainly, but they didn't help to clarify my mind.

The auction was still scheduled for Thursday 17 July. Sandy hadn't rung about the china. That meant she'd changed her mind and she'd expect me to go ahead as if nothing whatsoever had happened. But a proposed completion date for 10 July had arrived in the post, which made a complete nonsense of the date of the auction.

'Five weeks since the funeral. Two weeks to completion. I'll be back in London before Matthew even leaves Maharajpur.'

The thought gave me such a shock, I spoke the words out loud. Only two weeks left. And no Matthew to help me with the auction, or the final clearing out, or the necessary goodbyes. It had never once occurred to me my job at Anacarrig could be finished before the eight weeks of his study leave in India.

But, for the moment, the future would have to wait. I heard a vehicle change gear at the foot of the drive. With any luck, this would be the central heating man. After working intermittently for the last couple of weeks the boiler had finally packed up.

I glanced round the kitchen. Piles of bedroom curtains and bedlinen parked on the work surfaces stared back at me. They'd been there

201

since Friday, waiting to be ironed and rehung or folded and put away. If it was him, there was nowhere to put anything down. I snatched up an armful of curtains and hurried upstairs to Sandy's room.

As I laid them on the bed, I saw the shiny blue van pull up below the window. A tall, broad shouldered, bearded young man unwound himself from the driving seat. As he straightened up, he looked round. Ignoring the front door right beside him, he walked along the terrace, stopped and studied the garden, the rose covered arch and the small wrought iron gate on the path to the back of the house. He seemed to be looking for something, but at that moment, he turned and retraced his footsteps. I hurried downstairs and arrived at the front door just as he knocked.

'Mrs Weston?'

He was paying more attention to his clipboard than to me, but he seemed shy rather than unfriendly.

'Yes, indeed. Do come in. You're very punctual. I'm not used to this in London.'

He looked at me in surprise.

'You're not long moved in, then?' he said slowly.

'I'm not moved in at all, I'm afraid. I'm moving out.'

'Ah, that's it . . .'

Relief spread across his face. He gave me a great beaming smile and held out his hand.

'Shure, when I saw "Weston" on the ticket, I thought you'd be the new lady, for the house has been empty a long time now. But you're Miss Henderson, an' if I'm not mistaken, you'd be Deirdre.'

'Yes, I am.'

I can think of few occasions in my life when confirming my identity has been the cause of such unambiguous joy. He shook my hand vigorously and beamed yet more broadly.

'Well, Deirdre, I'm pleased to meet you, for many's the time I heerd tell of you. I'm Bill Coulter.'

'Wee Billy?'

It was my turn to feel a totally unexpected delight. And amusement. I couldn't help seeing the ridiculousness of addressing this young giant as 'Wee Billy', but 'Wee Billy' he had been to his grandfather, William Coulter, and 'Wee Billy' he had remained; the only son of William's widowed daughter-in-law, a figure in my life, significant and yet unseen until this moment.

'I can't understand why I never met you, Bill, when I went to Portadown to see William,' I said, as I pulled two stools from under the kitchen table so we could sit down.

'Och shure, I was football mad. I useta be out an away every minute I wasn't at school. My mother says I only went to school for the football. An' it was Saturdays you useta come to see Grandad

202

before you wint to London, wasn't it?'

We talked excitedly, like old friends meeting by chance, people who knew each other at one remove, loved and valued by the same trusted person. Like cousins, separated by geography, we still had a shared history, precious to both of us.

I liked Bill Coulter instantly. There was something so open, so disingenuous, about him. He was not like William at all in manner, far more extrovert. Lively and quick to laugh. Transparent in his pleasure. Though there was something about him which did remind me of William, even if I couldn't yet put my finger on it.

'Would you like a cup of tea, Bill, or am I keeping you back?'

'No, not-at-all. I'm me own boss, since January twelve-month. Shure, what is there to life if you haven't time to pass the time of day? But I'll tell you what, Deirdre, let me just look at the gentleman over thonder first, in case I might haveta go over to the wholesalers for a part.'

'Fine, Bill. And while you do that I'll go and make a couple of phone calls. I'd enjoy my tea more if they were done. There's been an awful lot to see to.'

He nodded sympathetically, took up his tool bag and began to unscrew the metal covering on the boiler.

I went upstairs, sat on Mother's bed and got started. The date of the auction I rearranged for Monday 7 July. I was just in time to change the date on the insertions in the local papers.

'Shure, what is there to life if you haven't time to pass the time of day?' I repeated quietly to myself as I waited for the auctioneer's office to ring me back about setting up a private view for the china.

Yes. That was it. That was his grandfather. For all their differences they shared the conviction that there is more to life than doing, or having done, the job.

As I put the phone back on the bedside table, I noticed the edge of a magazine poking out from under the bed. I picked it up about to add it to the boxful ready to go up the hill to the hospital, when I saw a name I recognised in the list of contributors. I flicked through to see what he'd done. It was the regular feature, 'Clothes for the life you lead.' Great pictures, as Terry's always were. Pin sharp, beautifully composed and lit. But, oh my goodness, those faces. So bright and brittle.

It would have been one thing if they'd been models, but they weren't. These were supposed to be ordinary women doing a job or running a home. They posed in immaculate kitchens with colourful vegetables tastefully scattered on the work surface, or sitting rooms with bowls of flowers on polished tables, as if all life were about cashmere cardigans, entertaining the boss, little dinners for two, or happy families; you, me, and one of each, in cleaner than clean designer casuals. Even the obligatory dogs looked immaculate.

I went through the entire magazine. Yes, with the exception of one 'heartbreak' story, they had managed successfully to exclude grief, loss, disappointment and despair from the texture of the life they demonstrated. My commissions often took me to the offices of this particular magazine. I was used to the bright good mornings, the ritual enquiries about one's health which expected only the answer 'Fine, just fine.' Oh yes, I could exchange the common currency of talk about projects, colleagues, holidays. But where was the time to pass the time of day?

In that world, the world I belonged to, there was only this hectic doing. But old William had passed on to Wee Billy a sense of something more, something lying beyond the getting and spending, without which one's living added up to very little.

I dropped the magazine into the box and hurried downstairs to put on the kettle. Bill Coulter sat at the kitchen table, his head in his hands. The room smelt hot and peculiar.

'Bill, are you all right?' I cried, as I threw open the windows and the back door.

He raised his head with an effort. His face was ashen grey. 'Aye. The smell's only the jointing compound. It's non-toxic. Woudya have a couple of aspirin?'

I ran a glass of cold water and fetched the tablets from the bathroom cabinet. He swallowed them listlessly. Poor man. I'd had bad heads myself, but I'd never seen anyone look like this even with a full-blown migraine.

'Do you often get headaches, Bill?'

'Aye. Doctor says it's migraine. Comes on all-of-a-sudden. I'm supposta carry tablets.'

The voice was flat, his dark eyes had lost all their animation. He glanced round the room restlessly, as if he were trying to avoid looking at me, and yet it came to me so strongly that he needed me to help him.

Then words spoke themselves sharply and clearly inside my head: 'Do what you can, do it in love, it will be more than you think.' There was one thing I could do.

'Bill, I have a friend who can ease my migraine. She puts her hands on my shoulders and it seems to help. Would you give it a try?'

'Aye, surely. I'd give anything a try.'

I walked round behind him as he sat slumped over the kitchen table.

'Now sit up straight and lean back against me,' I said with a confidence I certainly didn't feel.

I put my hands on his shoulders and gasped for breath. Through the light fabric of his shirt came a throbbing so fierce it seemed as if my hands might be thrown off by the force of it, yet I knew instinctively however strong the pulses of pain I must keep my hands where they were.

I pressed a little harder and then a glance upwards showed me what Bill must have seen. Neatly folded on the work surface lay a pink candlewick quilt. Immediately I knew that that was what had upset him.

I was so taken aback that I didn't even notice when my hands moved to his temples. The throbbing increased so violently I nearly cried out. Surely this could be no ordinary headache. And whatever did I think I was doing? The poor man needed a doctor, quickly, or something dreadful would happen.

'No, it won't. Keep your hands where they are.'

Like that moment in my room after I'd broken the pen, the words were so sharp, so clear, it was as if Deara had spoken in my ear. I even wondered if she could possibly be watching me as I had watched her the evening when Alcelcius produced the manuscripts. And then I saw what was necessary: yes, I could help Bill, but only if I set aside my own fear and followed the promptings of my hands and my heart.

I went on standing behind him and still had no very clear idea of what I had to do. Just holding on to the pain was taking all my energy, but something told me I mustn't let go. And then, quite suddenly, after a few minutes more, the throbbing grew less violent and I felt I could breathe more easily. It came to me then that I had to ask him about that pink quilt.

The instant the words shaped in my mind, all the sensible and rational ways of dealing with the world I'd used so effectively, for so many years, came back into play. Like the mechanisms that fall into place to defend some delicate piece of machinery, they printed out warning signals. Don't be ridiculous. How could a pink quilt make someone ill? But the sheer storm of protest I experienced encouraged me to defy sense and reason: 'What is it about the pink quilt, Bill?' I asked softly.

He didn't reply and for a moment I thought he hadn't heard. I felt such relief that my foolish question had dissolved in the air between us, as if I'd never been silly enough to utter it.

And then it came. A strange, strangled cry which took me by surprise, for it was so distorted I could hardly connect it with the feverish body on which my hands still rested. He put his head down on the table and wept, his body shaking uncontrollably. I put my arms round him and held him, trembling myself as if the pulsing energy I'd been exposed to had drained all the power from my body.

Then I began to see images, flickering on the edge of consciousness, like the rerun of one of those pieces of film, so familiar from news broadcasts over these last years. Army personnel in camouflage. Police redirecting traffic. A body, unmarked and apparently undamaged, lying against a low wall, like a sack of potatoes fallen from a lorry.

Slowly, the sobbing subsided. At last, I could make out what he was trying to tell me.

'Shure, that's what the woman brought to put over him, an' I diden know it was him, for Nora told me he'd meet me at the field.'

Mike was his best friend. He had been his best friend since they were wee lads together. As mad about football as he was. They had got a club going for youngsters on a Saturday. Training them. Till last October. Mike worked for a taxi firm that did weddings. They were short-staffed, so he stood in for someone else, a part-time UDR man. Went to take the car out and put the satin ribbons on ready for the driver. The garage door was booby trapped. Blew him clean across the main road.

I felt the tears trickle down my cheeks as I remembered seeing the one brief clip on the national news. It had been just long enough for me to recognise the road and the buildings I had passed every day on my way to and from school, but not long enough for Matthew to run in from the kitchen when I called to him. We had to wait for the next news broadcast, because I simply had to see it again. It was as if I would be able to do something about that crumpled heap, simply by looking at it.

Bill sat up and shook his head silently, calmer now, his face streaked with tears and dust from the boiler cupboard. And then, it was as if I heard Deara's voice again. 'There's more to come,' she said. What surprised me even more than her prompt was my own instant response. 'Yes, I know.'

I would have sworn she had been there all the time to guide me and encourage me. Reassured, I felt my legs stop trembling and my stomach muscles begin to unknot. Then I said simply: 'Tell me about the pink quilt, Bill.'

He sobbed again, his words so distorted I couldn't make sense of them. But his movements and gestures seemed to describe a journey, going somewhere, stopping, speaking to someone, then driving on. I waited patiently until his words grew clear again.

'. . . the road was blocked and the police told me to pull in. So I did, along wi' everybody else. Then I saw this policeman I know well. "What's happened?" seys I to him. "Is it bad?" "Aye," seys he, "bad enough, young chap dead. The ambulance is sent for, ye can get through in a minit." So, I seys to meself, "I hope Mike doesn't think I'm not coming, for I'm always the early one." Then I see the woman carrying the quilt and I think it's a funny thing for a woman to be carryin' a quilt down the road on a Saturday afternoon. An' I hear the ambulance coming and think, "No use crying over spilt milk, there's them wee lads to think about." And then as soon as the ambulance is thru', the police wave me on.'

I had come to sit beside him and he was looking straight at me now, speaking as if every word was of the utmost importance, a deliberateness about the way he described every detail. I was no longer anxious because I knew it was going to be all right, but my body was still rigid with tension as if I were waiting for a blow to fall.

'So, I starts the van and eases forward towards the roundabout. You know where I mean, don't you?'

I nodded.

'An' just as I draws level, they gets out the stretcher and one of the men lifts the pink quilt outa the way. An' I see the ginger hair, an' his face as white as a ghost . . .'

He covered his face with his hands, but no sound came.

'What did you do then, Bill?' I prompted gently.

'I came on back round the roundabout, instead of going out the Moy road and wint over to the officer. "Officer," seys I, for it wasn't one that I knowed. "Officer, has that man's next of kin been informed?" "No," seys he, "we haven't identified him yet." "Well," seys I, "he's Mike Laverty from Portadown an' he has a wife, Nora, an' two children an' they're expecting the two of us back for our tea at half-five." So he looks at me very straight an' seys, "You'll have to make a formal identification at the hospital before Mrs Laverty can be informed. Are you prepared to do that?" Seys I, "I am."'

'And did you?'

'I did.'

'And told Nora?'

'Yes.'

'And then?'

'I hurried away out tae the field tae catch the wee lads afore they went home an' told them we'd meet as usual next Saturday, an' Mike would be mad at them, if any o' them missed.'

He fumbled in his pocket and pulled out a handkerchief that had clearly seen action while he was working on the boiler. He wiped his eyes and blew his nose.

'I'm ashamed of myself, Deirdre, behaving like this. I'm shure ye've niver seen a man cry.'

'Oh yes, I have, Bill. Many's the time. If more men cried, we mightn't both be weeping for Mike. And Nora. And the little ones,' I replied, as I got up to fetch a piece of kitchen paper to dry my own tears.

'Ah niver shed a tear, till the day. Isn't that a strange thing? And that quilt o' yours should be sittin' there.'

He looked at me, his eyes bright, their gaze quite steady. When he spoke again there was a kind of excitement in his voice. 'Would you believe me, Deirdre, if I told you something?'

'I'm sure I would, Bill,' I said with a smile.

'That migraine of mine, it's gone clean away. There's not a sign of it. Now how do ye account for that?'

I laughed lightly: 'Shure there's no accountin' for it at all man. So we may just give thanks.'

Bill's face lit up.

'I haven't heard anyone say that for years, not since Granda died. He was always sayin' that, wasn't he?'

I looked over my shoulder at him as I filled the kettle and took mugs from the shelf. It was hard to believe it was the same man I'd found hunched over the table less than an hour ago.

'I haven't thought of it for years either,' I admitted. 'It's funny how things come back to you, isn't it?'

'Oh, it is that,' he replied. 'And always when you're a hundred miles away from the thing. That's when it comes to you.'

Easy and relaxed now, as if after a great effort, we talked about William, his passion for horses, his love of the countryside and the way he could twist and curve metal to make horseshoes or cartwheels or gates. I told Bill how I used to stand in the forge where the other children were afraid to stand, because William had explained to me which sparks could burn and which were merely fragments of light. We both felt sad that we'd not known him better, for Bill was still too young to appreciate him, and after Daddy died I was caught up in a life that gave me little chance to visit him.

'Bill, have you time to come into the garden? I saw you take a quick look when you arrived. You must see William's arch and his garden gate.'

We walked out into the sunlight and stood under the mass of pink roses that almost concealed William's handiwork. We traced the swirls on the little gate to the back garden and looked at William's mark, a squiggle that might have been the letter 'S' backwards or a small snake. We agreed neither of us would ever need an identifying mark to recognise William's work.

It was when Bill spoke about Nora's love of flowers, it suddenly dawned on me Mike and Nora were Catholics. I'd been so successful in putting out of mind the clues every Protestant is taught to look for when identifying strangers who might be 'the other side' that I'd managed to miss the obvious. What I hadn't missed, however, was the relationship which had developed between Bill and Nora since Mike's death.

Walking across the lawn to the hawthorns, I looked across at Bill and found it easy to imagine Nora finding comfort in his arms. They'd known each other since childhood, after all. It occurred to me that Nora might even have chosen Bill in the first place had he not been a Protestant.

Bill was so happy talking about their plans for the future, particularly for the two boys whom he already treated as if they were his own. But as I listened, anxiety descended upon me like a thundercloud. How many 'mixed' couples like Bill and Nora had been killed or injured simply for the crime of daring to love across the tribal boundaries?

I was so preoccupied with my sad and angry thoughts that I didn't hear the question Bill asked me.

'I just asked which one it was yer mother tried to cut doun,' he repeated.

The sudden shock of his words instantly drove away all my anxious preoccupations.

'You mean, which hawthorn?' I replied incredulously. 'You mean she tried to cut one of them down? Why on earth did she do that? This is one story I haven't heard, Bill.'

He stood staring at the hawthorns and at the two fragments of stone sunk into the ground. The kingcups were over, so I'd filled a large earthenware jar with buttercups from the lane to keep me company in my sitting place. He studied them as if they were a piece of the boiler still in need of a small adjustment and then sat down on the grass.

I sat down beside him and gazed across to the chestnuts I'd helped my father plant. In a fortnight, I would be gone. That far off day when a child, a man in his prime and an old blacksmith drank tea from a Thermos after planting a row of trees would become but a fragment of memory, to survive only as long as the last witness.

'I'm trying to recall the right way of it, Deirdre,' he began slowly. 'Ye see, when Granda didn't like someone, he woulden say a bad word about them, he just woulden speak of them at all. An' he niver mentioned your mother, but for this one story and he told it a brave few times. It seems there was a row between yer father an' mother one Sunday night. Your mother said if he diden cut them hawthorns down she'd do it herself when he was away at work.'

'Oh yes, she would too,' I agreed. 'How did he stop her?'

'Well, your Dad diden, to begin with, it was Grandad that stopped her,' he replied quietly. 'It fell out that he was workin' in the forge and he gets this idea he ought to go up to Anacarrig. It was a Monday mornin' an' he'd seen your father go past on the way to work, for you could see up from the forge in them days. Anyway, up he goes, an' as he comes up the drive he hears the saw.'

'Mother?'

'Oh aye. She'd started. But she was in such a hurry she'd got the wrong saw an' it was blunt forby. "Good morning, Mrs Hutchinson," seys Granda. "You've a hard job there I'm thinking." "It is," seys she. "But if Sam won't do it, I will. Superstition, that's all it is. I have to put up with him not goin' to church like a dacent man, but I'll not have him listenin' to a lot of superstitious nonsense." That one, of course, was meant for Granda, for he and your father would sometimes talk about the olden days. But Granda seys nothing. He just takes out his pipe and takes his time about lightin' it.'

I had to laugh: the image of William lighting up came back to me so vividly, I could almost smell the haze of Mick McQuaid on the fresh morning air.

'I suppose she gets on with the sawing?'

Bill nodded and I looked behind me at the hawthorns just to make sure they really were still there. Not a lot survived mother's anger, once she got going.

'Well, Granda just stands there quietly watchin' her and that starts to annoy her. Then he seys, very slow, "You know, Mrs Henderson, in the olden days, it was a crime in this land to cut down a chieftain tree. It was actually a capital offence, punishable by death. Isn't that a remarkable thing now?"'

'Goodness, Bill, that would have been like a red rag to a bull. What on earth did she say?'

'Granda niver wou'd tell that, for I asked him too. All he said was that, by a great misfortune, in her hurry to get on with the job the saw blade broke.'

I laughed with sheer relief.

'You know, Bill,' I said, still smiling, 'he was a wise old soul. No argument in the world would have stopped her. He must have known that.'

'Aye, and he knew a thing or two about saw blades.'

'So what happened then?'

'Well Grandad seys, "I'm afeard, Mrs Henderson, ye'll need a bit of weldin' on that blade before it's much more use to you," an' he takes up the bits and goes off back to the forge.'

'And welds them?'

'Aye, and sharpens the teeth forby, but he doesn't come up again till evenin', till he sees your father out down by the hawthorns whittlin' away with a knife. Up he comes and sits himself down. And it seems neither of them seys a word for a long time. Granda seys your father was graftin' a sign with beeswax and strips of old linen. When he'd finished, he seys to Granda, very quiet like: "William, did you ever notice how ignorance and arrogance go together?" "No, I can't say I have," seys Granda, "but I'll give it some thought." Then he seys to your Dad: "Do you think your trees will thrive?"

'"Oh yes," seys your Dad. "But at a price. There's a price for everything, even a tree. But you have to pay it because if you don't you might as well be dead. If your heart is dead, you've only your head to keep you walkin' round and talkin' to folk and doin' your work, as if you were alive."'

Bill stopped suddenly and looked at me uneasily.

'Deirdre, I hope I'm telling you the right way of this. Maybe I'm not mindin' it the way he had it. He told it often, but then I was only a wee lad.'

'Carry on, Bill,' I responded, reassuringly. 'I can hear the pair of them. I can almost see them the way you're telling it.'

'Well, Granda agreed that there was a lot of people walkin' round dead that thought they were alive and then he seys: "I hear in the church they tell you you reap what you sow. I wonder maybe they don't teach you to respect what another man has planted in his garden, or his mind."'

'William said that?'

'He did indeed.'

'I never thought William would be so direct. What did Daddy say to that?'

'Granda seys he went very quiet. He thought he wasn't going to say another word. Then all of a sudden he comes out with it: "That's what gets me, William. They know it all, these church people. Catholic, Protestant, Baptist, Elim, Pentecostal, Brethren – not one moment's doubt, the whole damn lot of them. They know it all. They do. Everything. No thought that anyone else might have a point of view as good as theirs. I'm not against religion, mind you, nor against belief, nor against Christianity, even though I've been told I'm this and I'm that. But I've had my say tonight, William. I told my wife that there were good and holy people before Christ was born or thought of and they worshipped Him by respecting His things, even though they knew nothin' about Him, and if I meet my Maker tomorrow I'd expect him to appreciate my point of view."'

Tears sprang to my eyes. Dear Bill. My father's words suddenly made clear for me something I'd never yet been able to work out for myself: the tension between the quiet pleasure and sense of rightness I so often felt in holy places and the violent hostility I always experienced whenever I was confronted with the whole idea of church. Had my father lived, I'm sure I'd have worked out the tension. I'd have seen his struggle with my mother and been able to decide for myself where I stood. But he had died and I'd not been able to resolve the tension and at times I felt it would tear me apart.

I rubbed my eyes surreptitiously and asked Bill when he thought all this had happened. But he didn't know and couldn't work it out.

As we stood up to go, I had a sudden thought. 'Bill, where would you start if you were going to cut them down?'

'Was she right-handed?'

I nodded and watched him size up the trees.

'That's the easiest one to come at.'

'And whereabouts would you cut?'

Bill looked puzzled. 'It would havta be before the branches spring off, but not too near the ground. If that low branch weren't where it is, I'd say just about there.'

I put my hands on the trunk of the tree. I think I was feeling for a scar, or a mark, but there wasn't any, the hawthorn was simply rough in the manner of old trees. But as I touched the branch Bill had pointed to, I had a sudden recollection of holding the tin of beeswax for my father as he wrapped strips of linen round one of William's old apple trees.

'Bill,' I cried, 'it wasn't a sign, s-i-g-n, that Daddy left,' I said excitedly; 'it was a scion, s-c-i-o-n. Look, he grafted this branch into the saw cut, to heal the hurt, and it took. If you hadn't remembered the story, no one would ever know it had been damaged.'

After we'd agreed to arrange an evening when he could bring Nora over for supper, Bill drove off and I went back down to the hawthorns. I stood and looked at them for a long time. There was no trace whatever of my mother's efforts. The hurt had been healed and something new had grown from the damage.

The thought comforted me and then I recalled what Merdaine had said to Deara when she was dying. To my amazement, the words came back to me without effort just as they always did for Deara: 'Here, I give you a parting gift of what you already have. For you both, and for all of your kind, who have love in your hearts, I give you the sign of healing.'

22

Beside one of the massive stone troughs placed at intervals along all the major routeways in Niall's kingdom, the party from Emain made their noon halt on the third and last day of their journey to Tara.

Deara dismounted gratefully, handed her reins to one of the warriors who rode a few paces behind her and turned away from the throng of people leading their mounts to drink. The talk buzzed around the watering place as women distributed dawn baked bread and courtiers and warriors stretched and eased weary limbs, but Deara had no heart for company. She caught up the folds of her cloak and picked her way over the hummocky grass that stretched away from the dusty trackway to where a small, stunted hawthorn enclosed by some rough boulders offered shelter from the chilly March wind.

For the last three days, as they drew ever nearer to Tara, the excitement had grown amongst the ambassadors and court officials as the time for the final talks drew near. Each day messengers from Tara had ridden out to greet them bringing gifts of wildfowl and fruit. All the signs were good. Before nightfall, Tara itself would welcome them. Within the next week a treaty to keep Ireland in peace for the long future might be achieved. Or it might not.

She sat down on the south side of the boulders, closed her eyes and held up her face to the warm sun. She felt its restoring touch, drew her hands from beneath her cloak and let them lie, relaxed and open, by her side. Whenever she felt her healing power diminished by overuse or fatigue she must seek soil, sand or rock, or the sun itself, to restore her power. That was what Merdaine had taught her all those years ago.

The sight of pure, blue sky filled her with longing. How she wished for a real end to winter, for warmth and wildflowers and the freedom of mild mornings and sunny afternoons. Not that the winter had been hard, as winters go, but it had been wearisome with the calls of duty, the constant travelling, the entertaining of ambassadors, the continuous comings and goings that the work of negotiating the treaty had brought with it.

She leaned back against the rough and twisted trunk and accepted the weariness which flowed over her. It was not simply three days of travel, nor even the demands of the preceding months, that made her feel so weary, it was something more difficult to name.

Stillness was a part of it. There had been so little time to be still. No time to tend her garden, or read a manuscript, or make a note of something she had observed on one of her visits to the healing sanctuary she had set up in the buildings that had once been Alcelcius's villa. There was never time to sit in the sun, or by a fireside. Always there was some call of need or duty. She sighed as men and horses settled to rest and the sound of their activity faded away into silence.

'My Lady, I have brought your noonbread.'

'Patrick!' she exclaimed, surprised he could have approached without a sound.

She turned towards the slim, white-clad figure who leaned towards her. With the light behind him, she could not see his face, only a radiance surrounding him and his long, pale fingers offering her bread wrapped in a clean cloth.

'I saw you walk apart, my Lady. But you must eat and drink. There will be feasting at Tara, but the warriors tell me it is many hours away yet.'

Deara looked up at the strong lines of the lean, weather-beaten face. Of the boy who had offered her a woven cross on the hill of Brolla a mere four summers ago, there was little trace. In his place, there stood a young man with all the presence of a warrior. But the strength which all felt and some had come to fear sprang from his dark, far-seeing eyes, his litheness of body and mind and not from any prowess with stave or sword, nor any skill learned on the Long Field.

She smiled wryly and broke the bread in the cloth. 'Did they also tell you that the distance from their gates to the door of their guest house is likely to take just as long?'

'No, my Lady,' he replied honestly, 'they spoke only of feasting and music, chariot racing, sports and entertainments. And of the splendour of Niall's court.'

She looked up at him and smiled. Sometimes, looking at him, she felt a love more sudden, more compelling even than her love for her son, Brendan, now always at his father's side, their looks and their manner so alike no stranger ever had to ask if they were kin.

'Patrick, I fear the welcome of Tara more than the weariness of this long road from Emain.'

'Fear, my Lady.'

She heard him repeat the word softly, not as a question, but rather to test it better. Often he was so sharp he reminded her of Merdaine, for as each year passed it seemed he possessed yet more of her seeing eye. Patrick's gaze penetrated the swirling mists that surround the surface of things to reach what is otherwise unseen. He was looking at her now in the way that so many feared. But she was grateful.

214

From Patrick, she had neither the wish nor the need to conceal the burden she carried.

'Yes, Patrick. Fear. I have confessed to none save you and our God. But I can give you no reason should you ask me. There is no cause I could point to. Why, even Sennach, the most cautious of friends, insists that all the signs are good and that he has never seen more hope of a binding treaty. And Lord Morrough, God rest his soul, was sure that a treaty would be signed. Indeed, he believed that once it was, Father Patrick would himself be given a hearing. That was not the judgement of a sick man, Patrick. While you were at Candida Casa, studying with the good fathers, Morrough spent as many hours with the ambassadors as did the King and his judgement was his own till the hour of his passing.'

Tears sprang unbidden to her eyes at the thought of Morrough and the devotion with which he had spent his final years in the pursuit of peace.

'I wish I could feel more hope,' she continued. 'On such a day as this, when all rejoice in the sunlight and the promise of newness of life, why should I feel such a shadow on my heart, Patrick?'

Patrick unhooked a grey metal cup from his belt, poured wine from a leather flagon and handed it to her, his eyes never leaving her face: 'Perhaps, my Lady, Tara is still a place of unhealed memories. When your sister welcomed us to the church at Meevay, Father Patrick told me of your mother's captivity. It must be hard for you to go to Tara.'

She nodded, touched by his perceptiveness. 'You would have been right the first time, Patrick. And the second. And perhaps even the third. But it is thirty-five years now since my mother took horse for Emain, riding to her death and my birth. I still grieve for her grief, but how can I continue to mourn my own loss, I who have everything of which she was deprived, my freedom, my work, my home and my loved ones?'

'And so, being thus aware, you feel all the more deeply the grief of others,' he suggested, 'for all the misfortunes which can come upon them through no fault of their own.'

'You are thinking of Lisbane and Carnbanna?'

'Yes, my Lady, I am. And every settlement put to the sword, burnt, pillaged and despoiled, in future years, should this treaty fail.'

Deara fell silent. In those first weeks after the great battle with the lake raiders, Patrick had followed her like a shadow. He had seen her weep as the bodies were piled high on the funeral pyres and hold herself rigid as the procession of women and children threw herbs and flowers into the flames that consumed the mortal remains of those they loved.

Until Father Patrick returned from his new foundation that autumn and the school was reopened by some of his followers, she had cared for him, taught him Greek, given him charge of Alcelcius's library and her own notes and manuscripts. In the year that followed, when he had outstripped his fellows and asked if he might go to study in Albi, it was she who made it possible for him to go and she who had missed him more than anyone.

Now she was to be parted from him again. In a few months' time, at the end of summer, he would be going to Gaul to study at Lerins. It might be years before she saw him again. She forced herself to return to the present, took the cup of wine he handed her and asked him if he had eaten.

'No, my Lady,' he replied. 'Each day of this Holy week, we fast till sunset.'

She nodded and considered what she should say. Good man though Father Patrick was, his rigorous use of fasting disturbed her. He seemed to live on air himself, eating only when to refuse to eat would give offence to a host or a patron. But it was hard on those who followed him. Patrick, son of Milchu, once a round faced and plump country boy, was now a shadow of his former self, though fasting was not the only reason for the change. Father Patrick's constant journeyings through the length and breadth of Ireland would tax any man, but so devoted was Milchu's son, he would not be parted from him.

'Very well then, Patrick. Till sunset you fast, as Father Patrick bids you. Tonight, at the feast, you will eat carefully, but generously, as I bid you.'

'And you, my Lady?' His voice was soft and in his eyes she read a question far deeper than any enquiry as to her physical well-being.

'I have no appetite,' she replied flatly.

'I wish your kinswoman were here. She would see what I cannot see and find the means to salve it,' he burst out unexpectedly.

'My sister Julia?'

He shook his head. 'No, my Lady, not Julia. The kinswoman I mean is Deirdre of Anacarrig, she who brought you from Emain to the hill of Brolla . . . after the fire.'

Deara felt her heart leap. It was not that she had not thought of Deirdre. Often and often she had gone back over their meetings and their talk together, as the years had passed, but hearing Deirdre's name spoken by one who had actually known her brought an unexpected joy.

'You remember her, then, Patrick? I can hardly believe that, you were so shocked and distressed by all that had happened and she was with me so short a time.'

'I shall never forget her, my Lady,' he protested vigorously. 'You had comforted me and said many wise things, but when she looked

216

at me, I knew she saw what it was I had to do. She sees what should be and asks us each to play our part, even if she does not know what her own part is. That is why I offered up my sword, there and then, though I did not understand why I had done it till I was away in Albi.'

Deara nodded, a smile on her lips. He was right, of course. Deirdre didn't know what her part was, yet she had power to make things happen, but only when she had faith in herself. As she had said herself, she had used her mind in ways that were wrong for her. It was her heart she needed to listen to before she allowed her mind its proper part.

'When will she come again, my Lady?' Patrick asked, after a little silence.

'In my deepest need, if I trust that it will be so,' she found herself replying. 'Pray that my faith be strengthened, Patrick, for my spirit is so weary. However brave we are and however much love we give, sometimes, there are times when all we can do is wait. Wait and pray. Not struggle to understand and act. Simply be still and accept that, for the moment, our part is done or has not yet come.'

From the road below, the long rousing notes of a horn echoed and vibrated. She stirred herself and said: 'Come, my dear, let us share this cup. I shall eat my noonbread by and by.' She thought of Deirdre as she raised the cup. 'To our journey and our purpose, and to all who wish us well, wherever they may be.'

She drank half the wine and passed the cup to Patrick. Without taking his eyes from her face, he drained it.

'My Lady, let me go before you to pick the gentlest path,' he said, as she rose and they set off down the rough slope to where the rest of the company were assembling for the next stage of the journey.

It was late afternoon when they halted briefly for the last time to let the horses drink again before the final stage of the journey. Deara turned to her companion and smiled: 'Thank you for your company, Sennach, it has shortened the way and eased the weariness, but I think I may have to leave you now.'

'I suspect your son brings you news,' Sennach replied, nodding towards a small figure approaching them on a grey mare.

Deara watched Brendan rein in his horse and bow to them both. For three days now he had ridden with his father and the warriors and the change in his bearing was clear to her. It was Niall's wish that Brendan be fostered at Tara as his father had been before him, and Brendan well understood it would be the equivalent of a hostile act to refuse this honour at such a time.

'Greetings, Mother. Greetings, Sennach. My Lord the King asks me to bring you this message, Mother. The road is ever dustier and will be worse when the escort arrives, but if you can bear it for his sake, he would wish you by his side.'

'Thank you, Brendan. Tell your father I will come as soon as my mare has drunk her fill.'

They watched him ride back, the sun glinting on his metal collar and inlaid belt, an upright figure, tall for his eleven years, yet seeming so small on the full-grown mare of which he was so proud.

'My child is now my son, Sennach,' she said, a hint of sadness in her voice.

'And your old teacher, even older,' he replied easily.

Deara smiled at him, grateful for the lightness of his remark, though she knew well enough he read the heaviness of her heart. Dear Sennach. She had been wrong, quite wrong about him. She had feared she would lose him through illness, this man who had always looked pale and thin. But Sennach had flourished in these last years. Still just as pale and thin, his hair long gone grey, he looked older than his sixty summers and yet he never flagged.

When Ferghal himself had come from the Hall of Council and lain upon her couch, exhausted from the demands of the negotiations, Sennach would shortly appear, documents in hand, freshly drawn, to ask for his signature, even before he had recovered himself enough to ask for a cup of wine. She often wondered how Merdaine would account for Sennach's stamina, or whether she would say that it was not something to be explained, simply something to give thanks for.

'You teach me still, Sennach,' she said gently, as she drew her young mare from the watering trough and turned her towards the rough margin of the roadway where Ferghal waited. As she approached, they parted to let her through to his side.

'Thank you, my love. It will be very dusty, I fear. Look!' He ran his hand along the neck of his stallion. Where he had rubbed, the skin showed black, the rest was grey.

'Perhaps if we are very travel stained, Niall will shorten the speeches or even ask for less of them.'

Ferghal laughed and signalled to his herald. 'Unless Niall is a changed man, more probably he and his Lords will blow our dust away with the wind of their rhetoric.'

Only minutes later, the noise of their progress was drowned by the arrival of the escort. In full regalia, preceded by horns and banners, the choicest warriors of Tara galloped towards them at full speed, swirled round them and urged them to make speed with cries and shouts. Thus, as custom required, the guests were hastened towards the gates of Tara to begin the elaborate rituals of welcome, which always left Deara longing for a solitude and a tranquillity that she knew lay more than a week away.

'Greetings Ferghal, son of Brendan, of the noble house of Ui Neill, King of Ulster, victor of Lisbane and Carnbanna, defender of the freedom of our land.'

218

Thus were the members of the Royal party greeted, each by name, genealogy, rank and epithet, one by one. And one by one, they responded with greetings and compliments and a concern for the health of the one who had greeted them. The elaborate procedure embraced not only Ferghal and Deara, and their son Brendan, but extended to the counsellors led by Sennach and Deirchu, the warrior guard, the poet, the bard and the scribes. It also included Father Patrick and his small entourage, Patrick, son of Milchu of Voclut and Patrick, son of Dairmid of Dalriada. Only when it was all completed were they able to dismount. By then Deara felt wearier than she had ever felt before, after such a journey.

It surprised her, for she had ridden with Ferghal as far and further over these four summers past, visiting every corner of the Kingdom of Ulster and its immediate neighbours. She wondered if it was just the noise. As the years passed, she found the noise of the crowds, the press of so many people, albeit well-wishers, harder and harder to bear.

At this moment, wherever her eye rested there was a tumult of people. On every vantage point overlooking the great courtyard, servants and slaves had gathered to see the arrival of the largest of the delegations to the talks. Every warrior in Tara stood in attendance on their arrival and a line of grooms awaited the moment when they would be permitted to dismount.

Then the speeches began.

Deara listened carefully, but not to the words. They were familiar enough and not significantly different from what she had heard many times before. It was the tone she was trying to gauge. Laoghaire always welcomed them with true pleasure. Committed to Ferghal since the days when Ferghal's fosterage was more in the nature of hostage taking, Laoghaire now looked on them as his dearest friends. Only with Deara had he been able to shed tears of grief and despair for his beloved Cumenora, the wife who died in childbed only two years after their marriage. He had refused all pressure to remarry and provide heirs for the throne of Tara. Like Morrough, with whom he had struck up a strange, close friendship, only the bringing of peace was of any importance to him after Cumenora's death. This task seemed to comfort a loss that he could neither heal nor forget.

As the speeches continued, it soon became clear that Laoghaire was no longer alone in offering generous words of welcome. Speech after speech made reference to the victory at Lisbane and Carnbanna and Ulster's role in seeking to protect the whole island from any danger that might threaten any one part of it.

As she listened, Deara began to wonder if she were being foolish, if she had allowed her fatigue or her imagination to stir up some deep anxiety of her own, some sense of dread that rose unbidden, whenever

219

she thought of Tara and of all that hung upon the events of the coming week.

The guest cups were brought at last and then it was the turn of Ferghal, as leader of the Ulster delegation, to deliver an elaborately formal and suitably extended address, thanking Tara for the welcome they had provided. Much interrupted by cheers and the drumming of swords on shields, he made the best of the more creditable achievements of Tara and carefully overlooked the various attempts to put an end to the talks that had emanated from that source, including the attempt to create dissension among the smaller kingdoms. Of the most serious matter of all, the finding of Tara gold in the money belts of the raiders from the great lake, together with the mystery of who had attacked and sacked Emain, he said nothing at all. When he embraced Laoghaire in the customary manner at the end of his speech, the cheers of the assembled company brought tears to her eyes.

It was not unusual for Niall to delay his appearance when guests were being greeted. Deara often wondered if he found the rituals on which he insisted as tedious as she did herself. As time passed, however, and he still did not appear, she found herself growing ever more tense. The sense of dread Laoghaire's warm welcome had softened came upon her again. And then, as the sun sank, turning the sky from blue to pale gold, the great doors of the King's Hall were thrown open, horns rang out and amid the deafening roar of Tara's massed warriors, Niall appeared.

Deara felt the blood drain from her face as silence fell. The tall, powerfully built man to whom she had bowed only a year ago, now tottered towards them, bent and wasted, his hair and beard white, his bony hands clutching at his sleeves. The hush was so intense she could hear the tiny clicks of the wooden shingles on the roof of the King's Hall contracting in the fresh evening breeze. Further off, she could even hear the squeak of a spit in one of the kitchens and further off again the lowing of cattle from the water-meadows beyond the Royal Hill.

Niall hesitated, his steps faltering. He looked bemused. At Emain, any man as reduced as this by the crab sickness would be in the care of the healing sanctuary, unless it was his express wish to die by his own hearth. Why had Laoghaire sent no news, why had he not told them that Tara would so soon have a new King? Looking at the bent and emaciated figure, gazing so helplessly about him, she judged that no more than a few weeks of life could be left to him, and yet it seemed as if Niall were not at all aware of his illness.

At that moment, another figure strode from the dark space of the open doors. Dark-haired, bearded, red-faced and stout, he came to the King's side and offered an arm. Niall took it gratefully. Together, they moved slowly to where their guests stood waiting.

Niall's watery eyes were bloodshot and unfocused as he looked at them unseeingly, his voice weak and hesitant as he said: 'I greet you Morrough, King of Ulster, and you Merdaine, Lady of Emain, and you my son-to-be, Ferghal, Prince of Ulster.'

Deara took Ferghal's arm as she curtseyed low to the stricken King. Without it, she was sure she would never have been able to rise again, for her heart had leapt so that she felt she could not breathe. A dark tide of fear and apprehension swept over her as she recognised the man on whose arm Niall leant his frail body and from whom he drew his strength. They had not met for eighteen years, but she would never forget the man who had demanded her death and had fled Emain in disgrace when she had won the favour of Morrough.

The man who now stared back at her was Conor, son of Art, sometime King's Druid to Morrough of Emain.

The talks did not begin the following day as they had expected. Niall had given orders that his guests were to be entertained for three days, that they might rest and recover from their journey, and Laoghaire was delighted to carry out his wishes.

The warm spring sunshine, the holiday atmosphere and the good spirits of all around her merely served to increase the burden Deara felt she was carrying. She had to make an effort to smile and to be friendly and forthcoming, not only with the women of the court, but equally with the Lords and Princes from the far corners of the land, many of whom she and Ferghal had visited in the four years since the victory over the lake raiders.

The saddest part of her distress was Ferghal's lack of response when she told him about the anxiety Conor had called up in her. He had held her in his arms, stroked her hair and been gentle, as they whispered in the darkness of their bedchamber, knowing full well guest houses have paper-thin walls and eavesdroppers to profit from them. He had reminded her how weary she was, because of the effort she was making, day by day, to strengthen the bonds they had forged with friends and allies. But he could see no danger himself. Niall was old and ill. He had always been preoccupied with signs and omens. Given he had only a short time to live, his dependence on a fat Druid was hardly a matter of substance. In effect, Laoghaire was already King of Tara and neither of them could doubt his commitment to the cause they all held dear.

Deara had made an effort to collect herself and when Laoghaire suggested they ride out to view the first foals of the season, she welcomed the opportunity gladly. Perhaps away from the oppressiveness of the court and the continuous noise and bustle as each new delegation arrived, she might feel more herself.

The morning was beautiful. The sun was warm, but the air still had that new-wine freshness so soon lost as the season moves on towards summer. The trees were leafing at the southern end of the enclosure where the mares stood with their foals, the buttercups already knee-high round their long legs.

Laoghaire's party dismounted and moved in twos and threes along the hurdle fence. Some had brought titbits for the mares to coax them closer. To her surprise, Deara found the large figure of Laoghaire himself at her side. He waited till the others had moved away and then spoke quietly to her: 'Deara, my friend, a word while we can. There is a matter I could not speak of when we were at table, something that may have caused hurt between us, and I cannot bear it so.'

Deara looked up at him in surprise. The most open of men, Laoghaire was never one to hide his true feelings. She loved him for it, but knew that, like Ferghal himself, it was not a strength for many of the tasks that fell to him. Often, she thought his openness would leave him exposed to those who did not wish him well, the shadowy figures who inhabit every court, breeding intrigue and mischief amongst those jealous of his claim to the throne. Of Niall's many sons, only Laoghaire had been born in wedlock, to a woman Niall had bullied and mistreated for most of her short life.

'You were shocked, Deara, were you not, to see my father's state?' he continued.

'Yes, I was. Has it been a very sudden failing?'

'Yes, I think you would say so,' he replied quietly. 'But its beginning is not recent. The first signs appeared last summer. You must wonder that I did not send you word or ask your advice.'

'Advice, no, Laoghaire,' she said gently. 'Your healers here at Tara have long taught me. But word, yes. We should have shared your concern and held you yet more closely in our thoughts.'

'You mean your prayers,' he said with a gentle smile.

She nodded. 'You must know that we pray for you.'

'Yes, I do know. Even if I cannot pray for myself, I could never reject your prayers or the love Emain holds for me.'

Deara saw the shadow pass across his face as he spoke, the sign of a sadness she knew well. Two years ago, when the hurt of Cumenora's death was still sharp, he had asked to see the church at Brolla. She had taken him, knowing what his thoughts might be, for Cumenora had come from a Christian family in Cambria. She had seen him moved by the simple service, but later he said he could not bring himself to believe in a God who would strike down so good and holy a woman as Cumenora.

'Deara, I could not send you word,' he explained, 'because Niall would not allow it. When the illness first appeared, he made me swear a vow, both on the seal of Tara and on the grave of Cumenora, that no hint of his weakness go abroad. He was so strong in his demands, I feared to deny him. Will you forgive me for that?'

'There is nothing to forgive, my dear,' she reassured him. 'It is often thus with the mortally ill, their wishes brook no denial. Often indeed, a denial can hasten the course of the illness.'

She watched the relief spread over his face and easement come to the set of his shoulders, as he nodded vigorously: 'So I was told by Maeve and this young man, new come from Gaul, whose name I cannot bring to my tongue.'

'Aesclepius?' she offered, smiling to herself.

Laoghaire was no scholar. Only on the most delicate of matters could he bring himself to use manuscript. News from Laoghaire still came in the old way, by herald.

'That is but one of his names,' he replied. 'He is not content with one name like ordinary men. He has three or more and I can command none of them. What think you of him?'

'As a man, vain, petty and conceited,' she pronounced firmly. 'As a doctor, well-read, keen as his own scalpel, but never to be found guilty of pity.'

Laoghaire looked at her sharply: 'You are right. As you always are about such things. I felt my judgement false, because I so dislike the man, but it is so. He told me last month I should measure my head to the crown, that it would not be many weeks before I had it from the bier.'

'And does Niall know of this judgement?'

'Maeve tells me that he did speak with Niall. He was angry when his medicines were refused, as Maeve's were too. Niall does not believe he is ill. To him, the illness is an illusion, the cause of which will soon be made clear to us all. He has forbidden anyone to speak of his illness except his Druid, who interprets the signs for him. That is why he will not let anyone else care for him now.'

Deara leaned on the wooden fence to look out over the green hillside where the foals stood by their dams, long-legged and gentle eyed, watching the moving figures. Almost pure white and still unsure of the capacity of her four legs, the smallest and newest foal nuzzled at her mother. The mare bent down and began to lick her.

'Laoghaire, did you know that this Conor, son of Art, was once King's Druid to Morrough?' she asked quietly.

'No. I did not.' He looked suddenly grave.

'Nor then could you know that he demanded my death in the Hall of Council three days after the death of Merdaine.'

Visibly startled, he wanted to know what could have led to such an appeal.

'He argued that I was a witch. I had bewitched Merdaine when she was spirit-lost and had called upon Nodons to carry off her soul.

223

I owe my life to Morrough and Conor owes a debt of malice to Emain for so dismissing his council. Laoghaire, I am afraid that in some way I cannot see he will come between you and Ferghal and between Tara and Emain. Already I feel his shadow lies between Ferghal and me.'

'Ferghal and you? But that cannot be,' he protested. 'You are as dear to Ferghal as life itself. He would be half the man he is without your love and your counsel.'

The deep concern in his voice, the hand that moved to touch her shoulder, was almost too much for her. She wiped a tear hastily from her cheek and tried to collect herself.

'It is nothing, Laoghaire. Forgive me,' she managed to say, steadily enough. 'I am just anxious because Ferghal cannot see any danger. He thinks I am tired, which I am, and being womanish, which perhaps I am too, for we are all subject to our own weakness, but I cannot lift this fear from my heart, that there is some malice waiting to strike down all we have achieved.'

'Have you spoken of this to anyone save Ferghal?'

'Only to Patrick of Dalriada,' she replied, 'who sees into my heart whether I like it or not. He is wiser than his years and absolutely to be trusted.'

Laoghaire nodded his agreement and after a long pause, said: 'Deara, I have been foolish. I have been so concerned with our plans and with the obvious threats to them from within Tara that I have neglected this man. I know nothing of him, who his friends are, or where he has come from. I will make amends this very day. I will set my most trusted friends to find out all they can. But what can I do to make amends to you, my dear friend, who have borne this anxiety since your coming?'

Deara smiled and shook her head. 'Your words are all I need, Laoghaire. I have felt such a burden on my heart and now you help me bear it. If my fears are groundless and if we are toasting the new treaty in a week's time, why, I shall be the happiest woman in Tara.'

'And I the happiest man, Deara.'

They had been walking slowly along the boundary of the field, keeping away from the clusters of guests who were coaxing the mares to the hurdles and feeding them titbits. Suddenly, Laoghaire caught her arm. 'Look, you can see all the foals from here,' he declared. 'Which do you favour? Give it a name and it is yours. Let it be a successor to your beloved Sabu.'

'Oh Laoghaire, you can't,' she responded laughing. 'I might pick your favourite.'

'So be it,' he said gaily. 'Name it and I shall be happy again.'

She looked at him and then pointed to a foal, close to the hurdle fence they stood by: 'That's the one, Laoghaire, the small, white one. I name her Hope. If Hope should flourish, then in a year's time I shall take her from the King's hand.'

'Meanwhile, Hope will be lovingly cherished for your sake.'

All afternoon Deara and Maeve, the most experienced of the healers at Tara, had been sitting in a sheltered corner of the herb garden, talking about herbs and healing; of the new eye medicines that had come from the east; of the work of the healing sanctuary near Emain, the infusions which Maeve had found so effective with the most recent outbreak of summer fever; and of the skill of Aesclepius, the surgeon.

They were deep in talk when the trumpets and horns rang out once more and from the halls and kitchens, storerooms and guardrooms, the court gathered to greet the latest and last arrival, Cathal Rhu, Prince of Oriel.

Deara had been surprised when Laoghaire's half-brother had not appeared sooner. Unlike the Princes from Connaught, he did not have a long journey, nor, like the Princes from Munster, a difficult one, for his princedom lay close by between Tara and Emain. She wondered if perhaps he enjoyed making an entrance like his father, Niall. From the tumultuous noise she could hear, it sounded as if his delay had indeed produced the desired effect.

They paused in their talk, as the sound rose in great roaring cheers and then subsided. Then Maeve said, quite sharply: 'Would that Aesclepius had been free to ply his craft last autumn, my dear, that we might be spared a while longer the tumult of Niall's passing.'

'Do you think he could have saved him?' Deara asked, surprised.

'He could have done much more than I could,' the older woman replied briskly. 'The tumours of this sickness can be removed, I have heard, if the sufferer is still fit and well, and the surgeon has as sharp an eye as this young fellow has.'

'So how did you advise the King, Maeve?'

Maeve laughed a short, hard laugh. 'No one has advised Niall these six or seven years since, except a certain Prince of Oriel, I might guess. And his Druid, whom I hear does ever join the hunting party, but is never there at the kill. Conor, his name is. A man of smiles and a smooth tongue. Last autumn, he came to Tara and since then he has fed Niall vain hopes, though to what end I cannot guess. He is not a man to act in kindness and I can see no benefit it might bring him.'

Deara nodded. Maeve had neither the vision of Merdaine nor the sympathy of Grannia, but of the few women she could speak to freely, Maeve was the shrewdest. She had known her for twenty years now, since that first meeting when Merdaine had brought her to Tara and set her to work collecting seeds while she and Maeve talked in this same sheltered corner.

'I know this man Conor, Maeve. I am sure he has some evil scheme afoot. I am sure it will bring great harm to us all, but I cannot see what's to be done.'

She paused and fell silent. A dark suspicion had re-entered her mind. It had come often enough in the weeks after the raid on Emain. Now it returned with a flash of certainty. The raid on Emain had come from Oriel. In vain the scouts had followed the day old tracks, only to find them double back, disperse and disappear, so that no direction could be guessed at. No survivor was left to tell of any favour the raiders had worn, or any battle cry they used. In their headlong flight to the safety of the woods, no woman or child had caught even the merest glimpse of them.

Deara recalled Aillech telling her mother that Niall's father was so superstitious he would rather face an army twice the size of his own than risk a woman's curse. Perhaps superstition ran in the family. If it affected Niall and his favourite son that would explain the ease with which Conor had been able to establish his hold over them.

She looked up and found Maeve watching her with concern: 'But why should you see?' she asked. 'It will no doubt end on a battlefield. The evil of men usually does.'

'And what of the evil of women?' Deara retorted.

'The same place, but by different steps,' Maeve replied promptly. 'Show me the man that lusts for power as does Niall, and I will show you the woman who has infected him. You did not know Niall's mother. Had you done so, you would understand for yourself.'

Maeve stopped speaking, looked at her young companion closely and shook her head. 'Come, what we cannot change, we must bear,' she continued. 'I have had such pleasure from your company, I would not see you distressed by this talk of ours. Shall we have a cup of wine together to lift our spirits?'

With an effort, Deara put all thought of Conor and the fiery Prince of Oriel out of her mind: 'I should like nothing better than to sit here while the light fades away,' she said. 'But the Great Hall is laid with yet more tables and I must prepare myself for such a distinguished company.'

Maeve reached out and took her hands: 'At this moment, I wish I were a wise woman like Aillech or Merdaine for they would offer you words of counsel. But you see further than I already, for I know only of herbs.'

She paused as if she had just remembered something. She walked a little way into the herb garden, peered at the plants in the fading light, bent down to pick a small, branching spray and brought it to her.

'Here, my dear,' she said, as she handed it to Deara. 'Put a leaf of this in each of your shoes tonight and each night you are here at Tara. It has no curative properties that I can find, but an old man I once met vowed that each leaf is made of three hearts – one for courage, one for

226

love and one for faith. Take it, and good fortune be with you. Come again when you can and we shall talk only of poultices and preparations.'

Deara looked down at the spray of tiny leaves in her hand. *Trifolium Minus*. True, she had never found it to have any special properties, but she was touched by Maeve's gesture and pleased by the old man's words: 'Thank you, Maeve,' she said gently. 'I'll do just as you say. And I will come again as soon as I can.'

Leaving her friend, she hurried between the wooden buildings of the east side and made her way north and west, through narrow ways and across dusty open spaces, towards the guest house that stood beyond the Great Hall. Suddenly, a white-clad figure appeared at her side and offered her greetings.

'Patrick!' she exclaimed, delighted to see him. 'Where are you going? The tables are not yet laid.'

'And the sun is not yet set, Lady,' he replied gravely. 'I go to Cumenora's chapel. Laoghaire has said that all who wish to keep the holy days and hours of this week may do so there without fear. Each day, more of his people come to be with us. As they have no priest, they ask Father Patrick to baptise them. He has baptised over a hundred in these three days.'

'That is good news, good news indeed.'

'But you, my Lady, have had bad news,' he said, looking at her closely.

As he spoke, she caught the merest glimpse of a figure moving in the shadows beyond where they stood. She brushed her finger across her lips, as if a stray hair had blown in the slight evening breeze.

'See, Patrick, I have been given a gift,' she said quite clearly.

His eyes met hers and studied her face as she showed him Maeve's offering.

'Courage. Faith. Love,' she said quietly, touching in turn each of the three leaves of the one sprig.

'Father, Son, and Holy Ghost,' he replied quickly. 'Three in One. One in Three. The love that will triumph even over Death. My Lady, spare me a leaf, I beg you.'

'Willingly. Here, put one leaf in each of your sandals as Maeve bid me do, then you and I will stand with seven hearts apiece.'

She dropped her voice to the barest whisper. 'Patrick, we shall surely need them, this night, or hereafter.' Raising her hand in farewell, she spoke in her normal voice again. 'Go in peace, my dear. I shall look for you in the Great Hall.'

'I shall be there, my Lady, with all the strength I can bring,' he replied solemnly, as he disappeared into the lengthening shadows and was gone.

23

It was several days after Bill Coulter's visit before I could believe something had really happened when I'd put my hands on him. Agreed, I hadn't 'just touched him and made him better' in the magical way I dreamed of when I was a child, but I couldn't deny healing had occurred, even if he'd felt much worse to begin with.

He said as much himself when I rang to make sure he was all right and to see which evening would suit Nora best to come over for a meal.

'Aye, as right as rain,' he said, laughing. 'Mind you, when you put yer hans on my shoulders, I thought ma head was goin' to blow off. An then, shure a while later, the pain just disappeared as if it had niver bin there atall.'

I was delighted to hear him in such good spirits. We made our date and I went back into the kitchen to mark it down on the calendar. I took it down and stood staring at the large coloured numbers. Sometimes I felt the only way I could keep track of time was to fix it firmly with my eye as if it were a leprechaun clutching his pot of gold.

There was no doubt time was playing tricks. One day I'd get up with a list of jobs as long as my arm and find I'd got through them with hours to spare; the next, I'd find myself dropping down exhausted somewhere after five, the perfectly sensible list I'd made at breakfast not even begun.

I knew I was preoccupied but that didn't seem a good enough reason to explain why my progress so often bore no relationship to my own estimates and predictions. It worried me. On the bad days, I thought I would never be able to finish all that had to be done before the auction, while on the good days, instead of being cheered by my progress, I felt apprehensive in case it wouldn't last.

Two weeks before my planned departure from Anacarrig, I booked my return flight, came back into the kitchen to circle it on the calendar and panicked.

Today was Thursday the twenty-sixth. There were only four more days left in June. I turned the page, ignored the soothing image of cricket on The Mall and ran my finger across the first week of July. I'd promised to spend two nights with Helen in Belfast before she went abroad. Mary and Hector were coming for a meal and to say goodbye to the garden. Mr Neill was on holiday, so I'd have to mow the lawns myself and Mother's car had to be sold . . .

The day of the auction was Monday 7 July. The auctioneer's men would remove the larger items the next day leaving me a day to clear up before my morning flight on the Thursday, the day Carol and Robert were moving in. In fourteen days' time I would be back in London, a whole week before Matthew had even left Maharajpur.

Tears came to my eyes as I caught up a white Biro embossed in gold. 'Hendersons of Armagh – for all your garden and leisure requirements' I read as I stroked off the previous day.

'And what about Deara?' I whispered to myself.

It was five days now since we'd been together at Emain, but it had felt more like five years. I thought about her continuously. Now, more than ever, after my experience with Bill Coulter, I needed to talk to her, to ask her about this gift of healing that we shared.

I stood by the window, thinking how I could possibly make contact with her. As far as I could see there was no formula for getting to Deara, no magic words, no trick or spell. At various times I'd tried closing my eyes, focusing on her, imagining her in the room, but although all these strategies brought a kind of comfort, they hadn't had the slightest effect in bringing us together. I had to accept my meetings with Deara had a logic to them I couldn't perceive.

And if that were so, and I was now sure it was, there was nothing I could do, absolutely nothing. And I couldn't bear that because I so hate feeling helpless. Surely there must be something I could do.

I stared out at the sunshine pouring down on the deep borders full of spicy smelling lupins and peony roses, deep pink and sweetly perfumed, until the silence was broken by a large bumble bee, who zoomed in through the open window, did a circuit of the kitchen, changed his mind and tried to fly out again. He landed on the central pane of the window, buzzed angrily and made frantic efforts to escape.

'Come on, silly,' I encouraged him, as I used one of my many lists to shepherd him in the right direction. But he wouldn't have it. The open window was a mere three inches from the fixed pane he was climbing up so ineffectually.

'Oh well, if you insist,' I said, laughing at his determination.

I fetched a postcard from the letter rack, a dry tumbler from the cupboard, and caught him without knocking the pollen off his legs, the way Daddy had taught me to when I was a little girl. Buzzing furiously still in his glass prison, I carried him to the back door, stepped outside and took the card away from the mouth of the glass. He roared off into the blue at enormous speed and left me laughing at myself.

Deara would enjoy the joke. I would tell her I had been buzzing furiously, trying to get to her, when all the time there was an open window right beside me. Assuming always that there was and that I could find it.

The thought calmed and comforted me, which was as well for only hours later, just as I'd arrived back from Armagh with a stack of velvet curtains from the dry cleaners, the phone rang. It was Sandy.

'How's it going, Dee? You must be fed up washing down all that white woodwork.'

This was Sandy in her helpful mode, so I didn't point out that I'd finished cleaning that weeks ago. But I did tell her about the central heating and reassured her it was only a small repair, sketched out how things were going forward and told her that I hadn't forgotten about Mother's car. As she seemed to be in such good spirits, I even risked asking her advice about selling it.

'You do whatever's easiest, Dee,' she replied warmly. 'You've had enough hassle. You must be dying to get back to London. Aren't you missing Matthew dreadfully?'

Of course I was missing Matthew dreadfully. I'd been missing him dreadfully all the time I'd been at Anacarrig, but I couldn't really imagine Sandy phoning me in working hours to enquire if I was lonely. I waited patiently and in due course the object of the call revealed itself.

'Dee, have you managed to start on the roof space yet? It must be a hell of a sweat.'

She couldn't have missed the moment's shocked silence at my end of the line, so I didn't try to cover it up.

'I didn't even know Mother used the roof space. I never remember anything being up there except the big suitcases and she got rid of those.'

'Oh, don't worry, Dee. I should have mentioned it sooner. I think she only started using it after you went to Queen's. I'll pop over and give you a hand with it,' she said cheerfully.

'Yes, you can go up the ladder, you know my head for heights,' I said, laughing.

I thought she was joking about giving me a hand, but she wasn't. A few minutes later she asked me to collect her from Aldergrove on Friday night and drop her back on Sunday afternoon in time to connect with her German flight from Heathrow. And had I another pair of jeans she could wear or did she need to bring some with her?

I have to confess that my weekend with Sandy was far better than I'd expected. After skating round most of Friday clearing her room, which I'd been using as a parking space for the stuff I was sorting, shopping for more food and cooking something proper for supper, I just managed to arrive at Aldergrove as she was picking up her suitcase from the baggage carousel. She was still in the best of spirits.

She enjoyed her supper, thanked me for bothering to cook, asked for a tour of the garden and later, picking up some of my library books from the table in the sitting room, wanted to know if I was working on a commission for Robert F. or if this Celtic stuff was a new interest of my own.

It was nice to be reminded of the best side of my variable younger sister and when I went to bed on Friday night I found myself hoping against hope that her good mood would continue once we started on the serious work in the morning.

'Is there anything there?' I called from the foot of the ladder as she slid the trapdoor aside and flashed her torch around.

I blinked rapidly as a small shower of dust and plaster descended. Then, to my surprise, a light came on, Sandy's blue bottom disappeared from view and I heard a muffled exclamation: 'God Almighty.'

The roof space was packed with cardboard boxes full of papers. It looked as if every letter, document, bank statement, stock list or inventory relevant to Henderson's since our father's death had been parcelled, labelled and stored. Each box had a detailed list of contents on the outside. When we started opening them, we found duplicate lists on the inside as well.

It took us the whole day to get them all down, shred them by hand and drop the remains into dozens of waste-paper sacks, but it took Sandy only about ten minutes to find what she was looking for.

'Can you grab this one if I lower it as far as I can?' she said, peering down through the open trapdoor. 'The light's not great up here. Anyway, I'll need a Stanley knife to get through all this Sellotape.'

I climbed halfway up the ladder, clutched the box and ducked as Sandy's legs dropped back into view.

'Cross your fingers, Dee. This box might be worth a bob or two,' she said, grinning.

Inside, we found all the correspondence relating to the sale of Henderson's to the consortium. And that was the really big shock, for we discovered Mother hadn't sold out at all. She'd retained fifty-one percent of the shares. It explained why there was no document at the bank, and removed all question of there being tax to pay. It also meant there would be a sizeable sum coming to each of us in addition to what we were getting from the sale of the house.

Sandy insisted on taking me out for a celebration dinner 'on our prospects' and offered me cash to keep me going till the sale of the house came through. And she worked feverishly right through Sunday morning, so I wouldn't have all the mess to clear up by myself.

All through Saturday and the Sunday morning she talked about what she would do with her half of the shares. On Saturday she favoured selling them and adding some higher risk investments to her existing portfolio. Whereas by Sunday morning, she had moved on to the idea of claiming her seat on the board of Henderson's and using her skills to increase the value of the shares before she sold them.

When I finally dropped her at Aldergrove I was so exhausted from humping boxes and having had someone talking excitedly to me all weekend that the thought of driving to Belfast for my two days with Helen appalled me. But I spent the rest of the day very quietly and by the time I set off on Monday morning I was in good spirits, only a little dimmed by the fact that I had still had no contact with Deara.

We all know you can only say some things to some people but the contrast between what was sayable to Sandy and what to Helen hit me hard during my two days with her. In the whole of my weekend with Sandy, I never once considered mentioning Deara.

When I confessed my anxiety that I'd not see her again before I left, Helen was such a comfort. She told me I mustn't worry about meeting Deara. I'd simply have to trust that either I would get to her, or she would come to me. She was sure it would happen, but probably when I was least expecting it. She was absolutely positive that 'thinking' was not going to help me find a way to her.

'After all, Dee, you've said yourself, you've got into habits of thinking that tie you up in knots. You don't sit down and "think" when you write in your notebooks do you? And you're certain that's some of the best stuff you've ever written, aren't you?'

I had to agree that she was right. I also had to confess to myself, if not to Helen, that by Wednesday morning when we said our goodbyes, I could hardly wait to get back to Anacarrig to sit down and write.

For the first time since I'd arrived a whole week had passed and I'd written nothing. All I wanted to do was write and write without having to think about people or practicalities or what had to be done next. I felt so agitated, so desperate to get to my table, I didn't even register what the parcel was parked by the back door, till I'd carried it into the kitchen, ripped off the heavy-duty wrapping and saw the familiar letterpress. I stared at it blankly. How could I have forgotten? I looked at the copy date and groaned.

I worked late into the evening and got up early next morning. By four o'clock I'd finished, by five o'clock I'd despatched it first class from the temporary post office in Armagh, walked on past the bombed out remains of the old one and made my way up Abbey Street.

After hours of sitting at my table, it was so nice to be outdoors. The afternoon was warm and pleasant, the shadows of the tall stone houses were just beginning to lengthen across the pavement as I climbed the hill.

At the top, I stopped in front of the deanery and looked both ways across the wide tarmacadamed space between the hospital and the cathedral gates. Not a car or a van to be seen. Apart from the noisy chatter of sparrows in the dusty gutters on Vicarage Hill, all was silent. Then I remembered – only ambulances were allowed through the security barriers down in the town on their way to the hospital that now occupied the site of Alcelcius's villa.

I crossed into the shadowy graveyard and walked between the worn stones to the low wall at its further edge. I stood looking down on Irish Street below and then gazed out across the sprawling suburbs to where Emain lies, hidden behind the low ridge of Legacurry Hill.

Shivering as a sudden breeze caught the light fabric of my shirt, I turned back towards the graveyard. The sunshine had vanished. I stood on a bare windswept hill, the ground hard with frost, a few flakes of snow blowing in the wind. To my right, a small stone building had to be a church, for dozens of white wooden crosses sprouted round it. Within a small arch over the main door, a bell hung on a chain.

As I caught my breath in the bitter wind, a party of monks appeared to my left. They were moving slowly, winding up the hill from a single storey building a little distance away, bearing a coffin towards the door of the church. Behind the procession of monks, a party of richly dressed figures followed, their clothes and gold ornaments in sharp contrast with the bleak, grey light, the bare trees and dark robes of the monks.

My heart leapt as I recognised Deara, a long purple scarf tied over her dress, beside her a dark-haired and dark-eyed man with gold on his breast and round his waist. Immediately behind him walked a young man, his mirror image. Ferghal and Brendan. At Brendan's side a young woman walked, strong faced and pleasing to look at, but not in any way resembling Deara. Brendan's wife, perhaps, for this young man was certainly in his twenties.

I watched patiently, for I knew I could watch Deara but could not reach her, just like the evening I had stood in the shadows at Alcelcius's villa. I longed to go to her and comfort her, for she looked sad and cold, her face drawn and weary.

The last of the figures entered the church and I was alone.

'Greetings, lady.'

The voice was light, but firm. I spun round and found myself looking into a pair of dark eyes I could never forget. But the man who returned my gaze was as far from the boy who had stood with me on the Hill of Brolla as I was myself from the child who had once decorated her exercise book with vivid green shamrocks.

'Patrick!' I exclaimed.

'As always, you come in our hour of need,' he began, 'as you came

234

to Emain and to Tara. Father Patrick is dead and dissension and strife threaten our infant church.'

He looked at me as if he were expecting me to say something wise. He was carrying a crozier by his side and before I thought about it, I asked him if he was now Bishop. He seemed surprised by the question, explained it was Father Patrick's crozier, which should have been brought to the church with his coffin from the healing sanctuary where he had died. He had noticed its absence and hurried back to fetch it.

I shook my head firmly as I replied: 'No, Patrick, it is yours now. Was that not his wish?'

'Yes, it was indeed, lady,' he admitted gravely. 'But in Ireland we are not masters in our own house. I am too young for the liking of those who make decisions for us.'

I looked at him steadily and what I saw was a different Patrick: not as he now was, but dressed in rich vestments and carrying the crozier upright, as he would were he Bishop indeed. I was quite certain the crozier should be his. What is more, I realised I was angry. That Patrick's Ireland was not master of its own spiritual life made me as furious as if someone had discriminated against me because I was a woman.

'Claim it, Patrick, as Father Patrick would have wished and let the future judge the rightness of your act.'

The moment I spoke, I was looking out over the city once more, my teeth chattering furiously, my arms covered with goose pimples. I had to go and find a sunny spot and sit there till I thawed out and felt my legs would carry me back down the hill to the car.

Driving out to Anacarrig I went through and through the details of our brief meeting, but it was only that evening I registered something I'd missed completely. Patrick had said I always came in their hour of need. But he had spoken of Tara as well as Emain. So it would be at Tara that Deara and I should meet again. But nothing in his words gave a clue as to when that might be. I would simply have to get on with my own life at Anacarrig and await the moment as patiently as I could manage.

On Saturday morning I sat down at my table to make a fresh list from the much scribbled over one I was working from and found to my amazement that I had done all I could. When I copied up the jobs that hadn't been stroked off, one lot were things I wanted to finish in the garden and they could be done on Sunday, the remainder were odds and ends of shopping I could do when I went into Armagh to have my hair done. After that, the rest of the day was mine.

Suddenly, I decided I would spend my last afternoon in Armagh as a visitor. I would hang my camera round my neck, instead of hiding it in my handbag, as I always do when I'm working, and pretend I had come for the day. I would go and take all the pictures visitors take, the ones people who live here never think of taking.

The idea appealed to me and I set out in excellent spirits. As I came into the town, there was a real feeling of gaiety in the air. In Scotch Street, bunting flapped in the gentle breeze, women wore summer dresses, children licked dripping ice-creams and teenagers in shorts and bikini tops laughed at each other's jokes and looked in shop windows. The mood was infectious. I felt my spirits rise yet further.

When an Army patrol vehicle pulled out in front of me, I had to brake sharply and follow it to the control point that bars entrance to the main shopping area. Hot and sweating in their camouflage, six soldiers sat in the vehicle, their self-loading rifles under their arms, the outline of their bulletproof vests visible through the fabric of their battledress.

'If you lived here, you'd just have to get used to it. There's no use thinking about it.'

My mother's voice. It seemed weeks since I'd heard it. My good spirits evaporated like dew under a hot sun. A sudden anger took their place, the very same anger I'd felt when Patrick told me the Irish church was answerable to clerics in a different country who could impose their choice of Bishop without any respect for difference of culture or a different tradition.

It was people like my mother who allowed themselves to 'get used to' bitterness and violence, rather than act against it. It was they who created an atmosphere in which nothing could change. For half my lifetime, both communities had mourned their losses. Time and time again I had dared to hope, as people of goodwill set aside their own grief and pleaded for a different way. But so far, every peace initiative had failed, despite the passionate longing for peace felt by everyone I knew. The more I thought about it, the more it seemed to me it wasn't bombs and bullets themselves that defeated the peacemakers, it was the selfishness of people of both communities, like my mother, who would have nothing to do with any way of looking at things other than their own.

The policeman on duty at the barricade waved the army vehicle through. As I drove past him, I saw under his thin, blue summer shirt his bulletproof vest, even more obvious than those worn by the soldiers. I followed the route away from the control zone, through the area which had once been the horse market, past the jail, and down the far side of The Mall to find somewhere to park.

They were playing cricket as they had played cricket every summer Saturday of my thirty-five years. Thirteen dazzling white figures, together with the lumpy shapes of the umpires, were set like toys against the smooth green of the grass. Crowds of spectators sat in the shade of the trees, or lay on rugs in the rough grass beyond the

236

boundary. Just like the picture in the milkman's calendar on the kitchen wall at Anacarrig, it was the very image of a perfect summer's day.

I managed to park outside the Orange Hall and that was when the penny dropped. Sometimes I'm amazed how easily I can miss the blindingly obvious. The bunting, the flags, the holiday atmosphere. Next Saturday was the Twelfth of July, so today was the beginning of the Twelfth Fortnight. All over the province, factories and workplaces had shut down for the annual holiday. I'd managed to forget the one day in the Ulster year no one is ever allowed to forget, wherever they stand.

'Your kinswoman has need of you.'

I stopped abruptly and stared at the sunlight on the stone facades in Thomas Street. The cracked plaster of bomb-damage seamed the frontage of a shop I knew well.

'Your kinswoman has need of you.'

'Yes, I've got the message,' I whispered. 'But I'm not sure who needs who most.'

If it hadn't been for the hairdresser I'm sure I'd have turned on my heel and gone straight back to Anacarrig, so much was piling in on me. I passed the place where a car bomb had exploded, killing two people before the centre of the town was barricaded off. I thought of all the others maimed and killed since 1969, and then of the bodies at Emain, at Lisbane and at Carnbanna.

I felt a black curtain of despair descending on me as all my bright hope for the future drained away. And then I heard the voice again: 'Despair itself is the enemy. Do not despair. Your kinswoman has need of you.'

As if my legs were moved by the voice itself, I set off for the hairdresser's once more. If Deara did have need of me, the least I could do was keep hold of myself till we met.

It was an effort, a real effort, however, to be friendly to the girl who did my hair, for my mind was wholly preoccupied by the third repetition of the fact that Deara needed me. But she did do a wonderful job on my hair and when I stepped out again into English Street, I felt steadier.

I fingered the case of my camera as I tucked away my purse and decided to go back to my original plan. I imagined sharing the afternoon with Matthew, one dark winter evening, so I set myself an assignment to try and capture the feel of this particular summer afternoon in the city.

I needed a panoramic view to begin with, so I retraced my steps towards the cathedral grounds. I moved slowly up the steep hill, surprised to find withered leaves and sepals already drifting in the gutters. A reminder of autumn to come, here in the midst of summer.

Beyond a door in the stone wall that led to the brownie hut I'd once attended, a newly open space revealed a different perspective on the 'new' cathedral. I can laugh when people call St Patrick's Roman Catholic cathedral 'new' when it's over a century old, but what doesn't amuse me is when someone insists upon calling it 'their' cathedral. Today, the twin spires were pure white, their edges ruler sharp against the deep blue of the sky.

I wondered what Father Patrick would make of it all, or Sceto, or even the fresh-faced young country boy from Foclut. Two cathedrals each bearing their name, perched up on their opposing hills. I took a lot of pictures and used my long lens to pick out my old school, nicely framed by trees I had known as saplings. Then I went back through the wrought iron gates into the churchyard and up to the west door of St Patrick's Protestant cathedral. I put my hand to the metal ring and found the door was locked. Dismayed and puzzled, I decided I must have got the wrong door. I went round the side into the dark shadow where the grave of Brian Boru is marked by a plaque in the wall, but that door was closed as well. All the doors were locked.

I felt so upset I had to go and sit on the wall. I couldn't stop myself reading the locked doors as a sign. Perhaps they were telling me I wouldn't be able to get into Tara either.

'This won't do, Deirdre,' I whispered to myself. 'There's no way forward through anxiety, or puzzling, and least of all through despair. Come on now, you'll have to do better.'

I waited patiently, but this time no voice spoke nor helpful vision came to me. I'd have to manage for myself. What should I do next? If I were a visitor, I'd do what any self-respecting visitor would do at a quarter to four on a warm Saturday afternoon in Armagh. I would go in search of refreshment. So I set off for Armagh's only department store.

As soon as I pushed open its plate glass door, I smelt freshly brewed coffee. I took the familiar route to the Wheel and Lantern, through Gloves and Handbags. As I ordered my coffee and home-made chocolate cake, I thought of the innumerable cups of coffee I had drunk here as a teenager, undergraduate and young married.

But as I sat at my corner table, listening to the familiar accents of voices around me, I felt a strange sadness come upon me. All afternoon I'd been putting together a picture of this city that had been my home; the buildings gone, the others propped up with steel girders; the City Hall, where once I'd gone to teenage dances blown to bits, the empty space now a car park. Yet much was still so familiar, so little changed with the passage of years; The Mall with its trees, taller and shaggier, the prospect from hill to hill, the streets with old stone houses and names of shops that had been there for decades.

I looked round and realised most of the people at the crowded tables really were visitors. Then it came to me with a devastating clarity that I too would be a visitor when I came again. I finished my coffee, but couldn't eat another morsel of my very nice piece of cake. The thought of being a visitor in the place where I was born and grew up left me with no appetite at all.

As I left the coffee shop, I remembered I wanted a present for Diana's birthday. My sister-in-law is passionate about flowers so I headed for China. As I turned under the archway into the department, I saw exactly what I wanted, right in front of me.

'Oh, how lovely!'

I actually said it out loud, but happily there was no one standing by the circular display to hear me. It was set out with a fine china I had never seen before. From tiny boxes to small vases, open dishes to plant holders, a whole range of delicate objects gleamed in the concealed lighting. They were translucent white, ribbed with an upward flowing texture and scattered all over with minute green shamrocks. I had never before seen an object decorated with shamrock that I'd had the slightest wish to possess.

'Can I help you at all?' The voice was timid, hesitant.

'I'm not sure you can,' I replied, as I turned and smiled at the young assistant. 'They're so lovely, I'm spoilt for choice. What are they? Belleek? No, they can't be, they're too lively for Belleek, aren't they? Are they new?'

I stopped myself. The girl who had spoken was very young, still awkward in her smart black skirt. It was perfectly clear she didn't know anything about them.

'They're very popular with visitors,' she offered.

'I'm not surprised,' I said, as I placed two small vases side by side. One was several inches tall and would take a single bloom, a rosebud or a miniature iris. The other was smaller, but wider. A posy of violets, perhaps.

'It's a birthday present,' I said, aware that the girl was waiting patiently. 'I suppose we give what we'd like someone to give us,' I added lightly.

She grinned broadly, revealing a metal brace on her teeth: 'My young brother gives me toffees for my birthday. He knows I can't eat them.'

'At least I know my sister-in-law loves arranging flowers,' I responded, laughing. 'She wins prizes for it, so I'm on the right track.'

'I'm sure she'd like one of those,' she offered. 'Maybe you should treat yourself as well.'

I looked at the small, fragile face, the dark eyes and badly cut hair. She was standing awkwardly on one foot and had a Biro mark on the collar of her slightly crumpled white blouse. She had no idea she'd said anything exceptional, but she had. The right thing, to the right person, at the right time, Deara would say.

'What a brilliant idea,' I exclaimed. ' Now why didn't I think of that for myself?'

But I knew perfectly well why I hadn't thought of it for myself. For all the years I'd lived in Mother's world, anything I bought, or was given, was commented on, disparaged or denigrated. I'd ended up never letting myself want things.

Matthew spotted it very early on in our relationship. At first, he'd thought my reluctance to buy the things I needed was merely the legacy of the very difficult years I'd had before we met. Being short of money was still relevant, he could agree, but he managed to convince me in the end my reluctance went far beyond the question of means. He said I'd taught myself not to want, for fear I'd be denied or disappointed. And in the end, I'd had to accept he was right.

Just knowing something, however, doesn't give you any power to alter it. Standing in that china department, watching the dark-eyed girl struggle with a fierce Barclaycard machine, I knew this simple act was important. No, I couldn't explain why, but I was certain the future would be different because I had bought for myself a small vase I really wanted.

When I got back to the house I put both little vases on a small table beside me in the sitting room and settled down to a quiet evening with my books. I did mean to fill them both with water and fetch something from the garden to christen them, Diana's vase as well as mine, but after my bath I must have dozed off. When I opened my eyes it was almost dark, and it occurred to me that going into the garden in Great-uncle Matthew's beautiful dressing gown was not such a good idea.

I sat and looked at the delicate shapes. Suddenly, it struck me that for the first time in my life I'd bought something without asking the price. Immediately, I felt guilty and had to tell myself not to be silly. But I still reached out and turned them upside down to look at the price tags. They weren't there, the little assistant had peeled them off and stuck them on my receipt. All I found was the maker's name scripted in the same lively style as the scattered green shamrocks. Just two words: 'Royal Tara'.

24

The noise and heat of the Great Hall burst upon Deara before she had even entered the doors. Never had she seen such a great concourse, even at Tara. Following one of Laoghaire's heralds, she made her way with Ferghal, Sennach and Deirchu to the high table at the raised north end of the long, high-beamed building.

Trumpets and horns sounded continuously as other princes, lords, nobles and ambassadors were conducted to their places, the long tables so extended that only the smallest spaces had been left through which the servants could enter the great hollow rectangle that custom decreed should echo the shape of this most ancient hall itself.

As they made their slow progress along the narrow passageway between the trophy-hung walls and the heavy wooden benches, they received the acknowledgements and greetings of allies and friends already seated on the left side of the chamber. Only when they came to the raised platform, and Ferghal offered her his hand to mount the steep wooden steps, was Deara able to see Laoghaire. Seated two places to the left of the empty throne, he rose to welcome them.

'Greetings, my friends. Come Deara, to your accustomed place. It is Niall's wish that you sit at his right hand tonight, as you have sat at mine these three nights past. Tonight I shall come between you and Ferghal, but only in love.'

Deara sat down. She felt the flesh creep on her bare arms and her heavy gold jewellery weighed upon her breast like lead. The further side of the hall was filled with princes and nobles she did not know, most of them dressed in the style and manner of Tara. Nearby, beyond the empty throne and the adjoining seat of state, sat a short, swarthy man, more richly dressed than any of them. He was staring at her. It was not so much the red hair and beard, but the light in the man's restless eye that told her who he was. With all the courtesy she could summon, she bowed to Cathal Rhu, Prince of Oriel.

The trumpets sounded yet again. This time, the whole company rose and the hunched figure of the King made his way to her side, blinking in the light of so many torches and candles. Bareheaded, he leaned on the arm of Conor, who carried the crown of Tara in his free hand.

Deara had never seen Conor so magnificently arrayed. A large, heavy man to begin with, his huge enveloping robe of darkest midnight blue made him seem twice his usual size. Embroidered in silver and clasped with a broad inlaid belt, the rich fabric swept the floor. On his head, a flashing circlet supported the symbols of his craft – the crescent moon, the stars and the signs of the terrestrial zodiac. These emblems were repeated on his silver collar, inlaid with precious stones to match his belt.

'There, my Lord, rest gently beside this Queen who has come to heal us.'

Conor's whisper was barely audible, but Deara read its message from the glinting eyes, which threw at her one quick, dismissive glance, before turning back to attend upon the King.

The Hall waited in silence as Conor attempted to put Niall's crown in place. Niall had lost all his hair and Deara could see that the weight of the crown would be too distressing for him. Besides, it was now far too big.

Conor was as patient as a nurse with a fretful child, but after some minutes, the crown was placed on the table. Niall lay back exhausted after his efforts, and Conor, bowing low to him, took the seat of state beside him.

The silence continued. Deara was aware of Laoghaire's uneasy movements at her side, but she did not look at him. For three nights now he had been host to the company, but tonight, when Niall sat upon the throne, only he could give the customary signal. Nothing could happen until he did.

The restless silence extended. Deara felt its unease grow more and more oppressive as they waited for Niall to speak. The dark blue figure leaned towards the frail body and spoke in his ear.

'What, what's that?'

Deara heard Niall's voice, a thin, petulant whisper, and Conor's reply, softly coaxing. She kept her eyes lowered, but even had they been tight shut, she would have been aware of Conor's pleasure as he rose majestically to his feet.

'My noble Lords,' he began, sweeping the Hall with a raised hand, so that the light gleamed on the silver devices of his robe. 'And Ladies,' he continued, a tone lower. 'My Lord the King asks me to bid you welcome, and . . . until he is presently returned to full health and former strength . . . to offer you his thoughts and wishes on this most auspicious occasion. Let the feasting begin.'

Conor sat down and a tumult of noise broke out immediately. Minstrels struck up in the gallery high above the great double entrance doors. From the east side, where the nobles of Tara and their allies were arrayed, a stream of servants appeared bearing laden platters. The hall filled with the smells of roasted meat and the noise of dishes and wine flagons.

'What think you, Laoghaire?' Deara whispered softly, as the Prince of Tara leaned towards her.

'Not good, Deara, not good. We had not expected half this following with Oriel. There is mischief in his eye, though I swear no weapon of any kind has come beyond those doors. Rest easy on that.'

'Those are not the weapons I fear.'

Deara turned away quickly from Laoghaire as a servant stepped between Niall and herself and began serving the King with the choicest cuts. The King appeared not to notice.

'You are the Lady who has come to heal me,' he said when his plate had been piled high with food.

His eyes were upon her. Indeed, he was staring at her, yet she could not be sure that he heard or saw her.

'I certainly come to wish you well, my Lord.'

The eyes were lustreless and watery. The skin around them was paper-thin and stretched tightly over the large bones. Niall had been such a big man, taller than Morrough, and in some ways not unlike him. But whereas Morrough had grown wiser and more merciful with age, Niall had not. His punishments were known for their subtle cruelty.

Twelve years ago, when Ferghal was commanded to bring his bride to Tara, she had felt fearful in his presence. Niall himself was civil enough to her and seemed friendly towards Ferghal, but there was about him a dark power she sensed rather than saw. It made her think of lightning, able to strike in a moment, without warning, and to destroy utterly.

'Do you still tell stories in Ulster?'

'We do indeed, my Lord.'

Niall muttered to himself. Quite oblivious of the food on his plate, he swivelled in his seat to survey the company and almost overturned the beautiful, jewelled goblet which stood by his right hand.

Deara did her best to eat a little and talk to Niall at the same time, but the task proved impossible, for the feeling of apprehension within her grew stronger with every passing moment and her stomach revolted.

'I like stories,' said Niall.

'Do you, my Lord?' she replied.

'What?'

'I asked if you liked stories, my Lord.'

'Yes, I shall have many stories, and then I shall be well,' he said, like someone repeating a well-learnt line. 'There is a woman coming to tell me stories. I never liked Merdaine, nor did my mother. She's dead now. She told me stories. She told me I would be King of all Ireland. You're a pretty girl, what are you doing here?'

'Listening to the harp, my Lord. Do you like the harp?'

'No.' He shook his head and wagged his finger in the air.

'Conor, I won't have it. Tell them to stop that noise. I want my stories.'

He pushed the untouched food towards Conor, who was pulling apart a roast chicken, having first done justice to the lamb and the beef. Conor licked his fingers and paused: 'Yes, my Lord, you shall have your stories. The Lady will be here very soon, as soon as you have eaten your supper.'

Deara turned away as Conor coaxed the King to eat a chicken leg. He himself continued to eat greedily, as if to persuade him the better.

Deara lifted her wine goblet and behind it murmured Laoghaire's name as gently as she could without looking at him.

'My dear.'

'If I leave this table, bid Ferghal and yourself, if you love me, to be patient beyond all bearing, else all is lost.'

She looked away before Laoghaire could make any reply. Then, as steadily as she could, she drank a few sips of wine.

As she put the vessel down, Conor wiped his fingers on his sleeve and got to his feet. Again, he raised his hand. One by one, the musicians unthreaded their melody, until only the ripple of the harp broke upon the quietened throng. Then it too was silent.

'My Lords and Ladies,' he bowed low to the company. 'My dear master, our noble and valiant King,' he bowed low to Niall, 'has asked me to make the following announcement.' He surveyed the Great Hall from corner to corner, drawing himself up to his full height.

'As you well know, we are gathered here from all parts of this land of Ireland to take council together, as to how we may heal the hurts of our native land. From all corners of the country you have come to receive the welcome of our noble Lord, Niall. The King acknowledges with gratitude your wishes for his health and long life. From nowhere do these wishes come more strongly than from Ulster.'

Conor bowed across the throne towards the Ulster party.

Deara sat motionless and felt the colour drain from her face.

'Ulster has not always been a friend to Tara . . .' There were angry murmurings from the Ulster delegation and from others, including Laoghaire, but Conor continued without pause. 'But for their generous offer to us at Tara, we will forever stand indebted. The Ulster party has come, bearing with them their new men of power . . .' He waved a hand towards the three robed figures who sat close by the steps to the high table. 'Power, my Lords and Ladies, greater by far, we are told, than anything I, or my humble colleagues, could ever offer to this ancient court and to this thrice noble King.'

He paused, surveyed the whole company, then with a dramatic gesture towards the Ulster delegation, continued: 'The men of Ulster have offered to heal our King. By the power of their new God and the

244

ministrations of their Queen . . . Deirdre . . . I mean, Deara, Lady of Emain . . . they have agreed to begin the healing of the whole country by the healing of our dear King.'

Expressions of amazement, cries of disbelief and angry protests, rose from the assembled company. Once she heard Conor's deliberate mistake over her name, Deara was deaf to everything else. Cold sweat broke out upon her skin and her hands grew icy. The challenge had come. She had known it would, but she had never imagined it could take such a form as this.

Conor waited till he had complete silence again.

'My noble Lady,' he cried, bowing towards her, his face a study in devoted admiration. 'I understand from my master that you have chosen to recount the heroic tales of Ireland, which, though I fear it is quite beyond my own . . . humble . . . understanding, are believed by Ulstermen to have great healing power.'

He bowed again. 'My Lady of Emain.'

Like a showman displaying a prize animal, he waved his hand towards her and sat down. As he did so, the King jerked awake.

'My stories. When am I to have my stories?' he demanded.

Deara leant towards the King, aware that the eyes of the whole gathering were upon her: 'What story would please you, my Lord?'

But he did not appear to understand her simple question.

Deara rose to her feet. Slowly, she made her way behind the chairs of state. Laoghaire, Ferghal, Deirchu and Sennach all rose as she passed. She felt their gaze, sensed their anxiety, but she did not look at them. She came to the wooden stair, took the hand reached out to help her, a warm firm hand, in which her own felt like a piece of ice.

'Thank you, Patrick.'

She slipped through the narrow space left for the servants and stepped into the empty space. Faith, love and courage, else all is lost, she said to herself, as she bowed low before the throne. She arose and turned to face the silent gathering.

'It is indeed a long tradition in Ulster, as in many parts of Ireland, that a story has healing power. But we cannot know exactly what this power is. Whether it heals the body indeed, or the spirit alone, or even, as sometimes is the case, only the fears and doubts of those who listen with open hearts, ready neither to praise nor blame, but only to seek the truth. It is thus, humbly, not knowing whence comes that power, that I, willingly and in love, offer my story to the King and to you all.'

She bowed to the company. As she turned again to face the King, she looked directly at Conor and walked slowly back towards the narrow space through which she had just come. Conor sprang to his feet: 'Your audience is here, Queen Deara,' he shouted.

But it was perfectly obvious to everyone else what Deara was doing.

First her heavy jewelled necklace, then her gleaming bracelets, finally, the circle of pale gold pinned on her long, dark hair. One by one, Deara laid them on the length of table where Father Patrick sat between Patrick of Foclut, in a plain brown robe, and Patrick of Dalriada, who still chose to wear the white tunic of the scholars of Emain, an act of remembrance for those who had fallen at the gates.

She saw the deep concern in Father Patrick's face. Impatient of politics almost to the point of foolhardiness he might be, yet she knew he recognised threat when he saw it. And so did Patrick, son of Milchu. Deara couldn't imagine what this good-hearted country boy would make of Conor and his magnificent outfit, but she noticed his hands clasp and unclasp with anxiety.

At the youngest Patrick, whose eyes followed her every move, she dared not look. She knew he saw all that was in her heart. She saw his hands move to the wooden cross which hung round his neck and rested just above the surface of the table. Before her resolve not to meet his eyes should weaken, she turned away. At this moment, no one could help her. Alone, she must do what she could, whatever was to come.

She walked back to the centre of the worn, wooden floor and spread out her hands in the age-old gesture which says: 'Draw nigh and listen.'

The Prince of Oriel leapt to his feet and addressed the King.

'My Lord, I crave your pardon. I am not familiar with the customs of Ulster, nor do I wish to be, but I beg my Lord to inform me by what traditions does this "Queen" fail to greet a Prince of the Royal blood, and now, in this Hall, submit us all to her undressing. Pray, what customs are these that some at this Court would have us follow?'

There was uneasy laughter from the right of the Hall and angry murmurs from those who had come from Ulster. Deara saw Laoghaire bend forward as if he were about to rise, his face dark with anger. Then he checked himself. In that moment, courage came back to her like a breath of cool air in a stifling room. She waited to see if the King would speak. He did not. She curtseyed low to the Prince of Oriel.

'My Lord. I do not know on what occasion this discourtesy of mine could have taken place. I see but two possibilities. Tonight, when I came to my place at this high table and saw you for the first time, on which occasion I bowed to you . . .'

There were murmurs of agreement from both sides of the Hall.

'Or this afternoon,' Deara continued steadily, 'when you arrived at this court. I was not present. But nor were any members of any court other than that of Tara. As I understand it, the custom of Tara has long been to welcome Princes of the Royal blood in a personal and intimate way, unobserved by others.'

246

Deara saw his eyes falter in their hostile stare as cries of 'True. That is true,' rose from both sides of the Hall. She paused and quite unexpectedly, the thought flickered through her mind that all would be well. She drew breath to continue her task.

'As for the other matter which you mention, I cannot make any apology, though I regret your distress. I came tonight to this ancient hall, dressed, as indeed my Lord are you, with such finery as would honour this noble King and all this great company. But if I am to deploy what skill I have, as a healer, I must be free of such impediments. Gold has a beauty which we all regard, but only the colour of gold has any place in healing. Gold will not buy, or purchase, or command, that which may only come of love, whether that love be the love of God, or the love of men and women. So, my Lord, as you willingly parted with your sword and dagger, to demonstrate your love, pray grant me pardon for taking that same freedom to set aside what is not fitting, now that I know what I am called upon to do.'

There was cheering and clapping from many parts of the hall. With a dark look towards Conor, Oriel sat down.

Deara moved back to the centre of the open space, rotated slowly where she stood and in a clear voice which dispersed instantly the sounds and movements of the whole company said:

'I am Tuan
I am legend
I am memory turned myth

I am guardian of man's courage and dreams
By turf embers many tongues have spoken my tale
But still I am keeper of this story

This is my story.'

In years long after that great gathering at Tara, by house-fires and campfires, the story of Tuan was told, often and often. But sometimes, whether in the farthest north, where the great ocean pounds the rocky coasts, or in the remote blue-misted mountains of the south-east, at the end of the telling, an old man or an old woman would speak up: 'Good man, well told, I give you joy. 'Tis a great story and power to you who have told it. But I did hear that story told once, in the court before the King at Tara, and told it was by a Queen. Never did I hear so much in a story or feel so much in both my heart and my head.'

For so it was. As Deara took her courage and spread her hands, faith came to her, that the words would return, across all the years since Merdaine had taught her this lengthy and potent tale. And return they did, in her hour of greatest need.

Nor was it simply the words that returned to her. With each line that rose effortlessly to her lips, came memories from the years of their learning. Her life passed before her, as if, like Tuan, she could take on shape after shape, eagle or bear, man or stag, and see all life, as he did, from many perspectives. And there, in the empty centre of the greatest gathering of nobles she had ever seen, in the hour or more of the telling of this long tale, she found the quiet and the stillness she had not dared to hope for, till Tara had been left many days behind.

The wine flagons were empty, for the servants, too, had leaned against the walls to listen. Torches burned low, for no one wished to break the spell of that single voice which commanded the whole company. Even on the highest table, the candles began to gutter, because no one moved to replace them. As the Great Hall grew dimmer and her own shadow lengthened, Deara became aware of a great weariness. Her arms began to feel heavy and her legs ached. But she went on to the very last words, as coolly and as steadily as if she had just begun.

> 'I am memory turned myth
> I am legend
> I am Tuan.'

As she sank in a low bow before the throne in the deeply-shadowed Hall, a great roar rose from all around her. Tables were thumped resoundingly, warriors beat their fists on their metal collars, women clapped their hands and servants stamped the wooden floor, till they remembered themselves and hurried off to replace the torches and the candles.

Deara raised her eyes and saw that the King was sleeping peacefully. Conor had tried to rouse him, unsuccessfully, and now turned to Oriel, whose face was etched with annoyance. Laoghaire had risen to his feet and picked up her wine goblet. He waited now for a servant to refill it, so that he could bring it to her where she stood, acknowledging the tumult of the audience.

Laoghaire had just reached the steps, when an angry voice rang out over the excited hubbub. Cathal Rhu, Prince of Oriel, was on his feet, his finger pointing at him.

'Hold hard, Laoghaire, Prince of Tara. By what right do you carry cups of wine to serve our enemy? The King has not bidden you. By what authority do you take this task? Have you forgot yourself? Or has Ulster so bewitched you, you think yourself King already?'

A hush fell again upon the hall and men hurrying to the doors to go and relieve themselves stopped where they were for fear of missing what should pass.

'There is another story that this Queen must tell, and my noble lords will judge if I have not cause. Someone must keep hold of all that is dear to us, if the honour of Tara is not to be set at naught. Draw back, Laoghaire, and give me leave to speak with this Queen Deara, who has so bewitched you.'

Thirsty and tired and longing to sit down, Deara saw Laoghaire pause. Were he now to offer her the cup in his hand after Oriel's challenge, it would mean he was claiming the Kingship. For that to happen while the King yet lived and before the meeting of the council could only lead to the bloodiest of struggles, and an end to all their hopes for a better time to come. She felt her whole body heavy, as if her last remaining energy had drained away with the final words of her story, but she knew she must do something to help Laoghaire, who stood staring at Oriel across the throne, the brimming cup still in his hand.

She rose from a final deep bow to the King and moved towards Oriel. The distance was not more than four paces, the width of Conor's chair of state and the space between him and his neighbour, but it took an enormous physical effort, like walking in deep snow, and she wondered how she could remain on her feet much longer.

She bowed to Oriel: 'My Lord, what story is it that you seek to hear?'

'The story of your plot against Tara, my Lady,' he replied, his voice dark, icily sarcastic in tone.

Angry shouts and sharp exchanges followed the gasp that rose from the company and Oriel's face softened with pleasure as a group of his followers began to encourage him and further harsh words flew across the hall but a few moments ago a scene of lively and harmonious fellowship.

'Do you deny, Queen of Ulster, that your followers have been meeting secretly with the connivance of *that* Prince, the one that would bear you cups of wine? Do you deny that secret signs have been exchanged in those meetings and oaths sworn in blood?'

In the stunned silence which greeted his words, Oriel paused, drew a deep breath and spat out his final accusation: 'Do you deny the desire of Ulster to overwhelm Tara? Do you deny that your spies have conducted ceremonies and sworn to their aid servants and nobles, aye, nobles who sit in this very hall?'

Immediately, there was uproar. Many allies of Ulster rose to their feet in anger. Deara could not see them, but she heard the sound of overturned benches. She caught a movement to her left. Ferghal and Laoghaire had risen together, their hands clasped, but this she did not see either, for she dared not take her eyes away from Oriel. Momentarily, the noise abated. Like the words of the story of Tuan, Merdaine's words came effortlessly into her mind: 'In your deepest need, help will come, if only you believe that it will be so.'

'Yes, my Lord, I do deny your charges,' she said quietly, with all the steadiness she could manage. She paused. Whatever she said would have no effect upon Oriel and his closest allies, as they had already made up their minds. She had no idea how many there were in the hall who had not. At that moment, she felt a movement at her side.

'Niall, my Lord, King of Tara, I pray you, give me leave to tell a story.'

The voice was young and strong. Startled, she looked round to find Patrick bowing low before the King.

'A story? Yes, a story.'

The King's eyes had jerked open. Refreshed, he showed a sudden flicker of interest. 'Who are you, boy?'

Oriel shut his mouth and sat down, furious, but helpless. The King was speaking, so he had to give way. Conor whispered urgently in the King's ear, but the King did not hear him.

'What story, boy?'

'My Lord, a powerful story, about a weakling boy, a brave woman and a mighty Prince. It is a good story, my Lord,' said Patrick encouragingly. He had risen to his feet, his dark eyes shining and his voice light and easy. He was smiling at Niall as if quite certain the King would say yes to his offer.

'That will be a good story,' the King replied, as he smiled back.

'My Lord King, I pray you . . .' Oriel said as he bounced to his feet, able to restrain himself no longer.

Niall blinked at him and waved his hand. 'Sit down, sit down. We're going to have a story. I like stories. There was a woman coming to tell me stories, but she hasn't come. You boy, what was the name of this weakling?'

'Sceto, my Lord.'

The King chuckled to himself and nodded: 'Weak. But fast, eh? Go on then, boy, I'm waiting.'

Patrick turned towards his audience and bowed. Only then did Deara realise he was wearing a warrior's cloak that looked very familiar, a very handsome one, woven in gold and green, with the red embroidery for which the women of Emain were justly famous.

With a single gesture, he unfurled his cloak, spread it on the bare boards and bade her sit down, just as he might have done at any noonday halt by some river bank. She looked up at the slim, white-clad figure the handsome cloak had concealed. For the briefest moment he caught her gaze, as if merely to reassure himself that she was seated. There was a light in his eye and a firmness that instantly rekindled hope in her heart.

She had never heard Patrick tell a tale before. Indeed, she wondered

250

if he had ever had the opportunity to practice. To read Greek or Latin texts, or take his part in a learned debate, perhaps, but traditional stories had not been part of his education at Emain and surely not in Albi.

The next minutes more than answered her doubts, for Patrick was a born storyteller. Not only had he the voice and commanding manner of the best tellers of tales, but through the litheness of his body he deployed a gift of illusion she had seldom seen bettered. He was successfully making the story happen before the eyes of the astounded audience.

For the first time in hours, Deara felt herself relax a little. With all eyes on Patrick, she could afford to look towards Ferghal and the Ulster party. She could see also that Conor had a face like thunder and Oriel was clutching his goblet so tightly his knuckles were white, though he was pretending to be bored with the whole affair.

A burst of laughter recalled her to the tale. Patrick had created the weakling boy, the youngest child with his large warrior brothers. Despite all her anxiety, she found herself drawn into the laughter by the sheer verve of his telling. As the weakling began his training as a warrior, tripping over his sword, dropping his spear, missing the target and hitting his instructor, she laughed as heartily as everyone else. Even the King was leaning forward, bright eyed, clapping his hands in childish delight.

Laughter again, as with slow steps the weakling bids farewell to the warriors and leaves his home, bound for a far encampment where other skills are taught. Now the weakling is sitting at a desk. He is writing so fast that it takes three scholars to keep him supplied with materials. He runs out of paper, writes on the floor, the table, the walls.

Suddenly, above the laughter in the hall, there comes the call to arms. The weakling drops his pen and puts on a sword. As ineptly as before, he runs with his fellows to man the walls. The defenders are few, old men, disabled warriors and scholars in white shifts. They look and listen. A great force is coming upon them, well armed warriors on great snorting horses. They carry swords and firebrands. The weakling draws his sword in readiness.

Throughout the hall, there is not a sound, not a movement.

'Sceto!' The voice is that of an old man.

'Here, Sir,' replies the weakling.

'Sceto, take this message to The Place of Birth. Tell the Lady to rest where she is. Bid her to beware of smoke and to pray for our souls. We are outnumbered and cannot hold. Run, boy, as you have never run before.'

A pause. Then the noise of horses at the gallop.

'To-me-to-me-to-me-to-me.'

The voice is a warrior's rallying cry, high, undulating, with a strange, high-pitched nasal note.

A murmur runs through the company.

With incredible speed, Patrick makes three circuits of the hall, runs down a narrow passage and arrives, gasping, at the edge of the cloak where Deara sat. Before she had time to think about it, Deara had put out her hands to steady him. He crouched in front of her struggling for breath in order to get his message out.

Silence.

With a few movements of his hands, Patrick called up the labouring body of Bregella and the weary figures of the women who rested nearby. Then he rose to run back to the fight and was held by unseen hands.

He stood up. Sniffed. Went to the nearest table, grasped the candlestick and circled the bright island where Deara sat quite still. He coughed, moved in every direction, but was everywhere driven back by the tiny wisps of smoke he had laid on the still air.

So did Patrick of Dalriada hold in thrall all the company in the Great Hall of Tara as he took them through the labour of Bregella, the night of hiding in the passageway and the slow journey to Brolla with a baby under each arm. One by one the women arrived and sank exhausted on the ground. Patrick took off the wooden cross he wore around his neck, put it on the floor by the edge of the cloak, and knelt down briefly in prayer.

Then he stood up, and turning his back upon the audience, stepped lightly towards the throne and bowed to the King who nodded approvingly towards him.

'My Lord, King of Tara. I am Sceto. I am the weakling.'

Niall nodded again and looked pleased.

'My Lady of Emain, Deara, Queen of Ulster, is the brave woman.'

'Yes, yes, I can see that. But where is the Prince?'

Patrick threw back his head: 'To-me-to-me-to-me-to-me.'

The cry rang back from the high beams so fearfully that the women sitting at the tables nearest the entrance were startled.

'My Lord, King of Tara, I never thought to hear that voice again, except in my nightmares. But I, Patrick of Dalriada, called Sceto, the only survivor of the defenders of Emain, when all the strength of Ulster had gone to the aid of Lisbane and Carnbanna and the defence of our land from invaders, I have heard that voice in this hall tonight. The mighty Prince is here, my Lord.'

There were angry shouts from the men of Ulster and cries of distress from the other side of the hall where the men of Tara sat. 'No, no warrior he, no Prince he. Out. Out with Oriel.'

Oriel leapt to his feet, bitter hatred twisting his face into a mask.

'He lies, he lies. It is all part of their plot,' he shouted, waving his

252

hands towards Deara and Patrick and then towards Ferghal and Laoghaire.

With a look of desperation on his face, Conor signalled him to be quiet. He leaned forward to the King and whispered in his ear.

'Where? Where is she?' said the King.

Silence descended once again as the King spoke.

'There, my Lord, awaiting your pleasure.'

'Oh good.'

'Come, my dear,' said the King, beckoning to Deara.

With an effort, Deara rose from where she sat. The floor had been hard and uncomfortable, her legs felt cramped and stiff. As she straightened up, she saw Ferghal and Laoghaire exchange uneasy glances. The King was smiling abstractedly. Though he was seated, Conor seemed to have grown to enormous proportions. Oriel's face leered at her through the haze of candle smoke which seemed to be thickening every moment. She took a step forward, not sure whether her legs would bear her or not. And then another. She looked up at the King, whose eyes gleamed brightly and caught the light with their perpetual moistness.

'You have come after all,' he bleated. 'Good. Now we shall have The Great Cycle. Seven stories to make me well, as you have promised. Make haste now and begin.'

25

Somewhere after eleven, when I finished making notes from one of my library volumes, I put down my pen, got up and stretched, and stood looking down into the last glowing embers of the fire. I remembered again I'd been going to fill the two little vases with flowers but it was too late now, it was properly dark outside. I put out my hand to pick up one of them just to look at it again.

Immediately I touched it, I found myself in darkness, my outstretched hand having struck against something wooden. It was a few moments before I could distinguish anything at all. Then I saw I was in a passageway, lit only by a single torch which smoked dully in its bracket some way further along to my right. To my left I saw a thin, vertical line of light. As I moved towards it, I realised that the enormous roar I could hear was the sound of voices.

Suddenly, the crack of light flew open towards me. I jumped aside, tripped and fell over the bottom step of a flight of stairs, as a group of young men and girls came towards me through double doors, carrying empty dishes and flagons. The sudden waft of roast lamb as the doors swung shut behind them made me feel quite hungry.

I sat down on the bottom stair and rubbed my bruised ankle, but when I heard sounds of people coming from the other direction, I decided I'd better get out of the way. Tentatively, I began to climb the stairs. They were steep, wooden and creaked loudly, but they seemed a better idea than waiting to be discovered in the corridor below.

At the top of the stairs, a door lay open. I could smell food and candle wax, but although the roar of voices went on, there was no sound from nearby. Suddenly, the voices from the hall below stopped completely. In the silence, I peeped round the open door and saw greasy plates stacked on the floor. There were stools and an assortment of musical instruments, and a most wonderful harp, carved in gleaming wood, its stem post the body of a woman, but no musicians.

It looked as if they had done their turn, eaten their supper and gone, so I slipped in and crouched in the dimmest corner away from the torches. Even without the harp, I hadn't much doubt that I was in Tara, but I was certainly not prepared for what I saw when I peered gingerly over the high wooden front of the gallery. I gasped in astonishment.

In the middle of a great, empty space, surrounded by tables and scores of people in jewel-bright clothes that glittered and winked with gold ornaments, Deara stood quite alone. She was wearing a long, pale green dress, exactly the same shade as the Indian dressing gown I was wearing, but unlike my enveloping gown, so richly embroidered, Deara's dress was absolutely plain, but perfectly cut to the curve of her slender body. She looked wonderful. As I watched, I saw her stretch out her hands as if in welcome. Then she rotated, very slowly, just like a dancer, as if to take in every one of the people filling the great high-roofed hall. Every eye was fixed upon her and not a word was spoken. After the roar of voices, the silence was stunning.

I wanted to look around, to see if I could recognise anyone, at least to get a look at the King and Queen of Tara, who were bound to be very obvious, but I found I could not take my eyes off Deara. Then it came to me that, for the moment, I had to concentrate entirely on her, on Deara, my kinswoman who had need of me. Though what that need might be I could not imagine, so in command of herself she seemed to be.

But as I looked down, her face and body wonderfully composed as she stood there in the candlelight, I was suddenly overcome with a sense of foreboding I simply could not understand. There she was, the centre of great attention, no doubt with Ferghal and all her friends watching her and wishing her well, and yet I felt a familiar anxiety clutch me, making my stomach muscles tighten and my palms sweat – so much so that I had to speak sharply to myself: 'Stop it and get on with the job. You have a job to do, after all.' It was absolutely clear to me now that whatever happened, I must not take my eyes off Deara for a single second.

Keeping my eyes on her wasn't difficult at all. When she began to speak, her gestures were so eloquent and her words so beautiful she held me enthralled. Smooth and perfect, like raindrops sliding into a pool making ripples that vibrate and send tiny wavelets to break where branches dapple the shadows, they reached out into every corner of that huge hall.

And they slid into my heart as well. I could not understand what she said, for she was using her own language, but as the sentences flowed effortlessly on, I felt them work upon me and dissolve some darkness deep inside me.

Clearly, Deara was telling a story of her own people, but somehow it was also my story. Me, as a child, as a young person, as a woman. Me, in joy and sorrow, in love and in despair. Me, in city streets and remote villages, in rain and sunshine, in mist over summer fields and in the chill fog of November gloom. Me, alone and friendless, struggling with my fear. Me, with a loving companion, overjoyed by my good fortune. On and on, that dear familiar voice flowed, effortlessly, until there was no fragment, no image, no fleeting moment of my life's experience that had not been woven into a web as fine, as intricate, as the golden stitches on the smooth and shimmering silk of the gown I wore. I realised that at last the pieces of my life spun like a kaleidoscope no longer. Something had come together.

The story was near its end. I could tell from the gestures, from the intense concentration of the listeners and from my own sense of anticipation. Deara paused. She raised her arm, made a final slow, lingering gesture with her hand and her arm, like a slow, dying fall of raindrops.

> You are Deirdre,
> This is your story
> Rest now in peace.

I heard the words in my heart and there was peace. A stillness such as I have never felt before, a sense of quiet joy and of a deep inner confidence. But all around me, there was tumult. I had never heard anything like it. Shouting and stamping and cheering and clapping. It didn't surprise me in the slightest. I should have liked to jump to my feet and wave madly myself, but something told me to wait my moment. Poor Deara looked so tired. In the last stages of her story, her face had grown so pale, though her voice had never faltered.

The hall was brighter now, for dozens of servants had appeared, bringing candles and fresh torches. By their light, I could see how dark the circles were under her eyes. And yet, tired as she was, she still moved so gracefully, to make so flowing and controlled a deep bow. No wonder all the men were on their feet, striking their gleaming bracelets against the deep burnished collars they wore, so that the hall echoed to the sound like a forge full of hammers.

'Beating swords into ploughshares.'

Out of the peace of my heart and the memory of the forge, it seemed so appropriate I should recall William Coulter's favourite quotation.

When I noticed a few men not on their feet, something told me to look at them more closely. The King was asleep, poor man. Like a puppet parked on a chair when not in use, he lay against the back of the huge carved throne, lifeless and unmoving, a great crown sitting on the table in front of him, beside his wide-rimmed silver cup inlaid with precious stones. He looked terribly ill. In fact, he reminded me of the man in the next room to Mother's, at the hospice in Belfast.

Next to the King, there was no Queen. Where she would have sat there was a huge man in blue, who looked more like a magician than anything else. He was very fat and his bulk made him somehow sinister, far more capable of evil than good. He was whispering to a square-shaped little man beside him, one of the few not clapping or cheering, a glowering character with a red beard and long red hair, wearing so much gold that he glinted every time he moved.

The magician bent over the King. It looked as if he were trying to wake him up, but the poor man was so still, he might have been dead, a poor wisp, paper-white, his mouth open as he slept.

While the bulky blue figure blocked my view of the King, something niggled at the back of my mind. Surely magicians ought to be lean and gaunt, like Merlin or Gandalf. Then it came to me quite suddenly that this was no magician, but a Druid. I remembered Deara had told me once: 'I am called Deirdre by no one, except a Druid who bears me ill will.'

If ever anyone was capable of ill will, it was certainly this man. He might not be the same man Deara had spoken about, but whoever he was, he was bad news and his little red-haired friend loaded up with the gold ornaments was no better.

The tumult of excitement and celebration was beginning to die down a little. I saw a tall, handsome man rise from his seat beside Deara's empty place on the top table and summon a servant to refill her wine goblet. He picked it up, to take it to her himself. Poor Deara, she must be dying of thirst. The hall was terribly hot. Even with the door open behind me and fresh air coming up from that corridor below I was perspiring. I had no idea candles and torches could generate so much heat. Between the smoke and the fumes and the lingering smell of food, I was thinking longingly of a stiff gin and tonic with masses of ice and lemon.

I decided the man who now carried the full goblet to Deara must be Laoghaire, Prince of Tara. That easy gesture of command to the servant suggested he was the host. Besides, there was the colour of his dress. Once, long ago it now seemed, I had worn Ferghal's first warrior cloak and it had been decorated with red embroidery. Looking to my left, I saw a very large group of men whose dress was decorated with just that same red, but the kind-faced man who carried Deara's wine cup was wearing blue. Then I saw Ferghal. Younger than when he followed Patrick's coffin, he was dark and intense. His eyes never left Deara for one moment.

I was still studying Ferghal, when there was a commotion from the other side of the hall. The red-haired man had jumped to his feet. He might not be very big, but his voice made up for it. A real bull-roarer he was, except that he had a nasal twang as if he suffered from very bad catarrh. And he was working himself up into a right state, shaking his finger at Laoghaire, as he came down the steps towards the floor of the hall.

I saw Laoghaire pause, uncertain of what to do next. I was so taken a-back. Surely he wasn't going to let anything this awful man said stop him.

Then, quite suddenly, the knots in the stomach and the sweaty hands which had disappeared completely while Deara was telling her story came right back, for the cheering and the applause stopped abruptly. All eyes were now fixed on Redbeard and Laoghaire, as Deara made a deep and graceful curtsey to the sleeping King.

Just then, my eye caught a movement at the foot of the steps, beyond where Laoghaire stood, apparently frozen to the spot. A slim, white-clad figure slipped up the steps and paused behind Ferghal's chair. No one noticed Ferghal nod briefly, put a hand up to the clasp of his cloak and lean forward slightly. The white figure disappeared from sight so quickly I didn't get a proper look at him before I had to turn away because that awful little square man was now pointing his finger at Deara.

I heard him speak her name with a nasty sneer in his voice and the word Emain followed. His tone of voice left me in no doubt at all of what he was saying. I knew he was accusing her of something quite dreadful, because it made the men of Tara gasp and turn to their neighbours, wide-eyed with shock and anger, while the men of Emain jumped to their feet and shouted across the width of the hall, waving their fists with fury. In minutes, the whole hall was enveloped in anger. Like a dark tide, it washed from side to side, the waves growing ever larger as Redbeard's words beat like a strong wind behind them.

Deara turned to face him. Such a small figure to stand against such a monstrous tide of anger. And yet I sensed her power, as if her stillness would never be broken by the anger of this threatening man, however violent it might be. I couldn't see why no one did anything to stop that ridiculous figure. He must be unbalanced to make an attack on someone like Deara. Whatever she was supposed to have done, I knew she couldn't have done it. She was just not capable of harming anyone. Besides, she was a healer. They must all know that harming people is against everything a healer believes.

Just when I was feeling quite desperate, a young warrior, resplendent in a magnificent cloak of gold and red, materialised a few paces away from Deara. He addressed the King loudly, but very politely, calling him by name. To my surprise, Niall woke up and responded to him immediately. He even began to question him. He must have asked his name, for I heard the young warrior reply: 'Sceto.'

I was so delighted and relieved that I must have popped up further than I intended from my crouched position. Perhaps I even cried out. But whatever I did, I saw the Druid look straight up at me and stare in absolute amazement. He'd seen me so clearly, there was no point ducking down again, so I just stared straight back at him. Very shortly, he began to twitch at his silver signs. I could see sweat gleaming on his face when he finally dropped his eyes.

As soon as he looked away, I shrank down below the level of the balcony again in case anyone else should see me. Fortunately, I discovered a large knot-hole in the wood, just where I needed it, so I could still see quite clearly without any further danger of being seen.

The moment the King had woken up and replied to Sceto's question, Redbeard had scowled furiously and sat down. The rule must be that no one could speak if the King were speaking. Were this so, then Sceto had been very clever in stopping Redbeard. But that still left the anger he'd unleashed to be dealt with.

The Druid leaned towards the King and whispered to him. But whatever it was he said, the King didn't want to listen. He shook his hands at him, like a fretful child, and beckoned to the young warrior. With a single gesture, the young warrior unhooked his cloak, sent it spinning in the air and revealed the slight, white-clad figure of Sceto. I could have wept with delight and relief.

Like a young troubadour, he settled the cloak upon the ground, helped Deara to sit down and began to tell his tale. Within minutes, he had his audience totally enslaved.

Vividly, I remembered a summer's day, aeons ago, when this same young man had stood at my side, so absorbed by the message Ferghal's herald had brought to his Queen that he had quite forgotten his task as translator. If Tannach were anywhere in this great gathering tonight, he might well discover ways of developing his art. Sceto was a natural. Every line of his body, every gesture of his limbs, every inflexion of his voice, helped to dramatise the more effectively the story he told. What he was able to bring into being was something entirely different from the deep stillness of Deara's presentation, but he held his audience just as compellingly.

Two people in the hall seemed completely unmoved by his tale, however – the Druid and his friend Redbeard, who glared at Deara all the while Sceto was speaking.

I was having a good look at the two of them, when the tone of Sceto's voice changed completely.

''To-me-to-me-to-me-to-me.'

It so startled me I nearly fell over, as much because of the sound itself as its suddenness. It was loud, with a distinct nasal twang. Immediately, I looked down at Redbeard. There were others looking at him too. For a moment he sat frozen in his seat. But for a moment only. Within seconds, his nose was deep in his wine goblet. Then he began to look round the hall, as if his only concern was to signal to someone to come and refill it.

It took me a little while to work out exactly what Sceto was up to, but when he started to run like the wind round the hall and dash down an imaginary passageway to arrive gasping and near to collapse by Deara's seated figure, I knew he had to be telling the story of the destruction of Emain. He'd been far too clever to point his finger at Redbeard directly, but he'd done enough, however, for many more guests to look towards him, to judge his reaction; and not just men of Emain angered by his attack on their Queen, but lords and nobles wearing the blue of Tara itself.

I tore my eyes away from Sceto to see how the Druid was taking it. There was a look of ill-concealed fury on his face, and he was sweating so much his face shone in the candlelight like the devices that covered his magnificent blue robe. He was turning to whisper to Redbeard, who nodded shortly.

I waited anxiously to see what would happen next. Sceto was kneeling in prayer for a brief moment, at the end of the journey to Brolla. He sprang up lightly, to face the King. The transformation in the King was extraordinary. Like a child playing a guessing game, he seemed unable to contain his excitement. With growing insistence, he seemed to be asking the same question, but Sceto gave him no answer, till, quite suddenly, the terrible cry came again: 'To-me-to-me-to-me-to-me-to-me.'

It seemed to come from all around me this time, and carry a menace that was quite fearful. I wasn't the only one. Looking down into the hall I saw a number of women below me cover their ears with their hands. The men of Ulster were tight-faced and grim as they hammered with their fists on the tables.

There were shouts from the men in blue. The shouts became angrier. The gestures were unambiguous. Clearly, they were telling Redbeard to get out, but he looked stonily straight in front of him and behaved as if he didn't understand their meaning.

As Sceto stood waiting for the King to dismiss him, the Druid leaned across the fragile body once more and whispered in his ear. Niall smiled and beckoned to Deara. Immediately, the shouts in the hall died down as he spoke to her. Slowly, Deara got to her feet. I felt her weariness as if it were my own. Clearly she was being asked for something and she couldn't refuse, because it was the King who had asked for it.

Beyond that, I couldn't make out what was going on. I saw my dear friend, tired beyond tired, bowing to the King. I saw Sceto looking as if he had just heard the most terrible news, and Redbeard and the Druid looking pleased with themselves. It was deathly quiet in the hall. It was obvious to me that no one was going to be able to do anything to help her, because the King had made his wishes clear.

Before I'd even thought about it, I found myself running lightly down the wooden stairs and slipping through the doors the servants had used. With all eyes on Deara once again, no one saw me, until I arrived at her side. I put my arm round her waist and made her sit down again. Then, I stepped over to the high table, nodded to the King, said 'Excuse me' and took his untouched goblet back to Deara. She seemed very reluctant to take it, but I put my arm round her

261

again and raised it to her lips. She drank the wine gratefully and a little colour came back to her cheeks.

I heard a great gasp break the silence and when I glanced up, I found every eye in the place staring at me. I returned their gaze quite calmly until I heard a scream of rage behind me. I spun round. The Druid was on his feet, his face contorted with anger. He was pointing at Deara and saying something. What it was, I've no idea, but the tone was full of menace and the stabbing finger told me the rest.

It was something about that hectoring tone and pointing finger that made me lose my temper.

'Sit down,' I shouted at him, probably in good, strong Ulster English. 'Sit down and shut up, you great bully. Can't you recognise goodness when you see it?'

He stared at me in just the same way as when he'd caught sight of me up in the gallery. Now that I was much closer to him, I could see the same look in his eyes; he was terrified.

In the silence, a long time seemed to pass, but I went on staring at him, determined he would drop his accusing finger. Then I realised the look in his eyes had changed. His eyes weren't seeing me at all. As if I were watching a slow-motion replay, I saw him fall backwards, his eyes wide open, his blue gown billowing round his huge body. He dropped into his chair of state and his massive weight swept both him and it off the raised wooden platform. There was a resounding crash as chair and Druid hit the floor behind the platform. When I was quite sure he would stay down and not pop up again, as magicians have been known to do, I turned back to Deara.

As I helped her to her feet I heard another commotion. I caught a fleeting glimpse of Redbeard, pale as a snowdrop, hurrying out through the servant's door.

I felt some tension go. How ridiculous of me to feel so tired when it was Deara's ordeal, not mine. I turned back to her and smiled. I asked her if I could help by telling the King a story so she would be able to have a rest.

She took both my hands, kissed my cheek and whispered to me: 'Thank you, my friend. I knew you would come to help me. Yes. You must tell your story, but this is not where your story is needed. This story will end happily now and all will be well. Go, my friend. Go now and I will find a way to come to you. I promise.'

I saw the relief and the weariness in her eyes and heard the soft movement of Sceto as he came to stand close to her. Again came the strange, sighing noise I'd heard as I'd helped Deara drink from the King's cup. But I didn't find out what it was, because the candles went out and I found myself standing in my own bedroom. On the table where I write, stood the two vases of Royal Tara ware. Both were full of flowers.

26

After my visit to Tara I woke late the next morning feeling strangely sad. I lay and listened to the doves and watched the light intensify as the sun moved towards the front of the house. Through the gap in the curtains, a sunbeam fell like a spotlight on the two small posies of flowers which had greeted me on my return.

Suddenly, I turned my head into my pillow and began to weep as if my heart would break. If any dear friend had been there to offer me their sheltering arms, or ask me gently what the matter was, I might have tried to say something about anxiety or loss. I might have spoken about going back to London, to a life that was a burden to me, or leaving Anacarrig and all that it had brought me over the last weeks, or worrying how I would ever cope with my life, if I didn't have Matthew to love and support me.

I might even have admitted I felt sure I would be cut off from Deara once I had left the Irish coast behind and that was a loss I could bear as little as the loss of Matthew. Loss, loss and more loss, was all I could see that morning.

When I thought of not having Matthew to love me and make a life with me, I was overwhelmed by panic. Where could I go? How could I exist by myself? Where would I find anyone else to tolerate the vulnerable, unstable person I was, given to ecstatic joy over a buttercup or a fledgling, or to devastating despair at the cruelty of a world where bombs and bullets ripped lives apart and hate destroyed the security and peace without which good things can seldom grow?

My sobs echoed so strangely in the empty house. Even the doves flew away. I heard the whine of their wings as I lay exhausted, the tears flowing noiselessly to make damp patches on my pillow. I made the effort to get up and wash and dress, but when I sat down on the edge of the bed and picked up my sandals I dropped them on the floor and lay down again.

With my cheeks still damp from the pillow, I found myself out of doors. I was standing barefoot on a low hill, surrounded by green countryside, on a morning in early summer. Nearby, there was an enclosure where mares and their foals stood or lay. The sun was high. It gleamed on the smooth, well-fed flanks of the mares and glanced off the mobile bodies of the foals. Round and round they went, playing, like children playing tag, full of the joy of their freedom.

I thought of William Coulter, as I always do when I see horses. Dear William, he took such joy in them. He didn't need to own them, or even to work with them, it just delighted him that they existed. It occurred to me that William asked so little of the world, only that it was itself and that he be free to experience it.

If only I could be like that, I thought, accepting what is given, instead of always striving after something more. Wanting the world to be kinder or gentler than it could ever manage to be. So often I felt a fool, a ridiculous fool, to be so at odds with the world the way it was.

I went and leaned against the hurdle fence which enclosed the field. Having worn themselves out by their exertions, the foals were resting now, some nuzzling hopefully at their mothers, others rolling in the lush grass. One little fellow, smaller than all the rest and almost pure white, looked across at me and came trotting towards me.

'Hello, little fellow, who are you?' I asked softly, as he nuzzled me. 'I'm afraid I haven't got anything to give you.'

He stood quite still and let me stroke his nose and his neck. I found the tears trickling down my cheeks again. There was something so trusting about the creature, so soft and vulnerable, so dependant on the whim of others, to treat him kindly or cruelly as they chose. Perhaps he knew he could trust me, because we were two of a kind: perhaps he sensed I could never find it in my heart to hurt him.

I was so absorbed with my new-found friend I didn't notice someone had come towards us. Only when my name was spoken very softly did I turn and see Deara's cup bearer, Laoghaire of Tara, tall and handsome, standing beside me. His Latin was less fluent than Deara's, but his easy manner made light of his difficulties. He explained that this foal had never come to anyone before, though he himself had been trying all the usual tricks for weeks now. He took an apple from his pocket and handed it to me.

'What's his name?' I asked.

'His name is Hope.'

I smiled wryly and looked at the apple in my hand. I thought I had nothing to give Hope, and now I had. Hope was delighted with his apple. He chewed every bit of it and then licked my fingers clean.

As Hope backed away and raced round the enclosure, tossing his head and whinnying in delight, I turned to Laoghaire and smiled up at him, saying words of thanks. What his eyes said in return, no woman could fail to read. He was silent for a moment, then he took my hand, so tenderly I couldn't think of taking it back.

'Deirdre of Anacarrig. I beg you, listen to me,' he began. 'I have looked at no woman since I lost my wife, Cumenora. I thought my heart would never heal, but you have healed it. You came to Tara and in a single night, I became King and found the woman I would make my Queen. Deirdre, stay with me. Stay and be my Queen and I will give you anything you ask. My love you have had, since the moment I first saw you. My life, my future, I will share with you. Peace you have brought to Tara already, in great measure. Stay and let us work to make it grow. Let us share the love we have to give, with each other and with those who go in need.'

I looked into his eyes and saw a warmth and a depth of feeling that overwhelmed me. If ever a man could cause things to happen and bring hope and joy into the lives of many, this was the man. Here was the chance to live in a world I could make sense of, where there was still the possibility of creating something good. While Laoghaire was King, hope and love would be mine and the power to do many things. He was offering me everything I ever wanted. The thought was so overwhelming, tears were trickling gently down my face once more.

'Your love is precious and I shall cherish it. I long to stay, Laoghaire. But it cannot be. I have something to do in another time, though I see so little hope for anything I could do. Perhaps the love you offer me so generously is what will help me to find the hope I need.'

I saw the sadness sweep across his face, as he grasped the truth of what I had said. I put my arms round him and felt the warmth of his sheltering embrace. For a few brief moments, I felt a comfort and a security I had dreamed of. I knew now it could never be mine. I woke to find my pillow sodden and my cheeks still damp.

The day that followed was long and empty. I decided I would just have to do the things I had planned whether I wanted to do them or not. I cried a lot and drank a lot of sparkling water, because I was permanently thirsty. I couldn't face eating anything.

Early in the evening, Diana rang to ask if I'd like to come up to Norfolk for the week before Matthew arrived back. It's so like her, to think of me being lonely in an empty flat when I'd just said goodbye to Anacarrig. I was quite surprised when I heard myself thank her warmly and explain that I had a great deal to do before Matthew arrived. After all my negative feelings about going back to London, it seemed there must be something apart from Matthew I wanted to go back for.

I began to feel better after that. I took out my notebooks and started to write an account of all I had seen and heard at Tara. Then I searched through my books and photocopies to see if I could make any connection between what I'd read and what I'd seen, but they had little to offer, except for a reference to the Kingdom of Oriel, which I'd never heard of before. I was sure someone had called Redbeard 'Oriel.'

However awful the man, I loved the name. I said it over and over to myself. 'I am Brigid from the Kingdom of Oriel,' I murmured, as I sat looking into the fire, so still I was hardly breathing, my eyes beginning to close.

Suddenly, I jumped to my feet, threw my arms in the air and shouted out loud: 'You fool, you fool, why don't you face up to it? You're as Irish as bedamned. You're a dreamer and a storyteller – you're as peculiar as they come – you see things that no one else sees – you feel pain that is someone else's – you want to heal the hurt of the world. Get wise, woman, you're mad. And once you *know* you're mad, it might be easier to live with yourself, even to live with the world.'

'The worst thing that ever happened to you was your mother. Poor woman, what an awful cuckoo in the nest she got landed with. No wonder she tried to straighten you out. What did you expect her to do with a passionate Irish sensibility when what she felt she had to produce was a well-socialised, secondary female and a true blue Prod. Poor woman. You'll have to forgive her, there's nothing else to be done about her.'

I paused for breath and laughed. Just once or twice I'd caught myself saying the odd quiet word in the garden or in the empty house, but this was the first time I'd really let go and talked to myself since the little girl who sat under the hawthorns was finally reduced to silence.

'No more silence, I vow. No more being told to sit down and shut up,' I began. 'That was what I said to the Druid, wasn't it? And look what happened to him,' I went on gleefully.

I did have to sit down then, because I felt rather dizzy, but it didn't affect my joy. I went on spelling out the good news that had just come to me.

'No more submitting to the pointing fingers. No more being bullied and brow-beaten. I've escaped. Where I've escaped from and who locked me in, I'm not sure. Maybe I did it to myself. Maybe it wasn't Mother's fault at all. Perhaps it was the community, the culture, or even the ethos of the times. Whatever it was, it doesn't matter now. Something locked me up. All that's important is that I've been let out. I'm free to be myself. Nothing and no one is ever going to lock me up again.'

I stopped, breathless, and realised I was absolutely starving.

'Rarely, rarely comest thou, spirit of delight,' I said aloud, as I made some bread and honey while I waited for the kettle to boil. 'And what an extraordinary sense of timing you do have.'

A day, saturated with tears, survived only by executing a painful self-discipline, was ending with this marvellous sense of hope new-born, hope flowing unbounded through every part of my being. At this moment, I really could believe anything was possible. I could transcend any weakness, cope with any problem, go forth in newness of life, write what would speak of hope to many. I could even hope

266

that I might heal in my own time as I had been able to heal Bill Coulter.

I paused to ask myself what was happening to me. Was this some sort of euphoria? No, I was sure it wasn't. I was sure it was the positive side of a true seeing. No doubt the negative side would turn up in due course, but what was important, here and now, was that this feeling was as true, as valid, as all the dark feelings I had ever had.

I had always given greater weight to the dark feelings, because they felt more real to me. But they weren't. They really weren't. I opened one of my new exercise books, bought in case I should run out of notebook, took up my pen and bang in the middle of the first page, that magical, yet to be written on first page, the one that could inspire me or intimidate me equally, right up to this moment, I wrote in my best handwriting:

'Never forget Sunday 6 July, 1986.
What was true then is true now and for all time.'

And then I sat for an hour or more, doing absolutely nothing, at peace with myself, knowing that it was the last hour when the Anacarrig I had known could be at peace with itself.

The three days that followed were even more unspeakable than good friends had warned me they might be. Whatever joy and insight Sunday had brought me, it helped me little with the sheer volume of practicalities that began to flow on Monday morning first thing, and continued unabated right up to late Wednesday evening. Like all days, however, good or bad, I knew they would pass, and I would be free to turn back to everything I'd been given in the weeks since my coming, gifts I knew were going to reshape my life and chart my course anew into the indefinite future.

Yes, I would survive these days, but there was one thing I felt I could not accept. I tried to be patient and trust that all would be well, but I had to admit I just didn't know how I could cope were I not to see Deara just once more, before I left.

She had said she would come and come soon, but where would she come to once I was gone? And what did 'soon' mean in the strange pattern of time we had shared over the summer?

It was after midnight on Wednesday when I put my large suitcase in the hall ready for Bill picking me up at nine-thirty a.m. for the late morning plane. I took a last look round the empty rooms, but they had nothing more to say to me.

Suddenly weary, I went upstairs, opened my bedroom door and saw Deara standing by the window. Without a word, I went to her and put my arms round her. I wept for sheer relief.

267

'I remembered this was your sleeping place,' she began. 'I could see you were going on a journey, but you would not leave those behind,' she said, pointing to the two small vases filled with fresh flowers, almost the only remaining objects in the room. 'I waited for you. Is it a long journey?'

'Yes, I am going back to London,' I said. 'To my home, my husband and my work, And I am sad, Deara, so very sad, for I feel sure you will not be able to come to me there, or I to you here.'

She put her arm round me and we sat down on the bed, side by side, as once we had done in this same room, long ago before she was Queen of Ulster. Looking at her in the light of my bedroom lamps, I could see no more difference in age between us now than there was between Helen and myself, who share the same birth month, but I had known her for six and a half weeks. She had known me for some seventeen years.

'It may be so, my friend,' she said, after a pause. 'But surely it will be possible for you to come to Ireland again.'

'Oh yes, it would be quite easy to come,' I agreed. 'But I might not be to able to reach you, even if I did.'

'Then I would have to reach you,' she said soothingly.

Deara spoke so gently and so consolingly that I realised I'd been behaving like a fretful child. In my weariness and my anxiety, I was forgetting all that had been between us. Deara had promised she would come and she had come. I had what I had so wanted. Now I was busy worrying about how I could hold on to it instead of accepting it gratefully, here and now, as one more gift given.

'I am so very glad to see you, Deara,' I said. 'Forgive me, I am tired and I have been anxious.'

'There is nothing to forgive,' she responded warmly. 'None of us can escape such weariness at times, whether it is the work of our bodies or of our minds, or even that part which some call soul. But I have much good news for you. That is often a salve for such weariness.'

'I have been longing for news, Deara,' I replied eagerly. 'You must tell me everything that has happened. You can be my herald and tonight I shall play the Queen.'

She laughed, a laugh so joyous I knew I'd never forget it.

'And I promise not to interrupt, if I can possibly help it.'

She began her story on the Hill of Brolla and shared with me all that had happened in the four years between that day and our brief meeting at Tara. It was an absorbing tale, full of joy and sadness, of great hope and great disappointment, of waiting and longing, of fearing and of an end to fear.

As I listened, I realised that our meeting in the Great Hall of Tara could have been only months ago, not years, but before she could speak of Tara she had to tell me the full story of the battle at Lisbane and Carnbanna. I had not grasped how decisive a victory this had been. As she spoke, it became clear to me that this was one of those battles that change the course of history, because it had revealed how vulnerable Ireland was to all such assaults. She spoke of the losses with great sadness and then reminded me that without the barbarity of the lake raiders and the heavy casualties, it was unlikely that Tara and the other more remote kingdoms would have grasped the need for cooperation.

The women and children of Emain had survived unscathed, the long-learnt hiding places in the woodland had served them well and because of the gratitude of all the encampments who had been spared, Emain had been rebuilt with remarkable speed. Craftsmen and labourers were sent from every one of them to work over a long summer, and the gold and other treasures stacked in the raider's boats had paid for the rebuilding of the school and for bringing the best teachers that could be found from both Albi and Gaul.

The raider's gold had gone a long way to restore what could be restored, she said, but only the work towards a treaty of mutual support and protection could offer any solace to those who had lost their loved ones and give any real hope for the future.

From all Deara said, it was clear that Ferghal had taken the lead. The once smooth-tongued courtier who had fallen in love with her at first sight had become a leader and a statesman spurred on by a commitment that would not let him rest. There was sadness in her voice when she said that at times she found him remote, so withdrawn into the affairs of state that she wondered if some part of him had been left to die on the battlefield of his greatest triumph.

The years since our meeting at Brolla had not been easy for Deara. The work of negotiation had been full of sudden, heartbreaking setbacks, which made it look as if nothing could ever be done with a people so volatile and so untrusting of those they did not count as kinsmen. Of herself, her own joys and fears, Deara told me little, but the change in her looks and the whole way she now carried herself spoke eloquently of a tenacity of purpose, a courage and an enduring patience I could only envy. As the story unwound and I remembered how I had seen her stand alone at Tara, I was convinced that she had played a major part in holding together the hope that had to be sustained.

I was near to tears when she spoke of the spreading of rumours and lies to undermine what was being attempted. There had been ambushes of ambassadors and plots to kill both Ferghal and Laoghaire. Good men had lost their lives and she herself had often come close to despair.

As I listened, I remembered how I too had hoped and prayed and been disappointed, time after time, when men and women in my own time attempted the same task of reconciling warring factions who would not forgive old hurts and old wrongs.

'And so the time came, at last, for the journey to Tara,' she said quietly. 'I thought of you so often and wished so much to see you. But you waited till the precise moment I needed you most.'

She smiled and went back a little way in her story to tell me how oppressed she was by foreboding, how even Ferghal had not taken the threat of Conor seriously, for indeed she assured me, my 'magician' was Conor himself, by then the trusted ally of Cathal Rhu of Oriel.

I was listening hard, waiting for her to tell me about the kind of plot I could well imagine between those two, when she stopped suddenly, near to tears: 'Deirdre, my foreboding was right. All would have been lost, everything we had worked for, if you had not come to my aid and acted as you did.'

'Me?' I was so amazed my voice came out as a squeak. I took a deep breath and tried again.

'But, Deara, how could what I did . . . ?'

She put her hand over mine and squeezed it gently, to reassure me. Then she reminded me of the time when she had come to me, anxious about a slave who had presented himself before Morrough.

'You told me, my friend, that I was to be myself and then what I had to do would be given to me, even though I might have no idea what I had actually done, till long after.'

I couldn't remember saying anything half as wise as that.

'But that is precisely what you did yourself,' she began. 'You did what seemed right to you. Now listen and I will tell you what you did.'

She smiled and shook her head slightly as if something were amusing her.

'Firstly, my friend, you appeared in the heart of Tara when Tara was so well guarded that I doubt if a bird or a mouse could have found a way in.'

I opened my mouth to protest, but she held up a finger and went on. 'And then you did what no woman has ever done and lived. You lifted up the Great Cup of Tara and gave it to me. That cup is the most storied cup in all the land. There are those that would say it is magical, others that it is holy. But every child in the land knows that he who drinks from the Cup of Tara will either die or rule the land. You gave me no choice but to drink from it. Did you not hear the gasp of horror as they waited for me to be struck down?'

I nodded silently. I had heard a noise, but I had been far too concerned for Deara to think about it.

'Not only was I not struck down as a result of what you had done,' she went on, 'but you then turned and destroyed my attacker with a few strong words. Oh yes, he created his own death, such men who feed themselves on hate and rich food often die as he did, but you were the agent of that death. It was fear that destroyed him. But it was your courage in facing him that called up his fear. By the time you disappeared, no one in that whole gathering doubted but that they had witnessed good triumph over evil.'

I spread my hands in amazement and stammered something incoherent. Then I asked what had happened after I'd gone.

Deara became very thoughtful. There was a long pause before she said: 'Several things happened at once and even I cannot be sure which came first. Laoghaire asked for a stretcher to be brought, so that the body of the Druid could be carried away. While this was happening, Niall saw the body and started to cry. He said something pitiable like, "I want Mummy to put me to bed", but only those who were close to him heard the actual words. Laoghaire sent for Maeve and her women and when they came, he took the crown and gave it to a herald close by, to carry it before the King, as is the custom. Then, from somewhere in the hall there was a great cry: "Put on the crown, Laoghaire, it is time, for it is now we need a King."

'From every corner of the hall,' she continued, 'the cry was taken up. "Laoghaire. Laoghaire to be King." Not a voice was silent whether of Tara or Ulster, but Laoghaire left the crown where it was. He saw that Niall was comfortable and then he called Father Patrick to him.'

'Did he?' I broke in quite sharply, for I really was surprised.

'Yes, he did,' she said. 'I too was surprised, knowing the hurt in his heart from the loss he had suffered. But he summoned him to come forward and come down from the platform where we had been waiting upon Niall. And then he summoned me too, with Ferghal, and we went down to stand beside him. And then he spoke.'

She took my hands, and looked steadily into my eyes. 'Deirdre, I have known Laoghaire as long as I have known Ferghal, and he is dear to me. He has told me what has passed between you. I understand what has to be and so does he, but it is only right you should know the part you played in what happened next.'

She paused and composed herself and then she recounted the speech that Laoghaire made to the assembled company. I was so absorbed by her retelling I felt as if I was back there, sitting in the Great Hall, listening to this good man make the speech that changed the destiny of the whole land.

In one way, he was issuing a challenge. He was saying: 'Look, what is it you want? Do you want hatred and bitterness to flow on, unchecked, or do you want to leave your mark on history by showing that there is another way? Do you want to destroy yourselves and all your kin with your quarrels and your feuds, so that your real enemies are free to overrun the land, whether those enemies are raiders and killers, or famine and disease?'

271

At the same time, he was telling them what he stood for. Tender-hearted Laoghaire most certainly was, but what he was offering now was a steely resolution, a toughness of heart and mind, that measured up to the demands of the Kingship. If you do want me to wear that crown, he was saying, be sure you know the temper of the man you are committing yourselves to.

As my friend recreated the speech for me, I began to see the part she believed I had played in all this, for here was a man who had been healed. A man who had come to some new understanding of himself during that brief time I was there in the hall myself. I knew Deara was sure the healing had come with his love for me, and yet the more she spoke, the harder it was to accept all I appeared to have done simply by being me and doing what I felt I was called to do.

As soon as Laoghaire finished speaking, a tumultuous noise broke out, clapping and shouting and stamping, amid continuous cries of 'Laoghaire, our King.' Gradually the noise died down, as he stood waiting, and when he had complete silence, he beckoned to Father Patrick to step forward.

'One thing more, my friends,' he said. 'This crown weighs heavy and I shall need strength to bear it greater even than the love of my friends, or the loyalty of my people. Tonight, for the first time, I have understood whence comes such a strength, now I shall seek it, as wiser friends have sought it before me. Will you, too, follow me and seek the help of God and open your hearts thereby to a future you cannot know?'

'Aye, Laoghaire, aye,' rustled through the whole company, a heartfelt sigh of relief at the end of a long and bitter struggle. Thus everyone present gave their assent, and watched in silence as Laoghaire knelt before Father Patrick, accepted his blessing, and rose a King and a Christian committed to peace throughout the land.

The tears were running down my face and it seemed pointless to dab at them. Deara could not know that all my books agreed, the reign of Laoghaire of Tara brought in a golden age which continued for several centuries, centuries that won for Ireland the true epithet, 'the land of saints and scholars'.

Books contain only the facts that survive, but those bare facts took on a wholly new life as I matched them to the words of Deara's story. They became a reality that would affect me far into the future.

'There is one thing more you must know, my friend,' she said slowly.

I nodded and tried to steady myself, for Deara's tone told me what she was about to say was something I should not ever wish to forget.

'The actual making of the Treaty took only two days. The third day was declared a holiday. It was, however, Easter Day. On that day, Father Patrick lit the Paschal fire on the Hill of Slane, the sacred place near Tara where once the Druids performed their rites.'

She paused and looked at me steadily: 'Deirdre, do you remember what Aillech said?'

And as she spoke, I heard the familiar words repeat themselves, before I spoke them myself: 'That together we might light a fire at the heart of Tara?'

'It seems we have done that, my friend,' she said quietly. 'We could not see our part when we read the words, nor had we any idea which acts were important and which were not. We puzzled over it, like a riddle, but we could find no answer. And now much of the prophecy has been fulfilled. We have played our part for the Ireland of my time, you and I. Now the question moves to the Ireland of your time.'

'I can't remember the rest of the prophecy, Deara,' I confessed. 'Really, I'm no use at remembering things, unless I write them down.'

She smiled and got up from the bed. There was a clipboard on my table with a list of things for me to remember in the morning. She picked it up and handed it to me.

'Come, then. Write, my friend, for it is almost time for us to part.'

She dictated the second half of the prophecy, the bit about her holding out her hands to a woman from another time, and healing that woman so that she would be able to heal in her own time. I scribbled away and thought how strange the words of the prophecy looked alongside things like 'Give keys to Bill' and 'Empty pedal bin and dustbin'.

I finished writing and looked up, suddenly aware of a familiar weariness which had begun to steal over me. I too sensed the time of parting was near.

'Deirdre, listen to me, before I go,' Deara said. 'You spoke once of a story that you wanted to write. And I know that stories have healing power. It is so in my time. It may be so in yours. I have thought and prayed for guidance, for this journey you go upon will be long and often it will be hard for you. What comes to me is this. You must write this story you want to write and then you must come back to Emain.

'However long it takes, and it may take a long time, come back to Emain and I shall find the way to come to you. Above all, however hard the way and however long it takes, do not despair, remember all we have shared, all the good that has come to us, and come about through us, the love we have for each other and the love we have from those who love us. Nothing can ever take that away.

'Go, my friend, go in peace. Do what you can, do it in love, and be sure that it will be more than you ever imagined. In some future time, I shall greet you again at Emain.'

I felt the touch of her kiss on my cheek and heard the soft rustle from her dress as she stood up. And then she was gone.

27

If someone had told me in 1986 that seven years would pass and my story would still not be written, I wouldn't have believed them. But that is what happened. And to me, it was all the more surprising because seldom a day passed that I didn't think of Deara and wonder if there was indeed some task I had to do in my own time, or whether I was simply letting my imagination run away with me.

And yet already by the time Matthew arrived back in London, I had planned the layout of my story. I still remember those late July weeks as one of the happiest times in my life. Even before I told Matthew about Deara and what I was hoping to write, he said he had never seen me so happy or so very much myself.

For a week or more after he came back, we turned every evening into a celebration. We lingered over our supper, drank a little more wine than usual and talked into the small hours about all the possibilities the summer had opened for us both.

We considered the possibility of finding a tiny cottage well away from London where we could hide at weekends and write and walk together and we looked at how I might reorganise my work so that I could create the time I needed for my story. I was planning to start as soon as I caught up with my regular commitments and dispatched the big special commission I'd agreed to nearly a year earlier.

And then Matthew's father rang to tell him that John had had a heart attack. Diana was with him and the boys had been sent for. John died a week later, leaving Diana and the boys the task of moving out of their large, cluttered Norfolk rectory and making a new life. We did what we could to help, for there was no one else within range except Matthew's parents, who had both been unwell for some time. Within a year of John's death, first his mother died, then his father, after a series of illnesses and operations.

The joy of my return and the possibility of writing my story did not entirely disappear, but the year of bereavements cast such a shadow over Matthew that I had no heart to go forward with my own project while he was so depressed. When the chance came for us both to go to India to begin work for a book on village health care and medicine, planned before Mother died, I jumped at it. I knew it would be a wonderful experience and something to help heal Matthew's loss.

And Deara went with me. There was little I observed or experienced in the world that I did not put to her, wondering what she would say or how she would react. Sometimes, as in those remote Indian villages where women were being taught hygiene, first aid and nursing, I knew exactly what she would say. At others, as I moved down crowded escalators, watched news broadcasts, pressed the keys on my computer, I had no idea at all how she would react.

I had completely underestimated the time and energy the production of our book would take. True, it restored Matthew's spirits and brought us both great satisfaction, but as the years passed I felt I had let Deara down, guilty that I was failing in my part of the pact we had made. When I felt really bad I would comfort myself with her parting words to me. Carefully copied onto a plain postcard, I carried them with me wherever I went:

You must write this story you want to write, and then you must come back to Emain. However long it takes, and it may take a long time, come back to Emain and I shall find a way to come to you. Above all, however hard the way and however long it takes, do not despair, remember all we have shared, all the good that has come to us and come about through us, the love we have for each other and the love we have from those who love us. Nothing can ever take that away.

What would have happened in the end if Uncle Hector hadn't had a fall in the summer of 1993, I really don't know, but when I heard Aunt Mary's voice on the phone I knew I had to go to her. I was with her when Hector died, just after midnight on Midsummer's Day, so peacefully that neither of us was quite sure he'd really gone.

In the week that followed, I did the things a daughter might do to help her. Dear brave lady, she shed tears often without any apology and then smiled at me.

'Hector and I made a pact,' she said. 'If we got our fifty years we wouldn't complain. And look, we've had sixty, even though I was so very ill ten years ago. I mustn't weep, Deirdre. I've had so much love and Hector's gone so gently. If you've been loved as I have been loved you must give thanks in whatever way you can. Now who shall we invite to Hector's party?'

Driving round Armagh in Mary's blue Metro, exactly like the one my mother used to have, it was hard not to relive the events of 1986. I made time to go to the museum, I shopped in the familiar places, I

276

thought of going to Emain. Every day, I thought of going to Emain.

When eventually I stood watching the light dapple the mounds of flowers and the smooth oak of Hector's coffin, I was so aware how close I was. For the jackdaws who carried on their noisy chatter in the trees above the open grave, Emain was but a moment's flight. I need only turn left from the ring road on the way back into the city and I would be there.

As the earth fell on dear Hector's coffin and I wiped away unbidden tears, I knew I could not go. However short the distance, however little time it might take, I could not go. The time was not right. I was overwhelmed with sadness.

I followed the line of cars back to town to the hotel Mary had chosen for a gathering far too large for the small bungalow she and Hector had recently made their home. The undertaker had found a route round the back of the cathedral which avoided the delays of the security control zone. Suddenly and quite unexpectedly, I found myself looking at the new shop front of Henderson's, twice bombed and twice rebuilt, each time larger than before. I knew then what I had to do.

Later that week, staying in Belfast with Helen, I phoned Matthew and told him I was selling my shares in Henderson's and giving up all my routine commitments for a year. And now the manuscript is finished.

I had hoped I could manage it in a year. All through the autumn of '93 and the winter months of '94 I had a dream of going to Emain at Midsummer and standing on the great mound as the sun went west casting enormous shadows on the longest day. I don't laugh at my dreams any more, I just accept that they cannot always be. At Midsummer, on the anniversary of Hector's death, I was reliving the sack of Emain.

Now it is August. London is hot and dusty after weeks of punishing heat. Already on the Heath the chestnuts have yellowing leaves. In Ulster, it has been a lovely summer. 'Warm and fine but never too hot to stop you doing the things you want to do,' it says on Helen's postcard from Donegal. Just like my summer of the hawthorn.

I am going to Emain next week. It will be September when I get there, Thursday 1 September to be exact. It will be an ordinary, unmemorable day, not like Midsummer or Beltane or even August Bank Holiday. But a day can become memorable in all manner of strange ways that we can never guess at.

Yes, I hope Deara will be there. I hope so much that she will. But I do not predict. What that day may bring I cannot tell, and even when it has come and gone, it may be years before I know, if ever I know, what its meaning might be in my life. It is ever thus. What I shall remember as I stand on the great mound is that I have kept my promise, I have told my story.

Somewhere, in some way, that story may heal, as once Deara's story brought healing at Tara. I may never know. But I have hope, great hope. That is but one of the gifts I was given in my summer of the hawthorn.

Publisher's Note

On Thursday, 1 September 1994, the IRA announced the cessation of hostilities in Northern Ireland.